WINGLESS
CROW

PART 1

MARINA SIMCOE
THE RIVER OF MISTS

Wingless Crow, part 1
World of the River of Mists

This book is a work of fiction. Names, characters, places, and incidents are a product of the author's imagination. Locales and public names are used for atmospheric purposes. Any resemblance to actual people, living or dead, or to businesses, companies, events, institutions, or locales is completely coincidental.
Spelling: English (American)
Editing by Cissell Ink
Proofreading by Nic Page
Cover image source Depositphotos.com and Period Images

Wingless Crow is the first book in the Wingless Crow duet. It contains graphic descriptions of intimacy, violence, and discussions on adult themes.
Intended for mature readers.

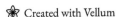 Created with Vellum

Wingless Crow

PART 1

MARINA SIMCOE

To all who need no wings to fly.

Chapter One

"**D**on't look just yet, but the hot guy on the other end of the bar is checking you out." Diane made big eyes, staring straight at me but tilting her head slightly to the right, where the man she was talking about must be sitting behind me.

As a rule, random hot guys didn't "check me out" for any good reason.

"Yeah, I left my pen in my hair." I yanked my ball pen out of the messy bun it held. My thick, chestnut hair unraveled, falling over my shoulders. It'd been making me hot in the office, so I'd used the pen to hold it up when my hair elastic broke. "He must be wondering what weirdo would come to the bar like that. Either that or he's just staring at those girls over there." I tipped my chin at a flock of giggling college girls at the table that would probably be in the hot guy's direct line of view if I wasn't sitting in the way.

Diane didn't look convinced. Her excitement didn't dim a bit.

"Nope. I think he likes you."

"Then he couldn't be that hot," I quipped.

There were far more attractive targets for a hot guy to stare at in this bar. It was Friday night. Most women were dressed nicely, with their hair done properly. They wore full make-up and smelled like fruit and flowers.

I was still in my work clothes—a simple dress and a gray cardigan I knitted years ago in high school, back when I had enough time for hobbies. I probably smelled like ink cartridges, dusty cubicle walls, and microwaved food. My hair was a mess, even without the ball pen stuck in it.

"He must be desperate if he thinks I'm his only option."

Diane rolled her eyes. "Fine. But would it kill you to smile if he comes over?"

I stretched my lips into something that probably resembled a tired, miserable scowl rather than a flirty smile.

"Whatever..." She waved her hand at me, giving up. "Play hard to get. Maybe he's into that."

I was too tired to play anything. It'd been a hard day at work. A hard week... A hard year, dammit. I'd worked late into the night today and was going back to the office first thing in the morning, despite it being Saturday tomorrow. I was too numb from exhaustion to even think about flirting. Trying to impress a hot guy felt like a chore at this point.

Sipping her wine, Diane slid another furtive glance over my shoulder.

"Well, he's still looking at you. God, he's so fucking hot." She moaned softly then clicked her tongue in appreciation. "You know in that rugged, dangerous kind of way. He's huge too. Must be a bodybuilder."

Diane and I weren't close friends, just coworkers who happened to live in the same apartment building and walked home together once in a while. She didn't know that bodybuilders weren't my type. Not that I had a type. But if I did, I didn't think bodybuilders would be it. It was safe to say I wasn't their type, either.

Despite that, curiosity stirred in me. I wished to steal a look at the guy, too.

"Uh-oh!" Diane gasped under her breath. "He's coming over here."

"He is?" Panic jolted me like an electric shock. It'd been forever since I'd spoken to a guy who was in any way interested in me. What the hell was I supposed to say?

I flicked my hair over my shoulder, then nervously tugged at my ear.

Did the pen leave ink marks on my neck or ear?

I drew in a long breath, trying to get my nerves under control. Maybe I could tell him a joke? I liked making people laugh. Even a bad joke could ease the tension of a first date and help break the ice. Unfortunately, I was too tired to come up with even a bad joke right now. My brain had been wrung out during the long day at the office.

But then again, this wasn't *a date*. The guy was probably coming over here to ask for my pen to write down another girl's phone number.

As pathetic as the thought was, it calmed me down instantly. Of course, that would be it. There was no other reason for him to come over here. Men didn't get attracted to women after seeing only the back of their heads, anyway.

Diane chugged the rest of her wine.

"Listen, I need to go to the bathroom. Don't fuck this up." She slid off her barstool and sauntered toward the bathroom to the left of the bar.

"Don't fuck this up?" I mumbled under my breath. "I wish I knew how..."

"Hi, gorgeous." A deep masculine voice rolled over me like honey, peppering my skin with goosebumps.

The barstool behind me squeaked as someone large and heavy, someone who smelled like spice and male, sat down on it.

I held my breath, turning around as slowly as was possibly appropriate without being considered rude.

The guy was massive. Even sitting, he towered over me on my

stool. He was clean-shaven and completely bald, but it suited the shape of his head and the strong, angular features of his face. His black t-shirt stretched over his wide, muscular chest, his thick biceps nearly bursting out of its short sleeves. Black lines of an unusual tattoo circled his neck, disappearing under the neckline of his t-shirt only to continue down his entire right arm.

"I saw you finished your drink." He tipped his chin at my glass. There was still a sip or two worth of wine left on the very bottom of it. "So I brought you another one."

He slid a tall, narrow glass my way. It was filled with a shimmering pink-and-blue liquid I'd never seen served in this bar before.

"What's this?"

"A cocktail." He casually lifted an identical glass to his lips. "See? I have the same." He appeared to take a sip and closed his eyes in pleasure. "It tastes like heaven. Try it." He nudged the drink toward me.

I took the glass, just to be polite. The cocktail sparkled with something that looked like pink glitter on the surface.

"It looks pretty." I sniffed the liquid. It had a pleasant scent of warm vanilla mixed with honey and a hint of something flowery. It made me think of a bakery, bringing up a warm feeling inside me. "Smells nice, too. But I'm not thirsty."

I set the glass back on the bar counter, however, without tasting the liquid. The man wasn't rude, but he was a stranger, offering me a drink before he even told me his name.

"As you wish." He smiled.

I appreciated that he didn't insist I accept his offering. Neither did he seem offended by my declining it. His smile remained pleasant.

"What's your name?" I asked.

"Trez."

"Trez?" It was a rather unusual one. "Is it short for something?"

"No. It's my full name. Do you come here often?"

"Once or twice a month."

The bar was on the way from work to my apartment, which made it convenient to stop for a drink every now and then. I only did it when Diane was with me, though. As much as I hated my job and loathed my life lately, I hadn't stooped so low as to drink alone yet.

"Lucky for me you came tonight." His smile grew wider, making him even more handsome.

I dropped my gaze to the drink he'd brought me. "I haven't seen you here before."

In general, I rarely gaped at the patrons in the bar and never spoke to anyone. Normally, I would just have a glass of wine, listen to the music, and enjoy having people around me for a while. It made me feel slightly better about myself, as though I too had some social life outside of work.

I would've remembered seeing Trez, though. He certainly stood out from the crowd—unforgettable.

"I'm new to the city," he explained.

"Oh, where are you from?"

He gestured vaguely. "From out west."

"West? Like the West Coast? Or closer?"

"Something like that," he replied evasively, leaving me guessing. "It's my first time here."

He leaned with an arm on the bar, shifting closer. His full-sleeve tattoo came into view. The intricate designs ran from his wrist up into the sleeve of his t-shirt, displaying images of a giant serpent with claws and other fantastic beasts. I wondered if the tattoo had a meaning.

"I'm all alone here," he said with a small shrug. "No friends, no family. It feels rather lonely at times."

The confession seemed real, intimate, and disarming.

"I know what you mean." I released a kindred sigh. "There are so many people in the city, one is never alone. But that doesn't mean many of us don't feel lonely. It's so easy to get lost in the crowd."

"I'm glad I met you." He lifted his glass and moved it my way as if to toast with me. "It already looks like the best night I've had here."

"Really?" I lifted my glass, too, clinking it against his. "I'm happy to share it with you, then."

"Thank you," he said before dipping his lips into his shimmering cocktail.

I did the same, barely touching the liquid with my lips. It didn't even reach my tongue but, somehow, I sensed its flavor. It tasted amazing, making me want to drink the whole thing in one gulp. Being careful, however, I forced my hand to set the glass back on the counter.

Trez watched me intensely.

"You missed some," he said softly. Leaning closer, he gently skimmed my bottom lip with his finger. "Just a drop." He held his finger at my mouth.

I wasn't sure what compelled me to part my lips and dart my tongue out. The gesture was rather intimate, but his expression was open with a hint of wistfulness that reflected the tone of our conversation. Maybe I sensed some camaraderie with him, remembering when I first came to the city? I'd felt so lost and out of place then. I still did.

What harm was there in sharing a drink and a conversation with a handsome, lonely man? We were in a public place, surrounded by people. I wasn't alone here. Diane was nearby. There was no reason for me to feel unsafe.

I smiled and licked the shimmering drop off his fingertip.

"Good girl," he murmured. The deep satisfaction in his voice caressed something inside me. Pleasure washed over me at his praise. "Now drink the rest, sweetie." He lifted the glass to my lips, and I found it impossible to disobey.

I opened my mouth and drank. Gulp after gulp. The more I

drank, the more I wanted. The cocktail proved immediately addictive, and I just couldn't stop.

"More?" He smirked.

The soft wistfulness was gone from his expression. The crooked, self-assured smirk he had in its place now should be concerning. Only I didn't feel concerned. A lazy indifference spread through me, sweet and gooey like a melted marshmallow.

"Sure." I nodded.

He set my empty glass aside and handed me his instead.

"Here you go."

I emptied it as well.

"It's really nice." I licked the fragrant liquid off my lips, idly wondering if the pink glitter looked like lip gloss on my mouth.

"It does the job." He shoved both empty glasses aside. "Let's go."

"Go where?" I should've asked but didn't.

For some inexplicable reason, the destination didn't really matter. The priority was to obey this stranger I'd just met and knew nothing about.

I got up as he tossed some money on the bar, enough to cover the price of my wine, and offered me the crook of his elbow. "Hook your arm in mine and smile."

I did as he said, my body no longer feeling like my own. I couldn't stop him from leading me to the exit. My limbs obeyed the will of this stranger, refusing to listen to me. Hopelessness fluttered underneath the hazy fog from the cocktail inside me.

As we were leaving the bar, Diane rounded the corner on her way from the bathroom. My gaze crossed with hers.

This was my chance to get help, to stop whatever was happening to me, and to regain some control over the situation. All I had to do was call out to her. Even the right gesture or a facial expression would alarm Diane and stop this stranger from taking me.

But he'd told me to smile, so that was all I did.

"Wave goodbye to your friend," he said.

Once again, I obeyed. I waved at Diane, with that stupid care-free grin on my face.

She wiggled her eyebrows, giving me a teasing smile in return, and mouthed, *"Have fun."*

And that was it.

Trez led me out onto the dark street, and my one chance for help was gone.

Chapter Two

Trez stopped his van in a deserted parking lot. The pale glow from the few streetlights left the place largely in the dark. This would make a perfect setting for a horror movie. Yet I didn't feel scared.

Deep inside, I realized I should be terrified, but fear never made it to the surface, smothered by the thick fog in my brain. The sweet cake-shop scent of the shimmering drink lingered in my nostrils. Idle, useless thoughts floated in my mind like clouds of cotton candy.

Trez turned off the engine.

"Get out of the van," he commanded.

I immediately opened the passenger's door and climbed out.

He had a white windowless van—the classic vehicle for a kidnapper or a serial killer—if it wasn't for a bright, yellow-and-red decal *Madame Tan's Menagerie* on the side.

Instead of dread, a giggle rose in my throat unexpectedly. I was in a dark, deserted parking lot on the outskirts of the city, with a man I'd just compared to a serial killer in my mind, and all I did was giggle about the situation.

"Come." He gestured for me to follow as he headed into the trees of the park nearby.

The soles of my black pumps slipping in the gravel of the parking lot, I hurried after him as fast as I could.

The main purpose of my existence had become to please this man, to do exactly what he said and as quickly as possible. I'd literally jump off a cliff if he told me. If he took a knife to my throat, I'd just tip my head back to make it easier for him to slit it.

Deep, deep inside, I knew it wasn't right. I had to fight for my life, to scream, to run away...

To do *something*.

But I just didn't care. I trotted after Trez with bubbling lightness filling my chest, as if being murdered by a serial killer would be the best thing to ever happen to me.

Stepping off the path, he led me to a duck pond behind the trees. The night had cooled the air, and I wrapped my cardigan tighter over my chest. The water in the pond had warmed up through the day, and now a milky steam was slowly rising from its surface.

Trez stopped at the water's edge and peered into the mist. Unsure what to do without his explicit instructions, I did the same.

To the left, the mist appeared pink. It shimmered slightly, bringing to mind the drink Trez had given me.

"There it is." Trez pointed at the shimmer. "The River of Mists. Let's go."

He wrapped his large hand around my upper arm, steering me into the water with him. With the first step in that direction, my shoes filled with mud. This wasn't a lake or a river, but a pond of dark, standing water and muddy banks. There must be frogs, bugs, and probably leeches too. My skin crawled with disgust, but it didn't slow me down. I waded through the murky water, dutifully following Trez.

The mucky bottom sucked my feet in up to my ankles. I managed to free them at the expense of one shoe being left behind.

Trez dragged me behind him. "Hurry up, will you?"

He sounded impatient, *displeased*, and that concerned me more than the cold, the mud, or the fact that he was clearly intending to drown me. Plowing through the duckweed and lily pads, I moved faster to keep up and make him happy.

The water rose up to my waist. My breath hitched from the cold, but I kept going and stopped only when Trez did.

The pink mist was right in front of us. I smiled, admiring the pretty sparkles shimmering inside it.

Trez drew me closer, enclosing me in his arms, like into a cage.

"Hold on to me as tight as you can," he instructed.

I obediently wrapped my arms around his middle and gripped the fabric of his t-shirt with both hands.

"Now hold your breath." He stepped into the pink mist and dove under.

The dark water closed over our heads. Cold enclosed me from head to toe. I'd scream if Trez hadn't ordered me to hold my breath.

Then, the chilly sensation of the water lapping against my face vanished. Pink light shimmered beyond my closed eyelids.

"Take a breath," Trez said, allowing me to release the air I held.

I opened my eyes, but all I could see was the milky-pink mist surrounding us. We were suspended in it. I kept smiling, but mostly because Trez never told me to stop. Deep under the thick blanket of artificial joy, however, dread stirred inside me.

This place was like nothing I knew. Holding tight to each other, Trez and I floated in the pink *nothingness*. There was no up or down here, no solid ground, not even gravity. But there was some sense of direction in the pink mist. It seemed to move in a slow, barely discernible current.

"Get ready." Trez shifted me to his left side, freeing his right arm.

Ready for what?

There was no time to ask.

A blast of wind tore the pink mist to shreds. Gray clouds

moved in. The lazy peace of the pink, misty stream was gone, replaced by the howling wind and screeching birds.

"Hold on," Trez gritted through his teeth, hooking his right arm over a rocky cliff.

Gravity returned with a vengeance, dragging us down, down to...

My feet dangled in the air. One had a shoe on, the other didn't. Both were wet and covered in mud. And below my feet, there was nothing but patches of gloomy gray clouds. As the clouds parted, the ground came into view.

Far, far below, stretched the bird's-eye view of a landscape with black mountains, green valleys, and hair-thin silvery ribbons of rivers.

Trez was hanging by one arm from a sharp, rocky drop high above the world. This wasn't a mountain peak. It was not connected to the world below, hovering high above it, like an island of rock above the clouds. Trez's arm around my middle was the only thing keeping me from plunging to a certain death.

"I'll swing you up, and you climb onto the bank," he said casually, as if hanging high above the clouds was a very normal thing to do.

Not waiting for my response, he swung his entire body forward, shoving me up. For once, I was glad for the muddling fog in my head. It left very little place for fear. I simply did what Trez told me to do. Letting go of his t-shirt, I gripped the rock of the cliff and climbed up and up until there was nowhere to climb anymore. The steep rock wall plateaued, and I sat on it, waiting for Trez to tell me what to do next.

He climbed up the cliff, too, then yanked me up by my arm.

"Let's go."

I got up without a word of protest, but I hoped we didn't have to go too far. Whatever this place was, the weather here was colder than where we came from. A biting wind blew incessantly, chilling my skin through my wet clothes. But of course, I followed

Trez without arguing, limping in my one shoe along the rocky path.

Either the effects of the shimmering drink were wearing off, or the shock of what was happening helped to thin the haze in my head, but curiosity broke through the numb indifference inside me.

Falling slightly behind Trez, I threw a furtive look around, trying to figure out where we were.

Somehow, it was day now, but the sun remained hidden behind a thick cloud cover above us. The cliff we'd climbed up was a bank of a river with the opposite bank barely visible in the distance. Instead of water, however, gray clouds rolled and churned between the two rocky banks. In the middle of the river, the clouds shimmered pink in a thin continuous ribbon of mist.

The duck pond and the park with the parking lot were now gone. A thick forest grew on each bank of the river.

Trez led me to a path between the trees, moving with the confidence that told me he'd been here before. The path started from a stone bridge built across the river of clouds and slithered between the trees, disappearing into the forest.

Trez dragged me by my arm, leading me away from the bridge and the river.

"Almost there," he assured me.

My bare foot ached, hitting the rocks that stuck out from the packed dirt of the path. The high heel of the shoe on my other foot made me limp. I didn't care about any of that, though, still under the effects of Trez's drink.

A tiny part of me had gotten free from the hazy feeling somehow. And it was fascinated by the place we'd come to.

The tall trees on either side of the path had gnarly, twisted branches, but that didn't make them look scary. Rather, it gave them unusual artistic shapes. They rose into the gray sky like fantastic sculptures with their lush crowns of green, glossy leaves. Tall leafy vegetation grew at the base of the tree trunks. I spotted a few colorful mushroom caps and a sprinkle of berries here and there.

Some things seemed familiar. The leaves on the trees had the shape of oak tree leaves. The plants on the ground looked like ferns with patches of grass and moss in between.

But other things were so different, they looked like props—pretty but not real. The brightly colored mushroom caps were dotted with neon colors or decorated with fluorescent spirals. The moths fluttering in the shade had wings that glistened as if dusted with silver-blue glitter.

"Hurry up." Trez kept dragging me along.

I realized belatedly that he wasn't speaking English. In fact, he'd been speaking a different language ever since we swam out of the pink mist. I had no idea what language it was, but I understood him perfectly.

I tried to move faster, tripping over the tree roots that crisscrossed the path.

"Where are we?" I asked, then gripped my throat with both hands.

I wasn't speaking English, either. The language I'd never heard before Trez flowed out of my throat as easily as my mother tongue.

"What... What's happening to me?" I mumbled. Some clarity returned to my mind, enough for me to feel worried this time.

Trez smirked. "You'll get used to it."

"Why? Why do I have to get used to this?" My voice rose to nearly a shriek.

He winced, clearly annoyed. "No more questions."

My mouth snapped closed as if on its own. Obeying his order once again, I asked no more questions. That didn't mean they weren't swarming inside my head like bees in a beehive, stinging me with worry and fear through the foggy intoxication.

The forest thinned. The trees grew shorter as we climbed up a hill.

"Wow!" I took in the green rolling hills that spread far and wide around us. Some were forested. Far in the distance, however, farmers' fields stretched between and over them.

The path snaked through the landscape toward the most fantastic structure of glistening towers and clusters of curved, spiky turrets up ahead.

The building was taller than the tallest tree or hill around us, its top disappearing into the low-hanging clouds. With its flowing lines and brilliant facets, it appeared to be constructed from crystal lace and wisps of mist. The pale daylight played in the intricate details of its twisted columns and turrets, and I could only imagine how magically it'd sparkle if the sun were out.

Trez tipped his chin at the magnificent structure. "That's Elaros, the royal palace." He scratched his chin. "It looks like they've finished rebuilding it already."

A palace?

For real?

Where were we?

Who were *they?*

I couldn't ask any of the questions out loud anymore, not since Trez had told me not to. So I just stared at it in silence.

The palace looked like nothing else in the surrounding landscape. Yet its smooth lines and sparkling crystals blended well with it. It clearly was a part of this world, whatever world it was.

A flock of large birds emerged from the clouds, and Trez's grip on my arm tightened.

"Wait," he said, as if I could go anywhere without his permission.

I couldn't physically move my feet even if an anvil was falling out of the sky onto my head, unless Trez told me to move out of its way.

It wasn't an anvil, however, but the flock of birds that descended our way. As they got closer, I realized these weren't birds at all, but people.

With wings!

I gaped at them as they made a slow circle above our heads,

15

then landed on the path in front of us. One of them stepped forward, folding his brown-gray wings behind him.

How did it work? Were the wings powered by a mechanism? Or did they grow straight out of his back? How about his clothes? Didn't they get in the way?

I furtively studied the man, fascinated by his unusual appearance. His skin was gray like pewter and it glowed warmly. I fought the strong urge to touch his cheek, faced with the newcomer's less-than-friendly expression.

His vivid green eyes glimmered with warning. He drew a sword from the sheath on his hip. A real, long sword. Not a prop by the looks of it. The dark blade sparkled with red when he thrust it at Trez.

"Who are you and what are you doing in the Sky Kingdom?"

At the sight of the weapon, Trez paled a little and spread his hands in a pacifying gesture. "Easy, my lord. Goddess Ghata sent me. I came to settle her debt with King Aigel."

The newcomer turned his head toward the four people that had landed behind him, all of them wearing identical gray coats with silver embroidery, and ordered, "Let the High General know about this. He should be close."

One of the group nodded and spread his wide, feathery wings. I watched, mesmerized as the wings beat the air, lifting the man off the ground. He soared in a graceful arch, taking off toward the palace. The movement of his wings was so fluid, it looked natural, as if they were simply an extension of his body.

But how could that be? Even with my mind floating in the invisible pink cloud, I had a hard time believing any of this was real.

Maybe I was sleeping, and all of it was just a dream?

That would actually explain everything.

The green-eyed man turned his attention back to Trez. "King Aigel has been dead for centuries."

"Has he?" Trez shrugged and deadpanned, "Time flies. So,

who's in there now?" He jerked his chin toward the magnificent sparkling structure in the distance—the royal palace.

"King Tiane is on the throne of Sky Kingdom, the grandson of King Aigel."

"And who are you?"

The man slid a measuring glance down Trez's burly frame, as if assessing whether he was worthy of an introduction.

"I'm Lord Alcon, the Head of the Palace Guard," he finally said. His eyes then paused on Trez's arm tattoo. "And you are one of Ghata's slaves, by the look of it. A *brack*."

"Right. Like I said, I'm here to settle the deal she's made with your late king." Trez shoved me toward Lord Alcon. "Take her to your new king, then, and my business here is done."

Take *me?* What business?

How dare they?

I opened my mouth, but not a word came out. Trez had told me not to ask questions. They burned on my tongue, pounding against my skull from the inside, but could not come out, no matter how hard I tried.

Lord Alcon kept his sword trained at Trez's throat.

"It'll be up to the High General to decide what to do with you both."

Trez huffed, visibly annoyed. "Where is he, then? I don't have all day."

"Then turn around and leave."

"I'm not leaving the human here without your promise to deliver her to the king."

"I'm not giving you any promises, *brack*." Lord Alcon spat the last word out like an insult. "Take her with you if you're in a hurry."

Leaving clearly wasn't Trez's plan. He didn't move, his boots rooted in place. The fight came to a standstill. And neither of the two asked for my input in the argument that was ultimately deciding my fate.

A winged figure appeared in the sky, rounding a nearby hill.

The man Lord Alcon had sent to inform the High General was returning. He flew low to the ground, following a lone rider on a horse that rode along the road. The horse was dark as night, as were the rider's clothes and the large bird that flew above them. The only pale spot was the rider's face.

As the horseman approached, Lord Alcon lowered his sword and stepped aside.

"High General," he greeted the horseman with a brief but respectful nod.

The newcomer ran his gaze over Trez's tattoos. He didn't look baffled by them as I was. On the contrary, he appeared to easily read the tattooed lines and images, the meaning of which was hidden from me.

Whatever he saw in Trez's body art didn't seem to please him. His dark eyebrows shifted close together on his already stern face.

"You're one of Ghata's *bracks*," the High General stated in a deep, calm voice. He sounded bored or tired, like someone who had a lot on his plate and didn't appreciate wasting his time on something so insignificant as my future. "I've no business with your goddess. Leave. And take the human with you."

He hadn't spared me a glance. I wondered how he even knew I was there.

Trez shifted on his feet uneasily. A prospect of a confrontation with the High General seemed to unnerve him much more than the argument with Lord Alcon.

"You may not do business with my mistress," he said, "but your late king did. On behalf of Madame Tan—as Goddess Ghata is now known—I made a deal with King Aigel yesterday. Well..." He rubbed the back of his neck. "To me, it was *yesterday*. But, as you know, crossing the River of Mists makes time crease and twist. So, it seems, centuries have passed here since." He glanced at Lord Alcon, then continued talking to the High General, "Anyway, the deal was made. King Aigel fulfilled his part of the bargain by giving me a saddlebag full of *camyte* powder in exchange for a human girl to be delivered directly to the Sky King. Well, here she is." He gave me a shove to the back that made me stagger forward, tripping and nearly falling over my one high heel.

The High General finally turned my way. His steel-gray eyes rested on me, and I felt trapped by his stare more effectively than even by Trez's orders.

"Take her back," he said firmly, annunciating every syllable.

"She's the payment," Trez insisted. "If you refuse to take her, my mistress will remain in debt to your late king, which she highly dislikes. You cannot stand in the way of the deal made between a king and a goddess."

"Take the human back to her world. And let me worry about the consequences." The High General never raised his voice, yet the force with which he spoke made me shiver even more in my wet clothes.

Trez rolled his shoulders back. The movement was jerky, he was clearly uncomfortable under the High General's heavy stare weighing down on us from the height of the saddle.

Yet Trez stood his ground.

"I can't take her back. You know the River of Mists would never deliver her back to the place and time where I took her from. She'd be lost, which would be a waste of a young, healthy female."

The High General raised an eyebrow.

"I also know that Ghata pulls you back to her every time you leave Nerifir. She will make sure you'll arrive to the human world at the same time and in the same place where she is and where you've left from."

Trez rubbed his chest, looking genuinely concerned. "Ghata pulls her *bracks* across dimensions, but no one else. If I jump into the River of Mists with this human now, we'd get separated. She'd be lost. She'd land elsewhere in her world, in a different time period, which can be cruel for a single girl her age."

I didn't believe for a second that Trez worried about my safety or wellbeing. But the High General paused, looking reluctant.

Trez jumped at his hesitation like a starving hound onto a

bone.

"It's best just to keep her," he insisted. "Why don't you want her?" He gave me an assessing stare, as if looking at me for the first time or seeing me under a new light. "Come to think of it, she is rather plain. Short and kind of chunky. I didn't think about that before. All humans equally repulse me, anyway. But if the king prefers someone else, tell me what he'd like to see in a human pet, and I'll find one to his liking. I'll just get rid of this one." He grabbed my arm.

The rider gripped the reins, making his horse twitch and beat the ground with a hoof.

"Get. Your hands. Off her."

Said in a grave, low voice, the words of the High General dropped like lead-laden punches. Trez jerked away from me. His massive shoulders curling in, he appeared to shrink under the cool gaze of the High General.

The horseman tossed aside the end of his long cloak and freed his foot from the stirrup. Swinging his leg over the saddle, he dismounted, gracefully landing on the path with both feet.

"If you can't take her back to her time and place, she'll stay here," he spoke to Trez while staring at me.

Even out of the saddle, the High General towered over me. I had to tilt my head back to see his face. His steely eyes peered at me from under his tousled hair, black like raven feathers except for a few thick strands of silver in the front.

"She stays," he said. "You'll leave and never come back. From now on, no one in Sky Kingdom will make deals with Ghata's puppets. Do you hear me? Don't ever bother coming back."

A corner of Trez's mouth crawled up in a smirk.

"In the present, maybe. But, with time travel, I'll always have the past."

The High General's gaze flashed with anger. I cowered, terrified of this man's wrath even though it wasn't directed at me. He regained his composure quickly, however. His expression turned so calm again, it bordered on laziness.

"Leave, *brack*. Or I'll kill you. Then you'll have neither the present nor the past, just the joy-sucking shadows in the World of Under."

A long, bejeweled handle of a sword strapped to the back of the High General was visible over his left shoulder. He never bothered to draw the weapon. Yet I didn't doubt he would deliver on his threat if Trez was stupid enough to disobey.

The *brack* retreated carefully, keeping his mouth shut. But when he was a few steps away from the High General, he spoke again.

"So, it's a deal, then? Give me your promise you'll deliver her to the king."

The muscles in the High General's jaw moved. His eyes narrowed in annoyance. He clearly had enough of the *brack*. But giving the promise must be important, because he kept in control and said what Trez had asked for.

"I promise to present the human woman to King Tiane. The deal with your goddess will be honored."

The wind changed momentarily. Instead of the brutal, ice-cold gusts, a warm swirl curled around us. It shimmered with a light of its own. The breeze puffed softly, blowing the wet strands of my hair, then settled down to the ground just as suddenly as it had risen.

Trez pumped his fist in the air. "The bargain is complete!"

The High General no longer paid him any attention. With a finger under my chin, he lifted my face to his. The butter-soft leather of his glove glided smoothly along my skin.

My hands felt numb, as cold as ice.

"I just want to go home," I whispered, pleading.

His eyes were like the sky behind him, gray and cold. The emotions I glimpsed behind them were even more chilling. I saw regret in the High General's eyes—regret for me, for all that I'd been and for all I would never become now.

A chilling regret for my entire life.

Chapter Three

T he High General held my chin in his gloved hand.

"I'm sorry, little bird."

What was he apologizing for?

Maybe he felt sorry about me being kidnapped by Trez? Or about my getting here, whatever this place was?

Deep inside, I feared he was apologizing for things he hadn't done to me yet.

I held my breath as he shifted closer. His lips parted as if for a kiss. I felt his breath on my face. It was warm and fresh, and it smelled like rain. His lips were but a hair's breadth away from mine. Only instead of kissing me, he inhaled deeply through his mouth.

I stilled, unable to move, unable to even blink as I stared into his eyes that were the same color as the sky. The longer I looked into them, the more it appeared like he didn't have any eyes at all. That they were just bottomless holes in his head, open to the sky behind him.

He sucked the air in through his mouth, and a part of me disappeared. I felt emptier inside. Something was missing, but I couldn't tell what it was.

I didn't remember what was gone.

"From now on, your name is Sparrow," he said.

Breath left me in a gush, as if my lungs had been punctured. At the same time, I felt relieved I could still breathe at all, that I could still move. That I was alive. For a few moments there, he seemed to have absorbed my entire being, leaving nothing left.

"I already have a name," I said, gasping for air.

Of course I did. I had my very own name, just like everyone else did. I hadn't lived all these years without one. How many years would that be?

How old was I?

What was the name that my parents gave me?

Who were my parents?

My family? Did I have them?

A heavy ball of dread formed in my stomach as I realized I had no answers to any of these questions.

I didn't remember. *That* was the part that was missing.

My past was gone.

What had he done to me?

I trembled in the wind. Tears rolled down my cheeks, leaving my skin wet and cold.

The High General calmly unclipped the crescent-shaped buckle that held his black cloak at his shoulder.

"Let's get you out of here." Taking the cloak off, he wrapped it around me. It shielded me from the weather, laying heavily on my shoulders. The wind had quieted down somewhat, but the cold remained bitter.

He led me to his horse.

"Do you ride horseback? Will you stay in the saddle?" he asked.

I didn't know anything about myself. In one single breath, he'd just erased everything from my past, even my name.

I glared at him. "I don't *remember*."

He winced, as if he'd already forgotten what he'd done.

"Right. Well..." He placed his hands on my waist. "Just hold on, then. I'll ride with you."

He lifted me up easily, as if I were a child, and placed me sideways on his horse. The animal snorted, stomping its hooves.

Its master calmed it with a single word, "Steady."

I tried to hold on as he'd said, but my hands tangled in his cloak draped around me. I swayed backwards and nearly fell. But he promptly hopped into the saddle behind me, gripping me around the waist.

"Steady," he said in the same tone of voice as he'd spoken to his horse.

Was this what I was supposed to be in this world? Something akin to an animal? Didn't Trez mention something about me being a pet? My heart squeezed with fear at the thought.

My brain remained fuzzy, however. Thinking hurt. But the fog seemed to be thinning slowly. I tested it by opening my mouth to ask a question. It still didn't work. The words wouldn't come.

The High General seemed oblivious to my struggle. He steered his horse along the path toward the beautiful palace shimmering in the distance. His people spread their wings. Taking off into the air, they flew ahead of us. Only the black bird remained, circling high above us like a vulture waiting for me to drop dead.

"We'll be in the palace soon," the High General said. "You'll get a warm bath and a meal."

A bath and a meal sounded great. My mind was too jittery with anxiety to feel tired. But my body felt weak and sluggish, like it hadn't rested in days.

Still, I wished he would just let me go home...

Where was my home?

I tried to remember, searching my brain for any clues that would trigger my memory, but found none.

Tilting his head, he watched my face. "Do you wish to say something?"

With his arm firmly holding me in place and his cloak keeping me warm, I relaxed a little, clearing my throat.

"I have questions," I said, glad that my voice came out strong enough for him to hear.

"Ask." He shrugged. "I may feel inclined to answer."

"I can't ask. I was told not to."

He raised an eyebrow. "Did the *brack* feed you some glacier saffron?"

Trez. I remembered him and everything that happened from the moment he'd offered me a drink. Except that my memories of that were submerged in a dense fog. There was Trez, and me, and two tall glasses with a shimmering liquid on a bar counter. But all of that was happening as if in a bubble. I didn't remember any of the surroundings. Where was that bar counter? Who else had been there?

"I don't know," I said softly.

"Glacier saffron comes as a pink, glistening powder. When ingested, it forces obedience."

"The pink glitter." I closed my eyes, focusing on those few images that remained from my past. "It was on the surface of the drink he gave me."

"What color was the drink?"

"Swirls of pink and blue. With a shimmer. It tasted like cake."

He nodded. "*Camyte.* The *brack* bragged about getting a saddlebag full of it from the late King Aigel."

Right. Trez got it as a part of the deal he'd made. And I happened to be the other part of that bargain.

"*Camyte* relaxes your mind," the High General explained. "It makes you care less about your surroundings. It can also impair your perception, making you think and feel whatever the person who gave it to you wishes you to feel."

"Sounds awful."

He didn't argue with that. "Both substances are extremely rare. But so are humans."

He gave me a curious glance.

I kept my mouth open, but the words once again refused to come.

He leaned over, taking my chin into his hand. Peering into my eyes, he said softly, "Ask."

There was a push of power in his voice. It reached inside me, dissolving the obstacle in my throat that prevented questions from leaving it.

"Will the haze in my brain go away?" The question left my lips easily, this time, freely like a breath.

"Eventually." He released my chin, taking the horse's reins into his left hand. His right one remained on my waist, supporting me as we rode. "Though you may wish it didn't," he added ominously.

Fear gripped my throat. I almost wished for more of Trez's *camyte* drink, missing the state of not caring that it provided.

"What are you planning to do with me?"

His chest expanded against my side with a deep breath. "I gave my promise to present you to the king. And that is exactly what I will do."

"Why? What does the king want with me?"

He petted my side soothingly, as if calming a skittish animal.

"Whatever comes, you'll be well taken care of. Chances are the king will keep you. You'll like the king. Everyone does."

A hard note in his voice and the way his jaw muscles ticked prompted me to prod.

"Except for you, right? You don't like your king that much, do you?"

His dark, elegant eyebrows moved closer together. He lifted his chin, staring straight ahead.

"I hold the utmost respect for the crown," he bit out.

"For *the crown*. But not for the king."

He slowly moved his gaze back to my face. I expected to find annoyance in his eyes, anger maybe. But they shone with interest.

"The king and the crown are one and the same," he stated.

"If you say so." I shrugged, letting him know he hadn't convinced me at all.

He huffed, shaking his head, but said nothing in reply. The silence depressed me more than his anger would.

"I bet you're regretting allowing me to ask questions, aren't you?" I prodded again. "Do you wish I remained quiet?"

Incredibly, a corner of that severe mouth of his twitched up in a pale resemblance of a smile.

"What would be the fun of that?"

It had not been my intention to amuse him. But I was glad to see him relaxed rather than angry.

"You'll do just fine at the Elaros Court." He nodded confidently.

"I won't stay," I warned. "You can't make me. I'm not going to eat or drink anything while I'm here."

He remained unfazed by my threats. "Starvation is a horrible way to die."

I wouldn't stay long enough to starve. I'd run the moment I could think clearly again.

The shimmering palace looked even more spectacular the closer we got to it. The sharp, sparkling turrets and lacy parapets crowned the faceted crystal walls. Ombre gray vines interwove in a delicate pattern, holding the tall wall panels together. Up close, it looked even taller, its highest towers piercing the cloudy skies.

I tilted my head back, trying and failing to take the entire palace in. Apprehension fought its way through the foggy remnants of *camyte* in my system.

"Please," I begged the High General softly. "Please just let me go home."

His features hardened. Any trace of a smile was gone. "I'm afraid you're here for the rest of your life, Sparrow, however long or short that may be. The sooner you accept it, the easier it'll be for you."

The horror of that statement was emphasized by that one word he'd said—*Sparrow*, the name he gave me, overriding the one I'd had since birth, the one he'd made me forget along with my entire life prior to coming here.

Resentment rose in my chest. Hot and bitter.

"Don't call me that."

"It suits you," he said firmly, as if the matter had been settled and no further arguments were allowed.

"But it's not my name," I wouldn't give up.

"It is the only one you have now."

Hot sparks of irritation burned through the layer of *camyte* fog that shrouded my mind like cotton. I wished I could summon more of that to burn through the placid haze and bring wrath down upon his head. Surely, I was capable of some screaming and foot-stomping before I'd taken that awful drink.

But the flash of anger settled down way too quickly. The calm indifference closed over me like dark water once again.

The High General seemed to take my subdued mood for acceptance. He made himself more comfortable in the saddle, settling me a little closer to him.

"It won't be easy, dear Sparrow," he said as we approached the arched bridge over a river—a real river with water in it, not fog or clouds. The bridge led to the tall gate of the city built around the palace. "You'll have little choice in what your life here is going to be. But I have faith in you. If you're as perceptive and resilient as I hope you are, you'll make it here, in the Sky Kingdom. For this is your only home now."

Chapter Four

SPARROW

I sat on the edge of a four poster bed under a lacy canopy and stared straight ahead. A numbness seized my mind and muscles. I couldn't tell whether it was the murky residue from the cocktail of magical substances that Trez had made me ingest, or the result of the overwhelming hopelessness, or both.

There was nothing to ground me. My mind was empty. Void of thoughts and memories, it floated like a soap bubble inside my skull.

The room inside the royal palace where they'd put me wasn't very big, but it had everything one would want from a bedroom.

It held a bed with a white comforter trimmed with frothy lace. A round crochet rug on the floor was also white, as were the light gossamer curtains on the tall window. Shiny, gold beetles decorated the curtains, weighing the gauzy material down.

There was also a small glass table by the fireplace with a pink upholstered armchair next to it and a carved-wood vanity with a mirror in a crystal frame. A tall trunk, painted with silver stars, stood by the wall between the window and a single nightstand on the side of the bed. A door on the other side of the bed led to a small wardrobe room with a toilet off it.

The space was neat and clean, though the air had that stuffy quality that came from places left unoccupied for a while.

The ornamental crystal in the window broke the sunset beyond it into geometrical shapes, which made the outside look like an abstract painting. Just like this world that I found myself in. It was a surreal, abstract place. A senseless dream that just wouldn't end.

The door to the room opened, and a woman entered.

Her short curly hair was neatly styled between a pair of curved horns positioned on each side of her head. She carried a silver tray with dishes, which she deposited on the glass table by the fireplace. She then trotted across the room to me, the staccato of her small, polished hooves slightly muffled by the rug on the floor.

Horns and hooves? As odd as the woman looked, she fit right in in this bizarre place. Whereas I did not.

I didn't belong here.

"Oh, by all the gods of Nerifir, just look at you!" The woman threw her hands up into the air, taking in my mud-covered feet, messy hair, and damp clothes. "Voron said you needed a bath, but it looks like I have to leave you soaking in lemon juice and vinegar overnight. What a mess." She shook her head accusingly, making her blonde curls dance around her horns.

I smoothed the polyester skirt of my dress over my thighs and tried to shove my feet further under the bed and out of sight.

"Who are you?"

"My name is Brebie." The woman straightened her frilly white apron over her powder-blue dress with a poofy skirt. "Voron sent me to look after you."

"Who is Voron?"

Her sandy-blonde eyebrows shot up to her hairline. "Why, he's our High General. High General Voron. He is the one who brought you here."

"Oh... Right."

Of course, he would have a name in addition to his rank. Everyone had a name. Everyone, except for me...

I drew in a breath and let it trail out of me slowly, like air from a deflated balloon.

Brebie fetched the tray she'd brought and placed it on the bed next to me. "Why don't you eat your dinner while we get your bath ready?"

The door flew open once again. Two men stomped in, carrying a full-size copper bathtub.

"Where do you want this, Brebie?" one of them asked.

"Right there," she gestured, "by the fireplace."

Both men had horns, too. The horns of one curled almost into circles close to his skull, like Brebie's.

The other one not only had horns, his entire head looked like it came from a bull, complete with large brown eyes, long face, and a wide bovine nose. He also had a long tail, I noticed, as he bent over to deposit the bathtub in the place Brebie had pointed at. His long tail with a tuft of fur on the end whipped around his legs as he turned on his hooves.

"Thanks, boys," Brebie blew them a kiss on their way out, then turned to me. "Let's feed you now or, I fear you'll pass out in the tub. You don't look very good, honey."

From a plate on the tray, she dumped some cooked chopped vegetables into a painted terracotta bowl, topped them with chunks of meat and fresh green herbs, then poured some red wine from a crystal carafe over the entire thing.

"There you go." She handed me a silver spoon with a delicate filigree handle. "Can you hold this on your own, or should I feed you until you regain your strength?"

She seemed kind, even if a bit impatient, nudging me with the bowl.

"I can feed myself, thank you." I gripped the spoon in my hand but didn't touch the food. "Except that I'm not going to eat anything."

Brebie propped her hands on her hips. "And why is that?"

"I've no idea what's in this." I eyed the bowl suspiciously.

"Turnips, carrots, potatoes, purple squash, braised venison, and fresh herbs from the royal garden, topped with cranberry wine from the Dakath Mountains," she fired off the ingredients in one continuous line of words. "Is any of that not to your liking, dear?"

The dish smelled amazing, with a tendril of a unique flavor I'd never sensed before. But that made it only more suspicious.

"Not to my liking are the things you *didn't* mention. Like the pink *camyte* glitter and stuff."

"Don't be ridiculous." She rolled her baby-blue eyes up to the ceiling—a rather unexpected gesture from a woman with horns and hooves and wearing an outfit that brought Alice in Wonderland to mind.

Alice in Wonderland...

I remembered the story. I knew what it was about. The images of the book's illustrations and scenes from several movie adaptations came clear to my mind.

I held my breath. Did I get my memories back?

Ignoring Brebie, I searched my brain. When did I read the book? When did I watch the movies? How old was I? Who was with me?

And... I had nothing.

I knew *of* the book and the adaptations, but not where I read or watched any of them. I couldn't tell what I'd thought of the story. There was nothing in my mind about my personal experience with it.

"The pink glitter is called glacial saffron," Brebie's brisk voice rolled over my head. "*Camyte* powder is iridescent and turns blue and pink when mixed with water. I assure you there are no magical substances in your food. They're too rare and expensive for me to randomly sprinkle them around."

Her assurance meant little to me. I didn't know this woman and had absolutely no reason to trust her. I put the spoon down on the tray.

"Thanks, but I'll pass. It's better to be safe than sorry."

More people entered the room—three women. Each carried a yoke on her shoulders, with buckets of steaming water hanging from each end. They poured the water into the tub. None of the three had horns, but they were no ordinary women either. One had a pair of double wings on her back. They were translucent, with a hint of pearlescent gray. The other two had neither hooves nor feet. Instead, a thick, scaly tail undulated under their wide aprons. They used their tails to slither along the floor, gracefully maneuvering around the tub as they poured fragrant oils and sprinkled flower petals into the water.

"Fine, don't eat," Brebie conceded, seething at my refusal. "See how long you'll last without food, the fragile little bird that you are."

"I'm not a bird," I protested. "Certainly not a little one."

If it weren't for Brebie's hooves and horns, we'd be almost the same height. And I was definitely much wider than her, especially in the hips and chest.

She ignored my argument and went to check on my bath.

"It looks lovely," she cooed. "Thank you, girls. Well, Sparrow, you may refuse the food all you want, but I can't allow you to spend another minute in that filth." She wrinkled her nose, tossing a disgusted look at my feet and clothes. "You need a bath."

I gripped the sides of my sweater, pulling it closed over my chest.

"I'm not taking a bath with all of you here."

"How else is a lady supposed to bathe?"

"I'm not a lady. I'll wash myself."

Brebie blew out an exasperated breath.

"It's even harder than I thought it would be," she muttered to herself. "You know what?" She glared at me. "I may actually consider begging Voron to force-feed you some glacial saffron. It'd make my job so much easier." She pursed her lips and folded her arms across her chest. "I'll tell you what. I'll send the maids out of the room, then turn away while you get undressed and climb into the tub. But I will have to wash your hair. It needs to be done properly."

Her hard stare and a slight stomp of her hoof told me this was the only compromise she was willing to make.

The other three women never said a word. As pushy as Brebie was, she seemed talkative. Maybe she knew something about getting my memories back and finding my way back home? Maybe I could get her to answer my questions? Or even help me escape?

"Fine." I got up from the bed and almost fell, tripping over the high heel of my sole surviving shoe.

"Oh, by all the gods of Nerifir," Brebie grumped, grabbing my arm to steady me. "This really needs to go."

Bending over, she yanked my shoe off my foot, then opened one side of the tall crystal window and tossed my muddy pump out.

"What are you doing?" I was too shocked to stop her in time. "That was the only shoe I had."

"And that was exactly the problem, wasn't it? Come on." She waved at the tub. "Get in. No need to get upset. The king will get you more shoes than you can wear in your lifetime. But you need to be clean and smell nice for him to like you."

I didn't care for the king or his shoes, but it would be nice to wash the mud off.

After the other three women started the fire in the fireplace, Brebie shooed them from the room, then turned her back to me.

"Now take your clothes off," she ordered.

I tiptoed to the tub, trying to leave as few muddy footprints on the pristine white rug as possible. Steam was rising from the bath. It smelled like summer flowers. The warmth of the water lured me. Bathing wasn't eating. Surely, there was no danger in getting clean and warming up a bit.

I stepped closer, peeling off my damp sweater. Making sure Brebie's back was still turned, I quickly got rid of the rest of my clothes and stepped into the tub. It was short but deep. Sitting on the bottom, I had to bend my legs, but the warm water covered my body up to the top of my breasts.

Leaning back, I exhaled and let my muscles relax in the soothing caress of the water. Pink and lavender petals floated on the surface, obscuring my submerged body from view.

"You can turn around now," I said to Brebie. "But you really can leave. Like I said, I'm fully capable of washing myself."

"That's what you think," she snapped, jumping into action.

Opening the trunk by the wall, she produced a wicker basket filled with jars, bottles, and vials. She then pulled the glass table closer to the tub and started taking the items out of the basket and arranging them on the table.

"A lot goes into washing a lady's hair," she murmured, lovingly lining up the bottles in some unknown to me order.

"But I told you, I'm not a lady."

"Doesn't mean you shouldn't look like one." She gave me an assessing look. "Who knows, maybe one day you'll even learn to speak and act as a lady, too?"

She finished with the bottles and grabbed the sad pile of my discarded clothes off the floor.

"Are you going to get them washed?" I asked quickly as she moved toward the fireplace.

I needed them. I had to return home wearing my own clothes. They belonged to my world, just like I did.

Brebie looked at the pile in her hands with clear distaste. "Dirty or clean, these clothes are dreadfully ugly. Wearing them is not going to help you impress the king."

"I don't care about impressing anyone." I gripped the edge of the bath.

But she was too quick. With one swift swing, she tossed my dress, my sweater, my bra, and my underwear into the fire.

"No!" I jerked forward, making the water splash out of the tub.

"Stay still." Brebie pressed a hand on my shoulder. With strength unexpected from a slender woman like her, she settled me back into the tub. "Look at the mess you've made." She pointed an accusing finger at the wet rug under the tub. "And we haven't even started washing you yet."

"I need my clothes," I almost sobbed, watching the flames engulfing the last pieces of what I used to be. The smoldering rags were the only things that connected me to the past I no longer remembered.

"You'll have lots of new clothes, honey. Trust me, you didn't need those rags," Brebie soothed.

Tears prickled behind my eyelids, but I couldn't break down in front of this woman. With my forearm placed on the edge of the tub, I buried my mouth in the crook of my elbow, silently watching my clothes burn.

"I'll get out of here," I promised to myself. *"One way or another, I'll get back home. I'll just need to remember where my home is."*

Brebie gathered my hair from behind.

"Your hair could be longer, but at least it's nice and thick." She took some silvery pink paste out of a jar on the table, then lathered it into my hair. "And you most certainly should care about impressing King Tiane, sweetie. The more the king likes you, the better your life here will be. Now stop sulking." She rinsed my hair, only to put some clear gel that smelled like almonds on it next. "Look at what you already have." She gestured around the room. "You'll be warm and comfortable here. You have your own dressing room, like every lady I know. It'll be filled with beautiful dresses and the nicest shoes you've ever seen. Court life can be tricky. But if you have the king's protection, you'll be safe..."

I stopped listening to her describing the "wonderful" life I'd have as the king's kept woman, and instead tried to remember the road the High General and I had taken to the palace.

The road wasn't that wide, more like a path, but from what I recalled, it was clearly visible between the hills and valleys. It hadn't taken us that long to get to the palace from the point where he'd met Trez and me. We'd traveled on horseback but, I imagined it'd be possible to cover it on foot in a reasonable time. We hadn't ridden that fast.

There would then be the trek through the forest that Trez and I had made. But I'd done that while limping in one shoe, tired, dazed, and confused. Surely, it wouldn't take me that long to walk it rested and properly dressed. If I followed the same road all the way, it'd lead me to the cloudy river with the bridge over it.

A chill of trepidation rushed down my back when I recalled how Trez and I had been hanging off the riverbank. The river filled with clouds had no bottom. If I jumped into it, I'd fall to my death.

But Trez went back somehow, didn't he? Unfortunately, I didn't remember much from his conversation with the High General about that. Drunk on *camyte*, I couldn't focus properly and a lot of what they had said didn't make sense.

"Brebie," I interrupted the chatting woman. "What is this place where we are?"

She glanced around us. "What do you mean? The room? Or the building? It's Elaros, the king's palace, located in the middle of the main city of Sky Kingdom. The city is also called Elaros."

"And where is Sky Kingdom located?"

She shrugged. "High above the clouds, of course."

"But there are plenty of clouds above us, too." In fact, it felt like the thick, gray clouds were everywhere in this gloomy place.

"Right. For those from the World Below, Sky Kingdom is above the clouds. They can't see our land from down there because we have our own plane, with our own sun, stars, and clouds." She jerked her nose up, obviously proud of that fact.

"And what's the World Below?"

"The rest of Nerifir. Several kingdoms lay on the surface of the Below, places like Lorsan, Sarnala, the Olathana Ocean, and the Dakath Mountains. And under that plane is the dark World of Under." She shuddered. "A ghastly place, really, filled with joyless shadow-creatures. It's a good thing they can't fly and keep mostly to their wretched kingdom."

She spoke casually, as if all of that was common knowledge when it sounded completely insane to me.

"So, where exactly did I come from?" I asked. "Where is the world of humans? Earth?"

Earth.

I remembered that world, the weather, the buildings, the countries... The people, in general, like Americans, Germans, Japanese, Brazilians... But I had no memories of friends or family. I had no idea what nationality I was or what country I used to live in. I knew I spoke English before, but that was it. I couldn't remember anything else.

"Humans?" Brebie wrinkled her nose, as if trying to recall anything about my kind and coming up short. "A very long time ago, all worlds of the River of Mists used to be one. You may find many similarities between Sky Kingdom and where you came from because of that. Now, your kind live in the human realm, connected to us by the River of Mists."

"Is that the only way to get there?"

She shrugged a slim shoulder. "As far as I know, yes. We don't get humans here very often. You're the first one to come in like..." Her dainty little nose scrunched up again. "Ever?"

I was a rare creature, indeed.

"Tell me more about the River of Mists, please."

She sighed, clearly growing bored with the topic she knew little about. "What do you want to know?"

"How does one use the cloud river to travel between places?"

"Oh, you really don't need to worry about that, sweetie." She waved me off. "You'll never have to step your foot into the dangerous mists of that river ever again. This is your home now."

Chapter Five

SPARROW

Colorful lights danced behind my eyelids, waking me up. I rolled in bed. It was a comfortable bed, not very wide, but warm and cozy. The bedding felt light and silky against my skin. I stretched. My leg muscles ached, as if after a visit to a gym.

But a gym wasn't what had made my legs ache. This bedroom was inside the crystal palace that belonged to someone they called King Tiane.

And the gym... The gym was far away, in another place.

The place where I belonged.

Keeping my eyes closed, I focused hard on that one word from my past. Gym. It came with the memories of smells of sweat, rubber, and metal. The sounds of weights clanking and treadmills running. Images of people exercising. None of their faces were recognizable, though. And none of them were me. I knew what a gym was. But I had no memories of ever using or even visiting one.

This was just a useless piece of knowledge, without any

personal connection to trigger my memory into remembering my past.

I opened my eyes and sat up in the bed with a sigh.

The room was dimly lit by the walls that glowed softly, aided by pale sunlight that played in the crystal window. Its facets broke the light up into pretty, colorful sparkles scattered all over the room. The sparkles were what had woken me.

Tossing aside the covers, I climbed out of bed, dressed in the long, light nightgown Brebie gave me last night.

The rug was dry now. The tub was gone. The fireplace stood unlit. I crouched in front of it, wondering if I could start the fire. A few neatly trimmed logs lay on a wrought-iron stand inside, but I couldn't find any lighters or matches to ignite them with.

My stomach pinched with hunger, and I had a slight headache, probably from dehydration. I hadn't eaten or drunk anything since that last fateful drink with Trez back in the nameless bar. But I couldn't stay away from food and water for much longer. If I ever wanted to leave this place, it had to be soon.

Other than the nightshirt I was wearing, there were no clothes in either the bedroom or the adjacent wardrobe room.

Before leaving last night, Brebie had told me to pull the wide silver ribbon hanging by the door to call a maid if I needed anything. I tugged at the ribbon. It didn't feel like it was connected to anything. But a soft knock came on the door soon after.

"Come in." I stepped back, giving room for the door to open.

A woman walked in, carrying a tray.

No... the woman didn't walk. She *slithered.*

Keeping her torso upright, she used her long, thick tail to propel herself forward. Like the two maids who had prepared my bath last night, she had no legs. Her tail was almost as wide as her body, being an extension of her torso.

She wore a pale purple blouse and a crisp white apron. Her backside remained exposed from her waist down, and it was all tail, like a giant snake. The deep green color of her tail turned to pastel beige on her face and arms.

"Breakfast, my lady?" the fantastic creature asked, setting her tray on the glass table by the fireplace.

The haze of the *camyte* drink had worn off overnight. The world around me was clear and crisp again, which made it even more incredible. Things looked real when my mind told me they couldn't be.

"What...um." I wanted to ask what this person was. A half-snake, half-woman. How did she even exist? But that would be rude. So I asked, "What's your name?" instead.

"I'm Alacine, my lady." She lifted a cover from the tray on the table. "The High General insists you eat today."

Brebie must have briefed him on my skipping dinner last night.

"The High General can bite me," I snapped.

Alacine blinked at me in shock with her eyelids trimmed with thick green eyelashes.

"I won't tell him you said that. High General Voron is not a man you wish to anger," she warned gently.

I didn't care if she told him. I would tell it to his face if he were here. What would he do to me? Send me back to where I came from?

But I didn't want to shock the poor woman any more than she already was. She seemed extremely disturbed by my lack of respect for their High General.

"Thanks," I said instead.

She returned her attention to the tray. "Following the orders of the High General, these are all simple foods and clear water."

Less likely to have been tampered with, I realized. Despite his demeanor of cool indifference, Voron must be worried about me starving myself before he'd had the pleasure to "present" me to their king.

There was no point in saying any of that to Alacine, whose serene expression had returned to her face. She seemed nice. Not as talkative as Brebie, but I hadn't gotten much info from Brebie last night either, despite all her chatting. Maybe I'd have better luck with Alacine?

"Do you know anything about getting one's memory back?" I asked.

She looked confused. "Getting it back from where?"

I decided to tell her the truth. What did I have to lose at this point?

"The High General took my memories. I don't remember anything about my past."

"He *took* them?" She kept staring at me, clearly dumbfounded. "But how?"

"I'm not sure... He just looked at me and breathed in." It sounded silly, but that was exactly how it'd happened.

Alacine smiled, shaking her head. "No one can do that. Maybe if he hired a hag to put a spell on you and made you drink a potion—"

"No," I exhaled, disheartened. It didn't look like Alacine would be of much help here, either. "There was no potion and no hags. Just he and I."

She shook her head adamantly. "No one has the power to do something like that with just one look. Aside from maybe the king? His Majesty has the magic of Elaros and is the most powerful man in Sky Kingdom. But..." she added, her voice lifting, "if the High General did that somehow, then maybe you should ask him to reverse it?"

"Right." I didn't think it'd be easy to convince him to reverse it. He didn't take my memories for the pure pleasure of having me beg him to return them.

I asked Alacine to bring some clothes before she left, then inspected the "simple food" she'd brought.

The tray held a silver plate with wafers baked with dark flour that would make pink glitter easy to spot had it been added. Another plate had whole fruit and berries laid out on it. An unpeeled egg was set into a metal filigree holder with a tiny spoon laid next to it. The water was in a clear glass carafe. Unlike crystal, the smooth surface of the glass had no facets to break the light or hinder my inspection of the liquid inside.

Whatever his actual intentions were, the High General clearly tried to make it easy for me to inspect the food. So I did.

I carefully lifted every item, sniffed it, and looked for any trace of glimmer or shimmer. Only when I didn't spot anything suspicious and didn't smell even a hint of vanilla cake, did I take a bite of a wafer. It tasted like rye bread. And since it was the first food that crossed my lips in a very long time, it was the best taste in the world.

I peeled the egg quickly and after a thorough inspection, ate it in just a couple of bites. Next, I polished off the grapes, strawberries, and oranges, washing them down with the fresh, clear water from the carafe.

After the food was gone, I sat in the chair by the unlit fireplace and tried to figure out if I felt any different.

There was no one here to test my obedience. So I had no way of telling if there had been any glacier saffron in my breakfast. But I was certain there hadn't been any *camyte* because I still cared very much about what had happened to me in the past twenty-four hours. I felt simply furious that I couldn't remember anything beyond that

I definitely wasn't indifferent about the loss of my memories. Resentment bubbled and grew inside me.

How dare he?

How dare Voron take a part of me like that? Who was I without my past? A nobody. Adrift. Cut off from my roots. Floating through this bizarre world I never planned to come to in the first place... Well, at least I *thought* I hadn't planned to come here. But I couldn't *remember* that either.

Everything here felt wrong. Nothing aligned with the frame of reference I had retained from the human realm. People didn't look or act like normal people. Eating carried a risk of being stripped of one's free will. The future that awaited me here was to be presented to the king... What exactly did it even mean?

I didn't care to find out. I simply wanted to leave.

B rebie stormed into my room like a lightning bolt of horns, hooves, blonde curls, and energy.

She gave me an assessing stare and nodded approvingly. "You look much better than you did last night, honey."

Grabbing the tray with the empty dishes from the table, she handed it to one of the two maids who came with her. "Take this back to the kitchen."

The second maid was Alacine. She was holding a bundle of silky fabric and a pair of embroidered slippers—clothes for me, I assumed. I would've preferred jeans and a pair of hiking boots since I'd have to hike back to the river at the first opportunity. But if those were all they had for me, I'd make do with them too.

"Time to get you ready," Brebie cooed.

"Ready for what?"

"High General Voron needs to see you."

"What for?"

She bounced on her hooves with excitement. "It's happening, honey. You are to be presented to the king at the ball tonight. But the High General needs to see you before that."

"Tonight? Why so soon?"

"Why wait?" She shrugged. "The king is having a ball tonight. It's a great opportunity for you to meet him and his entire court."

"Tonight?" I repeated numbly.

Something told me it was best to leave before the king of this place had laid his eyes on me. Which left me very little time to plan and execute my escape.

"Yes." Brebie nodded impatiently. "Voron will be waiting for you at noon. And we still need to get you changed, brush your hair..." She poked my naked arm, then pinched my skin. "This needs some oil and shimmer. Take off your nightgown, dear. We'll start right away."

"Now?" I folded my arms over my chest protectively.

She pinned me with a critical glare. "Trust me. It'll take time to make you look presentable to both the king and the High General. We'd better hurry."

I'd never met the king, but the idea of seeing the High General again brushed by my spine with a chill of trepidation. I wasn't looking forward to having those cold eyes of his on me again.

"What if I don't want to see either of them?" I asked.

Brebie huffed, propping her hands on her hips.

"Well, that's not up to you or me, is it? High General Voron is the most powerful man in this kingdom after the king. He runs the royal court and the entire household of King Tiane. Nothing happens in this palace without his knowledge and approval. He ordered you to be there. And you think you can just stomp your foot and disregard his orders? Who do you think you are?"

That was the problem. I had no idea who I was. Which was a hundred percent High General Voron's fault. He took my memories, my past, and my very identity.

Maybe Alacine was right? Since Voron was the one who did this to me, he would be the one to undo it. In any case, it wouldn't hurt talking to him, would it?

"Fine," I said to Brebie. "I'll see him."

Brebie made a face, shaking her head at my attitude. She clearly was fed up with my inability to act like "a lady." But I wasn't here to please her. With any luck, she wouldn't be putting up with me for much longer.

"Wait here." The guard placed a hand on my shoulder, stopping me in front of a tall carved door.

The other guard stepped in front of us. His russet-colored, feathery wings shrank, then appeared to melt into his back. There were no openings in his gray-and-silver uniform. I saw no slits or gashes in the fabric. His wings just disappeared, as if absorbed through the cloth by his body.

"Wow." I turned to the guard next to me. "Can you do that too?"

He gave me a puzzled look, saying nothing.

The first guard knocked on the door.

"The human woman is here as you requested, High General," he announced loudly to the door.

"Get her in," came from inside the room.

A shiver ran down my arms at the sound of that voice. I dreaded facing the High General again, knowing the horrible things he could do. He held the power to erase a person from existence, not by physically killing them, but by annihilating the very essence of what they were.

I drew the ends of the silk robe I wore tighter around me. It was the only garment I'd received from Brebie. After babbling all night about how many clothes the king would gift me, all I had to wear today was this long creamy-white robe, painted with pastel swirls, and a pair of blue silk slippers.

The guard opened the door and gestured for me to enter. The two didn't move from the corridor. Clearly, I was expected to face the High General alone.

I hesitated, but the guards poked my back, prompting me to move. The moment I crossed the threshold, the door slammed shut behind me.

"Hello, Sparrow." Voron leaned a hip against the dark-wood desk placed by one of the three tall windows in the room.

The large black bird I'd seen flying in front of his horse yesterday was now perched on his shoulder. The bird's ankles were circled with pretty silver rings, probably to let others know this was the High General's pet.

Bookshelves lined the walls between the windows. They were tightly packed with thick books in embossed leather bindings. Several long baskets on the floor by the shelves held rolls of parchment that looked like old scrolls.

An open scroll was draped over the desk with a world map on it. It was *my* world—Earth. It looked like the High General had been studying it, probably trying to learn what he had to deal with upon my arrival to Elaros.

Dressed in black pants and a black silk shirt with wide sleeves and ruffled cuffs, he had his arms crossed over his chest, studying me as I pressed my back to the door behind me.

He had no coat on. The black vest he wore over his shirt was open, giving him a slightly more casual look, which sadly failed to make him any more approachable. His silver-gray eyes remained as distant as ever.

"I trust you slept well," he said with a slight tilt of his head. "You look far less...um, *pitiful* today."

I didn't need his pity.

Shoving away from the door, I straightened my spine, standing taller.

"Thank you, I had a very good sleep," I said in a clipped voice.

A smile ghosted his lips. It melted quickly, like the first snow of the season after touching the ground.

What amused him? There was nothing funny or even friendly either in the words I said or in how I said them.

I shifted my gaze around, studying the room instead of its occupant who unnerved me. It was warm in here. The fire burned lively in the fireplace by the wall opposite to the desk. A chaise lounge, upholstered in royal blue velvet, stood in front of it with a fluffy blanket neatly folded on one end.

What was this room? It was spacious, but not large enough to be a royal library. Was it Voron's personal reading place? It was cozy. I could easily imagine myself curling up with a book by the fire.

Imagining the morose High General relaxing anywhere wasn't easy, though. Despite his casual pose, leaning with his hip against the desk, his body seemed rigid and his eyes remained guarded. He didn't trust me. That made two of us. I had no trust in him, either.

I didn't want to be here, but we needed to talk. Taking a deep breath in, I took a step in his direction. I might as well get straight to the point.

"What do I have to do to get my memories back?"

His dark eyebrows jerked up in surprise. "You came to negotiate, little bird?"

I winced at that nickname but didn't protest. There was nothing I'd want him to call me instead, anyway. The only name I now had was the one he gave me. And "sparrow" was essentially the same thing as "little bird."

"That can be interesting." He pushed away from his desk. His pet bird flapped its wings, flying from his shoulder to a gilded tree branch mounted on the corner of his desk. "What are you willing to offer?"

He stalked my way, stepping softly on the thick gray rug covering the white marble floor. I resisted the strong urge to flinch or retreat, standing my ground.

"What do you want?"

The question was a mistake. His features relaxed into a self-assured expression. He clearly took it as an invitation to help himself to anything his heart desired.

What were the desires of Voron's heart? It wasn't easy to tell with him, but I feared the price might be far greater than what I was willing to pay.

Significantly taller than me, he looked down at me as he came closer. He didn't say a word, just stared at me, with that elusive smile playing on his lips. His eyes peered into mine, reaching deeper. I felt naked in front of him, completely exposed, as he searched inside me for whatever else he could rip away from me.

Cold shivers of trepidation ran down my body. I gripped my arms with my hands. It was stupid to challenge this man. I was no match for him. He'd never let me gain from any deal we'd make. With him, I could only lose.

Breathing became a chore under his stare. I couldn't draw enough air into my lungs, no matter how hard I inhaled.

All I could do was beg.

I swallowed hard and licked my dry lips.

"Please..." I croaked. "I have nothing left to give."

"Oh yes you do. And were our circumstances different, I would've loved to help myself to the many treasures you possess, dear Sparrow."

His voice softened, easing my distress. The powers of this man were even greater than I'd thought. He could calm me down just as easily as terrify.

"I will take nothing more from you than I already have." He lifted his hand to my face as if to stroke it but stopped short of touching me, dropping his arm down again. "Instead, I'll give you something for free—a piece of advice. Now that your mind is void of the useless memories, you can start filling it with things you really need."

Useless.

How easily he dismissed my entire life experience. Bitterness burned in my throat.

"The last thing I need is your advice," I snapped, turning my head away from him.

"Oh, but you do need it. You need to get to know this world in order to survive here."

With any luck, I wouldn't stay here long enough for his advice to be useful. I'd leave, with or without his help.

He captured my chin in his hand and forced me to look at him again.

"Think carefully before making deals with fae, Sparrow," he

said slowly, measuring every word. "You risk to lose, with potentially dire consequences for yourself. We always come for what's owed to us."

The only deal I wished to make was for my freedom. Then, I'd be far away from this place for anyone to come for me, anyway.

Dreading to meet his eyes, I stared at his mouth instead. He had perfectly shaped, sensual lips.

"Made for kissing," flashed through my mind unexpectedly. Clearly, looking at his lips carried a risk, too.

I blinked slowly, regaining my focus.

"Is that your advice?" I bit out.

"Some of it."

"There's more?"

He shrugged, unfazed. "I'm in a generous mood today."

I huffed, trying to ignore the warm sensation of his fingers on my face. He held my chin for control. This wasn't a caress, even if it inexplicably felt like one.

"Generous? You simply trapped me, and now I have no choice but to listen to you imparting your wisdom to me." I instilled as much sarcasm into my words as I could muster.

A glimmer appeared in his eyes, as if he found my talking back exciting. Life as the High General must be a dull one if my snapping at him excited him.

He let go of my chin and stepped back. "Like I said, you need every piece of 'wisdom' you can get if you want to make it in Elaros."

"What if I don't? What if I'm not interested in *making* it here?"

"You don't have a choice, Sparrow." There was an echo of regret in his voice, the same regret I'd glimpsed in his eyes yesterday.

But if he regretted having me here, maybe he'd be glad to get rid of me?

"Help me, then," I pleaded. "Give me my memories back and let me leave. I won't even ask you to take me back to the river.

They say you're a powerful man, that you practically run this place. Tell the guards to open the gate, and I'll walk away. That's all you have to do, and I promise, you'll never see me again."

He regarded me with an expression that bordered on pity. "Where would you go, little bird?"

"Home."

"Where is home?"

I refused to falter under his stare, holding my head high.

"I don't *remember* that. Because of you. But I'll follow the same path that brought me here—"

"And you will never return to the same place or time," he finished for me.

I shook my head vehemently, refusing to let him weaken my determination. "I'll end up back in my world. Away from you. From this place. Back where I belong."

The muscles in his jaw ticked as he pressed those kissable lips of his into a sharp line.

"I can't let you leave, Sparrow," he said firmly.

My heart squeezed tightly at his words, crushing the hope inside.

"Why not?"

"For one, I don't want to. I far prefer having you around." He sounded so casual, I wished to slap him.

"Asshole," rushed through my head. *"A stuck-up, selfish asshole."*

"I quite look forward to watching you build a new life for yourself here," he continued, oblivious to the resentment seething inside me. "You're getting a pretty good start in Elaros, a chance of becoming the king's favorite. I want to see what you'll do with that."

Did he honestly think I'd find it enticing to serve as a source of his amusement?

"Sorry to deprive you of your future entertainment, but I have no desire to be a part of this world."

"But you already are," he pointed out. "The moment you

crossed the River of Mists, you became a part of Sky Kingdom. You have no choice in what your life here will be. But you do have control of your reactions to what is happening to you. You can fight it, be miserable, and try to escape. Or you can accept it and play the best game with the cards fate has dealt you. Either way," he made an elegant gesture in the air with his hand, "the end result will be the same. The only difference will be that the first path would lead you through more anguish and suffering."

"Not if I leave here—" I insisted, but he wouldn't let me finish.

"You won't leave. Not for long. If I let you walk through the gate, you won't make it a hundred paces from the palace before someone snatches you. The word that there's a human woman in the king's palace has gone out already. News like that spreads faster than a wildfire. Do you know how rare you are?"

I didn't answer that, but I remembered what Brebie had said about me being the only human here.

He didn't wait for my reply, anyway. "With one small, brief exception, your kind has never been to Sky Kingdom before you. There are no records of humans ever residing here directly from your world. If you leave, you'll be snatched, sold, and traded until you'll ultimately end up here, in the royal palace again. Do you know why?"

"Why?" I asked quietly, subdued by the fate he'd predicted for me.

He leaned closer, speaking softly in a voice that could be considered intimate if he wasn't talking of such disturbing things. "Because a rare thing like you, my dear Sparrow, can only belong to a king."

"But I'm not *a thing*. I don't want to belong to anyone."

"Sadly, it's not up to you to decide."

I balled my hands into fists to stop my fingers from trembling. As much as I hated to ask anything from this man, desperation forced me to beg again.

"Take me to the forest, please, to the bridge across that river. I'll do anything—"

His somber expression remained infuriatingly unyielding.

"The River of Mists is a capricious, brutal monster, Sparrow. If the crossing doesn't kill you, you'd return to your world, but it wouldn't be the same place or the same time as you left. You may end up thousands of years in the past. And you'd be alone, with no friends or family, with no means to support yourself, and no memories of where you came from in the first place."

Now I remember more from his conversation with Trez, who had said the same thing. I would go back to Earth, but back to *what?* No one could tell me what time period I'd end up arriving in. And like Voron had said, without friends or money, I'd risk far more than what I was facing here.

The hopelessness of my situation brought tears to my eyes. I sniffled, turning away from him. The last thing I wanted was for the snooty High General to see me cry.

He wouldn't let me hide, though. He couldn't give me even that little mercy. Cupping my face, he turned me to him.

"I can't give you your memories back, Sparrow, even if I wanted to do that. I didn't *take* them. I made them *disappear.* They're gone now. Gone for good. Irrecoverable."

Gone...

A huge part of me—my entire past—was lost forever. Sorrow gripped my heart. A tear I couldn't hold back rolled down my cheek, leaving a hot trail on my skin.

Voron caught it on his thumb and brushed it away.

"Old memories would be nothing but useless ballast for you here. Missing your past and the people you knew but could never see again would've only made you unhappy."

"I assure you..." I paused, willing my voice not to shake before continuing, "there is nothing *happy* about me without my past, either."

Keeping my face between his hands, he stroked my skin with

his thumbs. "Let's hope there will be soon. I sincerely wish for you to find joy in Elaros."

I stepped back, fleeing his hold. He couldn't return my memories and wouldn't free me. There was no reason for me to stay in this room any longer. I turned to the door.

"You can't go yet," he stopped me. "As much as I enjoyed talking to you, dear Sparrow, I didn't call you in here merely for a conversation."

"What do you want?" I threw over my shoulder.

"I'm presenting you to King Tiane tonight."

"Right." I released a long breath. "Do you really have to do that?"

"I've given a promise, which, as a fae, I cannot break. If I fail to bring you to the ball tonight, I'll end up in the Garden of the Cursed. Trust me, it's not a place I wish to be." He took a few slow, measured steps toward the chaise by the fireplace. "Everything and everyone presented to the king needs to be thoroughly inspected to ensure no harm comes to his royal persona."

"Inspected?" I wrapped the robe tighter around myself. "Please tell me you don't mean what I think you do."

"I'm afraid it is exactly that, little bird. A law stipulates a thorough inspection by the Royal Council. As the king's trusted advisor and the kingdom's High General, I was able to convince the Council that the inspection by just one person would suffice in your case." He leaned his hip against the high back of the chaise lounge. "That person is me."

Chapter Six

SPARROW

Voron flicked his wrist, and the flames in the fireplace sprung higher.

"Whoa!" I shrank back. "How did you do that?"

I couldn't even start a fire on my own this morning. And he did *this* with literally just a flick of his hand.

"Sky fae have the power to control light," he explained.

"And the fire, too?"

"Not exactly. Our magic can't start or extinguish the fire. But we can dim its light or make it burn brighter. Is this comfortable for you?"

For me?

Right. He had to *inspect* me. Was he hoping to make me at ease by setting the mood and making the fire burn brighter?

I clutched my robe to my chest.

"You're not touching me."

My heart pounded inside my rib cage. No way I'd let him go ahead with this ridiculous "inspection," or whatever it was he was planning to do to me. I had no idea how I would stop him, but I was ready to fight tooth and nail.

He didn't appear to be in a fighting mood, however, making no move to come closer. Resting his hands on the back of the chaise, he spoke calmly, "There is no need for me to touch you. But I do have to see everything, in order for the inspection to be considered complete."

"You're not *seeing* anything, either." I glared at him.

He held my stare, looking infuriatingly calm.

"Sparrow, I gave you a choice where you weren't meant to have any. Would you rather the Council conduct the inspection?"

I shifted from foot to foot awkwardly, considering my options. This wasn't much of a choice either way.

"How many people are on your Council?"

"Thirteen—" he cut himself off. "Are you seriously considering choosing them over me?" He sounded offended, like I'd hurt his feelings by not jumping at the opportunity to get naked for him.

I chewed on my lip. "It depends. If they are thirteen reasonably respectful women with a healthy regard for personal boundaries..."

"Only five of them are women. Most are shrewd and cynical. Many are judgmental and gossipy. None would hold back a snide remark or restrain from a poke, either physical or emotional."

"Oh boy..." I exhaled heavily. Unease crawled up my back like tiny spiders. The Council didn't sound like a friendly bunch at all.

Tugging at my ear nervously, I gave Voron an assessing look. He kept his distance, hovering by the fireplace as I remained closer to the door.

This man or thirteen complete strangers—that was my choice.

He still appeared to be sulking at my considering refusing him. "Just say a word, and I'll personally escort you to the council meeting room, where they all sit in their tall chairs in a circle, and you'll have to disrobe in the center for them to ogle you, measure, and judge."

He believed he was doing me a favor by volunteering to take over this particular duty of the Council for me.

Would I be wrong to reject his offer?

Voron was very much a stranger to me, just like the Council members were. Probably even worse, since I had plenty of personal reasons to despise him from stealing my past to refusing to set me free. But they said, "better the devil you know." Devil or not, I knew Voron better than the thirteen councilors I'd never met.

Maybe I could go through with it, after all? What if I looked at it as a visit to a doctor? I didn't remember who my doctor was, their name, or whether I even had one, but I knew that visits to a doctor's office were generally conducted in a detached, professional manner, with no emotions involved, which allowed for the patient to keep their dignity intact.

"Can you promise to be respectful?" I asked.

He adjusted a ruffled cuff on his black shirt. "I prefer not to make any promises at all. But if you insist..." He paused, looking straight at me. "I promise to do my best at refraining from touching you during today's inspection and try not to make any comments that I deem inappropriate."

A puff of warm air came from nowhere, just like it did yesterday when Voron promised Trez to present me to the king. It circled both of us in a shimmering twister, billowing my robe around my legs and ruffling Voron's bi-colored tresses.

"There you go." He twirled his hand in the air, following the shimmer. "You have my promise. And the magic is here to seal it."

I was new to this world, but even I could tell his promise had no weight, either sealed by magic or not. Too much of it sounded subjective and arbitrary.

Pursing my lips, I gave him a wary look. "What exactly is 'your best?' And what is your definition of 'inappropriate?'"

"Aaah." Satisfaction spread on his face, as if my catching him giving useless promises had been his goal all along. "Well done, dear Sparrow. Don't be assured by the shimmer of magic. Pay close attention to the words."

His praise shouldn't make me feel as good as it did. Pleasing him was not my goal. But pride glowed inside me when I caught a spark of genuine respect in his eyes.

"Well." I glanced aside. "How am I supposed to trust anything you say if you wiggle your way out of even giving me a simple promise?"

"You can't," he agreed, with amusement sprinkling his voice. "I'm telling you I won't touch you during the inspection and will keep my remarks to myself, but it's up to you to either believe me or not. The risk is yours."

I jerked my chin up in response to his challenge. The fight *was* happening between us, after all. Only the altercation wasn't physical.

Voron clearly enjoyed the game he was playing. Fine. I could play it, too. He wished to test me? I could do a test of my own.

"Or..." I stepped away from the door and strolled over to him. "You could prove to me that you can be trusted."

He tilted his head, looking very much intrigued.

"It's a test," I explained. "I'll let you 'inspect' me. And in return, you will show me how much I can trust you from then on."

"A test—" He stopped abruptly, his words clipped off by his sharp intake of air as I shed my robe.

In one quick, determined movement, I yanked it off my shoulders and let it fall to the floor. If I couldn't avoid this, it was best to do it fast and be over with.

"Go ahead. Look." I spread my arms out and lifted my head, staring at the top of a bookshelf.

Voron went so still, I couldn't even hear his breathing. After a few moments of complete silence, I ventured a look at him to make sure he was still there.

He stood in front of me, his gaze slowly traveling down my body. I had no memories of my relationships with men or even if I had any. I didn't know if a man had ever seen me naked. But if someone had before, did it make my skin tingle the way it did when Voron was looking at me?

Shaded by his long, jet-black eyelashes, his silver eyes appeared darker as his pupils dilated. His hands remained at his sides, far away from me. But he didn't need to touch me. He caressed me with his eyes. Not a single dip or curve of my body escaped his attention. There was curiosity in his gaze, appreciation, and... desire. It glowed softly, heating up the cool gray of his irises.

Awareness rushed down my body, pebbling the skin on my arms with goosebumps. This was far from the "detached and professional" that I'd intended for it to be.

I crossed my arms over my stomach. He didn't ask me to remove them. I wondered if he'd object to my covering the most intimate places of my body with my hands, but a part of me—an obviously deeply disturbed part—didn't want to hide from his attention. Light excitement skittered along my skin with waves of tingly pleasure, and I wasn't in a hurry to end it yet.

Instead of telling me to turn around for a full inspection, he slowly circled me.

I listened to his soft steps behind me, imagining where his gaze fell on my body. First, it might have slid down my arms to between my shoulder blades, then down my spine to the small of my back. I imagined it caressing my backside, wondering what his hand would feel like if he cupped me there...

"Lie down, please," he said quietly.

His deep voice yanked me from my rather inappropriate musings.

I turned to face him. "Lie where?"

"Right here." He pointed at the chaise lounge.

"What for?" I asked, unsure whether it was trepidation or anticipation that I felt at his request. My face felt warm. My entire body heated. My mind, however, cautioned me that this inspection was going too far.

"I told you, Sparrow, I need to see *everything*." His voice remained low, but it gained some new rasp to it that came from deep in his throat.

Everything?

It took me a moment to grasp what that meant.

"Are you going to look between my legs, too?"

His calm composure wavered, which was new and oddly satisfying to see.

He cleared his throat. "That is a part of the inspection, yes."

I cocked a hip, crossing my arms over my chest.

"Why? What do you need to see down there? What are you hoping to find? Tentacles?" Apparently, anxiety made me say stupid things.

He didn't laugh, however, just stared at me. His brow furrowed slightly as he blinked slowly.

Did he really believe there was a possibility of finding tentacles in my vagina? Had he not seen a naked woman before?

But then again, maybe he hadn't. Not a *human* woman, anyway. Since humans were so *rare* around here.

I couldn't possibly pass on this unexpected opportunity to torment him.

"What's the matter, High General?" I inclined my head, faking a concerned expression. "You didn't know? I guess they don't mention that particular part of human anatomy in those scrolls of yours." I gestured at the map of my world spread on his desk. "How does King Tiane feel about tentacles? Do you think they may dampen his joy at receiving me as a gift?" I threw my hands up into the air dramatically. "Maybe you should let me leave after all? Let me take my tentacles back to where they came from. And in return, I'll promise never to come back to terrorize your royalty with them."

I must've overdone it just a tad because the frown on his face smoothed out. He gave me an unimpressed look, shaking his head.

"Oh, but I had you there!" I laughed. "Admit it. For a second or two, you really wondered if human women had tentacles growing between our legs, didn't you?"

It felt so good to gain an upper hand over him, even if just for a moment and only because of a silly joke. Until now, the power had been firmly on his side. It was exciting and satisfying to have it tilt my way for once, to rattle his cool demeanor.

He heaved a sigh but didn't deny my victory.

"You really are *unique*, with or without tentacles," he muttered under his breath, then ordered, "now get your ass up here. We don't have all day."

He sounded grumpy, yet a barely-there smile curved his lips. He tried to fight it, but it didn't escape me. Now that I'd leveled the playing field somewhat, this whole "inspection" felt so much less humiliating. I even smiled to myself as I lay down on the chaise.

"Open your legs for me, Sparrow." His voice dropped a notch. The force with which he spoke made his words sound like another order, not a request.

Was he asserting his power over me again? After I'd wrested some of it from him with my joke?

"Show me," he demanded.

Breath caught in my throat at the velvety growl in his voice. This was Voron's bedroom voice. It had to be. That must be how he talked to women before making passionate love to them—it had to be passionate. Through his cool exterior, I'd glimpsed the smoldering heat of desire in Voron's steely eyes. And I could only imagine how bright it could burn if he let it burn unrestrained.

Now, I was thinking about Voron in his bedroom, climbing over a woman spread in his bed, with her legs open wide for him...

I drew in a deep breath, and it came out with a slight moan as I slowly parted my bent legs.

This definitely didn't feel like a doctor's exam or even as an inspection.

What was it, then? Why did it feel so natural for me to be naked in front of this man who was practically a stranger?

I wasn't trying to seduce him. I wasn't... Except that... What *was* I doing, breathing deeply and arching my back while hoping to look graceful and attractive?

Voron circled the chaise, stopping briefly to admire the view I presented with my thighs spread open. He spent but a moment or two there, standing between my legs, then moved on toward my head and stopped, separated from me by the back of the chaise.

Yet I still held my legs wide open, as if in invitation.

His throat bobbed with a swallow.

"You can get dressed now." He wouldn't look straight at me, staring at the corner of the blanket under my head instead.

I closed my legs so fast, my thighs slapped against each other, like my body was applauding me for coming back to my senses.

Apparently, Voron didn't need to add any magical substances to my food to cast a spell on me. Why else would I act this way? Why else would I feel anything for him other than resentment?

He picked up my robe from the floor and held it open for me while still having that odd detached look in his eyes, staring past me.

I dropped my gaze, stepping into the robe. He briefly stroked my shoulders, smoothing the material of the garment over them.

"The guards will take you back to your room."

I turned around slowly, keeping my eyes down. The massive bulge in his crotch was impossible to miss. The soft material of his pants stretched over his thick length pressed against his thigh.

I didn't remember if a man had ever had the same reaction to me before, but I knew what that bulge meant. Voron was affected by this "inspection" no matter how hard he tried to pretend otherwise. A hot jolt of desire shot down to my core at the sight of his hard-on straining to rip through his pants. I wished I could touch it...

I fisted my hands in the silk of my robe, lest they stray in his direction.

Voron was an incredibly beautiful man. But there was more

that pulled me to him. I wondered what sadness was hidden behind his cool exterior that would make it so difficult for him to muster a wide, open smile. I longed to find out. But I couldn't possibly allow any feelings of attraction between us.

My pull toward him was unexpected, insane, and so very wrong.

He'd deprived me of my past. He'd refused to set me free, mostly because he just "didn't want to." He'd put me through this ridiculous inspection, which was clearly meant to humiliate me, even if it failed to do so at the end.

But most importantly, Voron had brought me to this palace as "a gift" for another man. I should never forget that.

I stepped around him on my way to the exit.

"And?" his voice stopped me. "Did I pass your trust test, dear Sparrow?"

He'd kept his word. He hadn't touched me. Was he expecting to hear praise from me now?

"Trust?" I placed my hand on the door handle. "You behaved this time, but trusting you, I fear, would be a huge mistake. Of all the feelings I could have for you, High General, the only one I *should* have is hate."

His chest rose with a long, slow breath. He flexed his fingers, spreading them wide at his sides, then fisted his hands so tight his knuckles paled. Other than that one gesture, he remained perfectly composed.

"Of all emotions in existence," he said evenly, "hate is the wisest one to have between us."

Something pinched in my chest at him agreeing so easily, though I knew it was for the best.

I had but one more thing left to say to him.

"Yesterday, you mistook my state, induced by *camyte* or saffron or whatever that drink was, for 'pitiful' meekness of character. You may think of me as a weak *little bird*. But I am a person, and I am not weak. Sooner or later, I'll prove it to you."

There was more to me than my past. My memories didn't define me. I would figure out who I was even without them.

He raised his head, looking straight into my eyes.

"Please do, dear Sparrow. I'm very much looking forward to that."

Chapter Seven

SPARROW

As I followed the guards down the crystal corridors of the Elaros Palace, the grim reality that I was stuck here now settled heavily in my mind. The only way to fight the crushing weight of it was to search for any ray of light.

There must be a silver lining here, no matter how slim or threadbare. All I needed was a little bit of hope to go on. Something to look forward to in the future.

I'd lost my past, my name, and my entire world. But I kept the most important part—me. I might not know who I had been, but I could still become somebody. I'd lost my memories but retained my ability to think, analyze, and make decisions. I could watch, listen, and learn.

My life wasn't over just because my past was gone. Just because that man took it.

Since I didn't know who I was before, maybe I could try to be what they wanted me to be?

Could this place become my new home?

For the first time since I got to the palace, I looked around, noting everything.

The place where I met Voron was located a few levels higher than the room where I'd spent the night. The guards led me down a narrow staircase made of the light material with so many decorative cut-outs, it looked like hardened lace.

The stairs connected only a couple of floors, however. After that, we walked along a wide corridor with walls made of pale-gray vines that curved up in such smooth, organic lines, they appeared to still be alive and growing. The space between the vines was filled with white marble and the glowing crystals that illuminated the entire palace.

We took another tiny staircase down, then another one. There didn't seem to be a staircase or an elevator that would connect all floors from the ground floor to the top. The cute tiny staircases randomly appeared here and there, taking us a floor or two down, then we'd have to walk, looking for another one to take us to the floor below.

The guards must be leading me through the pathways reserved for servants, as many of them had passed us, rushing on their hooves or slithering on their tails.

The lower we descended, the thicker the vines in the walls got, and the more of them there were. In my bedroom, the walls consisted mostly of gray vines, with only narrow strips of marble and small entrapments of crystals that glowed no stronger than a nightlight.

Some light came through the window, but the decorative crystal panes distorted the view outside. The room was too dim. Setting my knee on the blush-pink cushion of the window seat, I yanked the two halves of the window open.

A gust of cold wind rushed into the bedroom, blowing my robe wide open. I gasped, catching the ends of the robe and drawing them closed over my chest again. Winged people soared around the palace. Thankfully, none of them appeared to be close enough to witness me momentarily exposing myself.

My room was somewhere in the middle of the palace, located half-way between the ground and the lacy tips of this unusual construction. This level was too high for me to jump down or even attempt to climb to the ground. Which was just as well. After talking to Voron, escaping the palace didn't seem that appealing any more.

What would be the point of risking my life while trying to escape Elaros, only to be captured and brought back here again?

Even if I could return to my old life somehow, what life would that be? For better or for worse, with my memories gone, so was the longing. I didn't miss the people or the places I didn't remember. I knew all about the world I used to live in, but I had no personal connection to it anymore. My homesickness had no purchase.

Any memories I now possessed came from here.

Instead of mourning what I'd lost, I focused on what I had. As Brebie had said, I had a roof over my head and enough food to eat. I was warm. And for now, at least, I was safe. No one threatened my life.

I suspected that my service to King Tiane might include giving him full access to my body. That was what Voron's inspection was all about, after all.

But I hadn't met King Tiane yet. What if I ended up liking him? Everyone else did, according to Voron. What if I enjoyed being the girlfriend of a powerful king? It wasn't the worst thing that could've happened to me, considering the circumstances.

I could go with the flow, at least for now. Maybe things might turn out not to be too bad, after all.

The door to my room opened with a blast of wind rushing from the window. It blew my hair back and whipped my robe around my legs. I turned around too quickly, slamming my shoulder into the window frame. One of the golden beetles fell from the curtains onto my shoulder and promptly scurried down my arm.

Shock zapped through me.

"It's alive!" I screamed, shaking my arm.

The beetle fell down.

Brebie carried in a tray with food and calmly placed it on the table by the fireplace.

"Of course it's alive," she said, looking at me like I was a complete idiot. "A dead one wouldn't be able to make those curtains for you, would it?"

"Are all of these bugs alive and moving?" I scowled at the golden beetles. There were at least a dozen of them on the curtains. They appeared motionless, but when I looked closely, I could see their little heads moving as they crawled ever so slowly along the fabric.

"*Firrian* beetles eat crystal dust and spin silk that our kingdom is famous for all through Nerifir and beyond. Look at it." Brebie lifted the edge of the curtain. The fabric shimmered in her hand, trapping the scarce daylight between its folds and breaking it into tiny rainbows. "Magic can be woven into it, creating the most wondrous of cloth. If done correctly, one can even look into gorgonian eyes through our spider silk and not be turned to stone."

Spider silk that was made by *beetles*. Just another thing about this world that made no sense.

Yet if I were to stay here, I had to find a way to understand it all.

"What is a gorgonian?" I asked.

"Not what, but *who*. It's another kind of fae. They live in the Below and can turn people to stone with their look."

I regarded the curtains with a new appreciation.

"What is such an extraordinary silk doing on my window?"

She shrugged. "Where else should it be? The beetles still need to add another layer for this cloth to be ready. It may as well hang here until they're done. The beetles get enough fresh air, sunlight, and crystal dust in the palace. A perfect place for them to be. Once they're done with this batch, we'll take this silk down and start them on a new one." Since I continued to eye the bugs suspiciously, she added, "Don't worry, they don't usually get too close to people." She picked up the one that I'd shaken off and gently placed it back on the curtain. "They prefer to stay on the cloth, unless people are clumsy enough to dislodge them from the silk." She shook her head disapprovingly. "Let's close the window now. It's chilly out there."

"Is it always this cold and gloomy in Sky Kingdom?" I asked as she closed the window and turned the little silver handle to lock the two halves together. "I haven't seen any real sunlight here yet."

Brebie had said Sky Kingdom was above the clouds, but it appeared it sat firmly right inside one, shrouding it in gray miserable mist.

She touched a crystal on the wall, and suddenly its glow grew. All the crystals shone brightly, illuminating the room.

"How did you do that?" I patted the wall and stroked the crystals, causing no change in their light whatsoever.

"Sky fae magic."

Right. Voron had explained that to me earlier today.

"If light is your power, then why is it so dark outside?" I gestured at the gray skies in the window.

"It's early spring. Cold is to be expected. Besides, King Tiane is a busy man. A lot of worries must be weighing down on him to think about the weather."

"What does the king have to do with the weather?"

She looked at me like I was a clueless child. "The Sky King controls the clouds, honey. His moods affect the weather in our kingdom and beyond."

"His moods? Really? Like he has to be happy for the sun to come out?"

"Well, we haven't had a whole day of sun in ages. It's not easy to run a kingdom, you know. Worries always cloud His Majesty's mind, I imagine. But maybe your arrival will cheer him up? Speaking of which, we need to get you ready for the ball."

Grabbing me by my arm, she dragged me to the chair by the fireplace.

"Why don't you sit here, honey, and eat your lunch while I get things ready?"

"What things?" I examined the food on the plates, paying far less attention to it than before. If Voron wanted my obedience, I believed, he had many means at his disposal to get it without resorting to adding magical substances to my salads and sandwiches. He possessed a great power, magical and otherwise, and I had little choice but to cooperate.

Brebie placed a quilted blanket over the silk coverlet on the bed.

"We will need to get it just right," she said. "You'll be presented to the king tonight, Sparrow. Your entire future depends on what he thinks about you."

I twisted a tiny spoon from the tray in my hands. "Talk about being pressured."

"The pressure is on all of us, honey." She arranged a battery of bottles, jugs, and small containers on the lid of the trunk by the bed. "We'll need to rub some fragrant oils on your skin, add some shimmer and body paint. We'll have to do your hair, get you dressed... Oh, there are simply not enough hours in the day for all of this."

With that, Brebie called to my room a flock of maids to help her, and I hurriedly shoved some food into my mouth before they took the tray away.

"You have to forget about your modesty, Sparrow," Brebie lectured me in a voice that disallowed argument. "Stop worrying about your privacy. It'd be highly inconvenient for us to work with our eyes closed—we'd never get anything done. Just take your robe off and let us do it properly."

If my future in this kingdom depended on tonight, cooperating with Brebie's efforts was in my interests. Besides, after having been closely inspected by Voron, I found undressing in the presence of the women much easier.

After they had thoroughly cleaned me and rubbed every inch of my body with something slick and smelly, they placed me on a stool by the fire.

A tall woman with lime-yellow wings arrived, carrying a pallet of paints and a small bucket of brushes over her arm. She lowered herself onto her knees in front of me.

"What should I paint on her?" she asked Brebie, not me. "The king's name?"

"No." Brebie waved her hands at the woman. "That'd be too presumptuous. And bad luck, too. The king hasn't claimed her yet. Just paint something pretty. But no words or letters."

Tilting her head, the woman stared at my naked breasts like an artist would look at a clean canvas envisioning the picture they were going to paint. Feeling self-conscious, I moved my hands to cover up, but she batted them away without raising her eyes to my face.

"Well, she has lots of space for me to work with," she said, taking out a brush from her bucket.

Lots of space?

That must be a reference to the size of my breasts, which were quite large compared to the fae I'd met so far. The woman's voice didn't sound like she was insulting or judging me, though. So, I chose to ignore her remark and said nothing when she put her brush to my skin.

She painted quickly, in skilled, confident strokes. Her brush tickled my skin, but I tried to hold still. Only when she dragged it over my nipple, I jerked away.

"Is *that* part really necessary to be painted over?"

Brebie leaned over my shoulder, leaving one of the maids to take over braiding my hair. "What's that, honey?"

"What's the point in painting the parts of my body that will be covered by clothes, anyway?" I shielded my nipples from the brush with my hands.

"Oh, but she isn't painting where it'd be covered."

My anxiety spiked at Brebie's words. "Are you saying my breasts will be fully exposed? Am I going to the ball topless?"

"Not exactly." Brebie dismissed my concerns with a vague hand gesture. "Sparrow, honey, please let the woman do her job, so we can finish on time. We all wish for King Tiane to like you, but the king hates to be kept waiting. He'll be furious if we're late."

I kept my hands in front of my chest. "Brebie, what is going to happen at the ball?"

"How am I supposed to know? I've never been invited to one. The royal balls are for highborn only."

But I needed the answers. "Is everyone going to be naked tonight?"

"Don't be silly." She shook her head, tossing her golden curls between her horns. "No one will be *completely* naked. You will be wearing a dress. The paint is a decoration, just like the jewelry. If anything, it actually hides your bits, covering them up."

"Is this really the only way? Why can't I have something like what you're wearing?" Her pastel-colored dresses were pretty but also provided decent coverage in all areas that mattered, including the chest.

She walked around the chair and crouched in front of me, shouldering the painter aside.

"Sparrow, the king gives beautiful parties. The highborn of the royal court love them. I'm sure you'll learn to love them, too. But you need to fit in to feel comfortable. Clothes like mine won't help you with that. We will dress you in the court's latest fashion. Trust me, no one will have a bad word to say about your outfit."

There'd be plenty of other reasons for the court to scrutinize me, I imagined, feeling every bit an outsider that I was. Maybe Brebie was right. I did need any help I could get to navigate the world I knew so little about.

"Fine." I removed my hands from my chest and flexed my jaw, allowing the woman to continue with her painting. She calmly twirled the brush around my nipple, laying swirls of gold paint in intricate designs on my bare skin.

So many things were out of my control here. Even my body didn't belong to me. I felt swept into a twister, carried to a destination unknown. Both Brebie and Voron had told me I had no choice. But there always was some, wasn't there? I could choose to drift along with what other people planned for me. Or I could fight it.

I could shove away all these brushes, jump off this chair, mess up my hair, and refuse to cooperate.

But what would that gain me?

They'd probably force me to obey. Or maybe the king would want to have nothing to do with me if I made a scene? What would happen to me, then?

I could always go back to my initial plan of escaping Sky Kingdom. I could find a way to jump back into the River of Mists and hope I didn't end up in the time period where I'd risk dying from plague or famine, be killed at war, or burned at a stake. That left me with a very narrow window of time, barely a sliver of a few decades in the entire human history. With my luck, could I even count on landing somewhere safe back in the human world?

Once again, it seemed safer to just wait and see what this world had in store for me. I didn't know enough about life in the palace to speculate on that.

"Tell me about the king," I asked Brebie. "What is he like?"

"The king? Oh, he's magnificent!" Brebie gushed. "Splendid and simply breathtaking. To be introduced to him is a huge honor. If you manage to impress him tonight and become his favorite, you'd never have to worry about anything ever again."

Did I have what it took to impress the mighty Sky King?

"What does he like to do?" I asked. "How does he spend his free time? He does have some free time, doesn't he?"

Leaving me in the capable hands of the maids and the woman artist, Brebie trotted around the room, putting away the items they didn't need anymore, like the oils and the blankets they'd used during my massage.

"King Tiane has impeccable taste," she said. "His parties at Elaros are famous all over Nerifir. His Majesty is an excellent dancer. He paints beautiful art. And he holds the highest appreciation for the best artists and performers. You'll hear the most exquisite music tonight." She paused her flurry of activities, giving me a curious glance. "Can you dance or sing? Paint maybe?"

My memories were gone. But when I thought about standing up and breaking into a song or a dance in front of a crowd, I felt no confidence. Instead, anxiety paralyzed me.

"I don't think so." I shook my head.

Brebie's lovely face fell with disappointment.

"That's a pity. It might have helped you gain a favor with the king if you did." She tapped her chin with her finger, contemplating something for a moment. "Of course, you'd have to be exceptionally good at that to impress him. Well." She shrugged, her voice lifting optimistically. "Maybe it's for the best. You're a human. Which makes you rare and special without you having to do a thing. We'll make you look pleasant to the royal eye, and you'll do just fine. All you'll have to do is to smile and act sweet."

Chapter Eight

SPARROW

"*Smile and act sweet,*" I repeated in my head when it was time to go.

Brebie opened the door to my room to hand me over to the guards who would take me to the royal ballroom.

"You're not coming?" I asked her, wishing to have at least one familiar face with me.

"No, honey. The royal balls are the affairs of highborn."

She straightened the gauzy layers of my skirts. The pink fabric was so light and frothy, it felt like a cloud floating around my legs. Despite the many layers, however, the fabric was so transparent, one could easily see the shape of my legs underneath.

"Have fun." Brebie smiled and wiggled her fingers at me before the guards whisked me away.

We headed up again, using the series of tiny little staircases. The vines in the walls grew thinner the higher we ascended. The crystal inserts grew wider, more brightly illuminating the space around us.

Servants rushed by. Many paused in their tracks to give me a quick once-over.

My face burned as I knew my dress left little to the imagination. The bodice consisted of four pink transparent scarves. The two in the front were attached to the waist of the dress and draped over my breasts. They were tied on my shoulders with the two similar scarves that crisscrossed my back. The thin material left my breasts almost completely exposed, with all the pretty swirls painted over my nipples shining through.

The only solid piece in my outfit was the belt. Made from light-gray leather, it was almost as wide as an under-bust corset, and just as tailored and stiff. It was laced with a golden ribbon on the back, cinching my middle in so tight, I could barely breathe. Or maybe my out-of-control nerves were the reason for my shortness of breath?

Either way, by the time we made it up to the wide, open space of the top floors, I feared I might pass out.

The vines in the walls up here lightened to ash white. Thinner than my arms, they held opaque crystal panels that flooded the space with soft, multi-colored light.

The walls retreated, opening the space for a wide, winding staircase in the middle. It circled the entire room, open to the floors above and below. This clearly was no longer the space meant for servants.

The vines twisted and curved into an ornamental railing, surrounding the glimmering white marble stairs. Leaning against the railing, High General Voron waited, looking effortlessly elegant like every other time I'd seen him.

He was wearing a white shirt this time. His black vest was stitched with silver shooting stars. It was shorter, reaching down only a little past his waist. Both the shirt and the vest were buttoned all the way up.

It appeared someone had spent time trying to tame his hair with a comb earlier today. However, their efforts had mostly been wasted, as Voron's hair refused to be tamed into absolute perfection. His raven-black tresses looked tousled, like ruffled feathers.

Swept back, the silvery-white strands over his forehead glistened like snowy ridges atop black mountains.

His massive sword was strapped to his back, with both the pommel and the guard ornately decorated and bejeweled. The sword's leather-wrapped hilt, however, showed some serious wear and tear, proving that the weapon was not a mere decoration. It'd been used, and often.

The fact that Voron had the weapon on him told me that even inside the palace where he apparently had full control, he didn't feel completely safe.

Over his right shoulder, a black cape was draped, falling all the way to the floor. It was too long, even for his height. A couple of feet of the darker-than-night material trailed along the marble tiles behind him as he took a step in my direction.

For a moment, I forgot all about our mutual resolution to hate each other or that he was here only to "present" me to someone else. I shamelessly admired his tall stature and his sure stride as he strolled toward me. Voron wasn't just breathtakingly handsome, he exuded an air of easy confidence, looking every bit the second most powerful man in the kingdom after the king.

Except that the very next moment, his confidence wavered. He stopped in his tracks, staring at me. I fought the impulse to cover my breasts with my hands. My gilded nipples must be winking at him through the fabric of the dress that concealed nothing. But he'd seen me completely naked before. This shouldn't be as awkward as it suddenly felt.

The outfit wasn't my choice, but the only dignified thing to do at this point was to own it. And since he just continued staring —taking in all of me from my hair, styled into cascading curls and braids and decorated with pink roses, to my light-gray shoes with kitten heels and golden buckles—I stood taller, cleared my throat, and spoke.

"Good evening, Voron... Um, High General, I mean," I said in a strong, clear voice, but dipped my head in a belated bow.

What was the protocol here? The guards who were with me just bowed their heads, without voicing any greeting at all.

Voron's throat bobbed with a swallow. He blinked. And just like that, his chillingly calm expression returned.

"Good evening to you, too, Sparrow. You look breathtakingly stunning today." His chest expanded as he inhaled deeply, as if recovering the breath I'd taken from him.

My skin tingled at the sound of his voice, just like it did back in the library when I had stood in front of him completely naked.

"Thanks." I ran the hands down my many skirts. The thin material flattened under my palms, only to poof right up the moment I let go. "But I can't take any credit for this. This is all Brebie's hard work, hers and her team's."

"Brebie is excellent at that," he agreed. "But she also had something remarkable to work with in your case." His eyes flicked down my body once again, but he promptly returned his focus to my face, offering me his arm. "Well, shall we?"

I hooked my hand in the crook of his elbow and splayed my fingers on his forearm, ready for him to lead me to my fate, but he didn't move.

My dress had no sleeves. Instead, my arms were decorated with lacy designs of vines, stars, and flowers painted by the talented artist back in my room. The swirls reached down to my hands and even covered the back of my fingers.

Voron traced a brush stroke on the back of my hand. He didn't appear to be aware of the gesture, circling my knuckle, then slowly following a line to my wrist. When he finally realized what he was doing, he jerked his hand away.

I immediately missed the gentle caress and the ribbon of tingly pleasure it left in its wake.

"We better go." Rolling back his shoulders, he led me toward the stairs.

The moment we stepped onto the first one, the stairs started to move. I gasped, gripping his arm.

"It's safe," he assured me softly.

This wasn't like an escalator where the steps were connected by a belt. Each stair here was a long, polished slab of marble suspended in the air and supported by nothing. As we walked, it floated up and around the room, pushing the stairs in front of it ahead too. The vines of the railing moved along with it.

I could see down several floors between the floating stairs. Beautifully dressed courtiers strolled on the floors below. A few flew by us, using their wings. They headed up to the top floor where the ball must be taking place. I followed their path of flight with my gaze, tipping my head back and nearly tripping.

Voron steadied me, catching me just before I would've fallen backwards.

"Oh, this staircase is dangerous." I gripped his arm with both hands, grateful for him being there.

"But beautiful, isn't it?" he replied. "It was designed and constructed by gorgonians."

"Those who kill with their eyes?" I remembered Brebie's story.

"Right. How do you know?"

"Brebie told me. She also said that the silk that the bugs make can be made into something that one can look through at gorgonians without turning into stone."

"Also true." He nodded. "Gorgonians haven't always been friendly with sky fae. There was an incident, over a thousand years ago, when our King Aigel, King Tiane's grandfather, made the mistake of kidnapping the gorgonian queen. Her husband got enraged, understandably so. With the help of the gargoyle king from the Dakath Mountains, the gorgonian King Consort got his queen back, burning down the old Sky Palace in the process."

"Wow." I whistled softly. "The tempers run high around here."

He glanced at me with that ghost of a smile on his lips.

"Royals tend to be swift and dramatic in their actions," he agreed. "As it happened, King Aigel didn't live long enough to rebuild the palace. His son, King Herane, the father of the current king, inherited still very much a ruin along with the Sky Crown. He was the one who finished the construction, using marble and crystals instead of relying solely on the *liliala* vines. It makes the palace far more resistant in case of fire."

"Was the old palace made exclusively from the vines, then?"

"Mostly, yes. The *liliala* vines are highly responsive to the royal magic that comes with the Sky Crown. The wearer of the crown becomes a part of the Sky Palace. King Tiane can move the walls or reinforce them if needed in case of an attack on Elaros."

"Interesting."

He stopped. And I realized the stairs had ended. I realized something else, too. By having a small talk on an unrelated topic, Voron had helped me calm down. My nerves had settled somewhat, and breathing became a little easier.

"The most significant part of this story, however," he said, helping me from the last step onto the marble of the top floor, "the most significant for *you*, I shall say, is that the gorgonian queen happened to be human. Just like you."

"Human?" I stopped, rooted in my place. "How long ago did you say it was?"

"Over a thousand years."

The hope of seeing another human woman died almost the moment it appeared.

"It was a long time ago." I sighed.

"It was. While the human queen was held in the Sky Palace, apparently, she managed to leave quite an impression on King Aigel."

"Is that why he made that deal with Trez, then?" It dawned on me.

"Precisely. King Aigel didn't live long enough to see the *brack* fulfill his end of the bargain. Which turned out lucky for King Tiane." He darted a glance at the white double doors up ahead. "Now, he gets to have you."

Anxiety rippled through my insides at the mention of the king. I tugged at my ear as we stopped in front of the doors at the end of the landing guarded by at least a dozen men in silver-gray uniforms. At the sight of Voron, they opened the doors immediately, without asking a single question.

Music rushed from the ballroom. The crystals in the walls and the floor glowed with pale violet light that slowly turned into magenta pink, then golden yellow, flooding the huge open space with light.

I gripped Voron's arm so tight, he winced but didn't extract himself from my fingers.

"Just breathe, Sparrow. This is supposed to be a fun, relaxing evening," he said. Then added, "For most of us, anyway."

Not for me. The room was filled with strangers who immediately turned to gawk at me. Nothing about it felt fun or relaxing.

"Just breathe..." Voron's words echoed in my mind.

I forced my lungs to expand, my chest heaving. Exhale. Inhale again. That was all I could do as Voron led me through the parting crowd.

People were everywhere. Some reclined in wide armchairs placed along the walls and by the numerous tall windows. Others mingled in the middle, stepping aside to make way for Voron and me. A fair number of the guests hovered under the ceiling, wings of all shapes and colors beating the air between the pale gray rafters made of intertwined vines.

All eyes were on me. My skin prickled with awareness. But at least, I didn't feel on display because of my outfit. The clothes of many of those present were even more revealing than mine.

Most men were shirtless. Some had on only prettily decorated loin cloths in lieu of pants. And with those men fluttering around under the ceiling, the tiny loin cloths really covered nothing at all.

Many women were topless as well. The rest had their breasts at least partially exposed, too, their chests painted with beautiful designs similar to mine.

As far as clothes went, I fit right in with this crowd. It was Voron who stood out as severely overdressed with all his buttoned-up layers.

Not only was his outfit out of place, his facial expression didn't match the cheerful mood of the room either. His eyes narrowed. His shapely mouth pressed into a firm line. He held his head high as if in challenge to everyone present.

The crowd split in two, parting all the way along the room for us. A round dais came into view, with the king sitting on his throne.

There was no doubt the man was the king. And it wasn't just because of the massive crown of gold and silver spikes he was sporting. The man's self-assured pose on the tall throne of interwoven vines, raised on the dais, betrayed the high position he held.

I drew in a breath and forgot to release it, struck by the magnificent picture King Tiane presented.

Splendid. Brebie hadn't been wrong in her choice of words when describing the Sky King.

His long, blond locks were so light, they appeared silver, spreading like rays of sunrise over his shoulders. He wore pearly-gray pants and a pure-white robe decorated with blue butterfly wings along the hem and neckline. The robe was open in the front, exposing the tan skin of his muscular chest painted with silver star bursts. Clusters of gold and silver stars also adorned his temples and cheekbones.

He turned his head slowly, sweeping the crowd with his gaze —the true monarch surveying his realm.

Regal. Gorgeous. High above the rest. This was the man I had to impress.

Where would I even begin?

Doubt gripped me.

The king's vivid blue eyes stopped on me, and a bright smile lit up his face.

"Ah, there she is! My grandfather's gift."

Chapter Nine

SPARROW

Awestruck, I stared at King Tiane like a deer caught in a car's headlights.

Voron bowed his head. "Your Majesty."

He tried to move away from me then, but I dug my fingers into his arm, holding on to him for dear life.

How pathetic of me was that? Using the man I should hate as some sort of security blanket?

But I'd known Voron for longer than anyone else in this room. He was at my side right now. The thought of him leaving me all alone, in the spotlight of everyone's attention, filled me with panic.

He placed a calming hand on mine and remained at my side. I exhaled a breath of relief even as my heart kept racing.

"Oh, isn't she adorable?" The king continued to study me. "So short and chubby. Like a baby chick. Come up here, my sweet. Let me take a better look at you."

His smile was bright. He sounded excited.

I glanced at Voron, who stared straight ahead, leaving me to make my own decisions.

"Come on, little human. Don't make me wait," King Tiane sounded impatient, clearly displeased by my hesitation.

Who was I to anger the king?

I unclenched my fingers, releasing Voron's sleeve reluctantly.

"Smile and act sweet."

I stretched my lips into a smile and took a step toward the royal dais.

People lounged on and around the steps leading up to the throne. The atmosphere was rather casual around the king. I seemed to be the only one intimidated out of my wits.

"Up, up you go." King Tiane waved at me to ascend the stairs.

The moment I approached him at arm's length, he grabbed my waist and hauled me to him, placing me between his knees.

"She feels nice, too," he murmured, stroking the side of my face.

He kept talking about me in the third person, and I looked around to see whom he might be speaking to.

A tall woman stood to the right of the throne. In the changing lighting of the room, her dark-green skin shimmered with blue and purple. Her violet hair was styled in spirals and spikes that fanned out like a halo around her head. The creamy, flowing dress she was wearing exposed her left shoulder and breast. The skin just above her areola was painted with a flowery rosette with the ornate letters P and T in the middle.

A man with dove-gray wings was hugging her from behind, kissing her neck. She stroked the man's arm and nodded to the king approvingly. She then turned her head to the man behind her to catch one of his kisses on her lips.

Most people around us acted just as affectionate with each other as these two. Many did even more, crossing the line of what would be considered an appropriate public behavior. A woman on the top stair to the left of the throne straddled a man's lap. She giggled as he slipped a hand under her skirt. Another couple reclined just a step below them. The man caressed the woman's bare breast as she played with his long, red hair.

Moans reached me from above, where couples fluttered between the rafters. Men and women chased each other, stealing kisses and more.

The king ran his hand down my arm, then moved it under my left breast. I held still, willing my body to relax. He lifted my breast, weighing it in his hand.

"Fascinating." He traced a line of the golden design through the scarf over my chest.

I dug my feet in, forcing them not to shuffle away. Voron's inspection should've prepared me for things getting physical between the king and me. But with Voron, it had been easier somehow. He'd warned me in advance what to expect from that inspection. He'd said he wouldn't touch me, and he'd stayed true to his words.

With the king, I had no idea what to expect. Was I supposed to accept this? I saw no way to refuse him. They said I had to impress him, only I didn't know what he found impressive. This felt like an interview for a job, when I didn't know exactly what the job was.

What was I supposed to be? The king's girlfriend? His mistress? What did he mean by calling me his "present?"

Did it give him the right to take me to his room tonight? What if he went ahead and made love to me right here, in front of his guests? It didn't seem that far-fetched, considering that some couples around us appeared to be there already, moaning and gyrating against each other.

I had no memories, no frame of reference that would work here, and no personal experience to go by. All I had were my feelings. And they betrayed me. The king was gorgeous, surprisingly easy-going, and fun. His fascination with me should be flattering. But something unsettling pulsed in my chest.

Maybe it was just my nerves getting the best of me.

The royal hand traveled up, gently brushing over my nipple. He stroked my bottom lip with his thumb.

"You have such kissable lips, sweet thing." He pinched my chin between his thumb and his finger, bringing me closer.

His warm mouth landed on mine in a light caress. The kiss was barely a peck, just a taste, as he eased me closer to him. My eyelids dropping closed, I inhaled a lungful of his scent. He smelled fresh and warm with a hint of pine, like sunshine in a forest.

My eyes remained closed even after he'd pulled back, which made him laugh.

"How are you so cute?" he mused. "Do I blind you? You can open your eyes, sweetie."

Hooking an arm around my middle, he pulled me into his lap.

"You're staying right here, with me, tonight," he announced. "I don't want you to leave my side."

I folded my hands on top of my thighs, awkwardly pressing my shoulder into his chest.

He laughed again.

"You're too stiff. Go ahead, hug me." He took my arm closest to him and draped it around his neck. "I allow it."

I carefully moved his shimmering locks aside, afraid I'd pull at them, then twined my arm over his shoulder and around his neck. Despite his permission, I remained rigid, afraid to lean into him too much or unwittingly get too close for his comfort.

All the while, I furtively studied the most powerful man in the kingdom.

The butterfly wings on his robe were real. When I touched one, my finger came back dusted with a delicate shimmer.

Up close, I realized, the tall spikes on his head weren't a part of his golden crown. King Tiane sported a full rack of antlers growing directly from his head. They gave him a truly majestic look, making the circlet of golden thorns gracing his head rather unnecessary. Painted with silver and adorned with beads and gemstones, his antlers looked like a crown on their own.

A servant with sleek black wings approached the dais, carrying a tray in his hands. He flew up to the throne.

"The first course of the evening meal, Your Majesty." He extended the arm with the tray toward the king. "Doe cheese soufflé."

There was a single plate on the tray, with a small, pale blob whipped into an aesthetically pleasant shape of a wave on it. A tiny silver spoon with an ornate handle laid next to it.

"Lovely." The king grabbed the plate with one hand. Since his other arm remained wrapped around my waist, he handed the plate to me to hold.

Using the silver spoon, he scooped off a small piece of the tiny portion and placed it into his mouth. The moment it happened, more winged servants appeared as if from nowhere. They weaved through the crowd, offering the guests tiny plates with small blobs of soufflé.

The royal court dined along with its king. Except for me. No one brought me any food, so I continued to hold the plate for the king as he ate.

"It's not awful," he concluded when there was only a single bite left. "You should try it." He handed me his spoon as the servant returned with course number two of the royal dinner.

It had been a while since my lunch. And I hadn't eaten it that well, wrecked by nerves in anticipation of the evening. Now, I was hungry.

Before the king handed me another plate to hold, I quickly swiped the remaining bite of the soufflé and ate it. It tasted amazing. I just wished I had a plateful more of that.

King Tiane made me hold the second plate for him, too. This time, he let me have a spoonful of his food before he had finished.

Another servant brought him a tall crystal flute of bubbling golden liquid. The king took a long drink, then brought the flute to my lips.

"Have some," he said. "You deserve it. You please me greatly, my little present."

I was relieved to hear that, but I wished I knew what exactly I'd done tonight to please him. I hadn't said a single word to him.

I'd been just sitting here, mum like a dummy. Was that all it took to please the Sky King?

He tapped my lips with the rim of his glass impatiently, and I tilted my head back obediently, parting my lips for him to pour some of the sparkling wine into my mouth. Its taste was light and pleasant. The bubbles played and popped on my tongue.

"How do you like it?" King Tiane asked.

"It's nice," I smiled, uttering my first words to the king.

"Hopefully, it'll make you a little more playful," he grinned.

Unsure what that meant, I just kept smiling in response.

Another course of the meal arrived, and I resumed my duties, first as the royal plate holder, then as the cleaner of the leftover food.

I quickly lost count of the number of courses served. All the food looked like tiny masterpieces on the plate. They tasted amazing but left me hungry, despite the great number of them. At least since I was eating from the royal plate, I could rest assured no one would feed me any magical substances.

The king never asked if I wanted more to eat than what he offered. Though, he shared his wine with me generously. By the time the dinner ended, I felt more drunk than sated.

"We have new dancers performing tonight," the king said excitedly after the servant had taken the last plate from me just before I'd managed to grab the one remaining crumb of desert off it. "I hope you'll like them."

Would it matter if I didn't?

Either way, I took his words as an invitation to stay and watch the performance. Since the king never told me to get off his lap, I remained where I was.

He grabbed my legs and threw them over the armrest of his throne, then beat down the layers of my skirt and rested his arm across my thighs, reclining against the back comfortably.

The guests, who hovered under the ceiling, produced musical instruments and started to play. The music gained strength, filling the room, as the remaining guests moved to the walls with tall windows, clearing the space in front of the royal throne.

A delicate clinking noise joined the music. Then, a group of six dancers flew into the open space. Their transparent wings moved rapidly as they danced, standing on their toes like ballerinas. Except that their pointe shoes were made from glass. The toe part of the shoes was as long as the dancers were tall, elevating them above the floor. From the distance, it appeared like they danced on crystal stilts that looked like long, sparkling icicles.

Their wings never stopped moving, keeping the dancers suspended and most of their weight off their delicate stilts. Every now and then, their wings would beat faster, the dancers would leap up into the air, bending their legs to make the crystals clink against each other. The melodious sound merged with the music, becoming a part of it.

I couldn't take my eyes off them. They looked every bit the magical creatures they were, only their magic was in the movement and control of their bodies, nothing more. Light and graceful, the dance they wove in the air was mesmerizing, blending seamlessly with the music.

"This is incredible," I exhaled in wonder and admiration.

"You think so?" The king had pulled a strand of my hair out of the weave of braids on my head and was playing with it by winding and unwinding it around his finger.

"Don't you find their dance beautiful?" I asked.

He drew in a breath that ended with a yawn.

"It's not terrible." He shrugged. "I guess I'll keep them around for another performance or two." He tickled my nose with the end of the lock of my hair he'd been playing with. "You're so easily impressed."

Maybe it was my lack of memories that allowed me to enjoy things that didn't seem to impress him? I had no recollection of ever watching a performance before. The novelty of it was exciting on its own.

But I also felt that I would've found this dance mesmerizing even with all my memories intact. The harmony of the dancers and their synergy with the music was extraordinary. It was pure pleasure to watch.

The king straightened in his throne suddenly.

"Let's show them how it's done." His voice lifted.

His face lit up with excitement as he grabbed me around the middle and spread his great, snow-white wings.

In one fluid movement, the king lifted into the air, taking me with him.

"Let's dance!" he exclaimed, his eyes glistening wildly.

"I can't dance!" I wanted to scream, but the words stuck in my throat as he leaped up to the ceiling with me.

Panic sliced through me when the ground lurched away. I gripped his robe, crushing the butterfly-wing appliqué.

The king laughed with glee, landing in the middle of the dancers. They scrambled away, shattering their crystal stilts in panic. The shards of crystal sprayed the floor, scattering around and shining like diamonds.

"Dance, my precious baby chick!" The king twirled in the middle of the room. His great wings created a twister that blew out my carefully arranged hairdo and whipped my skirts around my legs.

He dipped down, touching the floor with the toe of his right shoe, then leaped back up again, arching his back and extending one arm gracefully while holding me to him with the other.

The king was dancing, moving in a perfect rhythm to the music. I'm sure he presented a sight to admire. Me, on the other hand...

I clung to his shoulders, desperately hoping he wouldn't drop me, either by negligence or as a part of his choreography. I didn't even attempt to follow his lead, not moving a limb.

With the next dip, he set me down on the ground. My foot landed on one of the crystal shards, and I slipped, almost falling.

The king caught me, laughing. "You're so clumsy, it's adorable."

"I... I'm sorry. I can never dance like you, Your Majesty," I muttered, finally finding my footing on the solid ground.

"No one can," he boasted. "It's good you understand that. You're smarter than you look." Smiling, he flicked my nose with his finger.

As the dancers cleared the floor, the guests reclaimed it, dancing to the music that never stopped playing. Most of the courtiers moved with the grace of the dancers, too. Some flew up, using their wings and rising swirls of feathers in the air among their half-naked bodies.

"I shall let you retire for the night," the king said. "You must be exhausted. Crossing from another world isn't easy, I've heard. Off you go. I'll see you soon, my sweet baby chick."

He clearly wished to join his guests in the dance, without me slowing him down. The wine I'd drunk rose to my head. My mind was spinning along with the twister of the gyrating bodies floating all around me. The group dance looked fun, making me wish I had wings, too.

"I'm not tired," I protested.

But the king was already gone. His white wings beating the air, he joined the others.

Between the fluttering wings above, I caught the glimpses of fae chasing each other. Two women giggled, catching a man. One ripped his loincloth off, the other claimed his mouth in a kiss.

Another man dove headfirst under a flowing skirt of a woman passing by.

Two men twirled, hugging and kissing while hovering high under the ceiling with a laughing woman trapped between them.

The king had dismissed me. I should be leaving. But I feared I'd never make it out of the ballroom alive. With so many tall, hard bodies zooming through the air all around me, I risked being knocked down if I moved a step in any direction.

With King Tiane joining the crowd, the chaos intensified. The longer I stood there, the greater the danger of someone crashing into me grew.

Folding my arms over my head for protection against an unintentional kick of a foot or jab of an elbow by those flying above, I ventured a step toward the doors and immediately bumped into someone's hard abdomen.

The familiar silver buttons and the embroidered shooting stars on the black velvet betrayed whose hard abs I'd slammed into.

"Voron." I looked up to find the High General standing over me.

In all this mayhem, it seemed, some order remained. Among the chaos of light, music, and flying fae, Voron looked like a dark sentinel, keeping a watchful eye on everything, including me.

"Come, Sparrow."

Wrapping an arm around my shoulders, he raised the other one to shield us from those above, then skillfully maneuvered me toward the exit. Disoriented by the swarms of winged people flying around, I held my head down, giving him full control. He led me across the room and out onto the landing with the moving stairs.

"Thank you," I exhaled when he released me from his one-armed hold.

His expression was unreadable.

"Will you find the way back to your bedroom?" he asked.

I hesitated, trying to recall every little staircase the guards had used on our way to meet Voron at the bottom of the moving stairs.

He didn't wait for my answer, gesturing for a guard at the door to approach.

"Take Lady Sparrow back to her room." With a brief nod in my direction, he stepped aside, allowing the guard to lead me away.

"Good night, Sparrow." His voice chased me on my way down the magical moving staircase.

"Good night," I replied in my mind only, as the distance between us had grown too great for him to hear me.

Chapter Ten

SPARROW

The following day went by in a blur. Due to drinking too much wine and not eating nearly enough food at the royal ball, I woke up with a splitting headache the following morning and spent most of the day in bed, recovering.

Once I'd finally slept off the hangover and was able to climb out of bed the day after, Brebie and her small army of maids took over my bedroom. They marched in right after breakfast, carrying armloads of dresses, jewelry boxes, and trunks filled with furs and shoes.

The lifelong supply of clothes that Brebie had assured me King Tiane would provide for me appeared to arrive all at once. Apparently, the king had personally selected the pieces, instructing the maids on what I should wear the next time I was to see him.

Brebie was beside herself with delight that I'd managed to impress the king.

"He really likes you," she gushed.

"I'm not sure why," I wondered aloud. "I really blew it with the dancing, you know?"

She waved me off.

"It doesn't matter. He said you were delightful and so in awe of him."

I was in awe. It was hard not to be. King Tiane presented a splendid picture, blinding like the sun, especially, when residing on his marvelous throne. I couldn't pinpoint, however, what exactly he found so delightful about me.

With the aid of at least a dozen maids, Brebie jumped into action, organizing all the new treasures that had fallen upon me courtesy of the king. All the new shoes, dresses, and jewelry had to be sorted and put away in appropriate places inside the wardrobe room adjacent to my bedroom.

I tried to be useful by folding some things and putting away the others, but Brebie quickly put a stop to that.

"You've done it all wrong, Sparrow!" She threw her arms into the air, surveying the results of my work. "Everyone knows you can't store pearls in glowing crystal boxes. It makes them dull. And spider silk dresses need to be hung, not folded."

By the time the next day came and they were still not done with organizing, I'd had enough of the commotion.

"I want to go for a walk," I told Brebie. "To explore the palace or something."

She blinked at me, looking confused. "What's there to explore? You'll just get in the way and annoy both the servants and the highborn."

I rolled my eyes at her complete and utter lack of faith in me. "I promise to keep out of the way so as not to *annoy* anyone, including you. Don't you wish to get more space in here with me gone for a while?"

She considered that.

"If you really need a walk, go down to the gardens. That's what they're there for," she said. "My husband is the head gardener. I'll get him to take you there."

Everyone here, from a maid to the king, treated me like a toddler in constant need of supervision. From the moment I arrived at Elaros, I hadn't made a single step outside of my room without someone escorting me.

Sure, it was easy to get lost here with so many floors and countless staircases. But if I couldn't explore the palace at my leisure, how would I ever learn my way around?

This wasn't the best time to argue with Brebie, however. She already looked winded and irritated, making sure hundreds of shoes weren't accidentally put away with just as many gloves and my new barrettes didn't end up stored in the same box as silk handkerchiefs.

"Fine," I conceded with a resigned sigh, allowing her to call her husband in.

Brebie's husband turned out to be one of the men who had delivered the metal tub for my bath. He was the one with the head of a bull.

"Kanbor, honey," she said to him when he arrived. "Please take Sparrow to the gardens. She wants to walk a little while we're finishing up here."

Standing in the middle of my bedroom filled with piles of silk, heaps of ruffles, and trunks full of shoes, ribbons, and furs, the giant man looked rather lost.

"Sure thing, sweetheart," he boomed, carefully stepping around baskets and jewelry boxes lined up by the fireplace. Something cracked under his hoof, and he froze with terror on his large, bovine face. "Sorry."

"It's fine," I assured him, as Brebie retrieved the remnants of the pulverized tortoise shell barrette from under his hoof.

"Why don't the two of you keep going now?" She waved at the door impatiently. "Off with you both."

Kanbor retreated to the door promptly, clearly relieved to be leaving. I grabbed a pale-blue velvet cloak embroidered with silver dandelions from one of the open trunks and headed out, too. He pointed in the direction of the nearest staircase, and I turned that way as he heavily stomped beside me.

As we walked down the stairs, I tried to study Kanbor

without making it too obvious. He probably wasn't much taller than Voron, though his hooves and horns certainly added to his height. But he was so much thicker everywhere, his brawn made him look massive.

He didn't seem intimidating, however. His large, dark eyes trimmed with thick eyelashes gave him a kind, soulful expression.

Kanbor was dressed in a pair of long, brown pants and a light-green tunic with a simple embroidery around his thick neck. The extravagant, revealing clothing I'd seen people wear at the royal ball must be reserved for highborn only.

As the staircase ended, Kanbor turned toward another one and caught me staring.

I averted my eyes, but not quickly enough. "Sorry, I didn't mean to..."

"That's fine," he boomed good-naturedly. "I'm used to being stared at. There aren't that many of us *taureans* in Elaros."

"*Taureans?* Is that what your kind is called?"

He nodded his large head. His wide tongue lapped at the corner of his mouth.

"My folk tend to stay close to land, away from the big cities like Elaros. All my family are farmers. I have a farm, too, but I let my nephew run it while I'm here."

"What made you move to Elaros and leave behind your farm?"

"Not *what. Who.* Brebie."

His lips stretched in a smile. It was a bizarre image—a smiling bull. But the kindness and intelligence in his eyes set him far apart from the animal whose looks he shared. The more we spoke, the easier it was for me to think of him as handsome.

I tried to imagine these two as a couple. This slow, deliberate giant of a man and the prim and proper Brebie, who moved with the speed of lighting on her tiny hooves and probably weighed less than Kanbor's one burly arm.

"How long have you been married?" I asked.

"We celebrated our one-century anniversary two years ago."

"Wow, that's a long time to be together."

"Fae's lifespan is about five hundred years. We have a couple of centuries ahead of us still."

"Do you have children?" The question left my mouth before I could stop it. I bit my lip. Was it too rude to ask?

To my relief, Kanbor didn't seem offended.

"No. I'm a *taurean*. Brebie is an *arien*. Children aren't possible between us. But love doesn't know limits, does it?" He grinned again.

The pure happiness with which he spoke about his wife left no doubts he loved her. He also seemed to enjoy talking about her. The initial awkwardness disappeared from his demeanor. He chatted freely.

"Brebie started out as a chambermaid, but it wasn't her purpose. She's much better at leading and organizing than cleaning. Thankfully, High General Voron remembered her from when she worked for his mother. How long has it been now?" He scratched his chin as we arrived on the ground floor. "About a hundred and eighty years ago. Almost two centuries now. Time flies." He heaved a sigh, holding the heavy palace door open for me. "When the High General returned to Sky Kingdom, he allowed Brebie to come back to work in his family estate in Vensari. She's been running his household ever since."

"So, Brebie is not part of the royal staff, then?"

"No. I am, but she isn't. She moved here with the High General and is working for him, not the king."

I lived in the king's palace, but it was Voron's housekeeper who looked after me.

"They've known each other for a long time, then. How old is Voron?"

"Well, Brebie started working for his mother when he was a baby. So, he'd be about a hundred and eighty years old or so."

I exhaled a brief laugh in surprise. "He doesn't look that old."

"Compared to humans, maybe? Fae don't age until we're close to the end of our lives. How long is your lifespan?"

I sighed. "Less than a hundred years."

Compassion floated in his large brown eyes. "That's not long at all. You'll have to make sure to enjoy every year of it."

I smiled. "I'll try."

We walked across a large mosaic patio, then down a few wide steps to a stone path that ran between flowerbeds. Shrubs with luscious white and blue flowers grew in the middle of the flowerbeds, surrounded by short blooming plants arranged in an intricate pattern.

"This is so pretty." I appreciated the work that went into the design and maintenance of the neat, well-kept gardens.

"Thank you," Kanbor replied with pride. "They are a handful. King Tiane loves the most exotic, capricious plants. But the results are worth it."

"They certainly are."

Kanbor glanced up at the sky, then turned around slowly, studying the cobblestones under our feet.

"Is something wrong?" I asked as his forehead furrowed.

"There are no shadows at all again today," he muttered.

"Is that a bad thing?"

"No shadows mean there is no sun. The plants need sunshine to thrive."

He looked upset, and I felt the urge to comfort him.

"It's spring right now, isn't it? Summer is coming. The wind has calmed down already. I'm sure the sun will come out soon, too."

He heaved a heavy breath. "We haven't had a full day of sunshine in many decades. I phased out all the sun-loving plants from the gardens long ago." He waved his hand at the closest flowerbed. "These here tolerate shade well. But even they need sunshine once in a while."

We strolled along the path, then under arches of pale-gray vines with silver flowers that grew in clusters, like grapes.

Kanbor seemed distracted, lost in thought. He must have work to do. These gardens needed him more than I did.

"You can go," I told him. "I'll find my way back."

"Are you sure?" He looked concerned. "Brebie would tear my tail off if I let something happen to you."

"What can happen to me here?" I pointed at the sky above the arches with flowers. Winged figures soared around the palace in a wavy pattern, surveying the grounds below. "These are royal guards, aren't they? They'll keep an eye on me."

He scratched the back of his head, hesitating. "Well, if you're sure..."

I touched his forearm. "I'll be fine. I'll just walk a little and will be back in my room before lunch."

He looked worried but seemed relieved to be released from his babysitting duties.

"Honestly, don't let me keep you," I insisted. "I'm sure you have lots of work to do."

He nodded, then gestured forward.

"The gardens stretch all the way to the river this way. You can walk here freely, as well as to the right. To the left, the river comes close to the palace wall. I wouldn't go that way. There isn't much to see until the palace gate, anyway."

When Kanbor left, I proceeded on my way along the path. The gardens seemed enormous, but I kept the tall towers of the palace in my view at all times. There was no risk of getting lost and after staying in my room for the past two days, getting some exercise felt rejuvenating. Blood flowed to my arms and legs, warming me up. My cheeks flushed, too.

This was the first time I'd ever left the palace since I got here. Other than the brief ride with Voron that day, I'd never been to the city beyond these grounds.

Kanbor had mentioned the palace gate. Before I even finalized the decision, my feet had already turned to the left instead of continuing straight.

The gardens were beautiful with their intricately shaped shrubs and the variety of flowers in pastel colors, but I hoped to glimpse what lay beyond the palace gates. Or at least to see how well the gates were guarded.

Huddling in my cloak against the chill in the air, I walked briskly around the palace. Kanbor was right. The river came very close to the wall here, cutting sharply into the grounds. There was just enough space for a pretty path with border plants on each side.

I followed the path to the wide courtyard in front of the palace. It led to the gates, guarded both from the air and on the ground. People moved through, in and out. Most were merchants, with horses and wagons in tow. Servants were coming and going.

The guards stopped and questioned everyone coming in, but mostly ignored those going out.

This was my chance to test whether I was a guest or a prisoner in Elaros.

Pulling the fur-trimmed hood of my cloak a little lower over my face, I joined the stream of people leaving the courtyard.

I peeked around the backs of the people in front of me and could already see the streets of the city paved with pale gray and beige cobblestones. Some buildings appeared to be carved from marble, matching the palace walls. Others, more modest ones, were made from rocks painted in white and pastels. All of them were much shorter than the king's palace, only two to three stories high.

Most people moved along the streets either on hooves or tails, with highborn flying just above the crowd. But there were some highborn on the ground, too. With their wings hidden, they visited stores or strolled in the company of those who couldn't fly, like *ariens* and *snakanas*.

"Wait!" A guard rushed to me, and my heart sank.

I was so close to getting out.

"You're Lady Sparrow, aren't you?" he said.

I pushed back my hood. It was useless to hide now. "How did you recognize me?"

"You can't leave the palace without an escort appointed by the High General."

He didn't answer my question, but it was safe to assume my cloak had betrayed me. The silver-stitched velvet stood out among the simple fabrics worn by the majority of the people in the courtyard. That and the lack of hooves or a tail, too, of course.

I sighed. "Let me guess whose orders those were."

"The orders of the High General."

"Of course." This had Voron's controlling, hyper protective signature all over it.

The guard grabbed my arm. "I'll need to take you to him now."

He sounded grumpy, clearly annoyed having to interrupt whatever he was doing to deal with me.

"It's fine. You don't have to. I'll just go back to the gardens."

I had no plan to escape, anyway. Voron had outlined very clearly what waited for me if I ever made it out of Elaros. I just wanted to see if I could freely leave the palace, and now I got my answer.

"The High General needs to know about this." The guard dragged me by my arm across the courtyard toward the main doors of the palace.

"I'd rather not see him today," I protested.

The winged shapes flying above cast no shadows. We had no warning before two of them landed in front of us. Both were women. They folded their wings behind their backs. The wings of one were clear and iridescent. The other one had pure white feathers.

The one with the iridescent wings stepped forward.

"That's all right. We'll take her back to the palace." She placed a hand on my shoulder, addressing the guard. "You can go back to your duties, good man."

The guard considered her words for a moment, his eyes flicking between me and her.

Half of the woman's blue-black hair was arranged into an

intricate up-do, the other half hung down her back in a dark, silky mass. Her pearly pink skin shimmered faintly under the overcast sky.

The second woman brushed off one of her tight, snow-white curls from her dark as midnight face.

"She'll be fine with us, sweetie." She tapped the guard's arm with her finger. "You did good by stopping her from escaping. The city is not the best place for the king's favorite."

Now I was sure I saw these women among the courtiers at the king's ball two days ago, though most faces from that night had very much blended into a blur. There had been so many people there, and no one had been formally introduced to me.

"I wasn't trying to escape," I explained. "I just wanted to know whether I was a guest or a prisoner here."

The second woman tilted her head, making the stubborn curl fall over her forehead again. "In your case, it's kind of the same thing, isn't it? Out there, someone would snatch you within minutes and bring you back to the king for a reward. Or worse— they would sell you to a High Lord or something."

Well, Voron wasn't lying about that part.

"Come, Sparrow." The first woman tugged me toward the palace by my other arm.

I was stretched between her and the guard, until he finally relented, letting go of me.

"I'll tell the High General you took her, Lady Libelle," he yelled after us as the women led me away, probably just wishing to clear himself of any liability for me at this point.

"Yes, yes, tell him." Libelle waved him off. "He probably knows already, anyway. I swear he has eyes everywhere, watching us even now."

I dug my heels into the cobblestone of the courtyard.

"I don't want to go back to the palace yet. I came down for a walk in the gardens."

Libelle pursed her lips. "Then you should have stayed in the gardens, my dear."

"It's fine." The other woman lined up on the other side of me, matching Libelle's pace. "We can go back to the gardens if you wish, as long as we get out of the courtyard. It's always so noisy in here." She wrinkled her nose. "I'm Dove, by the way. And this is Libelle." She pointed at her friend as we turned toward the path back to the gardens. "We saw you at the last ball."

We rounded the palace, the busy courtyard no longer in our view. The women's wings trailed behind them like cloaks laid upon their shoulders, shielding them from the cold.

Libelle let go of my arm, finally trusting me to walk on my own. "The king seemed quite taken by you."

I couldn't tell whether it was meant as a compliment or an accusation.

"Did he?" I replied tentatively.

"It's a good thing," Dove assured me. "He hasn't had a favorite since Libelle bonded with Faisan last month."

I turned to Libelle. "You were with the king?"

"For nearly three months." She nodded proudly.

Her friend yanked on my arm to get my attention. "The king adored her. But no one can stand in the way of the magic bond, not even the king."

"Is it like marriage?" I asked.

Libelle huffed. "Much more than that. A magic bond happens when two halves of the same soul find each other."

"It's very rare," Dove sighed.

"Was the king heartbroken when you bonded with another?" I asked Libelle. "Is that why he's been sad and there hasn't been any sun in the kingdom?"

The women exchanged an amused look before breaking into a laugh.

"You're funny!" Dove blew her white curls away from her large violet eyes. "I can see why King Tiane likes you."

I hadn't tried to be funny. I blinked at them both, hoping for an explanation.

Libelle waved her hands in front of her face, fanning herself while trying to speak through her laughter.

"As much as I'd like to say the Sky King was *inconsolable* after losing me to Faisan, he was not. Sure, his lap was free for a little while until you came along. But he didn't have to miss out on anything else."

"What do you mean?"

"She means his cock could be well taken care of if he so wished," Dove stated bluntly. "The king is the most coveted man in the entire kingdom. He isn't bonded. He can have as many lovers as he wants."

That had to be expected. I'd seen the fun-loving company in which the king spent his time. He hadn't pledged me his undying love and loyalty, and it was safe to assume he never would. I might be the only human in the entire kingdom, which automatically got me the place on his lap. But it didn't put me into his heart or give me exclusive ownership of his body.

"I see." It was best to know these things as early as possible. It would make it easier for me to manage my expectations. "So, unless people are a bonded couple, there is no monogamy?"

"Exactly," Libelle confirmed.

I thought about Kanbor and Brebie. They weren't bonded. They didn't even belong to the same kind of sky fae. But their relationship appeared to be solid. Maybe monogamy just wasn't for highborn? Or specifically for the highborn of the Elaros Court?

Frankly, I wasn't sure I wanted the king's undivided attention, anyway. From what I'd seen, it might be exhausting. King Tiane both fascinated and intimidated me. I feared he might be overwhelming in large doses.

"The bond is boring." Dove formed her plump lips into an adorable pout as we reached the gardens, then continued to stroll between the flower beds. "All you have is your bonded mate, for the rest of your life. It's more fun without it."

"Unless you're the High General," Libelle laughed. "The man

has no bonds tying him to anyone, yet he has no fun at all. Such a prude. He doesn't even party."

Dove giggled.

"To be fair, he has no wings. It couldn't be fun without them." She glanced my way and added quickly, "No offence."

I didn't feel offended. I felt shocked.

"Did you just say Voron doesn't have wings?"

It wasn't easy to tell just by looking at him. People hid and displayed their wings at will. But I assumed all highborn had them and since Voron was a highborn, he would have them, too.

Then I remembered that he was the only one riding a horse on the day of my arrival. The rest of his people flew. He didn't just come on horseback for my sake, to pick me up. That must be his usual mode of transportation, since he couldn't fly.

Voron had no wings.

Could that fact be at least partially responsible for his moods that oscillated between somber and grumpy? It surely couldn't be fun to be the only wingless one in the king's court.

"Why doesn't he have wings?"

Dove shrugged. "I don't know. He never had them."

"Is it common for highborn?" I wondered.

"No." She shook her head. "As far as I know, he's the only one in the entire kingdom. I've never heard of any other highborn without wings."

"Of course you haven't." Libelle pursed her lips. "Because they don't exist."

But Voron did. I wondered how.

"Is that why he doesn't party?" I asked.

"Gods know why." Libelle made a face. "He doesn't party, doesn't dance, doesn't fuck—"

"At all?"

How had Voron managed to avoid sex in this place where the very air seemed to be permeated with lust? I knew for a fact that he got aroused. Blood rushed to my face at the memory of the bulge in his pants he'd sported after "inspecting" me.

"Well, maybe he doesn't *fuck*," Dove argued. "But he's not as cold and stoic as he wants us to believe."

"What do you mean?" I asked quickly.

Maybe it was wrong to pry for intimate details on Voron's life behind his back, but I soaked up every word about this man, dying to learn more about him.

Dove shifted closer, just as eager to share the gossip. "Susale, one of the ladies-in-waiting, was bragging just last week that she sucked him off after the ball a month ago, and that he returned the favor by going down on her that very night. She said he was great at that, too."

Libelle giggled. "So great that Susale has been batting her eyelashes at him ever since. Except that he's paid her no attention, going back to his austere, boring ways."

"Weird." Dove shook her head, sending her curls into a bounce. "It's like he's taken a hag's vow."

"*What* vow?" I asked, trying to keep up.

"Hags don't care about sex," she explained. "Just like Voron doesn't."

"There are no male hags, Dove. He couldn't have taken the vow," Libelle corrected. "Unless he isn't male? But then, Susale would've told the entire court if he weren't." She furrowed her forehead, rubbing her chin in thought. "Unless Susale lied about the whole thing, of course."

Dove propped her hands on her shapely hips. "If she lied, she wouldn't be so eager to get her mouth wrapped around his cock again, would she?"

The blatant way in which Dove expressed herself clashed with her angelic look of white locks, full lips, and huge violet eyes. But it weirdly suited her at the same time, too.

"Personally, I now think nothing happened between them," Libelle insisted. "Voron is so cold, his insides must be frozen. And his cock, if he has one, has probably long turned into an icicle."

I remembered the way Voron had looked at me, both with my clothes on and off. It had not been cold or disinterested. It had, however, been the look of a man who kept his desires in a firm grip of control.

A flapping of wings announced yet another arrival. I ducked as a large, black bird flew over my head from behind.

"Speak of the Lord of Under, and he'll appear," Libelle muttered under her breath.

Chapter Eleven

SPARROW

At the sight of the black bird, Dove unfurled her wings of pristine white. "We'd better go. I've no desire to run into the High General right now. We'll see you at the king's dinner tomorrow, Sparrow."

A dinner? It was the first time I'd heard about that. I didn't get an invitation. But maybe as the "king's favorite" I didn't need one to attend?

"Sure," I said, wishing I could fly away with them. The prospect of running into Voron unnerved me for reasons I didn't care to analyze.

As the women took off, the black bird made a wide circle overhead, then landed on the back of the nearby stone bench.

"And what are *you* doing here?" I asked the bird.

"The same thing you are," the familiar deep voice sounded behind me. "Getting some fresh air."

I turned around as Voron strolled out from under the arches with flowers. Draped in a black cloak, with his sword handle rising over his left shoulder, he looked very much the same as on the day we first met.

"Or did you come down here for another reason? I heard you tried to sneak out into the city, little bird."

He really had eyes everywhere. Was that why he came down here? To keep an eye on me?

"I now know not to try again," I said. "You don't need to worry."

"Good." He came closer. "And just to set matters straight, no part of me physically resembles an icicle."

Mortification chilled me from head to toe. He'd overheard Libelle talking about his dick. Was there something worse we'd discussed? But what could be worse than talking about his private parts behind his back?

"Oh, no... You heard?"

I wished the cobblestones would part under my feet for the ground to swallow me whole.

He appeared very much unfazed, however. Calm, like always.

"My dear Sparrow, someone is always *listening* in the king's palace. As a rule, it's best not to say out loud anything you don't want to be known by everyone."

My mouth felt dry as I replied, "I'll keep it in mind."

He sat on the bench and leaned against its back, crossing an ankle over his knee. He didn't invite me to join him, and I figured it was best to leave him alone. Drawing my cloak closer around me, I walked past him, fully intending to continue on my way along the path. After a couple of steps, however, I stopped.

Ever since I got to this world, it'd been overwhelming. New information had been coming at me from all directions and all possible sources before I even had a chance to process what I'd learned.

Voron, with his firm logic and composed manner of speaking, had the ability to sort things out for me. He could be helpful, and I should use him, as long as he let me.

Of course, he could always tell me off. Especially now, after he'd caught me gossiping about his dick of all things.

After a moment of hesitation, I decided to give it a try,

anyway, by starting with the most casual question I could think of: "What's the name of your raven?"

He turned to look at the bird, as if he'd forgotten it was there.

"Magnus." At the sound of his name, Magnus tipped his head, regarding his master with one of his beady eyes. "Only it's not a raven. He's a crow. From the Dakath Mountains in the Below."

"How long have you had him?"

He flinched, as if at a bad memory, but it was so fleeting, I wondered if I'd imagined it.

"For about a hundred and seventy years," he replied.

So, since he was a child, then.

"Do crows live that long?"

"This one does." Voron lifted a finger and Magnus hopped on it, digging his claws into the leather of his master's black glove.

"He listens well to you."

"No." For once, his eyes warmed with affection. "We just happen to like the same things and have a mutual understanding." He stroked the clawed feet of his pet with his thumb.

Voron seemed to be in a fairly talkative mood today, so I ventured another question. "Would you tell me about this place, please?"

Magnus flew off to the nearest flowerbed, where he scraped at the dirt, searching for worms.

Voron draped his arm over the back of the bench. His cloak opened at that gesture, revealing an all-black outfit underneath. "What place do you mean? Elaros? The gardens? Sky Kingdom? Or the entire Nerifir."

"Tell me about Nerifir. No," I immediately corrected myself. "Tell me about this whole entire thing. Starting with that pink mist that brought me here."

"The River of Mists."

"Right." I shivered, remembering the foggy entity that had almost dropped me to my death upon arrival.

"It connects our words."

"Earth and Nerifir?"

He shook his head. "Many more than that."

"How many worlds are there?"

"No one knows. The Royal Archives hold records of an Orc Kingdom and the Shadow Kingdom in the World of Under, as well as many more. All of them, including the human realm, used to be one world before. Now, they say each world has its own rules in how it's connected to the River of Mists. But no one knows exactly how accurate these records are."

"So, the River of Mists flows through all of them, snatching people at will and dropping them off at random times and places?"

Amusement sparkled in his eyes at my brisk summary.

"The River of Mists only *connects* the worlds. People are the ones who do the 'snatching.' The *brack* stole you from your world, Sparrow, not the river."

"You're talking about Trez, right?"

"Yes."

"Why do you call him *brack?*"

"Like all of Ghata's servants he used to be a werewolf once, one of those who live in the Below, in the Planes of Sarnala. He gave up his free will and control of his life when he became a *brack*, a monk of the disgraced Goddess Ghata."

I remembered some of these names from his conversation with Trez the day we'd arrived in Sky Kingdom. But I hadn't had the presence of mind to fully comprehend the full meaning of it, then.

Voron continued, "The werewolves banished their goddess from Sarnala long ago. And she escaped to the human realm. She had taken her *bracks* with her. But they keep showing up in Nerifir, fetching things for her to use in your world. As a goddess, she can pull them back to her every time they leave her. According to the archives, she wasn't in the human realm for very long—just a few decades. But the *bracks* keep coming from that time period and may keep coming still. Apparently, the things and substances they source in Nerifir have some value for her in the human world."

"They're trading humans for those things," I added.

If it wasn't for Trez and his deal with the dead Sky King, I'd be back in my home right now.

My heart pinched with longing. Voron had been only partially right when he claimed that getting rid of my memories would free me from homesickness. I might not miss specific people or places, but that didn't stop me from yearning for a place to belong.

The look in his gray-blue eyes turned somber. "Yes, it appears they've resorted to trading people, too."

I felt awkward, standing over him while he was sitting. There was plenty of space on that bench next to him, so I sat on the other end of it. His hand on the back of the bench ended up touching my shoulder. He left it there, and I didn't move away, either.

"Did the *bracks* bring the human queen of gorgonians that you told me about to Nerifir?"

"No. She came to Lorsan willingly," he said. "With her husband."

"Were they in love?"

"More than that. The records say they were bonded mates."

The magical bond that Dove and Libelle were talking about.

"I thought a bond wasn't possible unless both people were of the same kind."

"It's not possible between the different types of *fae*," he explained. "We all have different strains of magic that don't bond with each other."

"But humans have no magic at all."

"And that's what makes your kind so versatile. You have no magic, but some of you can gain something just as powerful."

"What is it?"

"Love," he said. "The Lorsan queen and her husband loved each other so much, her love bonded with his magic."

"Oh."

"You sound disappointed."

I shrugged. "I was just hoping for something more powerful than love. Something stronger that I could use for a weapon when needed."

"Some would say love is better than any weapon, in this case. A magic bond adds strength to the couple who have it."

We sat in silence for a few moments. Voron was watching Magnus pull out a fat worm from the dirt in the flowerbed. I traced the silver thread of the dandelion stem embroidered on my cloak.

"Do you believe in love, Voron?" I asked.

He tilted his head back and closed his eyes, like he was sunbathing even as there was no sun.

"Aren't you full of questions today, nosy little Sparrow?" he murmured instead of answering.

"Today and every day," I said. "Until just a few days ago, I'm pretty sure I didn't even know this world existed. And now, it looks like I'm spending the rest of my life here. I have years of questions to catch up on."

He hummed something indiscernible, keeping his eyes closed and looking like a cat basking in the non-existent sunshine. By ignoring me, he was clearly dismissing me, letting me know our conversation was over.

I itched to kick him in the shin to get his attention but settled on asking something else instead—something with enough bite to make it hard for him to ignore me.

"Tell me, Voron, what's the role of the High General in Sky Kingdom? One would think that the rank implies leading the king's armies into battle. Yet here you are, fetching girlfriends for him and working security in his palace."

His eyelids lifted slowly. Rising to his feet, he pinned me with his steely glare.

Unease gripped my chest. I wished I'd just kicked him instead of poking the beast with accusations. A kick might've enraged him less.

Faced with the wrath flaming in his eyes, I was ready to bolt. But he towered over me, blocking my escape.

"I've waged wars for my king," he growled low, somehow sounding more terrifying than if he shouted. "I *have* led his armies into battles. So many battles, you'd have to visit the Royal Archives to get the exact count. I've bled for him. I've nearly died for him. It is because of *me* that the king has absolute power in this kingdom. Because of me, peace has reigned in our lands for the past five years. It is my duty to keep the king safe, at war *and* in peace."

Voron hid his true self well behind the veneer of calm composure, but I'd gotten glimpses of the passionate man behind the mask. I'd seen the heat of lust in those gray eyes of his. I'd even caught the glimpse of insecurity in them before.

Now, I was witnessing Voron's wrath, and I feared he allowed me to see but a tiny spark of the real inferno burning inside him.

His cloak billowed in the rising wind, caging me. He appeared to be all around me, taking over the entire space between the ground and the clouds.

"Why, Voron?" My voice came out barely a whisper from fright, yet I had to know. "Why did you risk your life for King Tiane? Why is his safety more important than yours?"

The window to his soul slammed shut, locking me out. The usual unreadable expression settled over his face once again.

"Everyone has their purpose in life, Sparrow."

"What is yours? Sacrificing yourself for the king?"

He inclined his head, infuriatingly polite.

"Enjoy the rest of your walk, little bird."

He turned his back to me, and I watched him leave. Magnus followed, soaring above—his one and only companion.

"Yep," I muttered under my breath. "I should've kicked him."

The kick would've brought me some satisfaction in addition to this heavy feeling currently sinking inside me.

Chapter Twelve

SPARROW

A guard knocked at my door shortly before lunch on Tuesday to inform me that King Tiane wished to see me at his dinner soirée that evening. That was the official invitation I'd been waiting for. It was somewhat concerning that it arrived so last minute, but Brebie was immensely relieved that it had arrived at all.

I couldn't help but share her relief. My mood lifted. Everyone had been so excited about my winning the king's attention. Eventually, I had no choice but to believe it was what I needed to ensure my future.

I didn't even mind the hours of torture Brebie and the maids had put me through to get me ready for the "casual" event that tonight's dinner was supposed to be. After hours of bathing, oil rubbing, hair brushing, and dressing me into yet another outfit that had a lot of cloth but hid nothing, I was finally ready.

"Good luck," Brebie exhaled, adjusting a purple vine with glowing crystal berries in my hair. "Remember, smile a lot, say little, and do whatever the king says," she prepped me like a coach giving a pep-talk to his team before the most important game of the season.

I certainly felt the pressure like this was the most important game. In my case, the stakes were even higher.

The guards escorted me to one of the top floors of the palace but to a different set of doors than before. Several more guards stood by the doors, but I didn't see Voron among them. Disappointment knocked some air out of my lungs. I would've liked to see him before going in, though I wasn't sure why. Maybe it was because the last ball went well in terms of my gaining the royal favor, and I hoped Voron would be my "lucky charm" tonight as well.

Before I could cross the threshold into the room, however, the tall woman with dark-green skin and intricately coiffured purple hair exited.

"Sparrow, dear," she said, passing by and lifting her hand in a gesture for me to follow, "I need to have a word with you."

I stopped in my tracks, unsure what to do. I recognized the woman. She had stood next to the king's throne at the last ball. Her striking appearance made her impossible to forget. Just like the last time, she wore a dress that bared her left breast. The same design of the letters P and T was painted on it in gold.

She noticed I continued to stand by the door.

"Are you coming?" she asked sternly.

One of the guards nudged my side. "Her Majesty wishes to speak with you."

Her Majesty?

Shock jolted my entire body. Now, I couldn't move even if I tried.

This was the queen?

Why did no one ever mention to me there *was* a queen?

She pursed her mouth in a highly displeased expression and ordered to the guards, "Bring her over here."

Two guards grabbed me under my arms and practically carried me after her into another room down the hallway. They deposited me inside and left me at the mercy of the queen I hadn't known existed until now.

She strolled in, the long train of her ivory-white dress snaking behind her. A thin circlet of golden thorns lay upon her head, but it was largely overshadowed by her extravagant hairdo, decorated with much more prominent jewelry than her crown.

"We haven't been formally introduced," she started.

"*No one* has been introduced to me," I said.

She shrugged one slim, delicate shoulder.

"Well, you're a piece of property. There is no etiquette for that kind of introduction. You've been presented to the king, which was supposed to suffice. I want, however, to have this conversation to express my expectations of you."

"Your expectations?"

Didn't I already have enough of those to fulfill? The entire court was watching me, to see whether I'd fly or crash. King Tiane surely had his own expectations of me, which I hadn't even guessed yet. And now, the queen I never knew existed apparently wished to impart her expectations for me, too.

"Yes." She inclined her head in a very regal manner.

I found it stressful enough to please the king. If I also had a queen to worry about...

"Okay," I exhaled. "Let's hear it."

She winced. Maybe at my lack of enthusiasm? I didn't really care. Learning that the man I needed to charm was already married was hard enough to swallow.

No one said she was his wife, though. Hope rose in me. What if she was his mother? Fae didn't age. She could be his grandma even, for all I knew.

"I'm Queen Pavline," she said, annunciating every syllable of her name and title with obvious pride. "Wife and Queen Consort of King Tiane, the ruling monarch of Sky Kingdom."

With my hopes crushed, I mumbled, "Nice to meet you."

"It's nice to have you in Elaros, Sparrow." To my surprise, there was no spite or sarcasm in her voice. She appeared genuinely glad to have me here. "The king likes you, which is enough for me like you too."

She came closer and lifted my chin with her fingers. "Be sweet and cheerful for him, Sparrow. The entire kingdom wins when our king is in a good mood. Before his birth, a prophecy predicted the arrival of the greatest king of all. King Tiane was born with a crown on his head. He was meant to rule. But the prophecy says he will reach his greatest potential when he is fulfilled." She gripped my arms. "Please him in every way you can, my dear, make him happy. Give him anything he desires. Fulfill his every wish. And above all, bear him a child."

"What?" I choked on the word.

She let go of me, standing taller to emphasize the importance of her words.

"Every monarch needs an heir to pass on his legacy. Only then, the king can be fulfilled."

"Are you sure? There are many other ways of fulfillment, other than procreation," I suggested tentatively.

She shook her head. "He's tried them all. It's become my life's mission to ensure his happiness. Yet..." She wrung her hands.

In a way, I felt sorry for her. She looked genuinely crestfallen.

"Well, the king seems happy enough. Maybe he's 'fulfilled' already?"

She made a face, shaking her head at my incompetence. "True happiness is deeper than a smile, Sparrow. The sun can only shine when the king is happy, and our kingdom hasn't seen sunlight in decades."

"And you think a baby would help that?" I couldn't keep the doubt out of my voice.

"An heir is the only thing the king doesn't have."

"Why not?"

And why me? This all was just too much.

Now, I was supposed to have a baby? With a man I'd only just met? A *married* man?

I could barely breathe, not even attempting to organize my thoughts into any kind of logic.

The queen must have noticed I was about to pass out and took a step back, giving me space. She circled the room slowly.

"I come from a family of three children," she said. "Three! For fae, to have this many offspring is unheard of. Children are rare among our kind, but they have been more common in my blood-line. Our women are highly sought after because of that. I was betrothed to the king still in my teens. We've been married for a hundred and fifty years now, and the king still has no heir."

"And I'm supposed to fix that?"

She drew in a shaky breath. Clearly, I wasn't the only one under pressure here.

"Humans are more fertile than fae," the queen said. "Give Sky Kingdom its next monarch, and your place in Elaros will be secured for life."

"What happens if I can't? Fertility can be a fickle thing, even for humans."

For all I knew, I could even have an IUD in my uterus. I doubted they had an ob-gyn around here who could check for things like that.

She jerked her head nervously, raising her hand as if to stop all doubt.

"I'll arrange for the royal hag to see you. She'll make sure you're ready to receive the king's seed."

Her words left a foul taste in my mouth. "Do you really want me to have sex with your husband?"

She smiled, looking at me as if I were a clueless child, "Sweetie, my husband has had sex with this entire court by now, every male and female in attendance. If you're worried about my feelings on this matter, don't. I've learned long ago to deal with them."

That raised another question.

"If he's had so many chances to get so many women pregnant and it still didn't happen, don't you think the problem may be in him, not you?"

She snapped her spine rod-straight. Her delicate features hardened. Her eyes narrowed, as if I had personally insulted her.

"The king is blameless," she bit off. "Just do what you're told, Sparrow, and we'll pray to the gods for the most marvelous outcome." She leaned closer, malice slithering into her voice. "Fail me, and you'll regret the day you were born."

I staggered into the royal dining room, my limbs heavy with dread after the conversation with the queen.

Unlike at the ball a few days ago, the dinner was served at a table. That didn't mean everyone was sitting in their seats, prim and proper. The king's guests sat in each other's laps, moved their chairs, or flew over the table if they saw a seat they liked better than their own.

King Tiane occupied the high-backed chair at the head of the table. He wore a shirt tonight, but it was so thin and transparent, it would reveal his skin even if it was buttoned all the way up, which it was not.

A woman leaned over his shoulder, her lips joined with the king's in a kiss.

I paused half-way across the room, unsure where to sit. Could I just climb into the king's lap while he was kissing someone else? Or should I find an unoccupied chair at the table and let him be?

Queen Pavline was busy talking and laughing with a group of courtiers at the other end of the table. I couldn't count on her to provide me with guidance. Dove smiled from the other side of the table, and Libelle wiggled her fingers at me in greeting. It was nice to see their familiar faces in the room full of strangers. But the seats on either side of them were already occupied.

A man suddenly flew up from the chair closest to me and fluttered over the table to a woman sitting across.

"Nothing tastes as good as your kisses, my lady," he declared, hovering over her. She giggled before tipping her head back and catching his kiss on her mouth.

I headed to the chair the man had vacated.

"That's Lord Petuh's seat," King Tiane's voice rose over the table.

I paused, with my hand on the back of the chair in question.

"Come here, my sweet baby chick." The king petted his thigh in invitation. "Have you forgotten your place?"

People's attention turned to me, and I hurried to the king, relieved he'd called me after all. The woman who'd been kissing him flashed me a cheerful smile, moving away to give me space as he pulled me into his lap.

"You missed the first course of the dinner." The king pouted.

"I'm sorry, Your Majesty. I've been...um, delayed."

Should I tell him the queen wished to talk with me? She never mentioned that our conversation was supposed to remain a secret from her husband.

The king, however, didn't appear interested in hearing the reasons for my delay. He perked up as a servant placed a plate with a tiny pyramid of meat jelly on the table in front of him.

"I hope you like aspic. It's divine." The king cut his fork into the gelatinous mass with small cubes of meat and cooked vegetables suspended inside it.

Just like at the ball before, I had no plate of my own and was forced to watch everyone eat without any food served to me. Thankfully, I'd learned my lesson from the last time and had eaten well before coming here tonight. I wasn't hungry, using the time to survey the room and study the people.

The dining room was considerably smaller than the royal ballroom but just as opulent. White-gray vines held the marble wall panels set with pastel-colored crystals that illuminated the space with waves of soft color-changing light. The vines weaved into a tight pattern high above us, forming the ceiling.

I slid my gaze over the table toward the white double doors with gilded molding. Four guards stood at each side of the doors, watching over the king and his guests. But Voron wasn't there.

Again, I felt a pinch of disappointment.

But why?

Shouldn't his absence be a relief? After his outburst in the gardens, Voron had stormed away and hadn't been searching for my company. Which was exactly how I wished it to be.

Why did I feel disappointed not seeing him here now?

The king handed me his glass of wine between the meal courses. Careful not to drink too much this time, I barely dipped my lips into it.

"You don't speak much, do you?" the king said.

Was he complaining?

"Would you like to talk, Your Majesty?"

I set the glass down on the table, racking my mind in search of an appropriate topic. It had to be something exciting as the king got bored easily. To my horror, my mind grew completely blank. I couldn't come up with a single entertaining thing to say.

He made a face. "Long talks bore me. Especially when they come from the mouths of pretty women." He slid a finger along my bottom lip. "This mouth is better suited for far more exciting things."

My heart thudded in my chest. Was this it? Would the king make his move now? Or was I getting ahead of myself?

I didn't know if I had sex before, though the possibility of having it didn't scare me. Sex was generally considered to be a pleasurable activity, wasn't it?

But I was nervous. My heart leaped ahead in a wild gallop and my hands turned sweaty as the king drew me closer. He sucked my bottom lip into his mouth in a kiss. He tasted like the wine he'd just drunk. I tried to return his kiss, to show him I enjoyed it. But my mind buzzed with anxiety.

I had no memory of kissing anyone. How was it done? Did I do it right? What if he thought my efforts were lame? What if he realized I had no idea what I was doing?

The mighty king of Sky Kingdom surely wouldn't want a clumsy lover. What would happen to me if he lost interest? If he sent me away, where would I go if I couldn't return home?

He closed his teeth over my lip, no longer a kiss—a bite. I gasped at the sting of pain and shrank back from him, breaking the kiss.

"Don't move." He drew in a sharp breath, flexing his arms around me.

He kissed my neck, nibbling at my skin as he moved lower, over my collarbone and down to my chest.

Yanking on the end of the scarf, he untied the bow on my shoulder and let the thin material fall down, uncovering my breast. The spikes of his crown pressed to my painted skin as he kissed along one of the golden swirls of paint, then sucked my nipple into his mouth.

Avoiding his antlers, I tentatively placed my hands on the back of his head, my fingers sinking into his luscious, golden white locks. Lifting my eyes from his head, I glanced at the set of doors behind the throne, opposite to the ones I'd entered through.

My gaze crossed with the stormy-gray eyes of Voron, who now stood by the doors on guard. My breath hitched.

I knew I should look away, but I couldn't. His stare trapped me, searing me with heat that spread through my entire body. The king's hands and mouth caressed my skin, but it was the look in Voron's eyes that ignited me with desire.

My lips parted. My eyelids lowered. My face flushed with warmth.

And Voron saw it all. He knew exactly what his heated stare was doing to me. He skimmed his lips with his tongue, and my lips tingled as if he kissed me. A corner of his mouth lifted in a smirk. He was clearly enjoying learning how much power he had over my body.

Air rushed out of me with a moan I couldn't hold back.

The king leaned back. "Aren't you precious? With those little whimpers of yours."

Voron spun on his heel. His cloak whipped around his legs, lashing against the doorframe as he left the room. Only then could I finally look at the king.

He grinned. His mouth glistened with the gold paint from my breast.

"Look at you." He tapped the tip of my nose. "All hot and bothered and glowing with need. Desire makes you look lovely, my baby chick."

It was all I could do not to stare longingly at the closed doors behind which Voron had vanished. *He* was the man I wished would lap at my nipple, squeeze my breasts, and kiss my mouth.

Voron was the man I wanted, not the king, I realized with horror.

This was bad. Very bad. Inconvenient and potentially dangerous.

How did I let this happen?

I was supposed to charm the king. *He* was the man in charge of my future.

The king stared at me. Was I supposed to say something? What was he expecting?

I lost focus, feeling too flustered to gather my thoughts. I heaved a breath and forced my lips to stretch into a smile, tossing a glance across the room in search of a distraction.

The courtiers had mostly finished with the dinner by now. A few of them still leisurely picked at their dessert. But the rest seemed to be ready to move on to whatever was next on the king's busy entertainment schedule.

"Is there something else planned for the evening?" I batted my eyelashes at the king.

As I had hoped, the question diverted his attention from studying my face. He swept his gaze across the table.

"Oh yes. We shall move to the games room now."

"Can I come?"

I proved to be a lousy dancer. Now, it looked like I wasn't that good at kissing, either. Maybe I could at least learn the games the king liked to play and become a worthy opponent for him?

I didn't choose this life. But if I had any choice at all, I'd rather be King Tiane's game partner than his mistress or his breeder.

He grimaced. "You'd be bored."

Dove and Libelle got up from their seats. Lord Petuh, the one whose chair I'd almost ended up taking earlier, seemed especially eager to go wherever they all were headed.

And I was being left behind.

"What games will you play tonight, Your Majesty?" I asked.

"A round of War of Kings, for sure," he replied animatedly. "I'll be playing with Lord Petuh. He defeated all his other opponents the last time."

"He did?" I threw a quick glance at Lord Petuh, who puffed out his chest, beaming with pride at the mention of his name. "Is that why he's strutting around ever so proudly, like a cock in a chicken coop?" I said softly, only for the king to hear.

The similarities between a rooster and the lord with his meticulously styled red hair and his brightly colored shirt with a sea of ruffles on his chest were impossible to miss. The way he strolled around the table—his chin hiked up, his chest rolled out, the most arrogant expression on his face—only strengthened the resemblance.

The king squinted at Lord Petuh, then suddenly erupted into laughter that startled everyone around the table. The courtiers stared at their king. Some had tentative smiles flickering in and out of existence, unsure whether they should join him in his merriment even as they had no idea what had caused it.

"Lord Petuh!" the king announced loudly. "My little human thinks you look like a cock strutting his stuff in a chicken coop after winning the game last time. Not for long, though, my lord. I fully intend to beat you at it tonight."

I froze in mortification. The joke I'd blurted to the king in private wasn't meant to be heard by the entire room. I didn't mean to embarrass the lord in front of everyone. But it was too late to do anything about it now. Everyone joined King Tiane in laughter.

Lord Petuh glared at me. The next moment, however, he was laughing, too, to my relief.

"How about anyone else, Sparrow?" he challenged. "Surely, I'm not the only one who inspires your wit."

King Tiane eagerly shifted in his chair.

"What say you, baby chick? Anything else?" He stared at me expectantly.

Everyone laughed. The mood seemed cheerful, all in good fun. And I had plenty to say on the topic. I'd been watching them all evening, memorizing their names and faces, while comparisons had been popping up in my brain.

I turned to a man who'd been trying to impress the woman sitting next to him at dinner. Right now, he was standing up, fluffing his thick wavy hair with his fingers, and straightening the wide sleeves of his shirt.

"Lord Ara is preening and cleaning his feathers. I wonder if he'd break into a courting dance next in hopes of winning Lady Eleene's heart."

The lady seemed to be aware of the lord's advances and very much welcomed them. So I didn't feel like that would insult either of them. Both laughed, with the lady blushing slightly.

The king's eyes sparked with delight. "What else?"

I tilted my head up to the couple under the ceiling. The man held on to the vines up above, with the woman hovering in front of his crotch. Her brightly colored wings fluttered rapidly as she reached for the laces of the man's pants, eager to free his erection that swelled thickly behind the lacing.

"That's a thirsty little hummingbird in search of some nectar," I said with a wink.

Everyone laughed louder, including the king.

"And what do you think about me, my baby bird?" he asked next.

A smile played on his lips, but by the way the king's eyes narrowed with warning, I knew I had to tread carefully.

"You, my king, are a majestic swan, soaring high above the clouds."

This wasn't a joke, not a funny one, anyway. The syrupy flattery of my words made my own teeth ache. But the king's smile grew wider. I obviously said what he wished to hear.

"Aren't you a treasure," he cooed, kissing my cheek. "Now tell me what you think about my High General."

I should've noticed he'd asked that after glancing briefly over my shoulder, but I was too preoccupied with gauging the mood in the room to notice. I realized I was toeing the fine line between making people laugh and hurting their feelings. It was a delicate balance to keep, requiring all my concentration.

When it came to Voron, however, nothing I could say about him would be flattering at the moment. That man pushed all my buttons without trying, without even being present in the room. My body tingled with excitement at the mere sound of his name, and I wished to have none of it.

"The High General?" I said, my voice brimming with sarcasm disguised as glee. "Do you mean that buttoned-up, cranky old prude? He's probably sitting with his books right now, despising all of us from the bottom of his heart that's as dark as his clothes."

The king roared with laughter, the rest of the courtiers did too, and I didn't pay much attention to the change in their expressions or the way the king glanced behind my back once again.

I kept going, "Do you think that hanging out with his pet crow might be turning him into a grumpy old bird, too? What is he doing all day? Lurking around, glowering, and snatching things that don't belong to him?" Like my memories, my name, and now my sanity. My voice lifted dramatically to the delight of the crowd. "A gloomy, wingless crow, that's what he is."

"A wingless crow!" The king doubled over with laughter, folding in half over my lap.

I smiled, glad that I could please him even if at the expense of the anger rising inside me. I didn't want to think about Voron, but he just wouldn't get out of my head, infuriatingly persistent.

From the corner of my eye, I noticed Dove waving at me to get my attention. She stared at me pointedly, her big eyes growing even bigger as she flicked them toward the doors in front of the table. Since I was sitting sideways on King Tiane's lap, the doors weren't in my direct line of view.

Dread frosted my insides as I slowly turned in that direction, already knowing what, or rather *whom*, I would find there.

Voron stood by the doors, staring straight at me.

Chapter Thirteen

SPARROW

Why? Oh, why did this room need two sets of doors, one on each end? The last time I saw the High General, he was at the doors behind the king. Then, he left. How was I supposed to know he'd returned using the opposite set of doors?

Voron was leaning against the door frame, his arms crossed over his chest. His cape was draped over his shoulders like the wings he didn't have.

Everyone was laughing at him. Because of me. He could've fled the room, but he remained in his spot, taking it all.

He tilted his head with a rather amused expression on his face. As if it was *me* everyone was laughing at, not him.

"Is it because you're perched on the royal lap, dear Sparrow, that you think there is no consequence to your chirping?" he asked as the laughter had died down.

It felt like a challenge. This man could heat my blood in so many ways. It was infuriating and oddly exciting at the same time. Adrenaline shot through my system like I was faced with a life-or-death situation.

I sensed I should keep my mouth shut at this point, but I couldn't stop baiting him. It was like throwing stones into a volcano about to erupt. I knew I was playing with fire, but I longed for the light that also came with the explosion.

Words rushed out of me, impossible to hold back.

"Oh, how dare I!" I cupped my face with both hands, faking horror. "Pray tell, High General, what punishment should befall me for making jokes about you?"

I was inviting his wrath. But I felt I could take it, ready to fight him. I wanted his mask to crack once again. I longed to see the real Voron, no matter how devastating that might be for me.

He unfolded his arms, then rolled back his wide shoulders slowly, just like he'd done it back in the gardens. That deliberate way of moving before exploding into rage reminded me of the storm clouds gathering menacingly before the storm would hit full force.

His eyes flashed with heat, but it wasn't anger. Under his stare, I felt even more naked than I was with one of my breasts fully exposed, the paint having been licked off my nipple by the king.

The room stilled under Voron's glare. The laughter stopped entirely. His voice remained low, but in complete silence, it sounded like rolling thunder.

"Had it been *my* lips that smeared the paint on your skin, you'd be too breathless to speak, bold little bird. You'd be too busy moaning and screaming my name right now."

I'd expected anything but that. Threats, mockery, insults. I was prepared for all of them. But this... This...

His words knocked the air out of my lungs. A part of me—an obviously insane, uncontrollable part—wished it were just like he'd said, that *his* lips were dusted with the gold from my breast, that it'd been Voron who'd sucked, licked, and nibbled on my body. Everywhere.

Suddenly, it felt as if everyone in the room was gone. I forgot whose lap I was sitting on. It was just me and the man across the room, his steel gaze bridging the space to link with mine.

His lips moved again. "You have no idea what you're trying to start here, poor clueless Sparrow. You can't even fathom the devastation that you court."

The pity and regret in his eyes burned worse than any insults, rendering me speechless.

Lord Petuh appeared out of nowhere, pressing a glass of dark-gold wine into my hand.

"A toast," he announced, lifting a similar glass of his own. "To the king's delightful new acquisition. To the witty, little Sparrow!"

The dinner guests toasted, drinking their wine and other liquors, chasing away the lingering sense of unease that hovered over the room in the wake of Voron's words.

The king lifted his glass. With mirth twinkling in his sunny blue eyes, he tapped on the bottom of mine, urging me to drink.

And like a trusting fool, I did. I drank the wine. It was sweeter and richer in taste than the one we had before. The sparkling liquid prickled my tongue with flavors of overripe apples and honeyed apricots before sliding down my throat.

The cloying taste of the wine seemed to stick to everything it touched inside me. My mouth, my throat, even the lining of my stomach appeared to have a thick, gooey residue from it. No matter how many times I swallowed or licked my lips, it lingered.

The sweet tentacles of intoxication reached into my brain, permeating my mind. The room swam, awash in a champagne-colored glow. The faces of people floated like bubbles in a wine glass, making me giggle. The closest one to me, the king's face, stretched and constricted in a most hilarious fashion.

"How are you feeling, my baby chick?" The king sounded delighted.

Everything around me suddenly looked much brighter, bigger, and lighter.

I felt lighter, too.

"Weird... So weird," I muttered, grinning widely.

The bubble-faces appeared to float up. Did the people fly up to the ceiling? Or did just their heads fly up? The thought of floating balloon heads made me laugh uncontrollably.

"Oh, I want to fly, my king!" I tossed my hands up in the air, waving my arms like wings. Brown and gray feathers sprung from my skin, sprouting all over my arms. "I have wings!" I yelled, leaping off the king's lap. "I'm a sparrow. A bird. I can fly."

I climbed onto the table to get higher to the ceiling. I jumped but couldn't take off. The clothes weighed me down, so I tore at the silk scarves that served as the bodice of my dress. I ripped them off, tossing the flowy scraps of material back at the king, who was rolling with laughter in his chair.

People were hooting, guffawing, and cheering me on. The noise fueled me with energy.

"I will fly," I assured them, yanking at the layers of my skirts. Their material might be light, but like a spider web, it trapped me, keeping me on the ground. "I'll fly, you'll see."

I ripped my skirts off. The last thing I was still wearing, the gilded under-bust corset, proved much more difficult to take off. I tangled in the pink ribbons that laced it.

"You just wait..." I mumbled to all those laughing while I tugged at the ties. "You'll all see... I'll show you."

A hand reached up to me. "Come here, Sparrow."

"I'm not done yet!" I swatted the hand away. "This stupid ribbon..."

"Oh yes, you're done." Voron grabbed me around my waist and yanked me off the table. "Time to land, little bird." He heaved me up into his arms. "No more flying."

"But I didn't even make a turn around the room!" I protested, fighting against his hold. "You're such a party pooper! Just because you can't fly yourself, Wingless Crow, doesn't mean all of us have to sit on the ground with you."

The laughter rolled around us in swells. The king practically howled, doubling over and holding his sides.

"This is the best one yet, my human pet!" he shouted. "Well done, Lord Petuh."

Lord Petuh? What did *he* have to do with anything?

Voron adjusted me in his arms. "The fun is over, ladies and gentlemen."

He carried me out of the room.

"I don't want to leave!" I kicked my legs and shoved at his shoulders, but it was no use. The man was stronger than a bull, his arms holding me to his chest like a vise. "I want to fly!"

"Don't we all," he muttered under his breath, carrying me down the stairs, then into my room.

After kicking the door closed behind us, he deposited me onto my bed. With a flick of his fingers, the crystals in the walls shone brighter. Unlike Brebie, Voron didn't even need to touch them to illuminate the entire room.

My head was spinning so much, I didn't know whether I was flying or falling. I fell back into the pillows, but that only made the spinning sensation stronger.

"I'm going to be sick," I groaned, tossing my feathery arm over my face.

Voron was talking to someone at the door.

"I've got salt." He returned to the bed and sat on the mattress next to me. "Lick it." He opened the jar in his hands.

I laughed. It was a crazy, maniacal sound that I could hardly believe came from me.

"Oh, I'll *lick it*, High General." I sat up in bed. "I'll lick every part of your hard, strong body, darling Voron. All that muscly gorgeousness that you keep hidden under all those layers." I hooked my fingers between the silver buttons of his vest and yanked him to me.

He gave in, leaning closer. His eyes landed on mine and I held them, drinking in every drop of his attention, his surprise, and... his desire.

"What is it that you're doing to me, Voron?" I murmured. "Why do I want so much to see what you're hiding under your clothes? Why do I need to know what kind of heart beats in your chest? Why do I wonder what thoughts roam inside that handsome head of yours?"

I shifted closer, until my bent leg wedged between his thighs, my knee pressing down on the already familiar bulge in his pants.

He sucked in a sharp breath at the contact but didn't move away.

I brought my face closer to his. "Do you know how much I want your dick to rip through your laces, so that I could finally take a look at it, too? That'd be only fair, wouldn't it? You've seen me naked. When is my turn?" His lips were close enough to kiss. If only he let me... "Admit it, you want me to see you, Voron. All of you. To touch you. To lick you... And you want to taste me, too. Say it," I challenged. "Kiss me. Make me moan like you threatened you would."

He set the jar on the night table with force and snarled, "Do you really think I'd stop at kissing? If I kissed you, dear Sparrow, if I tasted you, I'd fuck you. And it'd be my ruin. Your ruin, too."

His eyes flashed. He gripped the back of my head, fisting his hand in my hair. I felt his breath on my skin, but I wished for more of him on me. I needed him closer, inside me. And I didn't care if it ruined us both.

This entire world could burst into flames, as long as Voron did something about the desperate need for him that burned in my chest and the heat that throbbed between my legs.

"I don't care," I begged in a hot whisper. "Damn it all. Just kiss me, Voron."

He drew in his next breath with a groan. Lifting his finger between us, he dragged his tongue along it.

"Lick. The fucking. Salt. Sparrow." He stabbed his finger into the jar, then shoved the salt-covered finger between my lips.

The moment I tasted the salt on my tongue, the curtain shrouding my brain drew back. The "feathers" disappeared from my arms. Clarity returned and with it, mortification filled me. I closed my eyes, like I could hide my shame this way.

"Thank you," I whispered around his finger that he left lingering in my mouth. "And sorry."

He chuckled. The sound came unexpectedly. I snapped my eyes open and searched his, trying to read him.

Was he laughing at me? Was he angry? If so, he had every right to be. I got carried away in my strife to please the king. I crossed the line by making fun of something Voron likely had no control over—his lack of wings.

Regret for my words reached deeper than even shame.

He removed his finger from my mouth but kept his other hand in my hair and his face close to mine.

"I'm sorry for calling you names," I said softly, my cheeks burning with shame under his gaze.

"My dear Sparrow. You didn't say anything I haven't called myself."

He sounded somber but kind, and I exhaled with relief.

"So, you're not offended?"

He released my hair and smoothed it down for me. The gesture was so gentle, it made my heart ache.

"I wouldn't be where I am now if I were so easily offended," he said. "But you have to be careful with the others. Lord Petuh didn't take your joke well."

The lord was the one who handed me the wineglass, I remembered. The wine didn't look or taste like anything harmful I'd had before. Yet it obviously wasn't harmless.

"What was it? What did he add to my wine?"

"Nothing. He gave you wine made from rotten fruit."

The sticky sweet taste of it had the flavor of overripe apples and possibly peaches or apricots.

"Is it the wine that made me take my clothes off?" I said with a bitter smile, a pathetic attempt to cover up my embracement.

His eyes flicked to my bare chest. The golden paint on one breast had been licked off by the king. On the other, the delicate swirls were now smudged and smeared, too. I crossed my arms over both to hide the mess the best I could.

Voron grabbed a folded blanket from the chair by the fireplace, opened it, and draped it over my shoulders, covering me up.

"Thank you." I pressed the blanket to my chest, suddenly acutely aware of my state of undress. All I had on was the corset-belt that covered nothing. And I'd been sitting like that, with my boobs on display, for quite a while now. Voron had seen me naked before, but that didn't make this situation any less awkward.

"The rotten fruit wine creates illusions and makes people who drink it act irrationally," Voron explained.

"'Irrationally' is a nice way to put it. I made a fool of myself."

"It's not as bad as you think," he tried to comfort me. "The royal court finds someone new to laugh at every day. By tomorrow, they'll forget all about today."

I fidgeted with the end of the blanket, avoiding his eyes. "I hope you're right."

"You know what?" He sounded like he'd made a decision.

Opening his vest, he reached for the top button of his black silk shirt underneath.

That got my attention.

My heart skipped a beat as he opened more buttons. His bare chest came into view—smooth pale skin stretched over the well-defined pectoral muscles with a generous sprinkle of short, raven-black hair.

With so much naked flesh constantly on display in Elaros, seeing a sliver of his bare chest shouldn't be this fascinating. But my mouth felt dry as my heart restarted with a thud. I swallowed hard, watching Voron open his shirt.

Sadly, he stopped after the third button. Reaching around his neck, he took off the necklace he wore under his shirt. It was a string of wrinkly, silver beads with a dark, smooth rock for a pendant.

"This is warded. I've worn it since I was a child." He placed the necklace around my neck. "The silver rowan berries and the hag's stone will protect you from pretty much every food or known curse out there, including the rotten fruit wine. No one will be able to take it off you without your permission. But some may be able to break it. Take care of it."

The beads carried the warmth of his body when they touched my skin. He was so close, his breath moved the hair on my temple. His fresh scent invaded my senses. His fingers skimmed my skin as he closed the necklace on the back of my neck. Warm shivers scattered down my arms from his touch.

I leaned forward until my forehead touched his shoulder.

"Tonight's dinner would be the one memory I'd actually *want* you to take away, Voron."

He briefly rested his chin on the crown of my head. "No more taking memories, little bird. From now on, you'll need every one of them to build your experience and to learn from it."

"Then, I should ask you to go around Elaros and erase the memory of me at tonight's dinner from everyone's minds. Starting with the king, please."

He exhaled a soft puff of a laugh into my hair, and I wished he would wrap his arms around me, kiss me, and tell me that everything was going to be okay.

But he quietly pulled away, leaving me to wallow in mortification and self-pity all on my own.

"You made the king laugh today," he said. "Wasn't that your goal all along?"

That was true. I'd tried to make the king laugh at the expense of others, and unwittingly proceeded to do so at my own expense, too.

"I got carried away." I rubbed my eyes, feeling exhausted. "Serves me right."

I felt so stupid for drinking the wine when I should've known better. I knew first-hand how dangerous drinks can be, but I let my guard down. I got distracted. By the very same man who was sitting in front of me right now.

Remembering his words about making me scream his name if I were his, I asked, "Why did you say the things you did? In front of everyone?"

He smirked, not looking very remorseful.

"Let's say I got *carried away*, too."

"And then when I threw myself at you, you promptly retreated." His rejection seemed far more offensive to me than his words.

"Would you rather I'd taken advantage of you? In your delirious state?"

Would I?

No.

But if I looked deep, under all the expectations, and pressure, and the glitzy façade of the palace life that had already rubbed off on me a little, what I really wanted would've been Voron taking me from Trez that day by the river and bringing me to his home in Vensari that Kanbor had mentioned. I would've loved for him to hide me there, away from the Elaros Court with its fake smiles and from the fickle attention of the Sky King.

As if guessing my thoughts, Voron gently touched my arm through the blanket.

"I saw you first, Sparrow. I gave you your name. But you are not mine and can never be."

As if I hadn't been rejected by him enough today already.

"Let me be, then," I said firmly.

He arched an eyebrow in question, and I blew out a breath.

"I'm trying, Voron. I'm really trying to make it in Elaros. I know it's not your fault that I ended up in Sky Kingdom. But you were the one who brought me to Elaros. You handed me over to the king. Everyone—literally every single person I meet—is telling me I *must* please the king. And the queen..." I pinned him with a glare. "Why did no one ever tell me there *was* a queen?"

He frowned. "What does it matter? Marriage is an arbitrary concept for highborn. Its meaning largely depends on the two people involved. For the queen, it's all about the position. There are no romantic feelings between her and the king. The royal couple haven't been intimate for decades."

"Really?" I sat back. "Well, that's not the way to go about it if they want an heir to the kingdom."

"An heir? Who told you the king wants an heir?"

"Doesn't every king want one? At least that's what Queen Pavline told me. And now apparently, I am Sky Kingdom's last hope." I scrubbed a hand down my face. A headache was pounding inside my skull after that rotten wine. I was so tired. "The queen wants me to have the king's baby."

"She does?" Voron's features sharpened with focus.

"I'm supposed to seduce King Tiane, get pregnant by him, and give Sky Kingdom the next king. How is that for a job description? I've been in this place for less than a week, and this is the pressure—the *honor*—that was bestowed on me. According to the queen, a baby would secure my place in Elaros for the rest of my life."

"Is that what you want?"

For once, someone actually asked what I wanted. Only what was the point, anyway? He'd said it himself that I would have very little choice in what my life here would be.

I exhaled a humorless laugh.

"Sure, Voron. Wouldn't that be wonderful? All I have to do is breed with royalty and voila! I have a clear path to a secure future. But you..." I pressed my hands into his chest, pushing him away. "You have to go. Please leave me alone. Don't say things you said to me at dinner tonight. Please, don't look at me the way you do. You have no idea what it does to me. And I can't... I just can't deal with it in addition to everything else."

"Sparrow..." His voice was soft, like a caress. He lifted his hand to my face, but I recoiled from him, jolted by panic.

"No. Please, don't touch me. I can't live the way the highborn in Elaros do. I can't smash my feelings into a million tiny pieces and sprinkle them like confetti on everyone at once. If I'm meant to be with the king, so be it. I'll try my best to do what's expected of me. But I can only do it with *one* man." I swallowed around a painful lump forming in my throat. "There is simply not enough of me for more than one of you. And it looks like it has to be the king."

That was what Voron wanted too, wasn't it? He'd rejected me enough times to get that point across perfectly by now.

His hand fisted in the bedspread, the knuckles turning white and the veins bulging. But he said nothing. I feared to see his face, choosing to stare at his hand instead.

He had to go. Yet a part of me wished he'd fight me on that, with the passion I knew he had in him. Just like he'd fought me in the dining room earlier.

But back at dinner, we hadn't been alone. I'd made fun of him in front of witnesses. He'd had to put me in my place to save face. That didn't mean he'd felt what he'd said.

"Go, Voron." It proved impossible to keep bitterness out of my voice. "Get out of my room and stay away from me."

He inhaled deeply, got off my bed, and buttoned up his vest.

"You speak with the voice of reason, dear Sparrow." He sounded calm. His usual frosty expression returned to his face. "Rest assured, I won't bother you again."

When the door closed behind him, I groaned, sinking back into the pillows. Grabbing one, I threw it at the door, wishing he still stood there to receive my wrath.

I'd told him to get out of my room and stay out of my life. Yet having him leave was the last thing I wanted.

Chapter Fourteen

SPARROW

A week later, I sat on my bed, with my knees drawn up to my chest, and watched Alacine clean my room for the lack of anything better to do.

The weather had been miserable for days, forcing me to cut my walks in the gardens short. It had warmed up a bit, and the winds were down, but the clouds remained as thick as ever. Hanging low and churning dark along the horizon, they promised a storm. Only no storm ever came. The air was heavy with moisture. But instead of a proper shower, only miserable drizzle came now and then, making being outside depressing.

Alacine wore a pretty cornflower-blue blouse today. The end of her long tail was enclosed in a soft cotton cloth. As she moved around, sleek and graceful, the tail trailed behind her, sweeping dirt from the floor and sneaking into every nook and cranny with the cloth.

There was a contentment on her face, as she softly hummed a cheerful tune.

"Do you like cleaning, Alacine?"

"Do you like breathing, my lady?" she retorted. A smile

appeared on her lips at my confusion. "That's what it's like for me," she explained. "I like making dirt disappear, putting things in their place, and taking care of others. It's my *calling*, which makes the tasks easy for me. When work is easy, it doesn't feel like work."

As she spoke, she never stopped moving. The tip of her tail twirled around the legs of the chair, under the trunk, and around the fireplace, picking up dust on the cloth.

"Is 'the calling' something one is good at?" I asked. "Like *taureans* are good at farming?"

She tilted her head, pondering my question.

"*Taureans* are good at reading the weather and picking up on the signs of plants' wellbeing. They enjoy the peace and quiet that working on the land brings. They're attuned to the slow cycle of a plant's life and often prefer working in solitude. All of that makes them suitable for farming." She expertly re-arranged the vials and hairbrushes on my vanity, somehow gaining a lot of extra space just by moving things around. "My people are called *snakanas*. We live in large communities and dislike being on our own. My entire extended family lives in Elaros. My mother is a maid here, too. My father takes care of the horses in the royal stables, and my grandmother used to be one of the royal nannies. She helped raise King Tiane," she added proudly. "I pray to every mother goddess that Queen Pavline is blessed with a child one day. I'd love to work in a nursery when that happens."

Anxiety scratched inside me at her mentioning a royal child.

In the past week, I'd seen King Tiane twice. Both times at dinner, like before. He'd feed me morsels of his food. We'd watch yet another breathtaking performance and listen to beautiful music. Then he'd leave to play a game with a selected group of the courtiers, and I'd be sent back to my room.

During dinner, his hands would stray into my neckline to play with my breasts or under my skirt to stroke my inner thighs. But he wouldn't take it any further. I was no closer to getting into the royal bed than I was on the day of my arrival in Elaros.

Maybe there was my fault in that, too. I didn't encourage him. I never touched him unless prompted, feeling rather awkward in his presence. He still liked bringing up the incident with the rotten fruit wine, laughing at me with the rest of the court. That didn't make me any more comfortable or trusting around him, either.

Queen Pavline hadn't spoken to me again. But she shot me urging, demanding stares across the dining table, as if expecting me to tackle her husband to the ground and force him to impregnate me right then and there.

All of it only increased my anxiety to the point that I actually enjoyed not having King Tiane in the palace for a while. He and most of his court left for the royal hunting lodge two days ago. They'd be gone all of next week, hunting wild animals in the woods, and it felt...lighter without them somehow.

I had no desire to hear anything about the royal nursery from Alacine and promptly steered her back to the topic at hand.

"What would happen if you were to work outside of your *calling?* Like what do you think about working in the kitchen?"

Concern shadowed her lime-green eyes.

"Is my lady not happy with the service I provide?"

"Alacine, please don't worry. This has nothing to do with your work. I'm thrilled you're looking after me, really, and I'm very grateful to have you. I'm just curious about life in Sky Kingdom. I'm new here and still have so much to learn. Would working in a kitchen, for example, make a *snakana* miserable?"

Her frown eased.

"Probably. We don't generally enjoy the heat of the cooking fire. And there are a lot of them in the palace kitchen. For me, one of the best parts about working here is that I don't have to cook, not even for myself. I'm fed from the royal kitchen."

She propped her hands onto the mattress, stretching to reach further under the bed with her tail.

"So, *snakanas'* purpose in life, or *calling,* as you put it, is service?"

"Yes. But don't forget, my lady, service has a very broad meaning. Quite a few of my ancestors were servants of the gods—priests and priestesses. My great-aunt's magic was strong enough for her to become a hag. She was one of the most esteemed healers in the kingdom."

"Does everyone have a calling in Sky Kingdom?"

"Pretty much."

"How about the highborn, then? What's their calling? Other than partying and being served?"

She giggled softly.

"Our king loves to be entertained," she agreed. "There are plenty of highborn who work as servants, too, or become hags if their magic is strong enough. But if they're born into noble families as lords and royalty, their only purpose is to govern."

She sounded almost sorry for the people she served. And maybe they should envy her. I'd never seen such serene contentment on their faces as the one that graced hers.

"And in times of war," she added, "the highborn fight and die."

"What do you mean? Do only the highborn go to war?" That was new to me.

She nodded.

"They start wars. They fight in them. They win or lose. But either way, many of them die. The rest of us are kept out of that, thank gods." She shuddered.

"Interesting." Where exactly did I fit in this bizarrely ordained life of Sky Kingdom? "What would the purpose of someone like me be, you think?"

She gave me a confused look. "Oh, but it's to entertain, of course, my lady. You're a human, the only one here. A rarity. You belong in the palace, with the king."

"And what if I lacked the ability to entertain? Or if the king didn't care for my kind of entertainment?"

"Well...um." She averted her eyes, going unnaturally rigid. Even her tail stopped moving for a moment.

"What is it, Alacine? Please tell me."

"If the king didn't want you by his side, he would…"

"Gift me to someone else?" I finished for her.

"No."

"No? But why would he keep me even if he didn't want me?"

"No one can have what King Tiane doesn't have. As long as you are the only human in the kingdom, you belong to him, and only him."

The conviction in her voice sent a chill of apprehension down my back.

"But what if he isn't interested in having me?" That was a possibility I absolutely had to consider when planning my future. I wasn't entirely sure what had earned me King Tiane's attention so far. I certainly had no clue how to keep it going forward.

"If he doesn't want you in Elaros for any reason…" Alacine said softly. "Not that it would ever happen, my lady," she added hurriedly. "King Tiane is really taken by you."

"Sure. He is. But what would happen if he wasn't anymore?"

She stretched her shoulders, looking uncomfortable.

"He'd send you to his menagerie, most likely."

"Menagerie?"

"It's just outside of the city of Elaros. He keeps many rare creatures there. Like a griffin from the Dakath Mountains and a few glowing turtles from the Lorsan Wetlands."

She glanced at me apologetically from under her thick eyelashes, as if it were her fault somehow that I would end up kept as an animal if I lost the king's favor.

"I'd be locked in a zoo?" My voice came out as hollow as my chest felt. "In a cage?"

"It'll probably be just a collar with a chain," Alacine rushed to assure me before catching my crestfallen expression. She grabbed my hand in an effort to console me. "Oh, my lady, you really don't have to worry about leaving Elaros. The king—"

"The king doesn't have a long attention span, does he?" I said bitterly. "No one can keep his affections for long. How many lovers did he have in the past year?"

Alacine shifted awkwardly, not even attempting to count for me.

"But he's had long relationships too," she defended him for my comfort. "He's been married for a century and a half."

"It's a state marriage. In name only. It doesn't bind him in any other way, I've heard."

"Oh, please don't be sad, my lady," she exhaled in sympathy.

My lady.

It was a fake title, too. Just like my name was also fake. Neither guaranteed me any kind of respectable position. No matter how hard I might try, it appeared my real future would still be a cage. Or a collar with a chain, as it may be.

"Parro!" Alacine suddenly exclaimed.

"What?"

"Parro, the royal jester. King Tiane had him for over five decades until he choked on a rainbow snail and died."

"Oh. That's unfortunate."

"Yes, but his death was an accident." She waved at me with both hands. "The point is that Parro retained the king's favor for decades."

"How?"

She shrugged. "By making him laugh. By entertaining him. Parro went everywhere with the king. He was there for every meal, every game. He went hunting, too. The king even took him to the battlefield."

"The jester went to war?"

"Not really. He just came with the king to inspect the troops or to accept a High Lord's surrender. High General Voron was the one who actually led the royal armies and fought all of King Tiane's wars."

"There were many?"

"What can I say, the highborn love to fight," she said matter-of-factly.

"Who do they fight with?"

"With each other. There were a few High Lords who dared dispute King Tiane's birthright to the crown. As the late king's nephew and King Tiane's first cousin, High Lord Bussard was one of them. But in the name of the king, High General Voron defeated the High Lord's armies and put an end to that war. The king then exiled High Lord Bussard to the Far Isles."

"I see. And why would anyone dispute the king's birthright?"

She shrugged again, not looking very concerned. "Everyone wants to wear the crown, I guess."

After Alacine finished cleaning and left, I stood in front of the mirror and studied my reflection. It had very much the face of a stranger, since I only had memories of it being *my* face for the past two weeks.

Hazel eyes. Medium-brown hair, reaching just below my shoulder blades. Not too many lines yet. I must be in my twenties. Mid to late twenties, maybe, as all traces of childhood appeared to have left my features already.

Who was this woman all her life? The life I didn't remember?

Would she balk at the idea of sleeping with a married man and having his baby only to give it up for others to raise?

Or would she look at what was expected of me as the opportunity to help a childless couple to start a family? To gift a queen, trapped in a loveless marriage, a new purpose in life? And to give the kingdom new hope?

I would never know what I would've thought about all of this in the past. I could only figure out how I felt about it now.

As it turned out, I wasn't in Elaros to become the king's girlfriend. I wasn't even his mistress. I was a *pet*.

The only way to improve my status would be to get pregnant. As the birth mother of the heir to the crown, I'd have enough respect from those in power to keep the collar off my neck.

However, that option came with emotional implications I wasn't sure how to handle. There'd be intimacy with the man who would never be mine and a baby I'd have to give up.

Besides, King Tiane didn't seem eager to bed me. I hadn't even seen his bedroom yet.

Taking off the silk robe I was wearing, I pressed my hands to my hips through the transparent material of my nightgown.

This was not the body of a fae. My skin didn't glow like theirs. But even if it did, I'd still look nothing like them. The ladies of the court were tall and waiflike, with delicate necks, graceful limbs, and small, perky breasts.

I was at least a head shorter than any of them. My hips were much wider. My full breasts rested heavily against my ribs without the support of a bra or the lift of a corset. I turned sideways, noting the visible swell of my belly and the thickness of my thighs.

The way Voron looked at me made me feel desirable. But was that really the case?

From the knowledge I'd retained about the human world, my body wouldn't meet the beauty standards there. How could I be considered attractive by fae who lived surrounded by perfection?

Trez had said I was short and chunky. Plain and unappealing. King Tiane had called me "short and chubby" when he first saw me. Those weren't the words used to describe conventionally attractive women.

Now I understood better why Voron named me Sparrow. He chose the name after a single look at me. Like Trez, he saw someone "plain and unappealing." Mousy, like the most humble bird of all.

How far would my "exotic" status of a human take me in Elaros? How long before the novelty of having a companion from another world would wear off for the king? What if I never became the mother of the royal heir that would ensure my status?

One thing was clear, I couldn't rely on the whims of powerful highborn for my future.

Everyone in this kingdom had a purpose.

I had to find mine.

Chapter Fifteen

SPARROW

"Can I help you peel the carrots?" I asked a young kitchen helper.

The smooth efficiency with which he was handling the knife was slightly intimidating, but I was determined to try doing the same.

Elaros was huge. The palace alone was populated by hundreds of courtiers with thousands of people serving them. All I needed was to find a task, a job, a chore that I could do to prove myself useful even if the king's attention went elsewhere.

The boy eyed me suspiciously, not giving up his carrots despite having two buckets full of them standing on the kitchen counter waiting to be peeled.

"Here, honey. Peel this turnip." Brebie placed the vegetable in my left hand and a small knife in my right one.

I'd begged her to bring me here today, wishing to see what working in the kitchen was like. I also secretly hoped the cook might have something for me to do, something that I could possibly make my main occupation with time.

There was no way I could ever compete with someone like

Alacine in cleaning rooms. But after having spent only five minutes in the kitchen, I doubted I could be as good as any of the people working here, either.

The head chef, a tall, elegant man with the grace of a dancer, was sculpting a giant snow-white swan atop a rose-pink crest of a wave on a marble platter.

"The ice-cream sculpture is for the celebration dinner for when the hunting party returns to Elaros," Brebie had explained to me when we'd arrived at the kitchen a few minutes ago. "It takes days to complete. And it's kept in a freezer in the cellar between the sculpting sessions."

"It's gorgeous!" I'd gasped in awe, which had earned me a smug glance from the head chef.

He had allowed me to stay and look around, though I suspected he was already regretting it. Wherever I stood, I seemed to be in the way of people working here. They moved swiftly between the tables, fireplaces, crates, and barrels, without bumping into each other. My presence broke the pattern of this well-coordinated choreography.

I squeezed into a gap between two tables and started peeling the turnip Brebie had given me. With the flurry of activity around me, I couldn't help but feel like a child who'd been given a box of crayons and some paper to occupy her while the adults were doing the real job. But I didn't complain. I'd peel a thousand turnips and then a thousand more if only that helped me keep the pet collar off my neck in the future.

"I finished!" I triumphantly displayed my peeled turnip.

The head chef didn't spare me a glance.

The kitchen helper just sneered in my direction. He'd almost finished a bucket of carrots by now. By smoothly rotating each root vegetable between his fingers, he managed to peel the entire carrot in one rotation. The sight was mesmerizing. I could just stay there and watch him work. Or watch the head chef manipulate a butter knife like a sculpting tool to whip the ice cream into shape. Or admire the way an *arien* woman deftly unmolded intricate shapes of jelly to be served to Queen Pavline and the few courtiers who hadn't left with the king's hunting party, choosing to stay in the palace instead.

Could I ever become as fast and efficient as the fae? Could I learn the skills most of them had been born to muster?

"Out of the way!" a woman carrying a tray full of dishes snapped, startling me.

I scurried back into my gap between two tables. Brebie hurried to me from where she was talking to someone by one of the giant stoves across the rooms.

"It's nice, sweetie." She took the turnip from me and placed it on the table where another woman quickly rolled it aside to make space for kneading bread dough.

"Can I do something else?" I asked.

Brebie shook her head. "You should go back to your room, now. We'll need to get you dressed for Lady Dove's tea party."

I inhaled, ready to argue when the head chef's cheerful voice reached me.

"Greetings, High General."

The breath stayed in my throat. With my back turned to the door, I didn't see him, but I *felt* with my entire being when Voron entered the kitchen.

My face flushed with heat as he greeted the head chef behind me. Blood rushed from my extremities, leaving my fingers cold and trembling. I carefully set the knife I held down onto the table, lest I drop it.

His deep voice sounded right behind my back, "The hunting party felled a stag this morning. The king wishes to have the venison served at the dinner celebration upon their return to Elaros next week."

Maybe he always spoke to the head chef in a clipped voice like that. But something told me Voron was curt because of me. Not because I wasn't supposed to be in the kitchen. But because he didn't expect to run into me here.

Ever since I'd kicked him out of my room, he'd been keeping

his distance, just like I'd told him to. He hadn't approached me, hadn't spoken to me, and hadn't searched out my company.

I did my best to avoid him, too. During the royal dinners, I'd refrained from looking around the room for him. No matter how hard it was, I didn't even glance at the doors where he usually stood watching over the king and his guests. But like now, I'd often sensed his presence. I'd felt his stare on me, even as I'd forbidden him to look at me.

The kitchen staff was busy with preparations. Among all the bustling activity, the silence around us grew that much more awkward. When I could no longer stand it, I turned around, against my better judgment.

His gray-blue eyes looked straight at me, robbing me of breath.

"Hello, Sparrow," he said evenly.

The sleeves of his black silk shirt were rolled up to his elbows. Clenching his right hand, he leaned with the fist against the table. The ropy muscles of his forearm bulged out, raising a thick vein under his pale skin. The short hair on the outside of his arm made me think of his bare chest I'd glimpsed when he'd taken his necklace off to give it to me. I'd been wearing it ever since. The smooth stone pendant nested neatly between my breasts, feeling like a gentle press of a thumb.

Raising my hand, I placed it against his necklace under my blouse, one of the very few non-transparent clothes I had in my extensive wardrobe.

"Greetings, High General," I finally found my voice.

I swept my tongue over my dry lips, forcing my eyes off his forearm.

My body buzzed with awareness in his presence. Heat pulsed through my chest, flushing my face and...pooling low in my belly.

I hadn't touched myself since I came to Elaros. I didn't know whether I used to do that in my past, but I knew masturbation existed. I knew it'd be a way to relieve the throbbing ache between my legs. And I knew I'd have the images of Voron's naked forearm and the sliver of his bare chest on my mind if I came on my hand tonight.

How pathetic was that? The man hadn't touched me, hadn't kissed me. He'd made it clear he had no intentions of ever doing either. And his body was the only one I fantasized about, lovingly cataloging in my mind every part of him he'd ever exposed.

I jerked my head, trying to shake off the inappropriate thoughts along with the highly inconvenient desire.

Cocking a hip, I lifted my chin defiantly.

"Fancy to find you in the kitchen, my lord." The snappy tone did wonders to calm my nerves and cool the stupid lust. "I see the duties of the High General also include supervision of food preparation."

A corner of his mouth lifted in a most charming half-smile. He ran his gaze over my face as if reacquainting himself with my features.

"Among other things," he replied. "The question is, what are *you* doing here?"

I straightened my spine, flicking my gaze across the spacious kitchen. The activity never stopped here. People continued to clean, peel, and chop. Few paid any attention to us.

Still, I leaned closer and said quietly, only for him to hear, "I'm just trying to find a way to exist, Voron. A way that doesn't involve moaning and screaming any man's name."

"I can't wait for the court to return to Elaros." Dove pouted, setting her teacup on her saucer with a loud clink. "It's so boring here without the king and his parties."

I took a sip of the flavorful concoction of steeped tea, doe cream, and imported lily honey with fragrant petals of jasmine floating on the surface.

Unlike Dove, I was enjoying the peace and quiet of the past

few days. Between my interactions with Alacine and Brebie and the afternoon tea with Dove, I didn't feel lonely. These few days had given me a chance to recharge and get ready to face the king again soon.

"You should've gone hunting, too," I said, setting my cup down.

Dove's suite in Elaros reminded me of my room with the explosion of whites and pinks. Only hers was much bigger. The silk upholstery on the furniture with carved gilded frames looked like it came straight from Princess Barbie's playhouse. The air smelled like candy and rose petals. Her suite was like a small world on its own, and I enjoyed coming here. Chatting with Dove helped get my mind off things.

She curved her lips in distaste.

"Hunting is gross." She leaned closer, as if sharing a secret. "There's dirt in the woods. And leaves. Pine needles and twigs get stuck in my feathers and hair when I fly through the trees. And bugs..." She shuddered. "I'd have to spend a week soaking in a tub to get all of that mess out."

"Libelle doesn't mind it. She went," I pointed out.

"Libelle doesn't have a choice. Her husband is an avid hunter. That's the pain of being bonded—you have to do everything together or be miserable away from each other." She picked up a tiny pastry from the three-tiered tray tower on the table between us and took a bite. "A few more days before King Tiane is back and life finally returns to normal. Balls, dinner parties, dancing, games..." She tilted her face up with a dreamy expression.

"What games does the king like to play?" I asked casually.

"Oh, there are so many. Some are naughtier than others." She hid a giggle behind her hand.

"Which one is the War of Kings?" I recalled the name the king had mentioned.

Dove's expression fell.

"Oh, that's a boring one. Everyone keeps their clothes on and just moves figurines on a wooden table."

"Like a board game, then?"

"Yes." She waved at me, faking a yawn. "Many, many boards. And even more figurines."

I shifted to the end of my chair.

"What can I do for you to teach me?"

I considered Dove my friend. But I'd also learned that at King Tiane's court everything had its price and favors were a hot commodity. No one did something for nothing.

She adjusted a butterfly brooch on her lilac dress. "Oh, I'd make a poor teacher, sweetie. I really don't like this game, and I'm not that good at it. To be honest, I only play because I want to be invited, and I never last past the first round."

"That's the reason I have to know how to play that game, Dove. I need to be *invited*, too."

"Why?" She cocked her head with a flash of curiosity in her violet eyes.

I exhaled slowly before confessing, "To spend more time with the king."

"Do you love him?"

"No."

That was easy. I didn't need to search my heart to answer that. My feelings for King Tiane had nothing to do with love. The most I counted for was lust and, hopefully, a lasting friendship after that.

"Good." She seemed relieved. "The last thing you want is to have your heart involved. Especially with the king."

"He doesn't fall in love?"

"Why would he? When there is so much fun to be had otherwise?"

I was fine with that. It was best not to expect the king's love or even his fidelity. After all, I was technically the other woman in his marriage. And it was safe to assume there would be more.

Deep inside, maybe I would wish to find someone who would genuinely care about me, be mine in every way, and love me like Kanbor loved Brebie. But I knew it could never happen in Elaros, and never with a highborn of the court. Here, games were the norm, and playing around could only be stopped by the magical bond that remained unattainable for most.

Sex was the most I could ever hope to get from the king, with possibly some residual affection that would compel him to keep me around.

"Do you know who King Tiane is sleeping with now?" I asked.

Her snow-white eyebrows slid up her dark forehead.

"You should know that better than me, Sparrow. You're the king's favorite. So, I assume it's you who warms his bed when he's in the palace."

I spun my tiny porcelain teacup on its saucer.

"Well, that's the thing. I haven't even seen his bed yet."

Since everyone had been telling me about the king's frivolous ways, I found it hard to believe he'd be staying celibate all this time.

"The king hasn't touched me," I confessed.

Dove shook her head, her angelic locks bouncing. "Nonsense. I've seen him touch you with my own eyes. He can't keep his hands off you."

"Right. In public. But he never gives us a chance to be alone. It never went past what you've seen." I fidgeted with the teacup before continuing. "Libelle was his favorite for three months. Do you know if they had sex?"

"Of course they did." She sounded almost offended that I would assume otherwise.

"Of course," I echoed. "It must be just me, then. Do you think he might see me as a pet more than a lover?"

The royal hag, an old woman wrapped in a dark cloak, had inspected me on Queen Pavline's orders and deemed me ready to "receive the king's seed." Only the king was in no hurry to make the deposit.

King Tiane didn't make me burn with desire the way Voron

did. But the king was the one whom I was supposed to be with. His lack of interest concerned me.

"I'm afraid he'll grow bored with me and will send me away to the menagerie."

"Oh, sweetie." Empathy floated in Dove's eyes. She leaned closer, covering my hand with hers. "The king likes you very much. There is no one else like you in the entire kingdom. But he also likes a good game. He probably is just postponing it, for it to last longer. It must be a delayed gratification thing for him."

"You think so?"

"Why not? King Tiane likes to play. Libelle told me the best sex they had was when he chased her. She flew out of his bedroom and he grabbed her so hard, he scratched her leg, drawing blood."

"Blood?" I repeated, hoping I'd heard her wrong.

"Just a scratch from his nails." She waved a dismissive hand. "It was an accident. She said he grew so hard, he fucked her out on the patio, not even bothering to get back inside. Come to think of it," she tapped her bottom lip with the tip of her slim finger, "that was the only time she told me about them having sex. Maybe the king prefers the chase to the actual deed."

If he only had sex once during the three-month relationship with Libelle, it might explain why he never got anyone pregnant yet. Chasing alone didn't result in babies.

I didn't remember the king ever getting hard for me, not even when he fondled me. Sitting in his lap, I would've felt if he did, wouldn't I? Did he even find me attractive?

Or maybe Dove was right, and he was postponing us getting together to savor it for longer. Maybe he knew once we'd do it, he'd lose interest quickly. Either way, with his track record, I couldn't count on remaining in his favor for long. I had to use something other than sex to keep the king's wandering attention.

After I'd come back to my room that evening, I thought about the game War of Kings again. I had to learn how to play it, and not just because it'd give me more time to spend with the king. I had to become a worthy opponent for him to enjoy playing it with me.

Being King Tiane's lover would never be enough. I had to become his friend, someone he'd need at his side for decades to come. When he'd lose any physical attraction for me, when I would inevitably grow old, the king would still have to find me irreplaceable—as a friend, as a companion, as his new jester. Whatever it took, I'd do it.

It was clear to me that there wasn't anything else I could do in the palace that mattered. Whatever chore I tried around here could be done faster and better by anyone else.

If my purpose in life was to entertain, then entertain I must. I should become the king's best friend. Someone he would never send away from Elaros or lock in the menagerie.

"Brebie?" I asked when my snappy housekeeping angel delivered my dinner that night, along with a briefing about the royal celebration I was to attend upon the return of the hunting party. "Do you know how to play War of Kings?"

She huffed. "Why would I? I have enough things to keep me busy without wasting my time on silly games."

"You see, but that's currently the favorite game of King Tiane. If I could learn how to play it, it may gain me more attention from him."

My mentioning the king's name made her take my words more seriously. "You really think you'll need to know how to play it?"

I released a long breath. "I'm afraid I need any help I can get at this point. Do you know about the king's menagerie?"

The way her eyes leaped from me to the wall told me she knew all about the place that waited for me if I failed in Elaros.

"It's not a suitable place for a sentient being," she muttered under her breath.

"You think?" I smiled without any mirth. "Trust me, I'll do anything to avoid being sent there."

She tapped a hoof against the floor, giving me a sideways glance.

"You know who is really good at that game? So good that he isn't even welcome to play with the king anymore?"

"Who?" I asked eagerly.

"High General Voron."

"Oh...him."

My enthusiasm dampened.

She propped her hands on her hips. "Something happened between you two, didn't it? Did you have a fight?"

"No." I rolled my eyes with more drama than was necessary. "We aren't close enough to have fights. Why would you even think that?"

"Voron has been acting weird lately when I tell him about your day."

"You tell him about my days?"

She nodded. "Every morning after breakfast since the day you got here."

"Is that why he put you here? To spy on me?"

"Why to spy?" She huffed again, clearly offended. "Voron just wants to make sure you're coping well. Coming to Sky Kingdom was a big change for you. He feels responsible for your wellbeing."

Responsible? To me, it sounded more like he was keeping control over everything in Elaros, including me.

"And? Do you tell him I'm coping well?"

She tilted her head, studying me with her clear blue eyes.

"Are you, though? You act mostly calm and quiet. But you snap at times and seem stressed and anxious. I'm not sure if that's your normal state because I've no idea what your normal is."

I definitely felt snappy right now. I wondered if it was her talking about Voron that had put me on edge.

"Funny thing, Brebie, I've no idea what my 'normal' state is, either. Do you know why? Because Voron took away the memories of my previous life. He erased my past. I don't know who I was before I came here. I don't even know what my actual name is."

"Is it not Sparrow?"

I flung both hands into the air. "Sparrow? What kind of name is that? It's not even a name! It's just a type of bird."

She shrugged. "It suits you."

"Not you, too," I groaned, plopping down on the bed.

"Oh, come on, honey." She sat on the bed next to me and hugged my shoulders. "Crossing the River of Mists is never easy. It's no wonder you lost your memories—"

"I didn't *lose* them. Voron took them."

"All right, all right, he took your memories." She didn't sound like she believed me, more like she was humoring me. "But do you really need to have them here? Our worlds are so different, you'd have to learn everything anew, anyway. Besides, who knows what your life back in the human realm was like? Maybe it's a good thing you don't remember it? Maybe there wasn't much to miss, anyway?"

I hadn't looked at it that way. All this time, I'd been mourning the loss of my past, my one true home. Never once had I considered my coming to Sky Kingdom as a fresh start. But Brebie might be right. There had to be at least parts of my past that were best forgotten. Who was to say that my life back home was much better than my life here could ever be?

Releasing a shaky breath, I relaxed into her side hug.

"I want to make it in Sky Kingdom, Brebie. I want to find my place here. I really do. I just wish I knew the best way to go about it."

"If you want to learn how to play that game, ask Voron to teach you," she said firmly.

It made sense that Voron was good at the game that required focus and concentration. He was the most level-headed, contemplative person I'd met in Elaros. He was also well-read and intelligent. His strategy skills had been honed in real wars and battles.

"He won't teach me." I sighed.

"Why not?"

"Plenty of reasons. First, I made fun of him in public. Then, I told him to stay away from me. I can't possibly ask him for any favors now."

She patted my shoulder soothingly. "Voron is a kind man. He'll forgive you."

"Kind? He's so distant, it's like he's worlds away even when he's close."

Brebie shifted her hooves on the fuzzy rug by my bed. "Life hasn't been easy on him. Especially in the beginning."

Other than the wars, I knew nothing about Voron's past, I realized.

"What do you mean? What happened to him?"

"His mother died when he was only ten. He never knew his father."

"Who looked after him, then? After his mother's death?"

She frowned. "I'm not sure. Our ways parted for a while. He was gone from Sky Kingdom for eighty years."

"Where was he all those years?"

"Down in the Below. He returned less than a century ago, during the time when Sky Kingdom was ravaged by wars. Voron joined King Tiane's army as a foot soldier. With no family and no connections, he had to start from the very bottom."

Kind of like me. It seemed Voron and I had more in common than I could've imagined.

Brebie continued, "He made it to where he is now by using only his courage, his mind, and pure determination."

"That is admirable," I agreed.

She squeezed my hand. "Talk to him. Ask him nicely. Make peace with him. I'm sure he'll help."

Chapter Sixteen

SPARROW

I knocked on the door with one hand, holding the plate with my peace offering in the other. The magnificent swan made of meringue, pulled sugar, and pistachios was set in a wave of whipped cream surrounded by fresh strawberries. The dish was personally created by the head chef himself and cost me a set of bejeweled hair combs for the chef's wife.

The swan was a true masterpiece. According to Brebie, meringue was Voron's favorite dessert. But would it be enough to make him forget all the harsh words I'd said and the demands I'd made and agree to teach me to play that damn game?

As beautiful as the dish was, it didn't seem enough as I stood by the door to Voron's rooms, listening for any sound behind it. He was the High General, after all, practically running this palace for the king. He could get anything he wanted anytime he wished. What if he laughed at me or scolded me for showing up at his door uninvited?

What if he got angry and shut the door in my face?

What if he...

I was almost ready to forget about the whole thing and bolt when the door flew open and Alcon appeared.

"Lady Sparrow?" He peered at me with curiosity.

I'd seen Voron's first lieutenant around Elaros often, but we'd hardly spoken. He moved his eyes from my face to the plate in my hand, and the curiosity deepened in his expression.

I smoothed a hand down my bright magenta skirts. This dress wasn't see-through for a change, but it made up for it by being so bright, it hurt my eyes, and having the neckline so deep, it barely covered my nipples. I'd arranged a white scarf embroidered with tiny parachutes of dandelions around my neck. The scarf covered my cleavage, making sure I wasn't sending any wrong signals by showing up here.

I'd been preparing myself to face Voron. Finding Alcon here instead was unexpected.

"I... Is Voron here? I mean the High General." I cleared my throat and held up my head, strengthening my voice. "Can I see High General Voron, please?"

"Is he expecting you?"

I swallowed hard, my throat dry with nerves knotting my stomach.

"No. He... I mean, I was hoping he wouldn't be too busy to see me this morning. Can he spare a minute to talk?"

Brebie assured me this was the perfect time of the day to catch Voron in his rooms—an hour or so after breakfast when most of his morning reports had already come in but before he left for his duties elsewhere in the palace.

"To talk about what?" Alcon inquired.

I hadn't expected to answer so many questions before I even saw Voron. Usually, he was far more accessible. One couldn't go through a day in Elaros without running into him.

"Um...a personal matter," I mumbled. "Could you tell him I'm here, please?"

If Voron refused to see me, I'd have my answer. Then, I'd eat his damn swan myself.

"All right. Come in." Alcon glanced at the fancy swan once again before opening the door wider for me to enter.

The space inside was a cozy sitting room with a fire burning in the hearth and some comfy seats arranged in front of it and along the walls.

Several men in the gray royal-guard uniforms lounged around. Four of them played a card game at a round table by the far wall. One reclined in a chair by the fire, his legs stretched out in front of him, an open book in his hands. One sat on a long couch with a plate of food in his lap and a steaming mug of tea on a small table nearby.

This seemed like a break room for the guards. But I assumed they were here to guard the High General instead of the palace.

"Wait here," Alcon instructed, heading to the door opposite to the one we'd entered through. That one must lead to Voron's private rooms.

I perched my butt on the vacant end of the couch. The guard sitting on its other end grunted something in greeting. I nodded in reply, and he continued eating his food. The rest tossed curious glances at me and my swan but didn't ask any questions.

Alcon returned.

"You can come in, Lady Sparrow." He held the door open for me.

Gripping the plate in my fingers, I hurried across the room, through the door, and into yet another sitting room.

It was roughly the same size as the other. Aside from the fireplace and comfy couch with armchairs, it also had a desk with a tall-backed chair in front of it. Three sets of crystal doors opposite the entrance must lead to a balcony or an outdoor terrace, but the view was obstructed by the designs etched in the crystal panes.

Ash-gray vines grew from the floor between the doors. Magnus was perched on one of the branches, eating seeds from the palm of his master, who stood by one of the crystal doors.

"Morning, Sparrow," he said, turning to face me.

Holy gods of all the worlds, but the casually dressed Voron, relaxing in his personal space, was the most fantastic sight.

He wore a long, silver-gray robe over a white, partially buttoned shirt and black pants. The outfit exposed his neck and a narrow strip of his chest.

I promptly dropped my gaze to the gray rug on the floor. There was no need to feed my imagination. It was bad enough that I'd been fantasizing about his forearms for days now.

With my eyes down, however, his feet came into view. Voron was barefoot. His toes sunk into the soft rug, and I suddenly wished I could kick my tight silk slippers off too.

"Is this for me?" he asked, since I hadn't uttered a word, not even a greeting. His eyes were on the swan in my hands.

I cleared my throat.

"Oh... Yes. Um... Brebie said you like meringue." I thrust the plate in his direction.

Magnus finished the seeds. Voron brushed his hands against each other before coming closer.

"Brebie sent you?" He scowled at the swan, then snapped its pulled sugar neck and dipped its head into the whipped cream.

I held the plate out for him, since he hadn't taken it.

"No. I came to ask you for a favor."

"What kind of favor?" He put the swan's head with the whipped cream into his mouth. The candied sugar crunched between his teeth.

I took it as a good sign. He'd accepted my offering. He didn't even question if I'd added anything to the food, which must mean he trusted me.

Or maybe he simply didn't care?

He must have some other protection against the harmful magic beside the necklace he'd given to me. The slim silver ring around his pinky, for example, could be warded, too. It looked too plain next to the other rings he wore, too simple to be worn by someone of his status.

Tilting his head, he looked at me expectantly.

"Well," I rubbed my chest. The beads of his necklace pressed into my skin under the scarf. "I wanted to apologize for being a bit abrupt with you last time... And the time before that—"

He blew out a breath, growing impatient.

"What do you want, Sparrow? You came to ask me for something. Just ask."

I gripped the plate tighter, risking snapping it in half.

"I want you to teach me to play War of Kings," I blurted out in one breath.

His dark eyebrows rose in surprise.

"And why do you want to learn it?"

My skin prickled under his inquisitive stare. Blood rushed to my face. That was the true price of his favor, not the swan, but honesty. I had to lay it all out for him, to explain my plans and to expose the fears that had led me to them.

I needed Voron's help. And if that meant potentially embarrassing myself even further in his eyes, then so be it.

I put the plate down on the small table by the chair in front of the fireplace, then turned to face him, my arms down at my sides, my head held high.

"My future in Elaros depends on my ability to hold the king's attention," I said.

His expression darkened at my words, his brow furrowed, but he didn't contradict me.

"To do so," I continued. "I can't rely solely on pleasing him in bed."

He winced, as if the very idea of me being in bed with the king gave him indigestion. But wasn't that why he'd brought me to Elaros in the first place?

I crushed my skirts in my sweaty hands. "I need to be more than just another one in the long string of royal bedmates. I can't be just his lover. I need to become his friend. Someone he couldn't easily replace. I want him to *need* me."

"Smart," he said softly. But there was no real approval in his voice or expression. I couldn't tell whether he truly thought this was a good plan or was agreeing with me simply to humor me.

"I need to spend as much time with him as possible. I need to learn the things he likes and do whatever he does well."

"But not *too* well." He smirked.

I snapped a questioning gaze at him.

"King Tiane loves winning," Voron explained. "If he sees you're better than him at the game, he'll make sure never to play with you again."

"Is that why you're no longer invited to the game? Because you're better at it than the king?"

He squinted at me. "Who told you I was any good at it?"

"Brebie."

"Brebie chats too much for her own good," he muttered, running a hand through his hair. "The problem is not that I'm better, but that I made the mistake of letting the king know it."

"You won?"

He shrugged. "Game rule number one, little bird—always let the king win."

That was ridiculous, like we were humoring a toddler, trying to avoid his tantrums.

"But isn't that kind of insulting to the king?" I asked, crossing my arms over my chest. The gesture pushed my cleavage up and above the scarf I'd used to conceal it. Voron's eyes flicked down to my chest, but he raised them almost immediately, as if catching himself staring at the things he didn't wish to stare at. "Isn't a real win more satisfying? Even if it's offset by a loss now and then?"

"True. And that is rule number two. Never let the king realize you're *letting* him win. Make it look like you fought hard before losing to him."

I released a breath with a huff.

"Well, that's just..."

"If you want to become irreplaceable for King Tiane, Sparrow, your main goal will have to be making sure the king has a good time during the game. It can never be about your winning it."

I wondered if that was how Voron got as high as he did. First, he won the king's wars. Now, he ran every aspect of the royal life. He had truly become irreplaceable to King Tiane. And if so, I came to the right person to teach me to be the same.

"All right," I nodded. "Does it mean you'll teach me how to play?"

That ghost of a smile appeared on his lips again.

"In a way, I've been teaching you all along, little bird. The strategy of War of Kings is very similar to real life. And the intrigues often mirror life in the royal court."

True, he had been teaching me already. Almost every time we spoke, he'd have some kind of advice for me. And all of that had proven useful, whether I wished to admit it or not.

"Will you show me the game, too?"

He strolled around me, the hem of his robe trailing behind him. Tilting his head, he peered at me from under his black-and-white strands.

"How about a daily lesson? One hour? Starting at about this time?" He glanced at the large, round clock over the mantle of the fireplace.

My heart beat with excitement. This was exactly what I was hoping for. But I had to be cautious when dealing with fae—that was one of the first things Voron had taught me.

"What will your lessons cost me?" I clarified.

"You've already paid."

He stuck a finger into the wave of the whipped cream, making the meringue swan tilt atop it. Hooking a blob of cream on his finger, he put it into his mouth. The gesture brought back the sensation of his finger in *my* mouth. I could almost taste the salt on my tongue again, feel the warmth of his body close to mine.

This was a dangerous game I chose to play. Seeing him daily wouldn't be easy, considering the effect his proximity had on my body.

He lifted the plate and took the meringue from it.

"I'll teach you how to play War of Kings, Sparrow. Brebie is right. I am good at it. I also know you're smart enough to make a great student. In a few weeks, you'll be able to beat the king. And in a few months more, you'll play well enough to let him win in a way he would never suspect that you let him win it. Deal?"

"What will you get in return?"

"This swan." He glared at the meringue bird before taking a huge bite out of it. "And the pleasure of your company," he continued after swallowing. "One hour a day, every day, until you no longer need me."

Chapter Seventeen

VORON

It was a mistake. One that a man of his age and experience should not have made. Yet he did it. He agreed to see Sparrow every day and spend an entire hour in her company.

The woman looked sweet, but he knew she could be dangerous. At first, he simply felt sympathetic to her situation. But somehow, she'd managed to get under his skin in ways no one had ever been able to do before.

She made his blood boil without even trying. He'd love to say all that boiling was happening due to anger, or annoyance, or something else equally benign, but he'd be lying.

There were other, far more risky reasons for his blood heating and his pulse speeding up when Sparrow was near. The same reasons that made his cock hard like marble with one look at her delectable curves or a whiff of her sweet, earthy scent.

The only way he could keep his full composure was *not* to be around her. Yet he now was destined to endure an hour in the same room with Sparrow. On a daily basis.

And he'd agreed to that.

Clearly, he'd gone insane.

He couldn't even accuse the little vixen of putting a spell on him. The poor thing had less magic in her than a doorknob.

The smart thing to do about it now would be to cancel the whole thing. Only that was the last thing he wished to do. On the contrary, he had lost his mind completely, as he was actually looking forward to the torture these lessons would undeniably be for him.

His heart—that old, dried out thing he'd kept permanently frozen in his chest for almost his entire life—suddenly started showing signs of life recently. His curiosity compelled him to go ahead with the lessons, if only to see how far he could let it go before caution dictated he put an end to them.

Besides, he'd already eaten the fucking meringue swan she'd brought as a payment. Now, he had no choice but to uphold his end of the bargain.

Backing out of a deal didn't carry the same consequence as breaking a promise. Sparrow had no power to enforce it, anyway. But his reputation was on the line. He hadn't backed out of a deal before, and he wouldn't do it now just because he wished to fuck the little human more than he ever wanted to fuck anyone in his life.

As the arms of the clock approached the time of the start of their first lesson, Voron found his pulse racing.

It amazed him that one young human female somehow managed to gain this much control over his body. But he didn't really worry. After all, he'd been practicing self-restraint for quite some time now. He'd very much perfected it over the past few decades.

Sparrow had caught him off guard last time, but today, he was prepared. For one, he was fully dressed—a shirt, a vest, and a matching black coat with wide cuffs embroidered with silver rain clouds and sapphire raindrops. The embroidery was not only expensive but beautiful, and just because he didn't share in the frivolities of the royal court, didn't mean he had to completely give up on all beauty in his life.

All his buttons were closed, all laces laced. He had a feeling, he'd need a girdle for his groin, a chastity belt, a fucking chain to leash his cock for the next hour. But all he had was his good old self-control. It had served him well all his life. It better not betray him now.

He had the game table brought in from the outside terrace. The spring had been slow in coming. The weather was still too cold for a delicate thing like a human woman to have the lesson outside.

From Brebie's daily reports, he knew Sparrow enjoyed desserts. He had a tray of the head chef's finest creations placed on the stand next to the game table.

He felt prepared. Yet a knock on the door jolted him. He straightened the ruffled cuffs of his shirt. It had been a while since he'd received a woman in his rooms. Still, he shouldn't be this frazzled.

"Come in!" he said, way too quickly.

Alcon poked his head in.

"High General, Lady Sparrow is here to see you."

This time, he counted to three in his head before replying, so as not to sound too eager.

"Let her in."

Sparrow appeared in his sitting room wearing an adorable smile on her face. Doubt seized him again, faced with her irresistible charm that, he'd bet his priceless sword, she had no idea she possessed.

"Good morning, High General."

She looked like the sunshine he hadn't seen in decades. Her bright-colored dress was printed with giant flowers that dwarfed her short stature. The style didn't suit her, but she wasn't the one ordering her clothes. King Tiane loved things loud and dramatic.

"Morning, Sparrow." He congratulated himself on making his voice sound calm and even.

She was clutching a leather-bound journal in her hands.

"Thank you again for doing this. I'm so grateful—"

"Pastry?" He interrupted her by pointing at the dessert tray.

The last thing he needed was to listen to her expressing her gratitude for his transgressions. Frankly, he should have known better than to agree to her proposal. But for some reason, it pleased him to give in to this woman.

"Oh, sure. Thank you." She shifted toward the tray. "I haven't tried this one yet." She took a bite-size tart topped with blue snowberry mousse and popped it into her mouth. "Mmm, it's so good."

She closed her eyes, savoring the pastry with a nearly orgasmic expression on her face. He made a mental note to stock up on those things before her every visit.

This girl was going to be the end of him.

And now he knew exactly what drew him to her—she was real. She ate with gusto, spoke her mind, and wasn't intimidated by people's ranks or positions. At least, she clearly was not intimidated by him.

He'd watched Sparrow during the many performances put on for King Tiane. She was the only person in the room who held her breath in genuine appreciation, enjoying the music and the dances that the highborn of the royal court took for granted, including the king.

There was pure, innocent joy in Sparrow that Elaros had lost to overabundance and pretense. Seeing it in her felt like taking a drink of cool, clean water, and Voron couldn't get enough of it.

Remembering his manners, he moved a chair away from the game table for her and shifted it slightly closer to the stand with the desserts.

"Have a seat. And have some more pastries. Feel free to eat them all."

"Oh, no more. Thank you." She laughed, sitting down. "I'm not like you guys. I have to watch what I eat."

He paused before taking the seat across from her, wondering what exactly she meant by that.

She answered his questioning glance in that no-nonsense tone of hers, "Sugar makes humans fat, Voron. I'm already twice as wide as any of the court ladies. I wasn't born with the fae beauty. The least I could do is try not to get any bigger."

Her eyebrows moved into a frown and her chest rose with a sigh as she leaned away from the dessert tray.

"You find fae beautiful?" he asked.

"Don't you? You guys are just so..." She searched for a perfect word to describe his kind and found it, "*perfect.*"

"Perfect," he repeated, the word leaving a bad taste in his mouth. "But true beauty is not the same as visual perfection, little bird. Far from it."

It pained him that such an alluring, conflicted, displaced but resilient person like Sparrow would find herself lacking in any way. Doubt floated in her eyes, the color of which he couldn't pinpoint. Green, blue, and brown mixed in her irises in an ever-changing combination.

He leaned across the table toward her. "Don't ever wish you were like us, dear Sparrow. If you'd ever peered into the souls of the royal court, you'd see nothing but ugliness. Don't try to be anyone else but you."

Her mesmerizing eyes narrowed at him.

"But who exactly is *me,* Voron? What am I without my memories? You've erased me—"

"No." He shook his head. "I've freed your mind from the memories of people you knew, places you visited, and events you witnessed. Things that you might've missed to the point of growing debilitatingly homesick. But I haven't touched the essence of you. Whatever your past life experiences have taught you—your beliefs, your personality, everything that makes you *you*—it all is still there, little bird. It's too precious to erase."

She must know it, too. She had to sense that the person inside her never changed.

Her cheeks turned a pretty shade of pink, but she didn't look flattered by his words. She looked lost in thought. Doubt, worry, some calculation—it was all there, playing out on her lovely face right in front of his eyes.

If she wished to thrive in Elaros, she'd have to learn to hide her emotions. Whether he liked it or not, Sparrow would have to become like the highborn of the court. She'd have to lose every fresh, sincere, real part of herself and replace it with fake smiles, words that meant little, and thoughts that were never on display.

She'd have to become like him.

There was nothing he could do to stop it. In fact, he'd been actively helping that transformation by teaching her to fit in.

The thought made his stomach churn.

"Do you still want to learn this?" he asked, hoping she'd change her mind and would release him from their deal.

No such luck. Her eyes lit up with enthusiasm. "Of course I do. Show me."

He lifted the first panel of the game from the table, then raised the rest. Each panel represented a playing field. They unfolded from the table like petals of a flower.

"There are thirteen of these," he explained, trying to focus on the lesson instead of his alluring student. "Equivalent to the current number of High Lords in Sky Kingdom. We'll start with two for now. But you will have to play all thirteen at the king's game nights."

"All thirteen," she repeated after him, opening her journal and sliding out a pencil from the loop on its spine.

"Are you taking notes?" This was too precious. His mouth quivered with a smile.

The pencil paused in her hand.

"Yes. May I?"

He nodded, watching her write as she bit her lip in concentration.

She couldn't be older than thirty, he decided. That was about the time when fae's aging stopped for centuries, to restart a decade or two before their passing. From what he'd learned about humans, their aging never slowed down. Every year would leave its mark on Sparrow's skin and add silver to her hair.

"All right." She set her journal aside, perking up like an eager little bird. "Now what?"

"The game requires focus and concentration. You'll have to pay attention when you play with the king."

Which wouldn't be easy with the king's hand up her skirt.

He groaned inwardly. Was that where his mind decided to go? Now? As if it wasn't hard enough not to search for traces of her scent in the air he inhaled.

Brebie made sure to bathe Sparrow in a variety of fragrances popular at court. But he knew her very own unique scent. She didn't smell like fae who carried the scents of fresh air, dew, and clouds on their skin. Sparrow's smell was warm and earthy, with a hint of salt he longed to taste on his tongue.

She stuck her pencil into her hair, as if there was no better place to put it, then touched the carved figurines nested in the velvet-lined compartments inside the table.

"Are these the game pieces?" she asked, thankfully oblivious to his disturbing thoughts and to the achy pressure gripping his cock under the table. "Will we need all of them?"

"Not today. Just take out the green and the brown ones for now."

Just like some of the colors in her eyes.

"This one looks like a king." She lifted a game piece carved from malachite.

He forced his attention from her face to the game piece in her hand. "Yes. That's one of them."

"Is there more than one king in this game?"

"Thirteen, just like the thirteen kingdoms they represent."

"I thought they were High Lords."

"In real life, they are. But this is a game," he said and murmured to himself, "supposedly."

She examined the figurine. Her other hand moved from her

neck down to her chest, her fingers tracing the outline of his necklace under her scarf. He didn't need to strain his imagination to envision both the necklace and her body underneath the scarf.

The necklace he had worn his entire life before giving it to Sparrow. Every bead of it was familiar, the stone pendant polished by the friction against his skin.

Her chest he'd had the pleasure of seeing completely bare twice by now. She looked very different from the women he'd known. And maybe that was part of what heated his blood and made his cock stand to attention in her presence?

Voron had trained himself to ignore all the naked female bodies at the king's events. He'd been doing well, content with only an occasional quick release, courtesy of a court lady's hand or mouth here and there. He hadn't expected the reaction his body would have to naked Sparrow.

What was worse, her curves teased him with fantasies that went beyond fucking. He could so easily envision resting his head on her chest or cradling her soft, pliable form in the curve of his body before drifting to sleep.

The confusing part was that he had no experience on which to base those fantasies. Even back when he was still allowed to fuck freely, he never cuddled. Sex in a war camp had been hot, messy, and lightning-fast.

What would sex with Sparrow be like?

He knew she was curious about him, too. The woman couldn't hide a thought to save her life. He'd caught plenty of heated glances she furtively cast his way. Knowing that she might be just as willing to explore his body as he felt about hers didn't make his predicament any easier.

He sighed inwardly.

"Voron?" Her voice snapped him out of his hot, sweaty thoughts. "Are you all right?"

"Of course." He blinked, retrieving his dirty mind from her cleavage. "Why, little bird?"

Had she asked him something?

"How about this one?" She held up another figurine. "What's this one supposed to be?"

"That one is a High General." He licked his lips.

"A High General?" Sparrow stroked the game piece.

He stared at her fingers, wishing desperately it was his cock clutched in them instead of the figurine.

This woman would be his ruination if he wasn't careful.

"What is the High General's role in this game?" she asked.

"To defend the kingdom from its enemies. And to bring glory to his king."

"To his king?" she echoed. "But how about himself? What does the High General get if he wins?"

"He gets to keep his head on his shoulders and his rank."

Wasn't that the truth? The game truly mimicked life way too closely. Maybe that was the reason King Tiane liked it so much without even being that good at it. Every win, real or fake, boosted the king's already over-inflated ego.

"But that's exactly what the High General starts with," Sparrow noted. "Which means when he wins, he really gets nothing."

She was too perceptive for her own good. And for his good, too, for that matter.

The hour he'd allocated for their game session ended way too soon. He couldn't believe the time when it was over and even considered having the wall clock in his sitting room checked.

As Sparrow rose from her seat, thanking him sweetly, misery descended upon him. The only thought keeping his mood from growing completely sour was that she'd be back again tomorrow.

He walked her all the way to the door out to the hallway. His men lounging in his receiving room stood to attention, sliding curious glances at Sparrow.

The moment the door closed behind her, Alcon turned to him.

"Her Majesty the queen wishes to see you, High General."

His spirit plummeted even further at the mention of the queen.

"When?"

"A man from her personal guard came by forty minutes ago with the summons. I told him you were preoccupied with an important matter."

Alcon knew him well.

"Good." He nodded.

Forty minutes ago.

Rumors traveled faster than storms or wildfires in Elaros. The queen would know soon enough that his session with Sparrow was over. There was no point in angering her by making her wait any longer than necessary.

"I'll go see her right now."

"Do you want to take a few men with you?" Alcon gestured at his guards, ready for his orders. Every one of them had been hand-picked by Voron from the men who had fought at his side during the many wars in Sky Kingdom's turbulent past. Every one of them he'd known for decades and trusted with his life.

There was no need to drag his men along, however. He had a feeling the queen would want to see him one-on-one, anyway.

"No." He headed to the door. "I won't be long." *Hopefully.*

Ascending the wide, decorated stairs to the queen's apartments, he didn't doubt that her summoning him had everything to do with Sparrow coming to his rooms. The timing was a dead giveaway.

Queen Pavline sat in a carved chair on a raised marble platform in one of her sitting rooms. Dressed in aesthetically arranged silks and precious jacquards, with her left breast exposed, she posed for one of the resident artists of Elaros.

She cut a cold glance at Voron, not turning her head.

"You made me wait."

"My apologies, Your Majesty." He bowed as etiquette demanded but offered no explanation as to the reasons for his delay.

She waved her hand at the painter and the apprentice impatiently. "Leave us."

The two women bowed before exiting the room. The queen relaxed her pose, dropping her shoulders. Her neck must be sore, too. The headdress set upon her purple hair was massive and looked heavy.

"What was the human doing in your rooms?" she went straight to the point.

It was about Sparrow, after all. Just as he'd expected.

Letting the queen wait for just a little longer, he strolled to the abandoned canvas. The artist was one of the most famous in the kingdom for a reason. Even unfinished, the picture already had the signs of a true masterpiece. The face of the painting, however, lacked the scowl that graced the queen's face directed at him.

"Lovely," he commented on the painting, not its subject.

"Answer me!" the queen shrieked. "What was the fucking human doing in your rooms?"

"She wasn't *fucking*. No need to worry, my queen."

"*Sadly*," he added in his head.

The queen ripped the majestic headpiece off her head, tossing it aside. "*What* were you doing with her?"

Sooner or later, she'd know the truth. There was no harm in telling it to her now. Especially, since it would likely calm her down.

"I'm teaching her to play board games."

"What?" The queen squinted at him in disbelief. "Why?"

"She asked me to. Sparrow is taking her role as the king's new favorite very seriously. She wants to please the king, in hopes that he'd take her to his bed one fine night and finally give the kingdom an heir."

The longer he spoke, the more bitter his sarcasm grew. Except that he could be as sarcastic as he wished, it wouldn't change the fact that every word was true. He was stealing a few hours of Sparrow's company now, in order to eventually lose her to the king completely.

He had no right to have any feelings on the matter. It shouldn't concern him. He wasn't involved.

The king was smitten with Sparrow. Sparrow was working hard to keep it that way. The queen cheered for them both. And there was not a single goddamn thing Voron could do about that.

He might've been able to organize this hunting trip for the king, making him believe it was his idea not Voron's. But he couldn't keep the king and Sparrow apart forever. Sooner or later, he would have to step aside and watch as the king led Sparrow into his royal chamber.

"Voron." The queen descended from the platform, moving his way menacingly. "Sparrow belongs to King Tiane. *Only* to him."

"I'm well aware of that. *I* was the one who delivered her to him."

His insides twisted. *These* words were also true. He saw Sparrow first, not the king. She should've been his, but he had no choice but to give her up. It was a bitter pill to swallow.

The queen was relentless. "No man's seed shall fill the womb of the human but the king's. Is that clear?"

He propped his shoulder against the heavy canvas and gave her a smile that felt like a scowl.

"As far as *my* seed is concerned, you and your husband made sure long ago it was never to fill any womb whatsoever."

"Right. It'll do you good to remember that." Pacified somewhat, the queen inclined her head toward him and lowered her voice. "The king and I aren't cruel. If you need to take care of your...um, *urges*, you may visit Lady Susale. I'll let her know—"

Voron stopped her with a jerk of his head. He'd accepted that offer before, when the "urges" had become painfully unbearable and the need for a woman's touch had grown stronger than the need for air.

Lately, however, he'd been too preoccupied by a certain, unattainable human to even consider a court lady as a substitute. Prolonged abstinence wasn't new to him. Refusing the queen's charity was easy enough right now.

He peeled away from the canvas frame, straightening his spine.

"Much obliged, Your Majesty, but I'll pass." With a brief parting bow, he headed for the exit. "Best regards."

"Voron!" she barked at his back. "Don't let lust get to your head and force you to make a wrong decision. The crown needs you well and alive."

And the crown had him. It held him, quite literally, by the balls.

He didn't turn around, speaking over his shoulder.

"No need to worry, Your Majesty. My *seed* will come nowhere near your precious human. I've had decades to practice my self-control. And if it fails," he lifted a hand over his shoulder, splaying it wide, then flexing his fingers. "I'll take the matter in my own hands."

"So crass!" He heard the queen gasp on his way out.

He smirked.

Better to be crass than sorry.

Chapter Eighteen

SPARROW

The guards led me out onto the wide terrace that surrounded the roof of the royal ballroom.

The winds were even stronger up here than down in the gardens. They tore at my creamy white cloak, making me hide my face in the soft fur of its hood.

Voron stood on the terrace, his expression as gloomy as the dark clouds above us. With his black cape billowing in the wind and his sword strapped to his back, he reminded me of a dark angel of doom, though he didn't intimidate me anymore.

On the contrary, my heart lifted at the sight of him. Despite getting only a brief nod from him in greeting, I smiled brightly in response. By now, he'd given me three lessons, teaching me to play the king's favorite game. The rules weren't overly complicated, but the sheer number of playing fields and game pieces created a nearly infinite number of strategies. After just three hours, I'd already filled a notebook with notes.

During the lessons, Voron had been his usual brooding, sarcastic self, but he'd also turned out to be a patient teacher.

With his help, I could already play up to six fields at once. I couldn't wait to eventually be invited into the king's game room to show off my new skills.

The royal guards stood at attention on either side of the terrace. I shuffled closer to Voron, clearing space for the royal party arriving from their hunting trip.

Their dark winged shapes stood out against the cloudy sky, as if painted in black ink on gray felt. They approached quickly, carried by their great, strong wings.

King Tiane was the first to touch the ground as his escort hovered over the terrace just behind him.

With a quick glance around the terrace, the king spotted me. A smile sprung to his lips as he headed straight to me.

His wings rested upon his wide shoulders. His long white-blond tresses whipped in the wind behind him. The cuffs and the front of his silver coat were stitched with hard, gold wings of *firrian* beetles, making him look like he was wearing golden armor. His antlers glistened, painted with silver and decorated with tiny strings of gemstones.

The sight of him was blindingly breathtaking.

"Did you miss me, baby chick?" The king scooped me into a hug, lifting my feet off the ground.

I felt awkward with my feet dangling in the air. Since he didn't set me back down, I wrapped my legs around his middle, just to get them out of the way.

"Yes, Your Majesty, I did," I lied.

I didn't miss the king during the ten days he was away. On the contrary, I quite enjoyed the peace and quiet in the palace without him. Thanks to Dove and Voron with his lessons, I hadn't been bored at all.

But I couldn't say I *wasn't* glad to see King Tiane, either. With the arrival of his magnificent persona, fun and glamor rushed back to Elaros in full force.

"Well, kiss me then," he demanded, offering his left cheek to me.

Careful not to smudge the golden sun painted on his skin, I pecked his cheek just above the corner of his mouth.

He carried me to the entrance of the palace but paused near Voron.

"Ah, there you are, High General. I need to talk to you."

"Your Majesty." Voron inclined his head, avoiding eye contact with me.

"I want you to bring all the cursed to Elaros this time," the king instructed. "I feel they need to be punished, and I wish to do so in the manner we disposed of the prisoners during the siege of Hollow Keep."

The king's tone remained light, the smile still playing on his lips. But Voron's expression hardened, turning darker than the stormy sky above.

"Those were the times of war, Your Majesty. You insisted on that kind of execution as a warning to your enemies. The kingdom is at peace now—"

"So?" the king interrupted with a shrug. "The cursed broke their promises. They deserve to be punished."

"They're already punished by the curse." Voron's voice came out hard and cold, matching the glare of his eyes.

The smile disappeared from the king's face. He stared his High General down. An argument was brewing. The tension thickened between them, ready to erupt.

Feeling uneasy, I dropped my legs down from around the king's waist and attempted to stand on my own. With his hand under my bottom, he heaved me up, forcing me to cling to him with my legs again.

"See? You're upsetting my pet," he snapped at Voron, soothingly patting my butt. "Tonight, we'll celebrate. Tomorrow, I want you in my sitting room first thing in the morning, not for a discussion, but to get my instructions on how I wish to proceed with this matter." He pinned Voron with his stare, his next words coming with added emphasis, "That's a direct order from the crown."

With that, King Tiane whipped around and marched into the palace, whisking me away with him.

Chapter Nineteen

SPARROW

"Don't come out here, Sparrow." Voron cut off my way to the outside terrace by placing himself between the exit and me. "Go back to your room."

Brebie had relayed his order for me to stay in my bedroom today while she was getting me ready this morning. Except that the king had sent his guards to fetch me shortly after. And the king's orders superseded those of his High General.

"King Tiane sent for me," I said quietly.

The royal guards escorting me walked around Voron and opened the doors to the terrace.

"Leave, Sparrow," Voron insisted, not moving out of my way.

The intensity in his stare and the grave weight in his voice made me wish I indeed could get the hell out of there. I had no desire to participate in whatever "punishment ceremony" King Tiane had dreamed up. The details had been kept secret for the entire week of preparation, but the name alone didn't sound very entertaining to me.

Unfortunately, the king had already spotted me from his chair out on the terrace.

"Come, baby chick!" He clapped his hands. "I've got a spot right here for you." He gestured at a low stool with a pink cushion at his feet.

Voron's hands fisted at his sides. He still wouldn't move from my path, squaring his shoulders.

"Sorry..." I mumbled, stepping around him and out onto the terrace.

Wind caught the hem of my cloak the moment I left the shelter of the palace. It howled between the banisters and turrets outside, yanking at the rich clothes of the highborn sitting in chairs along the terrace.

The king reclined in a high-backed armchair in the middle, with Queen Pavline on his right. She greeted me with a polite half-smile, which was a sign of favor since etiquette didn't dictate that she greet me at all. I had no rank and no title for the queen to have to acknowledge my presence.

I bowed to both royals and lowered my butt onto the pink cushion at the king's feet. He tugged off my hood and wrapped his hand around the back of my neck. The wind blew out my curls that Brebie had so carefully arranged for me earlier. I shoved the loose hair out of my face but didn't dare put the hood back on with the royal hand planted on my neck.

"Let me know what you think about this," the king said with a note of fervent excitement.

He often asked my opinion about things like food, drinks, or performers. Though, he rarely listened to my answers. I wasn't sure why he would even bother asking at all.

Dropping my head down, I cast a furtive glance back at the door. Voron stood there among the guards. All the guards wore identical uniforms, but a group of them, along with Alcon, tended to be hanging closer to Voron at all times. I recognized the men from seeing them in the receiving room where they took turns guarding their High General. Voron obviously trusted them the most.

Magnus made a circle around the palace, then landed on a

vine branch above Voron's head with a soft caw, as if letting his master know about his presence.

A moment later, wild screams and howls suddenly cut the air.

I jerked, startled, and the king squeezed the back of my neck lightly.

"Watch, Sparrow."

The terrace was located on one of the lower levels of the palace. It was only about two or three floors above the ground, which was unusual for the royal court. The highborn preferred the higher floors for obvious reasons, leaving the lower ones to those without wings.

The palace grounds on this side had no flowerbeds, just paths running between neatly cut lawns with fountains. Royal guards led horses dragging giant metal cages along the wide paths.

"What is this?" I shrank back from the wild noises coming from the cages and flattened myself against King Tiane's legs.

The cages were filled with creatures that looked like people but acted like animals. They growled, roared, and screamed. The horrible sounds reached through to my bones, chilling and terrifying.

Only a few of the creatures had some clothes on, mostly rags —torn, soiled, and splattered with blood. Red welts and deep gashes marred their bodies. They added more to their wounds by scratching themselves, tearing at their own skin like it burned them and they wished to peel it off.

"Who are these people?" I croaked.

"They're hardly people, my sweet." King Tiane petted my nape. "Not anymore. They're promise breakers."

"Why are they here? Who did this to them?"

"They did it to themselves," he said sharply. "They've made promises they couldn't or wouldn't keep. Now, they have to pay for that."

The poor wretches threw themselves on the thick bars of the cages, ripping their hair out and bruising their lustrous fae skin.

189

Their howls and screeching made me feel like my brain was being cut in two.

"Oh, please, make it stop," I begged the king, burying my face in the folds of his ivory cloak.

He gripped the back of my head and forced me to face the cages.

"Keep watching. You'll see, justice is so satisfying."

The guards dragged a woman from one of the cages. Smaller than the rest, she appeared to be only a teenager, though it was hard to tell with fae how old they were. Her peach-pink hair was matted, with patches of it missing. The remnants of her clothes dangled off her slim frame in frayed, soiled strips.

She screamed incessantly, lunging on the guards as they dragged her out of the cage. Foam dripped from her bared teeth. A guard's arm happened to come too close, and she threw herself on it, sinking her teeth into his sleeve. He punched her in the head, sending her to the ground. The other guard grabbed her by her neck, forcing her to stay down.

Her wings were broken and plucked, with only a few pale gray feathers dangling from the thin bones. She rolled on the ground, snapping a wing off completely. With a pained howl, she withdrew the remaining mangled wing into her back.

Even in her madness, she felt pain. Compassion pierced my heart at the sight of her torture. Hot tears streamed down my face, cooling off instantly in the biting wind.

"Oh, God, please," I sobbed. "What did she do to deserve this?"

"She broke a promise, just like the rest of them did." The king's voice was void of either the horror or compassion that wrecked me. On the contrary, there was glee in his tone that urged me to look up at him.

The royal court was somber. Most of them observed the scene below with some degree of disgust. A few remained impassive.

The king leaned forward, his eyes glued to the poor tortured woman with anticipation. He made a small gesture with the hand that wasn't on my neck.

The guards held the curse breaker down on her back and spread her legs. Four of them stayed on top of her, while two others lifted a long wooden spike from a pile of them nearby. The spike was at least twice as long as the woman was tall. They placed it on the ground between the woman's spread legs, the sharp end aimed at her core.

"No..." I whispered.

Horror spread through me with a swell of freezing cold at the realization of what they were about to do to her.

"No..." Blood rushed out of my legs and arms, leaving me trembling.

My stomach churned at the first slam of the giant hammer. They used it to hit against the dull end of the spike, forcing the sharp end to tear into the woman's flesh.

Sliding off my pillow, I hit my knees hard on the stones of the patio, but I barely noticed the pain. Scraping my knees and hands, I crawled to the low parapet at the end of the terrace, bent over it, and retched.

"Sparrow!" Voron's hands grabbed me, possibly stopping me from falling over.

He gathered my hair, wrestling it from the wind strand by strand, as I kept expelling the contents of my stomach until there was nothing but bile left. It rose to my throat, burning my insides.

"Baby chick, you're disgusting." King Tiane held a silk handkerchief to his nose, looking at me like I was a pile of vomit myself.

"Here. Take this, Sparrow." Voron yanked a piece of cloth from his wide sleeve, his handkerchief.

I grabbed it with trembling fingers, wiped my mouth and blew my nose in it, irreparably ruining the silky material.

He raised a hand, calling one of his men over to us.

"Take her back to her room, Farion." He handed me to his personal guard.

"She'll stay," the king demanded.

Voron straightened, rising to his feet.

"She will not." He calmly met the royal glare.

"The human is too weak-hearted. It'd do her good to watch. It'll make her stronger," the king insisted, but Voron was no longer listening. Turning his back to the king, he followed me and the guard.

"You cannot disobey my direct order, High General!" the king screeched, leaping from his chair.

"You gave me no formal orders," Voron said over his shoulder. "And it's not me who's taking her away."

That was true. His guard was leading me away, not Voron. Still, I feared Voron would pay for this, as well as for turning his back to the king.

The king snatched the weapon from the guard nearest to him. It was a crossbow that he aimed at Voron's back.

"No!" My throat seized with terror.

"Your Majesty..." Queen Pavline tensed.

In one smooth movement, Voron slid out his sword from the sheath on his back and turned. He stopped short from attacking the king, holding the sword out in front of him. But if looks could kill, his glare alone would have incinerated the king on the spot.

With an evil smirk, the king raised the crossbow, aiming it higher.

Voron's pale skin turned completely white at the soft "kraa" above his shoulder.

The king's bolt pierced Magnus's chest, sending the innocent bird to the ground at his master's feet.

"Magnus!" I gripped my cloak at my chest. My throat closed, making me choke on my next breath.

He fell and lay motionlessly, his wings spread wide. Ink-black feathers swirled softly over Voron's head then flew away, blown by a gust of wind.

The king's smirk deepened.

"Everything you own is mine, Voron. And you belong to the crown, too. Don't you forget that or you'll end up on the spike yourself."

Not a muscle moved in Voron's face. Not a word left his mouth. He calmly stepped over Magnus's motionless body on the patio stones and left the terrace.

Did he really not care about the poor bird? I had a hard time believing he didn't. He'd had Magnus since he was a kid. It must pain him to lose his pet this brutally.

But I also sensed that Voron would rather take a crossbow bolt through his own heart than reveal his true feelings to King Tiane.

Farion promptly ushered me back into the palace. Before the door closed behind me, I saw Alcon quietly swipe the dead bird off the floor, then carry it away.

SPARROW

Voron was not in Elaros, and the palace didn't feel the same without his quiet presence. For me at least, it didn't.

I used to see the High General everywhere I went. Even if it was just a glimpse of his black cape, a glint of his watchful eye, or a flash of his silver-black hair, I knew he was close, keeping order of the king's chaotic court from the shadows.

As infuriating as I found him at times, generally, his calm demeanor made me feel safe. Despite his outer bitterness and sarcasm, deep inside, our values seemed to align. With Voron, I never experienced the same anxious confusion as I felt with King Tiane.

The king's punishment of the cursed had shaken me to the core. The splendid image I had of the king had been cracking little by little, and I wasn't sure it could ever be whole again. I was glad he hadn't summoned me to dinner, because I wasn't sure I could act unaffected with him. The screams and growls of the cursed echoed in my ears all night, keeping me awake.

I jumped in panic at the sound of the knock on my door the

morning after that horrible day. I was alone in my room. Alacine had just cleared the dishes after my breakfast, and with Voron gone, Brebie wouldn't come to dress me until the king would send for me.

The knock sounded again, louder this time.

Please, don't let this be the king sending for me.

I wasn't ready to face him. Not while the tortured screams of the cursed still echoed in my ears.

"Who's there?" I asked loudly.

"It's Alcon, Lady Sparrow," came the deep voice of the Head of the Royal Guard and Voron's trusted man.

Had Voron returned? Hope sparked in my chest.

I opened the door.

"Are you here to take me for my lesson? Is the High General back?"

He'd left suddenly, without even saying goodbye. I'd learned he was gone from Brebie that morning, and somehow the world didn't feel quite right since.

"No, my lady." Alcon crushed my hope. "I'm here to inform you that High General Voron is not in Elaros and therefore won't be able to conduct your lesson this morning."

"How about tomorrow?"

His green eyes looked at me apologetically, glistening like emeralds in his dark-gray face. "Tomorrow, he won't be here either."

"Where did he go? When will he be back?"

"I don't know, my lady."

Wondering if his brief answers hid something he wasn't willing to share while standing in the open in the corridor, I swung the door wider.

"Come in, Alcon. We can talk in my room."

Instead of crossing the threshold, however, he took a step back.

"Sorry, Lady Sparrow, but none of us are allowed to enter your room."

"Really? Even if I'm inviting you? Who made these rules?"

"Her Majesty's orders."

Queen Pavline was serious about keeping me exclusively for her husband, it seemed.

"I see." I stepped out into the corridor to him and lowered my voice. "Just tell me, please. Will Voron be back at all?"

Alcon shook his head somberly. "He didn't say."

Worry tightened around my chest like a steel band.

What would Elaros be without Voron?

To me, it no longer felt safe at all.

B rebie rushed into my room two days later.

"Time to get you ready, Sparrow."

I looked up from the book I was reading. During my lessons with Voron, I'd discovered I could not only speak but also read and write in the language of the fae. It opened a whole new world of books and scrolls for me and gave me something to do while sitting in my room alone.

I'd read a few books already, trying to familiarize myself with the world outside of Elaros. I'd been in Sky Kingdom for over a month now but hadn't left the palace grounds yet. Reading was the only way for me to learn more about the people of Sky Kingdom.

"Ready for what?" I asked Brebie as she started getting out the gazillion things she normally used to make me look presentable for the king. Trepidation pricked my skin. "It's a bit too late for dinner, isn't it?"

I usually ate early, even on the nights when I had an invitation to appear in the king's dining room. The royal dinners were mostly for socializing; I never got enough food to eat during them. However, even by the royal standards, it was past dinnertime already.

"It's not for dinner." Brebie buzzed with energy, her short curls bouncing wildly as she rushed around the room. Even her horns appeared to be vibrating from all the action. "King Tiane wishes to see you in his chamber. Now."

"Now?" I echoed, my heart plummeting into the hollow of my stomach.

"Now, right now," she groaned, wringing her hands. "Gods, how am I going to pull this one off? With no notice at all?"

She rang the bell frantically, summoning maids to her aid.

I was no help. All I could do was stand there, as if struck by lightning. After waiting for this to happen for weeks, I finally got what I wanted—what everyone seemed to want for me—I got summoned to that sacred place, the king's bedroom.

Only now, it didn't feel like a win.

Apprehension seized my muscles, making it hard to move or even to breathe.

"Come on, come on, come on..." Brebie hurried, ripping my clothes off me. "There is no time to wash you properly. A quick sponge bath will have to do." She shoved me down on my bed as the maids got busy with sponges and buckets.

"I had a bath last night," I reminded them, numbly.

Everyone ignored me.

I tried to wrap my mind around what was happening. The king appeared disgusted with me when I threw up in front of him on the patio. Apparently, he'd gotten over it in the three days since.

"Why all this rush?"

"I don't know," Brebie snapped. "But do you really expect me to argue with the king?"

No. I certainly didn't expect anyone to argue with him on my behalf.

"He likes you," Brebie said, brushing my hair with the speed of an electric toothbrush. "He wants you. He can't wait to see you."

A flurry of activity rose around me like a twister. In seconds, my hair was brushed, braided, and pinned. My skin was rubbed clean, then oiled and powdered with shimmer.

There was no time for body paint, and that was fine with me. Except that without it, I lost a layer of coverage. All I wore now was an under-bust corset that lifted my breasts without covering the nipples and a pink gauzy skirt that reached down to my ankles but didn't conceal anything because of only one layer of fabric that was as thin as a spiderweb.

"Bring her a robe," Brebie waved impatiently at one of the maids while dusting my cheekbones with pink glitter.

She stepped back, giving me a critical once-over as I huddled into the luxurious magenta robe trimmed with flamingo-pink feathers.

"Well." Brebie clenched her hands in front of her nervously. "This will have to do."

"What mood is he in?" I asked, my nerves leaping out of whack.

"Who?" She blinked at me.

"The king. What did he say?"

"Oh." She rubbed her forehead. "I don't know, honey. I didn't talk to the king. He sent his orders through one of his guards."

I drew in a heavy breath, fisting my hands in the soft silk of the robe and crushing the pink feathers. Brebie must've guessed my unease as she stroked my arm through the long sleeve of my robe.

"Honey." Her voice softened. "This is good, *very* good, for all of us. King Tiane is fun, is he not? You like spending time with him. Tonight will just take your relationship to the next level and help you secure your place in Elaros."

I nodded to all the things she said. That was exactly how I used to think, how I was still thinking. Except that my thoughts were clashing with my feelings now. It wasn't the excitement and happy anticipation I was feeling. The trepidation that seized my muscles was too close to dread.

"You should be proud of yourself," Brebie kept talking in an upbeat voice. "We've been so nervous. So many people doubted you. But look, you did it! You made the king like you. He's besotted with you."

Besotted.

The word sounded ominous somehow.

With a knock on the door, the guards arrived, ready to lead me to the man I belonged to.

With an encouraging smile, Brebie leaned toward my ear. "King Tiane is a skilled lover, I've heard. He'll make it good for you."

I tried to hold on to her optimism while ascending the many stairs up to the tower with the king's rooms.

Despite some later developments, King Tiane had been kind enough to me. Because of him, I had a roof over my head, food was delivered straight to my room, and plenty of servants were there to do my bidding.

He hadn't asked for much in return. His attention hadn't been a burden. All I'd had to do so far was to grace his lap with my presence whenever he wished, which wasn't even that often.

After a month in Elaros, I still only had a vague idea of what kind of person King Tiane was under the façade of golden paint, wide smiles, and glamorous clothes.

Maybe tonight would bring us closer? Maybe I'd get to know him better, on a level that would endear him to me?

I brushed away the memories of the cursed in their cages, unable to deal with the dark emotions they stirred in me. But maybe I could get a better insight into the king's behavior that day, too? There must be an explanation for that cruelty. It had seemed so out of character for the smiling, easy-going monarch.

He waited for me in his bedroom in one of the tallest towers of the palace. And what a gorgeous room that was!

Snow-white vines created intricate designs between the opaque crystal panels of the walls. In the center of the high domed ceiling, the vines held a round clear glass. It would present a magnificent view of the starry sky, I imagined, had the sky not been so thickly overcast tonight.

The royal bed stood in the center of the round room, right under the glass dome. The bed was also round. The graceful vines that grew straight out of the floor served as the six bedposts. Gauzy curtains billowed softly around the vines, delicate like the river mist.

King Tiane lounged in a chaise by the bed, wearing a blush-pink robe embroidered with bright sunrise clouds along the hem.

He rose from his seat at the sight of me. The usual brilliant smile split his face.

"There's my favorite little human," he murmured.

The soft tone of his voice and the familiar smile put me at ease somewhat. I ventured a step in his direction, clutching my robe at my chest.

"Welcome, welcome to my bedroom, my baby chick." The king lifted two crystal flutes from a marble stand by the chaise. Coming closer, he handed one to me. "To many more nights together, shall we?" He winked, tapping the bottom of my flute to urge me to drink.

The sight of the pink and blue liquid shimmering in my glass sent cold shivers down my spine. The drink resembled closely the one I had with Trez on the last day of my past life.

"I can't..." I swallowed hard as my throat tightened. "I'm so sorry, Your Majesty, but I can't drink this."

The sensation of helplessness clamped around my limbs at the memories of the last time I drank this. I remembered what Voron and Brebie had told me about the drink, as well as the knowledge I'd added to their words by reading about it lately.

Camyte made one oblivious to what was right or wrong. It also made it possible for someone to impose their perception on you. Sometimes, permanently. If the pink glacial saffron had been added, too, it would make me a mindless puppet, numbly following orders of anyone who wished to boss me around.

"I won't drink it," I repeated, more firmly this time.

The king tilted his head in displeasure. I'd disobeyed him, openly and adamantly, for the first time ever. He clearly didn't like it. I pulled my head into my shoulders, bracing for his wrath.

"It's perfectly safe, my pet." To my surprise, he didn't sound angry. His voice remained soft and coaxing. "I wouldn't serve you something I wouldn't drink myself. Look."

With his finger under my chin, he lifted my face to his. Holding his glass in his other hand, he took a long drink from it.

I watched him closely. He didn't just dip his lips like Trez had done. He actually pulled the liquid into his mouth and swallowed, his lips immediately stretching into a smile right after.

"See? It's safe."

My surprise spiked, but then I realized that among the many pieces of jewelry decorating his hands, antlers, and chest, there must be at least one that was warded against the harmful effects of the magical substances. It protected the king from *camyte*. Just like the necklace Voron had given me would protect me from it, too.

"Why would you drink it?" I asked. "If not for the *camyte* effect?"

"Because it tastes good." He beamed. "It's like a dessert in a glass." He took another sip before setting his glass down. "But I'm not going to force you, my precious." He took my glass from me and placed it next to his. "I won't force you to do anything you don't like."

"Thank you," I exhaled with relief, dropping my shoulders as the tension released me somewhat.

"There, there..." He lifted my chin again, stroking my skin with his thumb. "I'm not angry. I understand. You don't trust me." He looked hurt, his bottom lip extended in a tragic expression.

"No, Your Majesty, I do. But..."

"Let's talk, sweetie. Tell me what makes you so distant. Are we not friends?" His voice flowed smoothly like a river. "Tell me what bothers you?"

Indeed, what the hell was bothering me? I had put so much effort into trying to become his friend. And now, when the king actually called us friends, I was risking ruining it all.

I often got tongue-tied around him. It couldn't be helped. The king was just so grand and majestic, it was impossible not to feel awe-struck in his presence. But there was something else tonight. It scratched inside me, echoing through my chest with screeching howls, like the tormented screams of the cursed.

"Three days ago," I said. "Those cages with—"

"Ah," he interrupted me. "You're still upset about my little event?" His perfect features distorted into a frown of disgust, possibly at the memory of me throwing up my breakfast in front of the entire court.

"Was it really necessary to have that 'event,' Your Majesty?" I asked. "Those people—"

"They're *not* people. Not anymore. A fae cannot break their promise without losing their mind and eventually their life. The cursed sealed their fate the moment they gave a promise they couldn't keep."

"But what kind of promise would do this?"

"*Any* kind, my dear. It could be that they promised to be faithful and loyal but ended up lying and cheating. Or it could be that they promised to arrive somewhere in five minutes and ended up taking six. There is just no way to tell now. They certainly no longer remember what brought the curse on their heads. The point is, they are no longer *people*. They don't know their names, don't recognize their loved ones. They're cursed to rage in frenzy until the wings of death close over them and they'll be judged by the gods."

"It's terrible," I exhaled. The images of that day wouldn't leave me. "That woman looked so young."

"Young and stupid," he bit out. "Regardless, she should've known better than to give promises sealed by magic."

The memory of the poor girl thrashing on the ground in torment, breaking her own bones, and trying to climb out of her skin assaulted me anew. Tears trembled on my eyelashes. Cupping my face, the king brushed them off with his thumbs.

"Aww, you have such a soft heart, my sweet baby chick. But there is no need to shed tears for the cursed. They feel nothing. And you don't have to worry about that woman. Seeing how it affected you, I showed her mercy." He raised his head regally.

"You did?" I pressed my hands to my chest. "Thank you, Your Majesty."

With his hands on my waist, he pulled me closer.

"You're very welcome, my treasure." He slid his hand into the neckline of my robe, caressing my skin underneath.

I gave him a smile, glad it felt like a genuine one. His fingers encountered Voron's necklace on my chest. He tugged at it, his warm expression instantly cooling off.

"This is Voron's, isn't it?" He frowned at the string of silver berries. "I've seen him wear it back at the camp during the last war." He fingered the beads, contemplating something. "Since you're not drinking with me, there won't be any harm in you taking this off, will there?"

Voron was gone, but his necklace kept protecting me, even in his absence. Taking it off felt like stripping myself of the only protection I had left.

I gripped the stone pendant through my robe. "Can I keep it on? Please?"

The king pressed his full lips into a hard line of irritation.

"Are you disobeying your king, Sparrow? Again?"

I couldn't recall him ever calling me by my name before. I wasn't even sure he knew it. His using it now highlighted his displeasure, even as his voice remained low.

"Your Majesty—" I tried to plead, but he stopped me with a kiss on my temple.

"Perhaps I should explain myself rather than demand. Forgive me, sweetie, I've been the Sky King for so long, I've grown intolerant to any kind of opposition."

I liked the change in his tone and the turn in our conversation. The king asked for my forgiveness.

"Thank you for your understanding, Your Majesty."

"Then maybe you would understand me, too. You see, I'm still cross with Voron. I'm sure he'll come around eventually and things will return to normal. But right now, it irritates me to see something of his around the neck of the woman I care deeply about. Especially tonight, when I finally have you all to myself."

He cared about me? Deeply? He never said anything like that before.

"I see."

"You do?" His voice lifted. "You understand, then? Will you take his necklace off? Will you do it for me? Please."

Not waiting for me, he ran his fingers around my neck and tried to open the closure of the necklace, but it wouldn't give. Like Voron had said when he gave it to me, no one would be able to remove it without my permission. But some might be able to break it.

The king tugged at it, getting more and more irritated. If there was anyone capable of breaking the necklace, I assumed, it would be the king with his strength and powerful magic.

"I'll do it." I reached back myself. "Here." I took it off.

He grabbed it from me and put it onto the marble stand next to our glasses.

"Excellent." He lifted his glass and took another drink. "The necklace will stay right here for you. You can have it back first thing in the morning."

With a gentle smile, he caressed the side of my face. Sliding his hand under my chin, he guided my face to his.

"Thank you for taking it off. It means a lot to me," he murmured against my lips.

His breath fanned across my skin. The sweet fragrance of *camyte* filled my nostrils just as his tongue parted my lips and invaded my mouth. *Camyte* flavor clung to his tongue, hitting the roof of my mouth.

Horror gripped me as the dreadfully familiar sensation of helplessness spread through my limbs. Without the necklace, I was defenseless, one on one with the man I now knew without a doubt I could not trust.

He leaned back, breaking the kiss.

"Now will you drink it?" he grinned, taking the goddamn flute from the stand.

"Please, don't..." I whimpered, even as my hand reached for the glass.

His blue eyes twinkled excitedly as he watched me drink. He practically bubbled with giddy anticipation.

"Oh, but I will, my treasure. I will do everything I've been dying to do to you for so long. Come now," the king murmured, taking me into his arms. "Let's fulfill the prophecy, my sweet, little pet."

Chapter Twenty-One

SPARROW

Light danced behind my eyelids. I opened my eyes, squinting and turning my head to evade it.

A ray of sunlight pierced the gauzy curtains draped between the vines above the bed—King Tiane's bed. The sunlight came from the round skylight in the domed ceiling.

There were barely any clouds in the sky. This was the first ray of sunlight I'd ever seen in this shadowless kingdom.

Propping my hands on the mattress, I rose in bed. The room was empty. The king wasn't here.

My robe lay on the floor where I remembered standing last. My corset was still on, leaving my chest bare. Several small round spots dotted my breasts. They were sore when I touched them. Then I realized the dots were bruises, likely left by rough fingers.

The memories of last night rushed over me. The king, the necklace, the drink... King Tiane saying something about a prophecy.

The last thing I remembered was the king leaning over me lying in bed.

"I will savor the memory of every minute of our first night

together," he'd said. "And I'll be looking forward to many more nights like this. But you..." He stroked my face. "You, my precious baby chick, don't need to remember any of it."

His lips had parted after that, and he'd inhaled one gentle breath in through his mouth. Then, oblivion had descended upon me like a thick, woolen blanket. And now I didn't remember how I got to bed in the first place, who took my robe off, or what happened in between.

My heart pounded anxiously. I tried to keep fear at bay the best I could and considered the worst.

Did the king rape me?

Why would he, though? He hadn't even tried to have sex with me before giving the drink. And if he had, I didn't think I would've refused him. He didn't need to force himself on me. I came to his bedroom mostly prepared to go through with it.

What happened, then?

I shifted my legs under the silk sheet covering me from my waist down and waited for my body to tell me what my mind had forgotten.

My inner thighs felt sore. But there was no ache anywhere higher between my legs. I ripped the sheet off me. My skirt was still on but torn from the waist down. Short, slim scars covered the inside of my thighs from my pelvis area halfway down to my knees.

The scars looked at least a week old, the cuts fully healed and only slightly sore, but the sight of them made my stomach twist in knots.

What had been done to me? Who cut me and why? How long had I been here for the cuts to heal?

I remembered nothing. And that made the whole thing even more disturbing and terrifying.

Untangling my limbs from the luxurious sheets, I stumbled out of bed and grabbed my robe from the floor.

No one was around. I was all alone in this gorgeous bedroom.

My silver rowan berry necklace lay on the marble stand next to my empty glass. I put the robe on, grabbed the necklace, and fled.

The guards at the door to the king's chambers gave me mildly curious looks but made no effort to stop me. I ran all the way to my room, clutching the robe closed at my chest, and didn't stop until I was inside my bedroom with the door firmly shut behind me.

First thing first, I put the necklace back on. Its slight press against my chest immediately made me feel safer. Then, I went to the toilet room and scrubbed my skin with a cloth and soap in the washbowl, getting rid of the phantom sensation of being touched, prodded, bruised, and cut.

Tears burned my eyes, but I refused to let them spill. I felt violated, helpless, and hurt. But I was also angry. Anger made me feel stronger, so I let it burn in my chest unimpeded.

I had no idea what happened to me, but I knew who was responsible. King Tiane betrayed me. I'd trusted him, and he crushed my trust under his foot, smiling and kissing me while he did it.

I put a clean robe on right before Brebie burst into my bedroom, bright and cheerful like the sunlight behind my window.

"Sparrow, what a glorious day it's promising to be!" She threw the curtains open, exposing the brilliant crystal of the window. It shone with a myriad of iridescent sparkles from the sun outside. "You did it, honey! They said the king was all smiles this morning. He insisted on singing at breakfast. The king was singing! For the entire court."

While I lay passed out in his bed.

Brebie noticed my less than gleeful expression.

"What happened, Sparrow? Why a long face? You should be celebrating. We finally got to see the sun for the first time in ages, and it's all your doing."

I stretched my lips into something hopefully resembling a smile, even as my insides twisted in nauseating uncertainty.

"How long have I been gone?"

Her smile wavered.

"What do you mean? You spent the night with the king. Several hours."

"That's it?"

How did my scars heal so fast? I didn't remember the night, but I knew I came to the king's bedroom with my thighs intact.

Brebie beamed at me again.

"Aww, he made you forget all about the time. You must be tired." She winked.

With a knock on the door, Alacine arrived, flanked by two other maids. They carried a giant basket filled with sweets, jewelry, and flowers.

"From His Majesty," Alacine announced with a wide grin.

Brebie and she unpacked it, oohing and aahing over each item, while I sat on the bed, huddling into a blanket.

It was tempting to give into the cheerful mood of the others. They viewed last night as something positive, and I wished with all my heart that I could see it as such, too.

If only it wasn't for the scars and bruises on my body, and no recollection about how they got there.

"Look!" Brebie lifted a tiny jar from the basket.

Glistening with gold and precious stones, the jar looked like a crown jewel, coming straight from the royal treasury.

"Do you know what it is?" Brebie gushed, uncorking it and taking a sniff. "It's a healing salve. It's made with werewolf blood and is absolutely priceless. Here." She handed it to me. "If you ever scratch or hurt yourself, use it. It'll make your skin heal within days, leaving no scars at all."

If you ever scratch or hurt yourself...

Only that wasn't the case here. I didn't inflict the wounds on my thighs. Someone else did.

"Aww," Alacine cooed. "The king must really care to send you such a gift."

How could I tell them what really happened? There was

nothing either of them could do about that, anyway. Besides, I had no idea what really happened.

Taking the jar with the precious healing salve, I gave Alacine a smile.

"I guess he does." I glanced at the pale pink gel in the jar. It had a faint scent of pine and copper. Had it been used on me last night? That would explain why the scars on my thighs looked healed and faint.

"Today, you rest." Brebie tucked the blanket around me as Alacine and the maids put away the royal gifts. "I'll get all your favorite foods brought up here. The king won't bother you today. He has an outing planned with the gentlemen of his court—bow and arrow practice in the gardens, might as well use the great weather. I also think you should cancel your lesson with Voron tomorrow. Relax—"

"Wait, what? Is Voron back?"

"He's coming back tonight. But if you need more rest—"

"I don't. Please don't cancel the lesson. I'll be fine."

This was the best news I got in days. Now at least I had something positive to look forward to.

Chapter Twenty-Two

SPARROW

Too excited about resuming our lessons, I didn't even realize I left my room way too early the next morning and ran to Voron's apartments way too quickly. Even the look on Alcon's face when he opened the door didn't clue me in how early it was.

"Morning." I flashed him a friendly smile, rushing by to Voron's sitting room.

I didn't knock and didn't wait, thinking he'd be expecting me. Shoving the door open with my shoulder, I just barged right in.

Turned sideways to me, Voron stood in front of the glass doors open to the outside terrace. The morning sun pierced through the perforated cloud cover in the sky, illuminating him from the side.

He wore a long royal-blue robe with silver stars scattered along the hem and on the wide sleeves. The robe was made from silk, a very *thin* silk, I realized, glimpsing through it the outline of his tall muscular body backlit by the morning sun.

At the sound of me entering the room, he whipped to face me.

His eyebrows shot up in surprise.

"Sparrow?"

I caught him off guard. He clearly wasn't expecting me yet. And for one beautiful moment, his face remained open for me to read his true emotions. He was just as glad to see me as I was to see him. His arms jerked aside as if ready to hug me.

There was nothing I wouldn't give for a hug from him. I needed his arms to ground me. For him to tell me that all was going to be okay somehow. I longed to feel his strength, for it to make me stronger, too.

Then, I noticed that Voron was wearing nothing under that robe. Nothing at all.

He remembered that, too, yanking the ends of his robe closed. But not before I got a glimpse of his entire, gloriously naked front. The wide planes of his chest. The hard, squared ridges of his abs. And the thin trail of black hair, as if painted with ink on his pale skin. It marked the way from his belly button down to his thick length, resting flaccid in his groin.

It didn't remain flaccid, however. As if led by my glance, it jerked, then rose toward me, swelling in both girth and length.

Even when Voron closed the robe, his hard-on refused to settle, poking against the thin fabric from the inside.

"I... I'm..." I tugged at my ear with one hand, clutching my notebook in the other. Forcing my eyes away from his crotch, I blurted out, "The lesson?"

If my sudden intrusion had knocked Voron's composure out of balance, he regained it quickly. Folding his arms across his chest, he gave me an amused look.

"I applaud your eagerness to learn, little bird. But will you at least allow me to put some pants on first?"

"Sure," I mumbled. "I'm sorry. I didn't realize how early it was."

The clock in a gilded frame over the fireplace showed I'd barged in here almost twenty minutes before our scheduled time. And now, I felt stupid.

"I can come back." I gestured at the door behind me.

"Stay," he said firmly in a voice used to giving orders. "There is no need to apologize, either. Normally, I'd be up and fully dressed at this hour. But I arrived late last night and slept in this morning."

His words didn't make me feel any better about my intrusion. The man came home late, after possibly a long exhausting journey, and there I was, springing on him first thing in the morning, before he even had a chance to get dressed.

I had half a mind to flee. Only the fear of making this even more awkward if I ran now kept me in place. That and the fact that it felt...nice to see him again. *Very* nice. I was really looking forward to spending the next hour in his room, the only place in the entire palace where I felt completely safe.

"If you'll excuse me." With a polite bow, he headed to the door that must lead to his bedroom or to his dressing room.

Sunlight slid down his back, playing in the shimmering fabric of his robe. The blue shimmer suddenly gathered into lines, forming the image of folded wings. They stretched from his shoulders all the way down to his backside, the tips curving over his firm buttocks.

I blinked, and the wings were gone as Voron strode through the door and into another room.

"Make yourself comfortable, Sparrow," he said from behind the wall. "I won't be long."

Was Voron aware of what had just happened?

He must have felt the light on his back. Only he didn't react to it at all.

Maybe nothing happened, after all? Maybe the sunlight just played a trick on my eyes. I couldn't even tell for sure whether the image of the folded wings had flashed on the back of Voron's robe or directly on his skin underneath it.

It had to be just an illusion. Voron wouldn't be acting as if nothing happened otherwise. My nerves were strung too tight. It was no surprise my jumpy mind would be conjuring up things.

Perching on the chair by the unlit fireplace, I opened my notes. I figured I'd go over them since it'd been a few days since my last lesson. My thoughts, however, refused to stay in the room with me. They wandered off, following Voron out through the door and feeding my imagination with the images of him getting dressed, separated only by the wall from me.

I happened to be one of the very few people Voron allowed into his suite. And even then, I had never made it past this sitting room. I wondered how many women had seen his bedroom. I tried to imagine what Voron's bed looked like—the bed where he'd slept in this morning. I didn't think he wore that long robe to bed. And since he hadn't been wearing any pajamas either, he probably liked sleeping in the nude...

Warmth tingled through my chest at the mental image of Voron spread out on his sheets, gloriously naked. Those long legs of his and his muscular arms—

"If I didn't know any better, I'd think you missed me." Voron's cheerful voice snapped me out of my daydream that was highly inappropriate on so many levels, including the fact that he was currently my teacher and I was his student.

He entered, straightening the silk ruffles of his cuffs over his hands. His black coat remained undone, but the same color vest underneath was fully buttoned. A pristine white cravat was tied around his neck. The lacy ends of the cravat were neatly held together with a pin decorated with a tiny feather carved from a black stone.

"You rushed in here first thing in the morning, dear Sparrow, catching me in a scandalous state of undress," he continued with an amused smile hiding in the corners of his mouth. "Please don't tell me you missed me."

"I didn't," I lied, quickly averting my eyes and likely fooling no one.

He chuckled at my flustered state but mercifully didn't call me out on the lie. With an elegant hand gesture, he made the crystals in the wall burn brighter. Their glow, however, could not compete with the sunshine spilling into the room through the open patio doors.

"I propose we do the lesson outside today," he said. "The weather is finally nice for a change. It'd be a shame to miss out on a day like today."

I didn't want to dwell on the reasons for the nice weather, following Voron outside to the patio and to the game table standing by the marble parapet. The wide pillars of the parapet were hollow and filled with dirt. White and pale lavender flowers grew from these outdoor flowerpots.

"These are pretty." I leaned over to inhale the delicate scent of the blossoms.

He watched me. "You like flowers?"

"Who doesn't?" I smiled as the delicate petals tickled my nose.

Ash-gray vines arched over the patio. A soft caw came from the one directly over our heads.

Voron glanced up, his features relaxing into a warm expression.

"Good morning to you, too, old friend," he said to a large black bird sitting in the vines.

"Is that..." I hesitated, afraid to say the name of Voron's last pet so as not to poke a fresh wound since he'd just lost Magnus.

Voron had acted cool and unaffected when King Tiane shot Magnus. That didn't mean he wasn't hurting from the loss of his long-time companion.

To my utter surprise, Voron smiled at me. A real, bright smile that lasted at least a second or two and nearly made my knees give in, almost sending me to the floor.

"Yes, it is Magnus. Come here," he beckoned the bird. "Come on over here, you rascal. You know it's breakfast time."

From a carved marble stand nearby, he took a glass jar filled with a mix of seeds, nuts, and dried berries. The bird cawed again, ruffling its feathers in anticipation of the meal.

"Speaking of breakfast," Voron said. "I need to get some food, too. I haven't eaten since forever, and I'm starving. Would you mind feeding him?" He handed the jar to me.

"Me? Will he eat from me?"

"He will, as long as I'll allow it." He flicked his wrist, gesturing from the bird to me, then walked back inside to order a breakfast through Alcon.

Flapping his big black wings, Magnus flew from the vine to the marble stand in front of me. He then tilted his head, looking at me expectantly with his beady eyes.

"Is that really you, Magnus?" I opened the jar and took a handful of the feed out, then offered it to the bird.

While he ate, carefully selecting seeds and berries from my hand, I studied him closely. I doubted I could tell one crow from another. I'd even mistaken him for a raven before. This one appeared just as large as Voron's previous bird. He also had the same silver rings circling his ankles.

But Magnus had been killed. A bolt as thick as my thumb had gone through his chest. I'd seen it with my own eyes.

"How did you survive, buddy?" I marveled.

"He didn't." Voron walked out to the patio again. "He most definitely died."

"Did you...replace him?"

He chuckled.

"Oh, no. Magnus is very much irreplaceable." He stroked under the bird's beak, speaking affectionately, "Aren't you, Magnus?" The bird glanced at his master, then rubbed the side of its beak against his finger.

"So," I blinked at them both, confused. "If he died, and this is him..."

"I brought him back from the dead," Voron replied matter-of-factly.

I leaned closer, squinting at the bird. Some feathers on his chest were missing, leaving a dent in his glossy coverage right where the king's bolt had struck.

"You can bring people back from the dead?" At this point, I

wasn't even that surprised. Voron was a mysterious man with many magical abilities.

"Not people, just animals. And not *me* personally," he admitted. "But I have a friend who can do it. For a price."

"Is that why you were gone from Elaros? You took Magnus to your friend?"

The bird finished eating, and Voron tenderly stroked the feathers on his head with his finger.

"I had to get him there as soon as possible. Beyond a certain point, a hag wouldn't save him. That'd be a job for a necromancer then." He winced. "And I really, really wouldn't want to deal with a necromancer, trust me."

He didn't show a drop of emotion when Magnus was shot. But without the court knowing, he rushed him to find the magic to revive him.

"How far did you have to go?"

"Quite far. Especially on horseback."

"Couldn't Alcon fly him there? Wouldn't it be faster?"

"Alcon would never find those who don't want to be found," he replied cryptically. Then added, "Either way, it's done. Magnus is well and safe now. He's a wise old bird. He'll know to stay away from certain people from now on. Won't you, Magnus?"

The crow cawed loudly and hopped up to the nearest vine. Voron followed him with his gaze, watching over his old friend.

"You really care about him, don't you?"

He gave me a small shrug, downplaying it. "We get along well, better than I ever managed to get along with any person."

I shook the remnants of Magnus's breakfast from my hands and closed the jar.

"But have you ever *tried* to make friends with a person?"

"People are impossible to make friends with."

"Why is that?"

He shot me a teasing look. "Because even the most promising of them ask way too many questions."

He made it sound like *I* was "the most promising" one to be his friend. And with Voron, this probably was the closest anyone could get to him.

His breakfast arrived. I noticed it had two of everything. He'd ordered for both of us.

"I'm not hungry," I said quickly as he unloaded the tray directly onto the game table with its playing fields still folded flat. "I already had breakfast."

"Just have some tea with me, then." He poured the fragrant liquid into two teacups.

As I took my place at the table, he brought a velvet cloak from the room and draped it over my shoulders.

"It's still rather chilly," he explained.

His kind gesture warmed my heart.

It wasn't just Voron's good looks that drew me to him, I realized. There were plenty of good-looking men at King Tiane's court to drool over, but I couldn't care less about any of them.

Voron stood out because he cared about me without having any agenda or special interest. I wasn't his breeder or his lover. He did all those little things for me that went beyond his duties simply because he wanted to see me fed, happy, and comfortable, without negotiating any price for himself for doing that. And if something bad happened to me, I believed, he would be the only highborn of the entire court, aside from maybe Dove as well, to be genuinely sad about that.

I blinked, glancing away.

The breeze was fresh, but the sun was out. Spotting our shadows on the stones of the patio, I thought Kanbor must be happy to finally have some sunshine for the gardens. Even Voron appeared to be in a much better mood today.

Everyone appreciated sunshine. But no one knew the price I'd paid to have the spring finally come to the shadowless Sky Kingdom.

Taking a sip of the warm delicious tea, I furtively studied Voron from under my eyelashes.

Did *he* know where I'd spent the previous night? Nothing

happened in the palace without the knowledge of the High General.

On the other hand, he'd come home late and tired. I'd caught him this morning still practically butt-naked. He might not have gotten the report yet. Frankly, judging by his bright and breezy mood this morning, I believed he didn't know yet.

I wished I could talk to someone about last night. But I didn't even know what to say and where to start, since I remembered nothing. Besides, after King Tiane broke my trust so heartlessly, I felt I should be far more careful about trusting anyone at all, even Voron.

That didn't mean I couldn't fish for some information from him. He'd been a great source for that so far.

"Well, spring has finally come," I said.

Topics on the weather were considered safe and neutral. Not in Sky Kingdom, however. Voron's brow furrowed.

"About time," he huffed into his tea.

"How exactly does it work? If the weather depends on the king's moods, why did it take this long for the clouds to part? I mean, I'd seen King Tiane laugh and smile before. In fact, he seems to be in a merry mood often."

"The weather isn't as fickle as the king's facial expressions, Sparrow. The clouds can't jump in and out with his every smile. I've read there are some differences from king to king but, generally, the weather is attuned to his overall state of mind."

"So, he could be partying and laughing, and looking like he's enjoying himself, but that wouldn't mean he's truly happy?"

He nodded. "Not all smiles are genuine, little bird."

Maybe he was right, but I had a hard time believing some deep sorrow was buried in King Tiane and that I somehow helped him overcome it last night.

"Queen Pavline said there is a prophecy about the king needing to be fulfilled to become great," I said, remembering the king's words about fulfilling a prophecy with me, just before the gap in my memories started.

"Right."

"What exactly does it mean? How is he supposed to 'fulfill' himself?"

"Don't we all wish to know that?" Voron smirked. "There are many interpretations. The one most favored by the queen and the king himself is that he's not to be denied anything."

"An excellent excuse for excess and indulgence."

"That's exactly what it is, dear Sparrow. Our King Tiane is heading to greatness by having as much fun as he can physically stomach." He set his teacup aside and flicked his thumb up toward the sky. "At least the rest of us get to enjoy the sunshine once in a while."

I finished my tea, too, and put down the dainty teacup onto the equally delicate saucer.

"Shall we proceed with the lesson?" Voron collected the dishes onto the tray and moved it aside to open the game table.

I'd asked him for these lessons with the intent of learning the game War of Kings, hoping to impress King Tiane one day. I never expected the lessons to become far more important to me than the end goal.

I smiled at Voron, helping him open the playing fields. "Sure. Let's see how many levels I'll last today."

Chapter Twenty-Three

SPARROW

I was dragging my feet on the way to the royal dining room. It'd been three days since the night I'd spent in the king's chambers. The sunshine hadn't lasted long. By noon of the same day, it was cloudy again, though the weather kept getting warmer as the spring had been gaining strength.

Despite the clouds, everyone around me still seemed elated. Brebie and the maids had chirped excitedly, getting me ready for dinner tonight. The queen was all smiles when I ran into her on my way to Voron's rooms yesterday.

"Your presence in Elaros is highly beneficial to the crown," she'd told me. The queen certainly approved my joining the court in their mutual striving to please the king at all costs.

Yet I entered the dining room with more dread than anticipation. When King Tiane waved for me to approach, I had to force my feet to move in his direction.

He flashed me a bright smile, dragging me into his lap. Before they even served the first course of the dinner, his right hand ended up under my skirt.

"How have you been, my sweet baby chick?" he murmured, stroking my thigh.

I stared straight ahead and gave him the only answer he'd want to hear. "I've been well, Your Majesty."

The tips of his fingers slipped between my legs. He prodded along my right inner thigh, pressing gently, as if searching for the cuts he'd left there. Only I'd already used the healing cream he'd sent to me. I'd slathered it on my skin several times a day until every trace of those scars was gone.

He nuzzled the side of my neck. "You please me greatly. If there is anything you wish for, all you need to do is ask."

The king was in a generous mood tonight, but all I really wished for was the truth.

"I'd like to get some answers," I said. "Can I ask you a question, please?"

His smooth brow furrowed, the dreamy expression gone.

"What kind of question?"

I met his gaze straight on. "What did you do to me the night I spent in your bedroom?"

His back snapped straight. The muscles in his thighs under my butt stiffened as his body went rigid.

"You don't need to trouble your pretty little head with that, sweetie," he bit off. Even the word of endearment came out sharp, like a warning.

"I wish I could forget it, Sire, but—"

"Oh, is that what you wish for? To *forget?*" He grabbed my chin, and I realized I'd made a mistake.

The king could make me forget this conversation and the entire past week. What if he erased whatever few memories I still had left? Every one I'd made since coming to Sky Kingdom? All of it, good and bad? Because there *had been* good memories, too, the memories I wished to keep.

"No. Please. It doesn't bother me at all," I lied. "I'm just curious…"

"Curiosity is not an admirable quality in a woman, Sparrow," he admonished sternly.

Fear gripped me, but anger burned through it.

What was he admonishing me for? For wishing to know what happened to my own body? What right did he have to hide that from me?

But I knew the answer to that—the right of power. King Tiane held absolute power over me, including every part of my body. I had no protection from him.

"Forgive me, Your Majesty," I gritted through my teeth.

But it was too late. He pursed his mouth, jerking his hand away from me.

"You soured my mood with your questions, human," he sulked. "I don't want you here tonight."

A week ago, that would be a devastating thing to hear from him. Now, all I felt was relief. I climbed off his lap quickly and bowed my head.

"Enjoy your night, Your Majesty," I said quickly, afraid he'd change his mind.

He wouldn't look at me, brushing off his thighs, as if trying to get rid of every trace of my presence from his white velvet pants.

"Now, go to your room and think about what you've done," he snarled. "Then make sure you do better next time."

With my head bowed, I left, trying hard not to run. Curious stares of the courtiers slithered after me. Some of them must feel pity for me. A few likely basked in schadenfreude, witnessing me falling from grace. But I didn't care. I simply had to get away from the suffocating presence of the king.

I craved fresh air.

Rushing into my room, I swung the curtains aside and yanked the window open. The night breeze blew in. It was warm but refreshing. I drew it in with long, gasping breaths.

A howl came in from the outside—a long, blood-chilling wail. Muffled by the distance, it was nevertheless terrifying.

I recoiled from the window.

"Water..." came the plea with the next scream. The word was distorted, skewed, and stretched, but clear enough for me to understand how incredibly thirsty the person was to beg for water through their suffering.

I recognized the howls. The curse breakers had screamed like that. But King Tiane had told me he showed them mercy. I assumed that meant he either ordered them released from the cages or, at the very least, granted them a quick death that ended their torment.

What was happening there now?

I shut the window, unable to listen to the screams. But they were lodged in my brain, echoing through my mind.

They said if a promise was broken, nothing would save a fae from the fate of the cursed. Releasing them wouldn't have helped them. They were doomed to die. But why weren't they killed? Wouldn't a quick death be better than whatever torture they were going through?

It had been seven days since the cursed were brought to Elaros. Had they been suffering all this time?

I hadn't heard their howls from Voron's terrace. But Voron's apartments were located on a much higher floor than my room and on the opposite side of the palace. And I hadn't opened my window until now.

Pacing around my bed, I couldn't rest. The echo of the tortured screams in my head tormented me, urging me to do something to relieve the poor souls' pain. Maybe I could at least bring them some water? What was the point in making these people suffer?

I grabbed a shawl from my dressing room and the pitcher of drinking water left for me by the maids in case I got thirsty at night. Then I headed out.

Wrapped into the shawl, I sneaked down the many staircases to the ground floor. No one stopped me. The king and his court remained busy with their after-dinner entertainment. I hadn't encountered that many servants on my way, either. Most of them must've retired to their rooms already, getting some rest before another busy day of fulfilling the king's every wish tomorrow.

I left the palace through the door that led to the gardens. It wasn't guarded like the main gates. The dark silhouettes of the night guards soared high above me, scanning the walls and the towers of the palace. But down under the flower arches in the gardens, the chances of someone spotting me in the dark were slim.

My silk slippers padded softly along the cobblestones of the garden path. It was quiet here. Only the breeze rustled in the vines of the arches. But as I rounded the curve of the palace wall, the howling of the cursed cut my hearing, curdling the blood in my veins.

A forest of tall spikes rose in front of me as I got closer. Spikes, twice as high as people, stood from the ground. Every single one held a body. Impaled through their pelvis and along their spines, they were held upright. It was a grotesque, morbid sight. Like a field of undead marionettes, waiting for the fingers of their puppeteer to get them moving.

Horror crawled up my back like a myriad of spider legs, chilling and paralyzing. Bile rose in my throat. My stomach spasmed at the stench of blood.

The bodies appeared partially destroyed. Huge chunks of flesh seemed to be missing, even around the spikes that held them in place.

"Water..."

The croak made me jump, my heart beating faster, as if trying to leap out of my throat.

At least one of the cursed wasn't dead yet. I searched the forest of spikes. Unlike the rest, a body at the very edge of it was positioned horizontally, the spike piercing through the chest. Stepping closer, I recognized the slim shape and the mangled remnants of the sole wing. It was the girl whose execution I couldn't stomach to watch.

She was the only one impaled through her chest. Such was the "mercy" the king had granted her.

Her fingers appeared to be missing, as well as her toes and most of her one remaining wing. Upon a closer look, however, I realized they weren't missing. They had turned transparent. The edges of her wounds and scratches frayed as if disappearing into the air, moonlight piercing right through them.

The girl writhed on the spike, her screams and growls garbled and choked.

"Water..."

She was thirsty. I had to give her some water. I could at least show her that little mercy. I lurched forward with my pitcher when something grabbed me around my waist, stopping me in my tracks.

Panic surged through me. My fingers spasmed, letting go of the handle. The pitcher fell to the ground, the delicate porcelain smashing to pieces on the cobblestones. The water splashed my slippers, chilling my toes.

I whipped around, shaking with fear.

The darkness in front of me solidified in textures of velvet and fine brocade. The familiar fresh scent of rain enveloped me.

"Voron?"

I cursed his uncanny ability to be everywhere at once. Wasn't he supposed to be in the dining room right now? Making sure nothing threatened the safety of their precious King Tiane?

"I need to go." I tried to sidestep him. "I have to get more water now—"

He gripped my shoulders, hissing into my face, "You can't be here, Sparrow."

"Oh yeah? And you can?" Terror turned to anger inside me. "Did you know they were here? Suffering all this time? Of course you did. Nothing happens in this palace without you knowing. Without you *organizing* it." My voice rose. Compassion for the poor woman burned so hot inside me, it hurt.

"Quiet." He slammed his hand over my mouth.

Flexing his arm around my middle, he dragged me away from the garden of horrors. I kicked my feet, clawing at his hand over my mouth.

Indignation shook me.

How dare he?

How the fuck dare he shut me up!

"Keep quiet, Sparrow." He gave me a shake, pivoting me around to face him. "Do you hear me? No screaming."

Muffled by his hand over my mouth, my screams of protest came out only as whimpers and groans.

He moved his other hand to the back of my head and fisted it into my hair. The sting at my roots only fed my anger. I kicked him in the shin.

He flinched but wouldn't let go of me.

"Listen." He gave me another shake, as if he could shake me into obedience. "Listen to me."

His eyes burned with the reflection of the glow from the pale flowers in the vines that climbed up the arches and over the garden path where Voron had dragged me to.

"Under the threat of death, no one is allowed to enter the Garden of the Cursed," he gritted through his teeth. "Do you realize I'll have to report you, now? I'll have to plan and organize *your* execution? I'll have to watch *you* being impaled on a spike?"

His hands remained firm but his voice shook slightly. He jerked my head closer, his eyes flicked between mine.

"I'll have to watch you die." His voice dropped, sounding soft like the rustle of a breeze on the vines above us.

His grip in my hair relaxed, but he didn't remove his hand, cradling my head. I stopped fighting him, and he dropped his hand from my mouth.

I panted, overwhelmed by his words and his closeness.

"Will you, Voron?" I whispered. "Will you kill me to serve your king?"

I waited for his answer, my breathing slowing. His gaze

dipped to my lips, then slid back up to my eyes with a caress over my entire face.

"Sparrow..." My name came from him like a moan.

He inhaled deeply, bringing me closer. Our foreheads touched. He slid his head down, the side of his face brushing against mine. Then I felt the press of his lips on my skin just below my ear—a kiss.

Here, under the double coverage of the night and the arches with flowers, Voron finally shed the armor he'd been hiding behind all this time.

My skin tingled under his lips. Warmth scattered through my body with sparks of desire.

"You aren't mine," he growled and added firmly, "but I saw you first."

His mouth descended on mine, robbing me of breath. Awareness rolled through me with a swell of bliss as our lips connected. I swayed in his arms, gripping his cloak just to stay upright. With his hand fisted in my hair, he angled my head to claim my mouth more thoroughly.

My heart pounded wildly. And Voron's resonated in response, beating against my hand I splayed on his chest.

I'd only been kissed by one man before that I remembered— by the king. And Voron's kiss was everything the king's wasn't. I was hardly aware of his tongue parting my lips, barely realizing I was kissing him back. My mind floated somewhere warm and fuzzy. My entire body appeared to join it there, too.

Another blood-curdling howl pierced the air, jolting me to my senses. There was no escape from the garbled screams of the tormented girl. The tender feelings melted away, crushed by the harsh reality.

Voron was right. I wasn't his. I belonged to a man who sent people to death by torture. And Voron was his head executioner. The man who took my breath away was the right hand of a tyrant.

I shrank away from him.

"I'm not yours. I don't want to belong to anyone. Definitely

228

not to a man who kills and tortures people. Or to the one who does it for him."

Another ragged scream tore through the night, invading our hiding spot under the flowers.

"Why does she have to suffer, Voron?" I gripped the lapels of his coat, displacing his carefully tucked and pinned black cravat. "Why for this long? What purpose does it serve other than cruelty? How can you allow this?" I shoved at his shoulders, but he wasn't ready to let me go, flexing his arms tighter around me.

"On the king's orders." His voice sounded flat and hollow, as if he just said out loud the words spinning in his head forever.

"The typical excuse of a coward." I shoved harder against him, twisting out of his arms.

He was no better than his king but even more dangerous because Voron also appeared caring and real. My attraction to him ran deeper than the superficial fascination I'd had for King Tiane.

I stormed down the path toward the palace. I expected to hear his footsteps behind me, but instead of following me, the sound of his footfalls moved away from me, dying in the distance. I paused with my hand on the handle of the carved door to the palace.

Where was he going?

Curiosity might not be a quality King Tiane admired in a woman. It might even be dangerous, especially in Elaros. Sadly, my curiosity about Voron proved unquenchable.

Letting go of the door handle, I quietly moved along the palace wall. Bypassing the tunnel of flower arches under which Voron had kissed me, I stayed close to the bushes that lined the glowing walls of the palace, using their shade to stay out of sight of the guards watching the grounds from above.

Voron strode out from under the arches and headed straight toward the spikes with the cursed.

He didn't enter the grounds, however. His warning to me must apply to him as well. He didn't want to be caught violating the king's rules. Instead, he circled the forest of spikes, getting closer to the one impaling the girl. Here, he paused, scanned the skies above, then looked over his both shoulders before finally closing the distance separating him from the girl.

His cloak moved, momentarily expanding before falling down his shoulders again. Then, he moved away from her promptly, heading back to the flower tunnel.

As his tall, dark figure disappeared under the arches, the screams and groans of the tortured woman died down before stopping completely.

What did he do?

Unable to resist a chance to find out, I came closer, to the very edge of the grounds.

The woman hung from the spike impaling her through her torso from behind. Her back arched, her head was tipped backwards. Her eyes were closed. But her mouth remained open, chapped and bitten lips parted, with no sound coming from them anymore. The night breeze moved the few remaining strands of her hair—the only movement on this stilled body.

Thick clouds obstructed the stars and the moon now. However, the glow from the crystals in the palace walls illuminated the girl's body enough for me to see the thin clear lines on her skin. They spread like spider webs from the wound around the spike, turning the skin and the flesh underneath transparent, just like the patches of the other corpses around us.

The girl was dead. They said the torment of the promise breakers didn't end with their death, that they still suffered in the afterlife until the gods or some higher power released them. But I was glad that at least in this world, her torture was now over. I hoped and prayed that her punishment in the afterlife wouldn't take long, either.

"May you have peace at last," I whispered, reaching to stroke the limp strands of her hair that turned transparent in my fingers.

Tears welled in my eyes, making my vision blurry. A spark glimmered through the fog. It came from the place where the spike pierced the girl's chest.

I wiped the tears off with my shawl, blinking the haze away. Something glistened in the open wound of the dead body. It was a metal pin. Tiny red sparks ran along its dark surface. The pin was made with Nerifir iron, the only metal that could kill a fae. And the top of it was decorated with a feather carved from an onyx-black stone.

The last time I saw a pin like that, it was sunk into the luxurious silk of Voron's necktie. Somehow, it didn't surprise me that he would wear a deadly weapon like an iron pin next to his neck.

Reaching over the torso of the dead woman, I carefully retrieved the pin. It seemed completely clean. If there had been any particles of gore or blood clinging to its surface, they must have already turned invisible and disappeared.

I clutched the pin in my hand and ran.

The girl was finally dead, and it was because of Voron. The only mercy this poor woman got didn't come from me. It didn't come from her king, either. But from his executioner.

And I'd called him a coward.

I caught up with Voron as he opened the door to the palace. The soft glow of the crystals backlit his dark cloaked figure.

At the sound of my footsteps, he let go of the door. As he turned, his hand smoothly reached behind him, sliding out his sword from the sheath on his back. In one swift movement, he faced me with the sword thrust my way.

"Wait!" I jumped back, barely evading the blade. "It's me. Sparrow."

"By the wings of death!" He shoved the sword back into the sheath under his cloak.

"Sorry, I startled you." I wasn't scared, even as I'd merely avoided being struck by his sword.

He stretched his neck. "I don't like surprises. Don't sneak up on me like that ever again."

"You surprised me, too, tonight." I stepped closer.

His cravat was undone, its ends hanging loosely on each side of his muscular neck. The collar that the tie was supposed to hold together was now open too, showing a narrow triangle of his skin.

I slid my hand down one end of his cravat, stroking the silky material decorated with fine black lace.

"Sparrow, what are you doing?" he lowered his voice.

"You're always so impeccably put together, High General. It's surprising to find your clothes in disarray." I flicked the end of the cravat. "What happened to your tie pin, Voron?"

He grabbed my wrist but remained silent. Only the sound of his heavy breathing came from him as I raised my other hand, the one with his pin clutched in it.

I pressed my closed fist to his chest. His heartbeat was as hard as his breathing, pounding against my hand.

"I believe this is yours." I opened my fist and sank the pin back into his cravat. "You helped that woman die, didn't you? Why?"

He drew in a long breath, pausing for a moment, as if wondering about it himself.

"Because you asked me to."

His reply left me speechless. Instead of taking my hand away, I slid it between the buttons of his vest and under his shirt.

He sucked in a breath when my fingers connected with his bare skin.

"What game are you playing, little bird?"

For once, I wasn't playing. I stopped pretending that he didn't affect me, that being this close to him didn't make me wish for more. I simply did what I wanted. And I wanted to touch him.

His skin felt warm; the short hair on his chest tickled between my fingers. I leaned closer.

"No games, Voron." A silver button on his vest popped open, and I opened the one on his shirt too, exposing more of his chest. "Just you." I placed a kiss on his skin. "And me."

With a strangled growl, he gripped my arms and staggered behind the bushes growing on each side of the palace doors, taking me with him. With a snap of his fingers, the wall of the palace next to us grew dimmer. Darkness shrouded us.

Here, away from any spying eyes, he drew me to him.

"Do you want me, Sparrow?" He buried his face in my hair. Trailing his lips down the side of my face, he kissed me. Tasted me. Breathed me in. "Tell me how much you want me."

I tilted my head to give him a better access to my neck, craving more of his kisses.

"I do. I want you so much," I confessed with a needy whimper. "So much, it hurts."

"Where does it hurt, sweetheart? Tell me."

I couldn't tell him. I couldn't find the words. He slid a hand between us, and I guided it to the spot in the apex of my thighs where the need for him throbbed most urgently.

"Let me make it better," he promised in a hot whisper. "Just this once."

He hiked up my skirts, his movements hurried and fervent. My entire body vibrated in response. My breathing was so rugged and heavy, it made my throat sore.

With his warm hands splayed on my naked backside, he turned us around, bracing my back against the wall.

If I had ever been touched like that by a man before, the memories of that were long gone. The sensation of Voron's hands on me felt entirely new. Holding me against the wall, he stroked up my thigh to the hot throbbing spot between my legs, the epicenter of my need.

"Is this where it hurts, my little bird? Is this where you want me?"

I released a tortured moan in reply, pushing my hips into his hand. "Yes..."

My mind might've forgotten what sex was like, but my body remembered. It seemed to light on fire under his touch, pleasure pulsing through me in waves. I dreamed about this, about Voron touching me, kissing me, loving me just like this. Being with him now still felt like a dream.

I hooked an arm around his neck. Our eyes met for a moment. His were hooded and dark, only a thin rim of steel-gray remained around his wide, dark as night pupils.

His hair fell over his forehead, black strands mixed with white in the front. Not really white, I noticed from this close, but clear. His silver strands were transparent. The scarce light of the night broke in them with iridescence, shining through them.

"Voron…" I parted my lips.

His mouth claimed mine, his heady taste invading my senses. I clawed at his chest inside his shirt. I wished we had fewer clothes on. I wished to feel him with my entire body, my bare skin against his. I wished…

He pressed firmly, working me with his deft fingers.

And all my wishes disappeared.

Only the need remained.

It swelled with hot pressure in my core. With Voron, I didn't feel shy or self-conscious. I felt wanton. I opened my legs wider, taking everything he was giving me. I tore at his buttons, peeling apart the layers that hid him from me.

"Touch me," I begged while touching him.

He tried to shift out of my reach, but I slipped my arms under his shirt and around his torso, pulling him back to me again.

"Stay." I kissed his chest. "Stay with me."

"Sparrow…" he moaned. "You'll be my demise, little bird, but what a sweet death that will be."

He slid a finger inside me, his thumb pressing on my clit. My hips bucked. I rode his hand harder, desperate for a release.

I'd wanted this for so long that the climax came way too fast. Pleasure crested and broke into white-hot fireworks of orgasm. It was a wonderful ending. But to me, it felt like a perfect beginning. A beginning of something more.

I held on to Voron, riding the last tremors of bliss. He swallowed my moans with his kisses, cupping me between my legs. I pressed into his hand, trapping it between us.

"More."

I wasn't ready to let go of him. Now that I finally broke through his barriers, I wished for it to last. I wanted to climb into his heart and live there.

But he shifted away from me. Setting me on the ground, he let my skirts fall down back in place. He adjusted the shawl over my chest, then buttoned his shirt, his fingers trembling slightly. As he closed the buttons of his vest, however, his composure returned.

"Voron?" I swayed his way, missing his body next to mine.

He gazed at me calmly, and I felt the doors in the walls around his heart slam close, locking me out again.

"Let's get you back to your room." His voice still sounded a little rough. But he acted with the usual calm demeanor of the High General I knew, not the passion of the man I longed to know.

My knees felt barely strong enough for my legs to hold me. My inner muscles spasmed deliciously with the aftershocks of the orgasm. Walking was the last thing my body wanted to do. Instead, it wanted to stretch languidly inside the loving arms wrapped around it.

But I rolled back my shoulders and took a step away from him, widening the distance between us. "I'll find the way on my own. Thank you very much."

He ignored my words. Falling in step at my side, he walked me to my room.

"Good night, Sparrow," he said with a brief nod before leaving me alone.

Once inside my bedroom, I shut the door, then leaned with my back against it and closed my eyes.

My muscles trembled from exhaustion. Warmth still tingled inside me after the one and only orgasm I ever remembered having with a man.

Voron took away my memories, but he now gave me a new one in return. And this one was all mine to keep.

Chapter Twenty-Four

SPARROW

My hand trembled slightly when I knocked on Voron's door the next morning. I had a strong urge to cancel today's lesson, unsure how to face him after what happened last night, but decided against it.

Canceling felt like a failure, as if I was hiding from him, when I hadn't done anything wrong. If we broke any rules or crossed a line, we'd done it together. Besides, I'd enjoyed it too much to feel guilty about what had happened between us.

His rejecting me right after still burned. But if I canceled our lesson, it would show him that it did. Instead, I borrowed a page from Voron's own book and pretended I didn't care.

My head held high, my shoulders squared, I willed my hand not to tremble and knocked again, firmly.

As Alcon led me to Voron's inner room, I breathed evenly. Only my heart fluttered nervously with anticipation. I wouldn't admit to anyone that one of the reasons I never canceled the lesson was because this hour spent with Voron had become the highlight of my day. The morning seemed brighter when I got to see him.

He met me at the game table outside.

"Good morning, Sparrow." His usual cool greeting helped me calm my nerves a little.

It was humid and stifling outside. Thick puffy clouds hung low, pressing the air to the ground and making it hard to breathe.

"Good morning, Voron." Avoiding his eyes, I stared at the carved feather of the pin in his necktie.

He must have more than that one pin, and I wondered if he was wearing this one on purpose. What purpose would that be? If it was to remind me about the mercy he'd granted upon my request, then it wasn't necessary. Acts of kindness couldn't be forgotten. They were rarer than precious stones in Elaros.

The tension around us wouldn't dissipate. It hung in the air thick with moisture, pressing heavily on my chest.

"Shall we?" I gestured at the game table. Maybe if we started playing, the usual friendly atmosphere of our lessons would return?

Voron didn't appear in a hurry to start the game, though. He looked rigid, standing by the game table. His thumb was tapping against the table's edge, and I wondered if he was even aware of the gesture.

"Sparrow." His voice sounded rougher than normal. "First, I want to make it clear. What happened last night can never happen again."

After the way he'd behaved right after, I assumed that much. Still, hearing him confirm that out loud added another stab to my wound. I'd rather we both pretended nothing happened, even as I doubted that would make it hurt any less.

My throat felt too dry, forcing me to swallow before replying.

"Of course, High General. You don't need to worry. I'll manage my expectations accordingly from now on."

His dark eyebrows shifted closer together, forming a deep crease in between as he studied my face. Evading his eyes, I pushed away from the game table.

"I know where I belong—in King Tiane's bed." I couldn't

resist a punch back, and I hoped it hurt him with at least a fraction of the pain his rejections had caused me. "Now, I think it's best to cancel this lesson. I have some oils to rub on my body in case His Majesty wants it tonight. At least, he's the one who has no qualms about touching me and has no remorse after."

I spun on my heel on my way to the exit but never got a chance to open the door.

Voron was right behind me. Grabbing the door frame on each side of me, he caged me.

"You told me once you wished to hate me, Sparrow." His hot breath hit the side of my neck from behind as if he were to either bite or kiss me there. "Do it. Hate me. Hate me so much, you won't stand being near me."

"Why don't *you* stay away from *me?*" I asked softly, staring at the door in front of me.

His breath traveled up my neck to my ear. He was so close, I felt the heat radiating from his body. But no part of him touched me.

"I wish I could stay away, little bird, but I can't. I pray you're stronger than me. Help me. Hate me. Gods know I've given you enough reasons to hate me."

Oh, I knew all the reasons perfectly well. I just couldn't summon a shred of hate for him anymore. My entire being reached out to him whenever he was close. And when he was away, my mind followed him wherever he went.

"I wish I could," I echoed his words. "Trust me, I still desperately wish I could hate you."

But I could only flee.

Turning the handle, I shoved at the door, practically flying out into his receiving room. Voron's men jumped to their feet, drawing their weapons.

I didn't stay long enough to hear whether Voron explained to them my sudden departure. Running to the door, I fled his rooms and made it to mine completely out of breath.

I wanted to ring for a tray of desserts and ice cream, then eat away the misery that was gnawing at my insides. But Brebie greeted me with a wide smile. A bathtub was already positioned by the fireplace, and the maids were starting the fire and arranging oils on a stand.

"Back so soon?" Brebie perked up. "Good. We'll have more time to get you ready for the king."

I t was hard to fake it. Hard to come up with jokes to make the king laugh. Hard to act sweet and merry when all I wanted was to hide in my room, eat a bucket of ice cream, and cry until I ran out of tears. It was even harder to deflect the queen's urging stares, like she had put a bet on my performance and I was her last hope to win the race.

I had to remind myself what all of this was for—to survive, to earn my place among people, instead of spending the rest of my life chained like an animal.

The palace had lost its shine to me ever since the Garden of the Cursed had been added to its grounds. I no longer viewed it as a magical place filled with beauty. Instead, I saw it for what it really was—a splendid monument to its owner's ego, filled with cruelty and pretense.

The hardest part of the dinner was to display any kind of warm feelings toward King Tiane. I searched hard for traces of the former awe I used to feel for the Sky King and couldn't find it. Even his beauty now seemed pretentious and over the top to me.

I held his plates for him, counting the courses and waiting for it to be over. After that, I listened to the performance of two incredibly talented singers whose voices interwove into a magical serenade of love and beauty.

I was physically present in the royal dining room, but my mind was numb.

"Well," the king huffed. "These singers aren't nearly as good as the siren I had a while ago."

Only now I realized he'd been fondling my breast through my poor excuse for a dress during the performance.

"You had a siren? A real one?"

"Yes," he replied proudly. "Straight from the Olathana Ocean. Sadly, she didn't last long."

"What happened to her?"

He shrugged. "She was a delicate creature, almost as weak as you are, my little human. But don't you worry." He flicked my nose. "We'll make you last longer."

My stomach sank with dread at his words, despite his smile and playful tone.

Holding my breast in the cup of his hand, he bent his thumb and scraped with the thumbnail against the fabric. The delicate material tore under pressure, his nail leaving a red welt on my skin.

I jerked away from the sting of pain. "What are you doing, Your Majesty?"

"It's not about what I'm doing, my sweet baby chick, but what I *want* to do. Come with me." He got up from his throne, making me slide off his lap to my feet.

Worry gripped my heart.

"Where are we going?"

"To my bedroom, of course." He wrapped an arm around my shoulders. "That was an excellent evening, everyone!" he announced loudly to the room. "Now, if you excuse me, I wish to retire." His eyes flashed with glee of anticipation. "Wish me an even more excellent night."

The court cheered for their king. People smiled and clapped their hands. I plastered a smile on my face, too, just to fit in. But dread had already slithered inside me, cold and gripping.

"I'm tired, Your Majesty," I said quietly, only for the king to hear. "May I be excused tonight? Some other night might be better."

"Nonsense," he huffed, leading me off the dais and to the door. "What can you possibly be tired from? From doing nothing all day? You have absolutely no use in the palace other than to make me happy."

That was the bitter truth. My only purpose in Elaros was to do whatever the Sky King wished me to do.

Voron wasn't in the room. Alcon stood by the door instead of him. But what could Voron do, even if he were here? He was the one who had handed me to King Tiane in the first place.

"Hate me, Sparrow." His voice, forceful and pleading at once, echoed in my mind.

Hate was what I had to feel for him. Nothing else. No lust, no trust, and certainly no hope of him ever becoming my savior.

Chapter Twenty-Five

SPARROW

The king left me standing alone in the middle of his bedroom while he headed to his bathing area through the arched entrance. King Tiane didn't have a bathtub brought to him whenever he wished to bathe. He had a pool carved out of marble right there in his bedroom suite.

"I'll be right back." He stretched his arms and shoulders before disappearing behind a decorative wall inside the bathing area. "Take that necklace off, will you?"

Panic struck me. The king was going to have his way with me again, and I would never learn *what* his way was.

I fisted the rock pendant of the necklace. If I refused to remove it, it was safe to assume he would find a way to do it for me, even if it meant breaking it. The king's attitude was far more direct and forceful tonight. He'd grown bored with charming me. Now, he simply went for what he wanted.

The sound of running water came from the royal bathing area, like he was washing his hands or flushing the toilet. He'd come back out here soon.

Hurriedly, I opened the closure of the necklace and took it off but didn't put it away. Instead, I loosened my corset, the only piece of clothing I'd kept on after my first night with the king. He didn't bother removing it the last time, probably because the under-bust corset didn't block his access to the parts of my body he wished to touch.

Wrapping the necklace around my waist, I closed it. It was just long enough to fit like a belt. Then I tightened the ribbons of my corset and tied them back up, hiding Voron's necklace under the corset.

The king strolled in through the arched exit from the bathing area.

"A drink?" He took a crystal carafe from a stand by his bed and poured two glasses of the dreaded shimmering blue-and-pink liquid into them.

His words sounded like a question, but he wasn't asking or offering. He shoved the glass into my hand, proving it was an order.

I feigned a smile and made one last attempt to avoid, or at least postpone, the inevitable.

"Would you like to play a game, Your Majesty? I've been learning how to play War of Kings. We can—"

"Now why would you bother learning that?" he cut me off.

"To be able to entertain you in more ways than this." I gestured at the glasses in his hands.

"You're too cute." He grinned. "But I already have lots of people to play War of Kings with. I need you for a very different game, sweet baby chick. Now drink." He tipped his chin at the glass in my hand. "Don't make me wait."

He took a few sips from his glass, watching me closely as I drank from mine. He didn't take his eyes off me until I finished it all, to the very last drop.

Holding my breath, I braced for the onset of carefree dizziness. But it didn't come. Voron's necklace on my body neutralized the effects of *camyte* and glacial saffron. Now, I hoped it would also prevent the king from taking away the memories of the upcoming night.

Despite the trepidation buzzing through me with warning, I needed to know what the king did to me. Maybe once I knew, I could figure out how to protect myself in the future.

The king took my empty glass from me, then trailed a finger around my neck where Voron's necklace used to be.

"Good girl," he murmured. "Isn't it so much easier when you just do what you're told?"

I kept smiling, not saying a word. The king didn't appear to care whether I answered, anyway.

From a trunk by the far wall, he produced what looked like a long jewelry box made from dark metal, with cut-outs shaped like swirls. A yellow glow filtered through the cut-outs.

"Today, I have something far more precious for my dearest pet than a simple hunting knife we played with last time. You deserve the best." Opening the box, the king took out a narrow black dagger. "It arrived just this morning. I can't wait to try it on you."

A knife?

On me?

My insides froze with horror.

The metal of the blade was dark, like Nerifir iron. Unlike the iron, however, the dagger sparkled with neon yellow light instead of red.

"Come, my sweet, little human." He grinned. "Let the fun begin."

He headed toward a tall shelf across from his bed, clearly expecting me to follow him. My feet rooted into the marble floor, however, and I couldn't move. Wherever he was he going with that blade, I didn't want to be there.

The king pressed on a vine on the side of the shelf unit, and it slid aside, opening a hidden staircase.

"Are you coming?" He squinted at me over his shoulder.

A shadow of suspicion drew over his blue gaze. If I didn't obey fully and completely, he'd know I was still wearing the necklace. I hurried after him, keeping the carefree smile plastered on my face.

The king led me down a white metal staircase into a round room below. All-white crystals in the walls here shone brightly.

A high metal table stood in the middle, long enough for a person to lie on. Its shiny gold surface had a raised edge along the entire perimeter, as if to keep the contents from spilling over. My heart sank into my stomach even before I could speculate on what those contents might be.

Behind the table, a large cross shaped like the letter "x" was attached to the wall, with a polished manacle dangling from each of its four ends. Next to it, a cluster of golden chains hung from the ceiling with bejeweled leather belts of various lengths.

My head was spinning. The huge amount of gold and gems packed in here made this room look like a royal treasury. Except that all these treasures were used in devices clearly meant for some sinister purpose. Tiny spikes were embedded into the polished surface of the cross and the sharp blades were positioned inside the belts, clearly meaning to harm the person wearing them. The vast collection of blades and spiky balls on chains displayed on the wall opposite from the cross also told me this room was meant for torture, not pleasure.

I froze at the bottom of the stairs, suddenly wishing the *camyte* had worked on me. Whatever the king was planning for me tonight, I would not be able to go through without the numbing effects of the drink. Obviously, that was the reason he made me drink it in the first place, to make me complacent and more manageable for him.

The king lovingly stroked the golden surface of the table.

"I'll tell you a revelation I had not so long ago, little pet," he spoke to me without taking his eyes off the table. "After decades of trying anything possible and beyond, I've realized that I enjoy making love to my own body far more than pleasuring anyone else's." He lifted his eyes to me. "There simply isn't anyone more attractive than me. Why would I waste my time on anything far superior than *this?*" He pointed down his torso with an elegant gesture. "I prefer my own hand to any slimy hole of someone else. But the queen insists I breed you." He shrugged. "So be it. Only I need to do it in my own way." He patted the table. "Hop on. Let's make it exciting, shall we?"

My legs felt like cotton. I barely made a step toward him without tipping over. He gripped me around my waist, then lifted me onto the table. Kicking my knees open, he wedged his hips between them.

"You see, my sweet, sex doesn't excite me much anymore. When you can fuck anyone you want in any way you wish, it becomes boring."

He knew he would make me forget this night, including everything he was saying right now. For once, he had no reason to lie or pretend. This was the most candid the king would ever be with me.

With the black and yellow dagger, he calmly cut off the scarfs that served as the bodice of my dress.

"You have the most magnificent tits. Truly, the best in the kingdom." He cupped one of my breasts, lifting it in his hand. "I know most of my court are salivating to get their hands and mouths on these." He kneaded my breast, smacking his lips appreciatively. "Only tits no longer excite me. Cocks were fun for a while, but I grew bored with them, too. That is the curse of having *everything*, my baby chick. Sooner or later, the novelty wears off and everything becomes dull." He leaned closer to me, whispering into my ear even as there was no one else to hear him, "But there is still something that makes my cock as hard as a sword. The *only* thing."

Without a warning, he slashed with the blade, so fast, I had no chance to scream. Pain seared my skin. Blood beaded from the hair-thin cut on my breast. It trickled down to my nipple.

I bit my tongue, trying not to scream, and fisted my hands so hard, my fingernails dug into the skin of my palms.

There was no way I could go through with this. No way I would survive this night.

A whimper escaped me, despite my best efforts.

"Does it hurt?" The king glanced at my face.

The tears welling in my eyes were impossible to hide.

"Good." He beamed.

Camyte would've dulled the pain, but it would not have eliminated it completely. Which was what the king wanted, it seemed. He thrived on my pain. The sight of my blood thrilled him.

My chest heaved with shallow panicky breaths.

"Mmm." The king moaned in pleasure. Lifting my breast, he licked under the nipple, catching a drop of my blood on his tongue.

"I can't do this to a fae," he murmured against my skin, his lips smearing blood over my areola. "My High General even took down my Garden of the Cursed this morning. I don't give a fuck what he thinks, but the Royal Council sided with him. They're afraid of riots. Apparently, my giving the cursed what they deserve upsets *my people*." Sarcasm curved his blood-stained lips. "The plain merchants of Elaros and the dirty peasants of Sky Kingdom are 'upset,' you see? I'm the Sky King, and I can't do what I want because of some lowborns from farms and villages!" His voice lifted with an indignant shriek.

He straightened his back, drawing in a long breath to collect himself. As he caressed the cut on my breast with his thumb, a smile appeared on his face once again.

"Thankfully, no one cares what I do with *you*. You're not a fae. You aren't even an animal. You're something in between, beyond our laws—a human, mine to do with as I please. And do you know what the taste of your blood does to me?"

He placed the dagger on the table next to me, then yanked at the laces of his pants.

"Feel this." He grabbed my hand and shoved it into the opening of his pants.

His erection jerked against my hand. Squeezing my breast, he dragged his tongue along the cut, lapping at the blood. His dick grew harder, trapping my hand in the tight confines of his pants.

"Do you feel it, my pet? Do you feel how much my cock loves this?"

Bile rose in my throat. There was not a trace of a smile on my face any longer. I couldn't manage one even if I tried. Horror and disgust filled me. The urge to flee pounded inside my head. It was all I could do not to bolt.

He raked his teeth down my breast, then closed them over my nipple, biting down so hard, I screamed in pain.

The king grinned, his lips smeared with blood, his erection hard as rock in my hand.

"That's right, scream." His voice came out hoarse with arousal. His sky-blue eyes darkened with need. He thrust his hips, riding my hand. "My cock will impale you like the wooden spike going through the asses of the cursed. Hard and unforgiving. I'll make you writhe on it, begging for mercy like they did when the wood drove through them, tearing through their insides."

He sounded delirious, lost to whatever perverted pleasure his own words plunged him into. Repulsion roiled through my stomach, making me gag.

He shoved harder against me, and I dropped my other hand to the table for balance. My fingers fell on the cold blade of the dagger he'd left there.

I had no time to think it through. No mental capacity to do it, either. My mind was reeling, shocked by the monstrous being King Tiane, the majestic swan of Elaros, had turned out to be.

Flexing my fingers around his dick, I squeezed hard, digging my nails into his silky skin.

He choked on his breath. His mouth dropped open.

With my other hand, I grabbed the blade from the table and stabbed the king in the chest. It scraped past his rib on its way into his flesh.

Either way, I was not going to survive this night. But at least

I'd go down fighting. Sinking the dagger all the way up to its handle, I shoved the king away.

He staggered back, shock swimming in his wide-open eyes. He hadn't expected this. He couldn't believe his meek, chubby baby chick had fought back.

"Hey, Your Majesty," I gritted through my teeth. "Want to hear a funny story? How about the one where a mousy sparrow cuts off the dick of a royal swan? I promise, there's lots of blood. Just maybe not in the way you like it."

I hopped off the table. There was nowhere to run. The guards stood at the doors of the king's chambers day and night. The king wouldn't let me get to the doors or the guards, anyway. As soon as he had recovered from shock, he would end me right here, in this weird golden room under his bedroom. He was a fae, after all, one wound to the chest wouldn't stop him.

All I hoped for was to make it as hard as possible for him to kill me.

I leaped to the wall decorated with the torture equipment and grabbed a golden knife in each hand, ready to slash at anyone who came at me.

But no one did.

The king took another shaky step backwards, his mouth agape, horror spreading on his face. Then, he crashed to the ground, flinging his arms aside.

He couldn't be dead. A single stab of a dagger wouldn't kill a fae, especially, since the blade wasn't even made from Nerifir iron. His chest was still moving with his breathing.

Was it a trap?

Was the king waiting for me to get closer, only to pounce on me when I did?

Holding my knives ready, I circled the room, careful to keep the table between the king and me at all times.

The yellow glow of the dagger embedded in the king's chest grew brighter. It shone through his flesh. Its handle pulsed with the king's heartbeat. But he wouldn't move. His eyes remained open, staring up at the ceiling. He didn't blink. Blood trickled from his wound, pooling under his back.

Did I really do it? Did I somehow kill the king?

I pressed the back of my right hand to my mouth. The dagger clutched in my fist trembled. I struggled to collect my thoughts.

This was unexpected, but the king seemed fully incapacitated. For now, at least.

Was this my chance to run?

If only I knew *where*.

I couldn't stay here, though. Sooner or later, someone would come in. I had to get out of here, not just out of the king's chambers, but out of Elaros. The moment they discovered the king dead, they would come for me. Everyone knew I was with him tonight. Everyone saw us leaving the dining room together.

Panic spurred me into action. I knew I would die the moment I came down these stairs. Every minute since was borrowed and an unexpected gift.

I had to use the time I won.

Carefully stepping around the motionless king, I ran up the stairs. Leaving through the bedroom door was not an option. The guards would see me right away. Someone might want to come in to check on the king, and I'd be caught.

I checked the floor-to-ceiling windows quickly. There were lots of them in this giant room. Two happened to be doors leading to a patio without a railing or a parapet. The king didn't need the railing since, unlike Voron or me, he had wings.

The river that ran in front of the palace bent around the structure on this side. The riverbank was so close to the wall below, I could possibly land in the water if I jumped from the very edge of the patio. The water in the river would break my fall, then I could swim across to the forest on the other side. *If* I knew how to swim, which I didn't remember.

But what choice did I have?

I ran back inside the king's bedroom and found the door that led to his dressing room, which turned out to be an entire suite of rooms on its own. Located on several levels interconnected by carved staircases, the king's wardrobe could've possibly housed his entire court.

There was a room only for his shoes and one just for his jewelry. Another one held a collection of various creams, gels, and jars filled with shimmering paste of every color.

Rummaging through the open trunks and dressers, I snatched the darkest cloak I could find, found a pair of pants made of a material that was neither see-through nor shimmering, and a short tunic that still reached down to my knees when I put it on.

Grabbing a satchel from one of the trunks, I stuffed it with the desserts from the snack tray by the king's bedroom. Then I tucked one of the golden knives from the king's room of torture into the tunic.

When I ran back out to the patio, however, fear descended upon me. Elaros Palace was an incredibly tall structure. The king's rooms took up one of its highest towers. The wide river looked narrow from up here. Even if I did land right in the middle of its stream, I risked broken bones, if not outright death.

What was better, dying by execution for murder or by breaking bones and drowning?

I didn't like the choice I faced. I never wished to have wings as much as I did now.

Crawling on my belly to the very edge of the patio, I searched for something I could use to possibly climb down the wall.

A door opened a few floors down, on a nearby tower.

"Fine, surprise me!" I heard the familiar feminine voice.

It was Dove. She sounded cheerful, as if she was in another world somewhere, where murders didn't happen and executions weren't a threat.

"I'm not looking," she laughed, walking out to the balcony. "I'll wait out here with my eyes closed, no peeking."

Completely naked, save for a bejeweled choker around her slender neck and a pair of matching bangles, she stretched in the glow of the palace crystals. She looked so beautiful, like an onyx statue topped with silky white curls and a pair of angelic wings.

Wings. Dove had wings. The height wouldn't be an issue for her.

But would she be willing to help me? Could I trust her not to call the guards?

I had no time to ponder. I needed help, and I had no one else. I had to take this risk.

She tilted her head back, and I called softly, "Dove."

"Sparrow?" she gasped, then smiled brightly. "Look at you up there! All the way on the very top."

Right. I'd made it high. So high, the fall would kill me. Literally.

The winged silhouettes of the guards patrolling the grounds came in and out of the palace glow. Afraid to attract their attention, I waved at Dove to fly up to me.

She arched a white-blond eyebrow, glanced over her shoulder at the closed door to her room, then shrugged.

"Sure, why not?" Spreading her wings, she flew up and landed on the patio next to me. "Where is the king?"

"Um...in the bathroom." I said the first thing that came to mind. "I need your help."

"Like what? Do you need some unicorn dust? It does wonders in getting men *excited*." She leaned closer, whispering in my ear. "I've heard lately it can take some effort to get King Tiane *up to the task*. If you know what I mean." She winked.

"No. It's not that..." How could I ask her to help me escape? Wouldn't that make her an accomplice in murder? I couldn't risk Dove's life. I couldn't drag her into this mess with me.

"Ooh," she teased. "You don't need any help to get him hard, do you? That means you've accomplished more than most. No wonder the king is so smitten with you."

He was smitten alright. Smitten all the way to the floor with a dagger sticking from his chest.

I drew in a shaky breath, coming up with the story on the spot.

"Actually, he isn't as much into me as everyone believes."

Dove's eyes flashed with excitement in anticipation of gossip. "He isn't?"

"No. Not even close. In fact, I think he's going to send me away after tonight."

"Where?"

Onto a spike. Under an axe. Onto a scaffold. Into a noose... However they would decide to execute me.

I closed my eyes, drawing in some air slowly, in an attempt to calm my nerves.

"To the menagerie, most likely," I said in a hollow voice.

"Oh, sweetie, that's awful." She spread her arms to take me in.

There was genuine empathy in her voice, which disarmed me. I leaned into her hug, trying not to break into tears.

Dove patted my shoulder. "Not all is lost. Maybe you're mistaken. Or he'll change his mind." I shook my head, but she continued optimistically, "We shall petition Queen Pavline to keep you here. And High General Voron. The queen is fond of you. And Voron is friendly with you, isn't he?"

Even if I hated Voron, I couldn't ask him to help me get away with such a grave crime like murder. I couldn't ask him to risk his life for me.

"He'll be returning to Elaros tomorrow," Dove said.

"Who? Voron? I didn't know he left."

"Yes, he did, this afternoon. On the king's orders."

"Where did he go?"

She hiked up a shoulder. "I don't know. Some boring state business, most likely. But he'll be back tomorrow. We can talk to him then—"

"No." I shook my head. "You know, Dove, no one can argue with the king if he has his mind set. I need to leave. That's the only way."

"Leave where?" She blinked at me.

MARINA SIMCOE

"There is a world outside of the palace and Elaros City, isn't there? We don't get to see it often, but it exists. People live there. I could find a place among them, too."

"Do you mean the human world?"

I didn't consider that yet. I was speaking of the rolling hills of Sky Kingdom, the farms and the towns I had no chance to see yet.

"Will you go back home?" Dove asked.

The human world hardly felt like home to me now. But I couldn't disregard that possibility, either. No one here would find me if I crossed the River of Mists.

I sighed. "If I have to. But I'll try to make it in Sky Kingdom first."

My priority right now was to get as far from the palace as possible.

"Can you fly me across that river below, please?"

"Across the river?" She glanced down over the edge of the terrace. "Why?"

"I'll hide in the forest on the other side."

She gave me a horrified look.

"Oh, Sparrow, that's insane. It's too dark. And there are bugs and wild animals in there."

I shook my head. "I'm not afraid of animals. Anything is better than being locked up."

The animals wouldn't hurt me just for fun. In that aspect, they were kinder than some people.

"Are you sure?"

She was clearly worried about me. But Dove didn't know how much more dangerous it was for me to stay. Or maybe she was worried about the consequences of helping me? In which case, her concerns were warranted.

"Please, Dove. I promise never to tell anyone you helped me, not even if they catch me."

"Pfff," she huffed with the typical self-assurance of a high-born. "I'm not afraid. They can't do anything to me. But I'm

254

concerned about how you're going to survive out there on your own."

"I'll have to try."

She rubbed her forehead.

"All right. Listen. You'll have to take these, at least." She unclipped a wide golden bangle from around her left wrist and snapped it around mine. She then did the same with the left, too. "They have enough gold and jewels in them to last you for some time. Go to Nalore Village. Do you see that high hill over there?" She turned my head all the way to the right, pointing at the large mass far on the horizon. "The Nalore Village is on the right side of it, in the foothills. Find the *snakana* Asfekadi. She used to be one of my nannies about two decades ago."

I didn't realize Dove was so young as to need a nanny just twenty years ago. She couldn't be much older than me, then.

"Will you remember?" she insisted. "Asfekadi from Nalore Village. Tell her I sent you. She will help."

"Thank you."

She glanced over her shoulder, watching the guards making their rounds in the sky. As soon as the closest group of them disappeared around the turrets, Dove grabbed me around my middle and leaped from the patio.

"Let's go."

A gasp stuck in my throat. I gripped her shoulders as the night air rushed by us.

Her wide white wings moved softly above us, like the wings of an angel. And right now, that was exactly what she was to me— my angel, taking me away from the murder scene I was responsible for and the deadly consequences I'd face if I stayed.

Instead of flying straight across the river, Dove covered the distance in sections. First, she took me to another patio, a few floors down, then down to a lower turret, moving closer and closer to the ground.

Her tactic served two purposes. First, it helped us evade the guards. And second, when she finally took me across the river, even if anyone saw us, no one could tell we came from the king's tower.

"Here is good?" Dove set me down on the opposite bank of the river behind the tree line. "Ew, bugs..." She shook her wings, running her fingers through her brilliant feathers to get rid of the few leaves stuck between them. "I can't stand flying through the trees."

"Thank you for doing it for me," I said sincerely.

"Do you want me to try and fly you all the way to Nalore Village? I mean, I'd need to get some clothes on, and such..."

That was a generous and a very tempting offer. I felt grateful for Dove even suggesting it, but I couldn't accept it.

"You already risked a lot, Dove." More than she even realized. "Someone may see you with me. Or they will notice you're gone from Elaros."

"Right," she remembered. "Lord Colomb is waiting for me. The poor thing is probably already wondering where I am. He can't even go look for me."

"Why not?"

She flicked her wrist with a shrug. "He's tied to my bed."

"He is? Why?"

She grinned. "He finds it sexy to make love that way. And I don't mind. He wanted to surprise me with a new position he's been practicing."

"While being tied up?"

"Mhm." She nodded, tousling her curls. "I better go before he twisted his neck or broke something. Well..." She drew me into a hug, wrapping both her arms and her wings around me. "Stay alive, little Sparrow. Send me a message when you've settled down, and I'll let you know how it's going in the palace. Sooner or later, things will calm down. You may come back still."

I doubted it would ever be safe for me to come back or even to send Dove a message without compromising her safety. But I couldn't think that far into the future. I simply tried to keep my head on my shoulders for a day longer.

"Thank you so much for everything, Dove." I let go of her reluctantly, then watched her take off into the air.

Her white wings moved gracefully. Her skin shimmered over her delicate curves, gloriously nude and dark like the starless night that eventually took her out of my sight.

Chapter Twenty-Six

VORON

He'd barely gotten off his horse in the courtyard of Elaros when Alcon landed softly in front of him.

"Greetings, High General. Glad to have you back. Her Majesty, Queen Pavline, demanded to see you the moment you return."

Voron tossed the reins to the approaching *snakana* groom, then took off his riding gloves.

"*Demanded,* did she?"

Alcon shifted his weight to another foot uneasily. "'Bring him to me the moment he arrives,' were her actual words."

Voron entered the palace and made sure they were a fair distance away from the guards before asking. "Where is she?"

"In the king's chambers?"

"Really?" He paused.

It'd been a while since the queen had stepped her foot into her husband's bedroom or since the king had visited hers.

"Did she say why I'm needed?"

"No, my general, but..." With a cautious glance around,

Alcon leaned closer and lowered his voice. "It must be about Lady Sparrow. She's gone."

The mere sound of her name sent a surge of thrill through his system, that specific mix of agitation and delight he'd been experiencing in any situation where Sparrow was involved.

This time, however, worry pinched his heart, too.

"Gone where?"

"No one knows. The queen ordered a thorough search of the palace, but we couldn't find her. The royal guards are combing through the streets of Elaros City right now. So far, no results."

"What happened? Did she leave by herself or was she taken?" He sped up, rushing up the stairs on his way to the top tower.

Alcon barely kept up with him, using his wings to give him a lift over the steps that Voron skipped over without flying.

"We... I don't know, High General," Alcon panted.

Voron growled in disappointment. He'd trained his people better than that. They were supposed to know *everything*.

"Lady Sparrow retired for the night after the dinner with the king." Alcon gave Voron a sideways glance, as if gauging his reaction to the news. "The king took her to his bedroom. That was the last time she was seen by the guards."

Bile burned Voron's throat. His hands flexed into fists, ready to punch something. The news of Sparrow spending nights with the king should not affect him so. She belonged to King Tiane. The very purpose of her presence at the palace was to entertain him.

He knew it, but it still wrecked him to learn she went to the royal chambers when he left the palace to save Magnus days ago.

Yesterday, the king had sent him on a mostly useless mission outside of Elaros, to deliver a message from the king to High Lord Morennor—an errand that a cloud owl could've accomplished just as successfully. Now, he understood why the king did it.

Voron had put an effort into keeping King Tiane away from his new favorite by organizing activities that didn't involve her and distracting the king. The king must have finally caught on to that and sent him away from the palace to enjoy her company one-on-one with no interruptions.

And now she was gone.

How the fuck had it happened?

He stormed into the king's bedroom. The queen might be demanding his presence, but he was the one needing answers.

"What's going on here?" He kicked the doors close behind him.

Dressed in a pale morning robe, her hair tucked into a colorful turban, Queen Pavline stood in front of the royal bed. The spider silk curtains were drawn close around the bed.

The queen wasn't alone. The High Priest and the royal hag were sitting in the chairs nearby.

"Ah, Voron. Finally," the queen huffed as if he'd been absent for his own frivolous reasons and not on the king's orders. He derived no pleasure in meeting that pompous, pretentious peacock High Lord Morennor.

"What happened here?" he asked again.

The queen threw her hands up in the air. "That's what we've been trying to figure out, High General. It looks like your nasty human protégé tried to kill my husband."

"Sparrow? Kill?"

It made no sense whatsoever.

"Who else?" the queen hissed, sarcasm dripping from her lips like venom. "Thanks for delivering that little viper to our home, Voron."

No one objected to Sparrow's presence in Elaros before. Queen Pavline used to call her "sent by gods." Whatever happened must be extreme to change her opinion so drastically and literally overnight. But "tried to kill?" Surely, that was an exaggeration. Sparrow wouldn't hurt a fly, would she?

"You may think of me as a weak little bird. But I am a person, and I am not weak. Sooner or later, I'll prove it to you."

The words Sparrow had said to him the day after they met echoed through his brain.

She had been mistaken, though. He never thought her weak. He saw her resilience the very first moment he laid his eyes on her on the road to the Cloud River on that windy, gloomy day. Stolen from her world and incapacitated by *camyte*, she never lost awareness and determination in her eyes.

He named her Sparrow as the most underestimated bird of all. Even back then, as she shivered in the wind, he sensed she had strength far beyond her short, gentle stature.

But an attempted murder?

He never expected that from her. *Underestimated* proved to be more accurate than even he could've predicted.

"What did she do?"

The queen frowned. "Come look for yourself."

He followed her closer to the royal bed, and she threw the curtains open.

King Tiane lay in the middle of his spacious bed, sinking into the white, silky bedding. His head, adorned with the majestic antlers, rested on a pillow. A luxurious bed spread covered him up to his waist, leaving his bare chest exposed.

A bejeweled handle of a dagger was sticking out from the king's chest, the blade buried deep in his flesh. A web of hair-thin lines spread from the dagger. These weren't the typical clear lines of sky fae's decomposition. They pulsed with a bright yellow glow.

The king's eyes were closed, but his chest rose and fell evenly with his breathing.

"Can I speak with him?" Voron asked.

The queen shook her head with a mournful expression. "He hasn't opened his eyes since we found him like this."

"Is he asleep? Unconscious?"

The High Priest stirred in his seat, smoothing the folds of his long golden robe over his blue *snakana* tail. "His Majesty is neither sleeping nor dead. He is not alive, either. He's—"

The queen interrupted him with a sob.

"See what that human girl did?" She snapped her teeth, as if wishing to sink them into Sparrow. "I need her found and brought to justice."

"Are you sure it was Sparrow who did it?" He really had a hard time wrapping his mind around that.

"Who then? She was the only one here with him."

He ran a hand through his hair, pondering what would drive Sparrow to such a drastic action.

"This dagger is not from Sky Kingdom," he noted. "It glows with the magic of Under."

The queen must've known that already. She threw her hand over her mouth, muffling her tortured gasp.

"Leave us," she snapped over her shoulder at the High Priest and the royal hag.

The two got up silently and exited the bedroom through the door that led to one of the king's many sitting and entertainment rooms inside his sprawling suite.

The moment he was left alone with the queen, she moved on to him.

"The human brought this vile weapon into the palace. I want you to find and bring her to me. She needs to answer for her crimes."

"The dagger isn't Sparrow's," he replied firmly. "I know every single contact she's ever made since coming to Sky Kingdom, everyone she's ever spoken to. There is simply no way she could've sourced a weapon like that."

"But she was the one who stabbed the Sky King with it!" the queen screeched. "I want her punished."

He pinched the bridge of his nose with his fingers. He knew the dagger didn't belong to Sparrow. But the queen was right on one thing: Sparrow had to be found. There was nothing but danger for a young human girl out there, unprotected.

"Who was the person who found the king? Can I speak to them?"

"No."

He raised a questioning look at the queen. "No?"

"No," she repeated quickly. "Those servants are no longer here."

"Where are they?"

She blew out a breath impatiently. "That's not what I need you to investigate, Voron. I want you to find the human."

"To do so, I need to know what exactly happened here."

Rubbing her forehead, she paced the spacious room.

"You can't know it all. No one can. Even I don't know everything," she kept muttering under her breath as if talking to herself, then stopped suddenly right in front of him. "The king was found lying in his own blood, on the floor."

"Where?"

"In one of the rooms he uses to entertain his guests in."

"Which one?" He was very familiar with the layout of the palace, including the king's suite.

"It's a secret room, reserved for special guests only. And no." She raised her hand, stopping his next question. "You can't see it. No one can."

He folded his arms across his chest. "It'll be hard to investigate the crime without seeing the crime scene, don't you think?"

"There isn't much to investigate. King Tiane retired to his bedroom with the human girl. The next morning, he was found wounded, lying in a pool of his own blood, with the perpetrator gone." She glanced back at the king on the bed. "According to the royal hag, the dagger is cursed. It can't be removed from the wound, as the king's life is tethered to it. His spirit can't leave for the afterlife, yet he isn't alive either. My husband is suspended between this world and the next. We're looking for a way to bring him back. Meanwhile, I need you to search for the girl. Take as many people as you need."

What use was having people if he didn't know where to direct them? He needed information.

"That 'special' room you were talking about. How many exits does it have?"

She shifted uneasily, wrapping her arms around herself and looking oddly uncomfortable speaking about that place. "One."

"Where does it lead?"

"Here."

He swept the bedroom with his gaze, not seeing any doors other than those he already knew about. Of course, the queen had mentioned it was a hidden room.

"The guards saw Sparrow coming in here," he said, lining up the events of last night in his mind.

"Yes, she came with the king."

He imagined the king leading her through the door, toward this very bed.

Against his best efforts to stop it, the images of them being together assaulted his mind's vision. The king kissing her, caressing her body that Voron had touched just once and never stopped wishing for more ever since.

He'd spend the rest of that night licking her scent off his fingers and pumping his long-suffering cock again and again until his arm ached and his hand cramped. He'd made himself come at least a half dozen times. And still, he hadn't satisfied his cravings for her.

He'd hoped that letting his restraints snap that one time in the gardens would take the edge off. That it would allow him to get on with his life just the way it was before the intriguing little human entered it.

After he'd kissed Sparrow and made her come on his hand, however, his thirst for her only grew. The cravings bordered an addiction. Even worse, so many other feelings blended in with lust, the feelings he never had for anyone.

Voron wanted Sparrow. Desperately.

King Tiane had her. He was free to enjoy her with no restraints, no promises to hold him back. Yet the king had blown it, horribly.

Now, the king was in a sad state, and Sparrow was gone.

"Is anything missing from the suite?" he asked the queen.

"What? Oh..." She glanced around, looking uncertain. "I don't know."

"Get the king's chamber groom, the maids, and the wardrobe master to go over everything to determine if anything is missing. I want every single item accounted for—clothes, shoes, jewelry."

"All right. We'll do it." The queen didn't even try to question him giving her orders.

He circled the bedroom slowly, paying attention to every detail. Not familiar enough with the king's quarters to notice if anything was out of place, he just tried to imagine Sparrow in this space.

Was she elated to be in the royal chambers?

Every woman he knew would be ecstatic to make it this high. Sparrow seemed enthralled by King Tiane, too, especially at the beginning.

But Voron noticed a subtle change in her lately. During their lessons, she didn't seem as eager to learn the game, content just to have tea with him and talk. She still seemed to enjoy playing, but she learned it at a more leisurely pace lately, without the fervent enthusiasm of the early days.

The way she looked at the king had changed, too. Instead of the wide-eyed admiration of before, her expression had turned more guarded. She acted and spoke far more cautiously. He'd written it off to her learning and adjusting to the life of court. Now, he feared something else might've been happening, something he'd been too distracted to notice. And now, it might be too late.

He inspected each window carefully. All of them were warded with magic. No one could enter the room through them without the king's invitation. Sparrow, of course, had been invited since the king brought her here himself. She could enter and exit freely. But she had no wings. She couldn't just fly out of the window.

He walked out onto the patio. The Elaros River glistened far below. The forest wedged into the glowing streets of the city, reaching the opposite riverbank.

Jumping from the patio would possibly land one into the river. Of course, the impact of a fall from this height would probably break every bone in Sparrow's fragile human body. But unless she was stolen by someone with wings, this would be the only way for her to leave this room.

He turned to the queen, who watched him nervously, crushing the precious fabric of her robe in her hands.

"I want you to promise me that Sparrow will not be harmed," he said. "She deserves a fair investigation and trial."

The queen jerked her head, her high turban swaying.

"You're not in the position to demand promises from me, High General. Find me that girl!" she yelled. "That's an order. The crown you swore to protect and whose orders you promised to obey is now mine. Do as I say, or you'll end up on a spike as a promise breaker."

He gritted his teeth, waiting for the rage from her words to subside. Thank gods he'd had a lot of practice controlling his emotions in general, including rage.

"I'll go alone. Call off the search in Elaros City."

"Alone?" She huffed. "It'll take you an eternity. You can't even fly!"

"Neither can Sparrow."

The queen's mention of his main shortcoming felt like a slap on the face, but he didn't flinch. He'd lived a lifetime without wings. He'd heard every possible insult already. He'd certainly learned how to hide the hurt well.

"Your Majesty knows the lack of wings has never held me back from succeeding where I wished to succeed." He marched to the door. "I'll find Sparrow. Dead or alive." *Alive*, he wished desperately. *Please, gods, let her be alive.* "And I'll bring her back for your merciful judgment."

Chapter Twenty-Seven

SPARROW

A drenaline kept me going. I had to get as far from the palace as possible. Yet every time I looked behind me, the glow of Elaros loomed against the cloudy sky, larger than ever.

On the other hand, the crystal light made the navigation easier. Both the moon and the stars were hidden behind thick clouds. All I had to do was to keep the multi-colored shimmer of the Sky Palace behind me to stay on course.

I was too scared to stop for a rest and walked through the night, listening to every noise. But as the sun rose behind the clouds, coloring the black skies gray, exhaustion weighed me down, making me stumble and trip.

The pampered life in Elaros hadn't prepared me for strenuous physical exercise. My walks in the gardens couldn't compare to the long hike through the woods. I needed to rest.

I'd been scared to sleep at night. But during the day, the forest didn't look as intimidating. Besides, the royal guards would probably be searching for me right now. It would be better to hide for a while.

By mid-morning, I stumbled onto a tiny clearing in the woods, with a tall tree in the middle. The tree's wide canopy sprawled over most of the clearing, shielding it from anyone who might be flying over it. The ground under the tree was covered in dark moss-like plants that climbed halfway up the trunk. Slightly taller than moss, the plants looked just as soft, with tiny black flowers at the end of each curved stem. It seemed like a good enough place for me to get some rest.

I spread the king's cloak over the flowers, then took out the food I'd stolen from the tray in the king's bedroom. Sugary macarons and crème-filled wafers weren't the most nutritious options, but they were all I could get my hands on before my escape. At least the sugar would give me some energy to keep going.

There was no water around, but I'd drunk plenty from a creek a while back. I ate a little, leaving some for later, then brushed the crumbs off my hands and licked the crème from my fingers.

Despite my utter exhaustion, I sensed that sleep would be hard to come. The thoughts about King Tiane didn't leave me. The fear and repulsion he'd caused in me were still there. But there was also a genuine sadness and regret.

I'd never planned to kill anyone. And despite everything the king had done to me, I wished he was alive. I hoped never to see him again, but I didn't want him dead.

The sound of a twig snapping sent me to my feet in panic. I whipped around, my heart pounding in my throat.

Voron!

Really?

He stood at the edge of the clearing, holding the broken twig in his hands.

With a smug smirk, he tossed the twig aside. He'd clearly demonstrated how easily he'd managed to sneak up on me. To add insult to injury, he led a horse by the reins. Magnus was sitting on the saddle horn, cleaning his feathers. I hadn't heard any of them approach, not until Voron deliberately snapped that twig to get my attention.

Unbelievable. The man was truly omnipresent—inescapable.

"How in the world did you find me?" I couldn't have hidden my shock even if I tried.

Leaning with his shoulder against the nearest tree trunk, he crossed his arms over his chest.

"You were so easy to track, little bird, it was an insult to my skills. You left a trail of clues as wide as a herd of wetland hippos."

I was annoyed he'd found me so effortlessly and worried about what he'd do next. But deep under the concern and irritation, I was actually glad to see him. Somehow, I'd been conditioned to associate Voron's presence with safety and security. The man might be dragging me to the gallows before the day was over, but all I could think about right now was how strong his arms felt around me and how much I wished for him to hug me.

The bastard also had the guts to smile, as if he, too, was happy to see me.

Scraping a hand over my face, I forced my brain to focus. If he came to arrest me, he didn't seem in a hurry to grab me, instead playing with me like a cat with a mouse.

I scanned the trees around the clearing.

Could I evade him if I ran?

His legs were significantly longer than mine. It was safe to assume he was in much better physical shape, too. But I was shorter. And without a horse in tow to slow me down, I could slip between the bushes and duck under the low tree branches that might slap him in the face or knock him out of the saddle.

He intercepted my gaze and guessed my intentions.

"Don't try to run, Sparrow. You won't make it far."

"Still worth a try." I inched closer to the trees and away from him. "What do I have to lose at this point?"

"Your life." He sounded eerily calm. "If I hadn't shown up, you would've been dead within the hour."

I propped my hands on my hips.

"That's what *you* think. I've made it through the night, just fine."

"But you wouldn't have survived the day. Were you planning to take a nap over there?" He tipped his chin at my cloak laid over the moss under the tree.

It looked like a makeshift sleeping pallet, which made it useless to deny it, so I said nothing.

"That's *ebon* weed," he said. "If you sleep on it, it'll suck your spirit out of your body and destroy your mind. Then, the night predators would finish whatever was left of your body."

Horror creeped up my back, sending me away from the plant. It no longer looked innocent. The black flowers glimmered ominously in the pale daylight.

"You're lying," I exhaled.

"Why would I?" He pushed away from the tree he'd been leaning against and strolled into the clearing toward me. "What would I gain by lying to you, little bird? In fact, of all the people in this world, you're probably the only one I'm inclined to be completely honest with."

"Are you?" I backed away from him. "Then tell me, *completely honestly*, why are you here?"

He stopped in his tracks. His darkened expression confirmed what I already knew.

"You came to take me back to Elaros, didn't you?"

"Yes."

Well, that *was* brutally honest.

I swallowed hard. My tightening throat felt rough and dry.

"Is the king...dead?"

"No. But he isn't alive either."

Some pressure let go of my chest—I wasn't a murderer after all. But his answer confused me.

"What do you mean? What happened to him?"

"I was hoping *you* would tell me that." His eyes searched mine.

I faltered under his intense stare. The memories of last night barged in unbidden. A hurricane of emotions assaulted me, all of them unpleasant. Pain, shame, terror twisted my insides into knots. I staggered on my feet, calling on whatever strength I still possessed to stay upright.

"If I tell you the truth in every detail, will you let me go?"

"No."

Why did I even expect anything else?

I exhaled, feeling defeated. "Will you at least make me forget again?"

"You want me to get rid of your memories, Sparrow?"

"Yes. Take away the ones from last night. Or you know what? Take them all if you wish. I don't care for any of them now."

Cruelly, he shook his head.

"I'll never take a single memory from you anymore, Sparrow. They are yours to keep, yours to learn from, and yours to cherish. Are there no experiences you've gained in Sky Kingdom worth cherishing?"

One of his black eyebrows twitched up in question. He looked at me with an odd glimpse of hope, as if he really cared about what my time in Elaros had been like for me.

Maybe not all of what I'd lived through had been bad. I'd met Dove and Libelle. I'd grown to like Brebie's company despite her constant poking, prodding, and stuffing me into way-too-tight corsets. And then, there was Voron...

Every encounter with him sparkled with crackling tension and tingling pleasure. With him, I was often both drained and elated —tired from toeing the line he clearly didn't wish to cross. The push and pull we went through was exhausting. But at the same time, if I couldn't have more with him, I wished to at least have more of the same.

Would I want to erase every memory of Voron from my mind? Good along with the bad? I didn't know. But I couldn't admit it to him, either.

"The few good memories don't outweigh the sad and the

outright scary ones," I said instead. "And if you drag me back to Elaros, I may as well not remember anything at all."

He came closer and placed a hand on my shoulder. Now, there was nowhere to run. I'd lost my chance.

"The queen wants to talk to you," he said.

I exhaled a humorless laugh. "I'm sure she wants to do far more to me than just talk."

"It's all part of the investigation." He sounded every bit his usual collected self. Why *would* he be stressing out? It wasn't like *he* had to worry about his life. "Sparrow, you can't survive outside of Elaros on your own. I admit, I'm impressed you've made it as far as you did. For a while, I feared you were dead after jumping into the river." He drew in a long breath as if my death would've affected him deeply.

I let him think I'd escaped by jumping into the river, though. He didn't need to know about Dove helping me.

"Come back with me." There was kindness in his voice, like he was giving me a choice.

I shook my head.

"Please, just let me go, Voron. Pretend you didn't find me. Tell the queen I did die in the river."

I wasn't asking him to save me. All I wanted was for him to look the other way. But I already saw it in his eyes, he wouldn't give me even that little leniency.

"I can't do that," he said. "I have an order, a direct order from the crown."

"Do you always have to follow the orders? Can't you be just a little bit less diligent?" I pleaded. "Just once?"

"I serve the crown. I swore my life to it." He picked up my cloak and satchel from the ground. "Come, Sparrow."

He wrapped his arm around my shoulders and walked me to his horse, ever so gently leading me to my doom.

The horse snorted when we came closer. It danced from hoof to hoof, but Voron stilled it by placing a calming hand on the side of its neck. Magnus flew up as Voron lifted me into the saddle. I gripped the mane of the horse and managed to stay in the saddle on my own this time.

"You'll ride. I'll walk." Voron took the reins, leading the horse away from the clearing.

The even trot of the horse was luring me to sleep. But I fought to stay awake.

"What will happen to me?" I asked.

"Like I said, there will have to be a thorough investigation and a trial. But since the king isn't dead, you cannot be tried for murder."

"Promise?"

He worked his jaw, glancing aside.

"Promise me, Voron, that I'll be safe," I demanded.

"I promise," he said, not meeting my eyes. "I promise to do everything within my power to keep you alive, Sparrow."

The magic swirled around us, sealing yet another promise Voron had made. It was a simple one, but it guaranteed nothing.

"Don't be assured by the shimmer of magic. Pay close attention to the words," his earlier advice came back to me.

Voron might have a lot of power, but not enough to go against royalty on my behalf. I took his promise for what it was— nothing. I couldn't count on Voron or anyone else for my rescue. If I wanted to live another day, I had to do it on my own.

I couldn't allow Voron to lead me to slaughter. I had to find a way to escape. With Voron on my heels, it couldn't be just one quick escape, either. I'd be running from him for the rest of my life. But at least I would *have* a life.

But he was also right about my knowing nothing about this world. If it wasn't for his intervention, I would be taking a nap on those deadly black weeds right now, never to wake.

Voron had always been an excellent source of information. Maybe I could get him to help me still? Only I had to find a way to do it without him realizing he was helping me.

I took a closer look at our surroundings.

"I'm hungry, Voron. Do we have a minute? I'll grab some of

those red berries over there." I pointed at the bush with juicy red clusters, then at the mushrooms with orange swirls on their cups that grew under the bush. "Or those mushrooms, maybe? It won't take long."

He gave me a suspicious look.

"Stalling won't help you avoid the inevitable, little bird."

But it might get me another day to live.

"Am I to starve under your arrest?" I huffed at him from the height of the saddle.

Voron blew out a breath and reached into his saddlebag, then took out something wrapped in a piece of clean cotton.

"The berries will make you vomit for days. The mushrooms will kill you. Here." He handed the bundle to me. "These have mushrooms, too, but not the kind you'll die from."

I lifted a corner of the cloth, finding a few stuffed pumpernickel rolls inside the bundle. The appetizing aroma tickled my nostrils. I took a bite of one and moaned in pleasure.

"Mmm. So good. They're stuffed with mushrooms and lamb, aren't they?"

He gave me an odd look, like he liked what he saw but wished he didn't.

"Yes. That's what Brebie said when she packed them for me."

Suddenly, I missed Brebie, and Alacine, and my little room. Regardless of what the future held for me, I could never return to that life anymore. It was now firmly in the past, with everything that was good and bad about it.

I bit into the roll fiercely.

"Sparrow, do you want to see how snowberries grow?" Voron suddenly asked, his voice lifting. "Look."

He crouched by a low bush under a nearby tree and plucked a plant from the ground. A pale blue berry, shaped like a glossy jellybean, dangled at the end of the plant's thick stem.

"That's the berries they use in Elaros to make the tarts that you like," he said. "These must be some of the last ones of the season. The snowberries come at the very end of winter and are usually gone by summer."

I took the stem with the berry from him, remembering our lessons with fondness. I'd managed to make him smile once or twice back then. We'd had tea and pastries. I never thought he'd noticed which ones were my favorite, but he clearly had.

Voron was right. There had been some nice moments in the short past I could remember. I couldn't give that up. I wished to keep those memories even if that meant I had to hold on to all the bad ones, too.

I bit into the juicy berry. The taste was so similar to the tart filling, it nearly made me cry.

"The stem is edible, too," Voron said.

He tore off the leaves from the thick, grassy stem, then handed it back to me.

"Try it."

Its taste was a milder version of the berry flavor, without any sweetness at all, filling and refreshing.

"The head chef of Elaros uses them in salads," Voron said, leading the horse along the narrow path back toward the palace.

"But you're not a chef. How do you know so much about berries and mushrooms?"

"It helps to know what is safe to eat if you're stranded in a forest for days or even weeks."

"Have you been stranded?"

He flinched. "A few times."

"During the wars?"

He nodded but didn't elaborate.

I wished he would talk more. I wanted to learn everything about his past. But it wasn't my goal at the moment. What I had to do right now was to find a way to escape him and for that, I needed to know more about our surroundings.

"These are huge leaves." I pointed at the large, flat plants under the horse's hooves. "Are they edible?"

"These? They aren't toxic, but they don't taste very good.

They're better for something else. Look." He ripped one off and lifted it for me to see. "They're thin but very sturdy. And their juice is sticky like glue. If you rip the edge off, like this." He tore off a thin strip all around the leaf, then folded the leaf in half, pressing on the edges. "The seam is waterproof, too." He tied the stem into a loop. "And now we have a water container. It'll only last for a day or two until the leaf dries. But it's good if one has no water bag."

I marveled at the ingenuity of this and filed away that information as well.

"Speaking of water. Would you happen to have some on you?" I asked. "The food made me thirsty."

He took a water bag from his well-stocked saddle pouch and gave it to me.

"There is a creek that way," I waved in the direction we were going since I'd passed this way already while running away from the palace. "We can refill it there."

He nodded, the silver strands of his hair falling across his forehead. When I returned the water bag to him, he tripped, grabbing onto the saddle.

"Are you okay?" I gripped his hand instinctively, as if I could stop him from falling this way.

"I'm fine." He took a drink too before putting away the water bag. "Just tired."

Only now I noticed the slight shadows under his eyes. His eyelids appeared heavy as he blinked, like it was an effort to lift them again once he'd closed them.

Dove told me Voron was gone for the night. To catch up with me today, he must've followed me all morning without stopping. Like me, he hadn't slept for over twenty-four hours now.

"We should take a nap," I suggested.

He glanced up at me, arching an eyebrow.

"What?" I spread my arms but then quickly grabbed onto the horse's neck, afraid to fall. "You're tired. I'm so exhausted, I risk falling from this horse and not just because I'm a lousy rider."

He gave me a knowing look. "You're stalling again."

"But can you blame me? I'm honestly not in a rush to get back to Elaros. What difference would a few hours make, anyway? Did the queen give you a deadline?"

"No. She didn't." He hesitated.

"Then why not take our time? The palace is still far away. It'll take us all day to get there because we'll need to ride along the river to get to the bridge. We may as well rest first."

With a soft flapping of wings, Magnus circled through the trees above us, then landed on Voron's shoulder.

"See?" I pointed at the bird with my chin, not letting go of the horse again. "Even Magnus is tired. We all need a break."

Voron cut a glance at his pet.

"He's just lazy," he said fondly.

He seemed to consider my suggestion, though. I was getting through to him. Encouraged, I pushed just a little more.

"Please, Voron. A nap may give me just a few more hours to live." I kept my tone light, despite the situation.

But he snapped his gaze to me, his expression turned stormy. "You won't die."

"I wish I could share your unwavering optimism."

"We'll stop," he conceded, taking me off the horse. "Tomorrow will be a big day. We'll need to be prepared and well rested."

Personally, I just hoped to live long enough to even see tomorrow. But I didn't say that out loud. He sounded like he was ready to go to battle for me when if he really cared, all he had to do was to let me go. Instead, he was delivering me straight to the queen.

I watched closely as he prepared a sleeping pallet. Behind a copse of nearby trees, he found a patch of the same large leaves he'd shown me how to make a water pouch from. Then, he pulled out a few large soft fern leaves and laid them on top.

It made sense. The flat glossy leaves were waterproof and would keep the ground moisture away from the sleeping person.

Putting the soft fern leaves on top added warmth and comfort. Next, he spread his cloak over the ferns.

"Looks cozy," I commented on his work.

He waved a hand at the pallet. "For you, my lady."

I didn't need to be asked twice. My head felt heavy and dizzy from exhaustion. To escape Voron, I needed a clear mind and all my strength. I climbed onto the pallet and lay down on one side of it.

Voron stood over me, looking uncertain.

"Come on." I patted the other side of the pallet. "Don't worry, High General. I won't try to seduce you. I'm too tired to try being sexy right now."

He sat on the edge of the cloak to take off his boots.

"As if you need to make any effort to be alluring," he muttered under his breath.

Did he mean he found me effortlessly sexy? Warmth rushed to my cheeks.

"Wow, Voron. That sounds very much like a compliment, especially coming from you," I teased.

He groaned. "Not a compliment. A complaint. Considering the circumstances."

Stretching on the pallet next to me, he dragged my cloak over both of us and turned his back to me.

I scooted a little closer but made sure no part of my body touched any part of his. As tense as he already was, I feared he'd bolt if even a strand of my hair touched him.

"Is it safe for both of us to nap at the same time?" I asked. "What are the chances of anyone finding us here? Should I stay up and watch while you sleep?"

I really didn't want to do that. I needed to sleep more than I needed to breathe right now. But I hoped I could fish out a few more useful answers from him before he passed out.

"We'll be fine," he assured me. "Magnus will watch."

The bird seemed to take his task very seriously. He took his place on the saddle horn, scanning the area suspiciously with his black beady eyes. Voron didn't even tie his horse, and I firmly believed Magnus wouldn't let the horse wander off, either.

"Are there no villages close by, then?"

"No," Voron said, hiding a yawn. "The closest one is in that valley between the two hills. It's about six hours through the forest for anyone to get here from there. Magnus will let us know if anyone comes too close."

I wasn't really going to sleep. All I needed was a quick catnap to clear my head and get some strength back into my muscles. But the moment I got warm and comfortable behind Voron's wide back, a deep, dreamless sleep claimed me.

Oblivion sucked me in. And when awareness finally returned, I felt like I'd slept for at least a year and a half.

I cursed under my breath. Did I sleep through my chance to escape?

Thankfully, Voron appeared to still be in a deep slumber. He had rolled almost entirely on top of me now, with his face buried in the dip between my neck and my shoulder. His arm was hooked around my middle, anchoring me to him. One of his legs was tossed across my thighs. I was essentially trapped. But at least he was sleeping, breathing softly into my neck.

It was warm here, inside my "Voron trap," safe and cozy, with his clean scent wrapping around me like a blanket. I really didn't feel like leaving. I had no desire to run from him. All I wanted was to close my eyes and relax with him.

If only it could last.

But it wouldn't.

Sooner or later, he would wake up and drag me back to the palace. I had to use this chance to escape. It could be my last one.

Carefully, ever so carefully, I freed my limbs from under him, one by one. Then I took my belt off and tied his ankles together.

"Sparrow..." Voron patted the side where I'd lain before.

I froze, afraid to breathe or to move a muscle. But he just scooped an armful of the cloak and grass underneath, then snuggled into it, going back to sleep.

He looked so different when he was sleeping. His facial features relaxed, losing his usual expression of either grim or snarky. He appeared peaceful and, with the imprint of my hair on his cheek and forehead, even adorable. The urge to cradle his head in my lap and kiss the shit out of him was so strong, I had to close my eyes to fight it.

I reminded myself that Voron was most likely taking me to my death, even if he didn't believe it. I couldn't trust him, no matter how adorably harmless he might look in his sleep.

For all I knew, he was dreaming about chasing me through the woods right now. That was why he muttered my name in his sleep. He might start jerking his legs next, like dogs did when dreaming about chasing a squirrel.

Regaining some determination, I swiftly moved on with my plan.

There was a reason I'd slept with my boots on. It saved me precious seconds. Voron's boots stood next to him, ready for when he was up. I took them and my cloak that he'd mostly tossed aside in his sleep.

Then, I padded to Voron's horse and climbed into the saddle, sending Magnus flying. The horse didn't even make a sound, likely just as shocked by my audacity as I was.

Shoving Voron's boots under my arm, I gripped the reins with both hands and steered the horse back the way we came, away from Elaros.

Not even a second later, Magnus cawed. The sound was so loud, it made me jump.

Clearly, I couldn't trust anyone in this world, not even a bird.

"Traitor," I hissed under my breath.

Tossing Voron's boots far away into the bushes, I hit the sides of the horse with my heels. With my miniscule experience at horseback riding, I wasn't capable of getting away at a full gallop. But I didn't need to be that fast. I only had to ride faster than Voron could run.

Gripping the reins tightly in my sweaty hands, I flexed my

thighs around the horse's wide back and let the animal wander out of the clearing while I concentrated on staying in the saddle and dodging tree branches.

Magnus's loud cawing behind me was suddenly interrupted by Voron's even louder laughter.

The man could laugh. Who knew?

As on edge as I was, I couldn't help a smile. Did I finally manage to do it? Did I make this man laugh out loud?

Running for my life, I kept smiling to myself as his hearty laugher faded into the distance. This was my favorite sound in the world, I decided. The best music to my ears.

Chapter Twenty-Eight

VORON

The little vixen tricked him!

The scent of her sleeping next to him had made him dream about her. It was the most magical dream, too. In it, he could touch her without restraints of deadly promises, and he didn't want it to end.

Magnus's signal had brutally yanked him out of it.

He jumped to his feet before he was even fully awake. Then... he tumbled onto his face, taking in a mouthful of fern and moss.

His legs were tied with the belt he'd last seen around Sparrow's waist. His boots were gone, and so was his horse, the sound of its hooves quickly disappearing in the distance.

The pieces of what was happening finally started to fall into place.

The clever little bird had tricked him and flown away.

The girl who was about one eighth his age, with most of her memories wiped clean, managed to outsmart him, the High General of the Royal Army of Sky Kingdom with decades of experience in dealing with far more cunning and powerful adversaries than a sly little human woman.

But she did it. She made a total fool out of him.

He didn't remember the last time he laughed so hard and with so much glee. Probably never.

And it felt so good!

Magnus cawed urgently from above, flying in circles.

"Yeah, yeah, I hear you. Aren't you a little late with your warnings, my friend?"

The bird wasn't to blame here. Magnus was used to seeing Sparrow with Voron. He'd even let her feed him. No wonder he'd grown to view her as a friend, not a stranger. She'd fooled Magnus, too. Only when she'd taken the horse had the crow realized it was bad enough to wake his master.

Voron could hardly blame himself, either. In addition to being tired from the sleepless night and long ride, his focus was also greatly impaired. His mind had been locked in the intense battle with his body's physical attraction to Sparrow. It took all he had to act unaffected, to ignore her pull and his cock's eagerness to jump out of his pants when she was near.

He should've realized her questions about edible plants weren't just idle chatter and that her insisting on taking a nap in the middle of the day also had more than one reason. He'd even told her where the nearest village was. What a fool.

Well, he'd found her once, and he'd find her again. Even with all the information she'd fished out of him, she wouldn't get far.

He freed his legs from Sparrow's belt, then got up and shook out his cloak.

"All right, Magnus, first things first. Did you see what she did with my boots?"

Chapter Twenty-Nine

SPARROW

The innkeeper twisted one of Dove's bangles between his slim, quick fingers. Thin red streaks marked the gray skin on top of his hands. The streaks continued up his arms and were also visible on the back of his neck and along his long *snakana* tail that he had looped under him.

His wife remained on the other side of the bar, leaning against the counter. Her light-green eyes never left the bangle as it sparked in the light of the thick candle in the carved-wood holder on the counter.

The bar served as both a restaurant and a reception room for the only inn in the village. With night approaching, the tables in the low-ceilinged dingy room were quickly filling with customers. Most of them were *snakanas*, but I spotted a few *ariens* and one or two *taureans* among them, too.

"How much do you want for this?" the innkeeper asked, weighing the bangle in his hand.

I wished I knew anything about trade or prices in Sky Kingdom. But I had no clue even what they used for money here.

"As much as it's worth," I said, trying to sound confident, manly, and gruff.

I'd introduced myself as a boy on my way to Elaros. I figured giving them the direction opposite in which I was traveling would throw Voron off track when he came after me. *When* not *if* because I was sure the High General was on my trail already.

Remembering how rare and "precious" humans were in this world, I pretended to be a highborn fae. With the hood of my cloak drawn low over my face and one end of it draped over my chest and shoulders with thick folds, I hoped to look like a short, plump fae boy, rather than a busty human woman. My clothes were baggy enough to hide my curves by adding bulk to my frame.

The innkeeper curved his thin lips, faking being completely uninterested about acquiring the bangle.

"I'll give you three coins for it."

"Gold coins?" I asked to a few snickers from his wife.

"Sure."

The bangle was made of gold. So even without the precious stones that decorated it, it should at least be worth its weight in gold. And I doubted three coins, even if those were very large ones, contained as much gold as the bangle.

"I'll take fifteen," I counter offered.

The innkeeper's wife stopped snickering, and her husband grunted, rolling his shoulders back.

"Ten is as high as I can go. It'll get you a horse if you need another one. Or will feed you for a month. I'll also throw in a free stay at the inn for the night. You can sleep in the stables with your horse, if you wish."

Judging by how quickly he'd more than tripled his first offer, I was clearly being screwed. But it was getting busy in here. People cast me curious glances. My skin crawled under their attention, urging me to get out of here, and the sooner the better.

"Fine. I'll take ten. Only because I'm in a hurry," I conceded. "And keep your accommodation offer. I'm not staying. But I do want my horse fed and watered, please."

The wife straightened her back behind the counter. "The night is coming, lad. It's not safe to travel in the darkness."

I'd already made it through a night in the woods on my own before Voron had found me. I'd been on foot and with no money, then. Now, I had a horse, some of Voron's leftover pumpernickel rolls, and ten gold coins.

"I'll be fine," I assured her.

Her husband produced a small trunk from behind the counter and counted ten shiny coins into my hand.

He paused, then suddenly shoved my sleeve up, exposing my forearm. Clutching the coins in my fist, I jerked my arm away from him.

A shadow momentarily blocked the dying daylight in the window.

Was it a bird? A crow? The omen of my doom?

I had to go. I couldn't stop running.

"Thanks. I'll be on my way," I mumbled, hurrying to the exit.

Things didn't look too bad. I'd survived one night in the woods on my own and was optimistic about spending another night under the thick cover of the trees. I had food. I'd stocked up on water in the village I'd just passed.

As the night fell, and the lights of the village disappeared behind the trees, darkness thickened around me. It was broken only by silent swarms of flying, glowing insects. They hovered around tree trunks and over the shrubs underneath, but their soft light illuminated the surrounding area enough for me to find the way without risking breaking the horse's ankles.

The eerie blueish glow of the insects made the forest look sinister, with grotesque shadows stretching between the trees. The branches appeared alive, as if reaching from the darkness to drag me off the saddle and into the shadowy canopy.

Fear trembled like a sickening haze around me, but I did my best not to let it in.

"We're doing great, buddy," I said to the horse. "You tell me when you get tired or hungry again. Okay?"

The horse didn't reply, of course, but the sound of my own voice made me feel braver.

Every noise sounded bigger in the darkness. I wasn't sure whether the rustling of the leaves up in the trees was caused by a breeze, some birds, or by something larger, sneaking out for night hunting.

I'd been warned about wild predators in the woods but hadn't met any yet. The possibility of running into them was probably higher here, away from the large glowing city of Elaros. To fight them off if needed, I kept the golden knife I'd stolen from King Tiane's creepy playroom under my cloak.

Rustling came from directly behind me. I jerked, turning to look back. Sadly, my skills on horseback were lacking, and I nearly fell out of the saddle.

"Shit," I cursed and gripped the horn of the saddle, regaining my balance.

Turning my head a little, I listened. All seemed quiet once again.

"Steady." I patted the horse's neck, trying to calm myself as well as the animal. My nerves were clearly all over the place, making me too jumpy.

The cracking of twigs and rustling of brushes suddenly appeared to come from all around me. The noise closed in from both sides, and several figures emerged from the darkness.

"Go!" I slammed my heels into the sides of the horse.

I'd send him into a full gallop if I had to. It was better to die falling off the horse than from the unknown horrors these woods held.

"Go!"

"Not so fast." A hand with gray skin and red markings yanked the reins out of my sweaty grip.

The innkeeper's smug expression looked outright evil in the bluish glow of the forest.

"Let me go!" I jerked at the reins, but somebody grabbed me around my waist, hauling me out of the saddle. "We had a deal!" I yelled, kicking at the two *snakana* men dragging me from the horse. "A fair trade. I owe you nothing."

The innkeeper slithered closer. "But was it really a fair trade between you and me?"

"Well, you did rip me off. But I agreed to that, so... Let me go."

He leaned closer. The blue forest glow flickering in his reddish eyes made him look terrifying. With a subtle hiss, he stuck out his tongue. Slim and agile, the tongue slithered in and out between his lips, the split tip of it fluttering in the air like a moth.

"The trade wasn't fair because I didn't know exactly how much you had to offer, *lad.*" The last word was said mockingly. He snickered, like he'd just made a joke.

The two other men who were with him chuckled, too.

The innkeeper turned to his buddies. "Or is he really a lad?"

Dread gripped my throat with icy fingers.

"What do you want? Your money back? Fine. Take it."

"Why would I take back the measly ten coins when every High Lord in the kingdom will happily pay me a fortune for you, *girl?*" He ripped the hood of my head and pawed at my breasts through my cloak. "Couldn't be easy to hide these." He smirked. "You've got the biggest tits I've ever handled."

I jerked away from him. "The way you *handle* them, it's a wonder any woman let you touch her at all."

Both men holding my arms snorted.

"She's funny, this one."

"She sure got you, Izux!"

"Shut up!" Izux snapped. "You too." He jabbed a finger into my shoulder. "Or I'll cut your tongue out."

"How would you sell me, then?" I challenged him. "High Lords love my tongue."

Izux's buddies guffawed loudly.

"You're too cheeky for a human," Izux muttered gruffly, untying a sash from around his waist. "Keep your tongue. I have other ways to shut you up." Yanking my head back by my hair, he shoved the sash between my teeth, then tied it around my head. "There you go. Now be nice and quiet."

The other two dragged me back into the saddle. Only instead of allowing me to sit up, they threw me across it, face down.

Turning the horse around, they headed back to the village.

"Great catch, Izux." Someone slapped my bottom as we made our way through the glowing forest. "You have a good eye."

"The moment I saw her hand, I knew she couldn't be a fae," Izux boasted.

Dammit. My skin had betrayed me. It didn't glow. Now I wished I'd had some of that shimmering powder Brebie used to dust me with. But it was too late. They knew who I was. And now, they'd sell me to whomever paid the most.

Izux petted my ass lightly, almost lovingly. "We'll see how much gold she'll fetch, the rare thing that she is."

I wouldn't give him the chance to find out my price. They hadn't tied my arms or legs, probably thinking it unnecessary— the three of them would easily catch and overpower me if I ran. I kept quiet, not willing to make them change their mind on that. But I kept thinking.

The night was dark, despite the glowing bugs. My captors might let their guard down. I had to be ready to slip from the saddle and run.

I'd lose my horse, the food, and the water bag. But I'd still have the gold and the knife. I could make do with those. I just had to find the best moment to take off and then make sure they didn't catch me.

All three men were *snakanas*. They didn't have legs. I mulled over scenarios where I could use that to my advantage. Maybe I could jump over a wide crack in the ground? Would they jump after me? Could *snakanas* hop over things without having legs?

Or I could run up a rocky hillside. It would hurt them to slither over sharp rocks, slowing them down.

The horse jerked suddenly. Coming to a stop.

"What the..." Izux muttered.

Then I heard a blade being drawn.

"Good evening, gentlemen." That voice. That so dearly familiar voice. "Or should I say *midnight*, since that's about the time right now."

Voron had caught up with me.

I rolled my eyes. That was all I could do at the sound of his deep voice dripping with sarcasm.

"Get out of the way," Izux barked.

"Certainly. Let me just take the woman, and I'll be gone in a flash."

Like a wingless angel, Voron had come to my rescue, only he had every intention of dragging me back to hell right after.

"She's ours," Izux protested.

"To do with as we please," one of his buddies chimed in.

"I'm afraid I can't let that happen," Voron replied politely, as if he were talking to the Elaros Court. Only I sensed that the sweeter he sounded, the more lethal he intended to be.

True enough. A blade swished through the air, followed by a grunt of pain and the sound of a body hitting the ground.

I twisted my torso, but hanging over the saddle with my face down and the horse's body in the way, I couldn't see much.

The horse stepped away from the action, possibly spooked by the swift blades and the noise. Wiggling around, I nearly fell head first. Grabbing the saddle, I shifted backwards all the way until I slid off and onto my feet.

Voron fought Izux, who had two long knives, each almost as long as Voron's sword. One of Izux's men lay motionless on the ground already, dark blood streaming steadily from a deep slash through his chest. The other one was slithering around Voron to attack him from the flank.

The *snakana* cracked his tail like a whip, aiming to knock

Voron off his feet. Voron twisted promptly, slashing through the air with his sword. The man's tail dropped onto the grass, blood spurting from the sliced-off end.

The *snakana* bellowed in agony. His wails cut through the night, bouncing between the tree trunks.

With trembling fingers, I found my knife, not to join the fight —neither of the men was truly on my side, anyway—but simply to have a weapon ready to protect myself if necessary.

Then, I ran.

Chapter Thirty

SPARROW

I bolted as fast as my feet would carry me through the underbrush and over the uneven ground. Jumping over the fallen trunks and ducking under the low-hanging branches, I focused solely on my next step.

I didn't look back. Not when the noise of the fight ceased. Not when the tapping of hooves on the grass came behind me. Not when the crow cawed above my head, spelling my doom.

The flying insects around me suddenly glowed brighter, illuminating the space around me as if plunging me into a spotlight. Sky fae had the power of light. There was no hiding in the darkness from them.

Gripping my knife, I had it ready. But I kept running. Until the horse lined up with me and a strong arm scooped me from the ground. Then I kicked and clawed and screamed through the gag I still had tied around my head.

"Hush, Sparrow." Voron easily removed the knife from my hand, then tossed me over the saddle in front of him. "Calm down. Or you'll fall on your head and break your neck."

But I couldn't calm down. I'd been so close to getting

free. I had done well surviving. Izux and his posse had been just a minor glitch in my journey. I would've escaped them. I could do this. I could run. If only Voron would stop catching me.

He grabbed a fistful of my clothes on my back, keeping me in place.

"If you won't stop squirming, I'll have to tie you to the saddle. Is that what you want, Sparrow? To ride all the way back to Elaros like a sack of potatoes?"

My head throbbed with all the blood rushing down to it in this position. The horn of his saddle dug painfully into my side. I blew out a breath through my nose, and let my limbs hang loosely.

"That's a good girl," he murmured approvingly. "Come up here, now."

He lifted me by the scruff of my cloak and sat me up sideways in front of him.

At the sight of the gag in my mouth, he flinched.

"Those idiots. They didn't appreciate your best feature—your smart mouth."

There was warmth in his cold eyes when he said it. How twisted was that? My current captor knew and appreciated me more than anyone else in this world.

He untied the gag and tossed it aside, then smoothed my messed-up hair, brushing it away from my face. His movements were kind and gentle. He acted as if he cared. But we were back on the way to Elaros again.

"Please, Voron," I begged softly. "Please let me go."

He took my face between his hands. The glow of the forest reflected in his silver eyes, making them look liquid, like bottomless pools of light.

"I can't."

Regret sounded in his voice, just like on the day we'd met. It was regret for my life. He knew even then that happiness wasn't waiting for me in Sky Kingdom. He'd always known.

Ever so gently, he brushed away a strand of my messy hair and tucked it behind my ear.

"Oh, to be free, my little bird," he said wistfully. "Free as you are."

"Me?" I couldn't believe his words. "How am I free? I haven't belonged to myself for a minute ever since I got to this world."

"Yet you have the freedom that I will never have again. You can't be bound by promises that rule my body and mind and tie my every move."

Finally, it dawned on me. The explanation for his reservations and all the contradictions was that Voron's decisions hadn't always been his own.

"What exactly did you promise to King Tiane, Voron?"

He stared ahead, steering the horse along the barely visible path. With a snap of his fingers, the glow of the insects around the horse's hooves brightened as we approached, illuminating our way, then dimmed again the moment we passed.

Holding the reins in one hand, he placed the other arm around me. Moved by compassion before I even heard his answer, I covered his hand with mine.

"I promised him everything," he said in a hollow, detached voice. "My life, my loyalty, my obedience, and a few other things that didn't matter much to me decades ago. Back then, I didn't think they would ever matter."

He tied himself to the king with all those promises. He didn't just *serve* the crown, he *belonged* to it. In more ways than even I did.

"Why did you do that?" I exhaled in shock.

"The payoff was too great to pass up."

"What did you get in exchange for your freedom?" What could possibly be worth giving up one's free will?

His eyes glistened in the darkness. "Power. Lots and lots of power, Sparrow. Back then, it was all I wanted."

"And now?"

His chest rose and fell with a deep breath. "And now it's too late to do anything about it."

The regret he carried, I realized, was for his life as much as it was for mine.

He'd given the promise to obey the orders of the royals. If he didn't deliver me to the queen, he'd end up losing his mind and eventually his life, just like the promise breakers King Tiane put up on spikes in his Garden of the Cursed.

"I have an order to bring you back to Elaros," he said. "And I will deliver on it, whatever it takes. There is nothing you or I can do about it, little bird. Wherever you hide, I will find you. If you run, I will follow. I'll follow you everywhere."

"I'll follow you everywhere."

He would, because he'd have to. He had no choice. And neither did I. There was no escape. The realization weighed heavily on my shoulders.

As if sensing my mood, he drew me closer to his chest. There was little comfort in that gesture, but I didn't refuse the little I could get.

With his other hand, he steered the horse around a dark object on the ground. It was the body of one of the men who'd taken me. The sickening smell of fresh blood invaded the fragrance of the night forest. My throat tightened as my stomach lurched.

"Did you kill them all?"

"The scum deserved it," he replied breezily, with no remorse whatsoever. "Don't look." Cradling the back of my head in his large hand, he guided my face to his chest to shield me from the gruesome sight. "Your stomach is too weak for these things."

He spoke from experience. Voron was the one who'd held my hair while I retched into the king's Garden of the Cursed in front of the entire court of Elaros. The memory of that was no longer as mortifying. I had way too many other things to worry about now to keep fretting about the courtiers' opinion of me.

"Are you afraid I'll throw up all over your boots?"

He chuckled. "These boots have suffered enough already. Did

you know that I had to pull out a slug from one after you tossed them into the *leatherleaf* bush?"

"Just a slug? What a pity," I quipped. "I was hoping for at least a toad and some very spiky thistle."

His body vibrated against mine from his soft laughter. "You're a menace, little bird. Your sweet looks are so deceiving."

I smiled, too. It helped ease the tension that was squeezing my chest like a thick, rusty chain. It helped me think more clearly, too.

Voron was too smart, too determined, and too motivated for me to escape him. He also had the power and resources to track me down, no matter where I went. He'd follow me anywhere, even to the Below if he had to.

But there was one place where Voron wouldn't go after me. He wouldn't follow me into the River of Mists. No one from Sky Kingdom would.

I had no memories of my life or my family back home, but I retained the knowledge of my old world and its people. I knew about its many cultures, the customs, and what dangers to watch out for. I was also generally familiar with its history and all the time periods I could possibly land in.

Going back would be extremely dangerous, but it would give me a chance to survive. A better chance than certain death at the queen's hand.

"Do you think Queen Pavline would show me any kindness if I asked her forgiveness and begged for leniency?" I asked.

Voron pondered my question way too long for my anxiety not to spring up in a new gear.

"You said the king didn't die," I prompted.

"No. But the dagger that you stabbed him with was cursed. According to the royal hag, the king's spirit is now suspended between life and death. He can't move or speak. No one knows if he can hear." He tilted his head to catch my eye. "Where did you get that dagger, Sparrow?"

There was no reason to keep that information to myself.

Maybe if Voron knew everything, he'd be able to advise me on what to do next. His hands were tied by his promise to the crown, but other than that, I believed he wished me no harm.

"The dagger belongs to King Tiane. He kept it in a black metal box in a trunk in his bedroom. He took it out to…" I swallowed hard, recalling that night again, and rubbed the sore spot on my breast where the king had scored my skin. "He planned to use it on me. For fun."

Voron went still. So still, he seemed to become one of the shadows in the forest.

"What kind of *fun?*" His voice came out hoarse and rough.

"The only kind that can get him hard, it seems." Bitterness burned my throat. Someone had to know the truth about the revered king of Sky Kingdom, and that someone might as well be Voron. "Apparently, your marvelous King Tiane likes to see people hurt. He thrives on it. Making people suffer is the one sure thing to get his dick up. He doesn't care about sex that much, unless it's with himself, but he uses people as foreplay props. I don't think he had actual intercourse with me, not even on the night when he made me remove your necklace, then sucked out all my memories of my time spent in his rooms."

"He did that?" Voron gritted out, holding his back straight like an iron rod. His entire body seemed stiff as iron, too. "You removed the necklace?"

"Yes. I know. Stupid." I hung my head.

"I didn't say you were stupid."

"Yet here I am." I spread my arms to the sides. "I've drunk the damn *camyte* twice now. Both times because I felt a hint of compassion for, or a connection with—or whatever the hell that was—with the men who poured it for me."

He brushed the side of my face with the back of his knuckles.

"You have a kind heart, Sparrow. The shame is on those who took advantage of that, not on you."

Having a kind heart, sadly, meant the same as being stupid in my case. At least, that was how I felt now. The only solution seemed to be never to trust anyone ever again.

"Either way, I was duped and taken advantage of," I concluded. "But I refused to fall for that again. The second night the king brought me to his bedroom, I wore the necklace, hidden from him." I fingered the berry beads through my clothes. Voron's necklace was back where it belonged, around my neck, with the rock pendant nestled between my breasts. "I remember everything."

"What happened that night, Sparrow?"

I released a long, slow breath, gathering my resolve.

"The king cut me," I said. "He was going to cut more of me and do other, God-knows-what horrible things to me. But I stabbed him before he could do them. He has a secret room off his bedroom, with a bunch of torture equipment in it. That's how your king gets off, Voron. He has hot, sweaty fantasies about impaling people. He revels in the gory details of tormenting others. He said something about making me last. But in the end, I'm convinced, he would've killed me in some torturous way, anyway. You see, I'm not fae. To him, I'm even lower than an animal. He believed there would be no consequence for him if he hurt me or even killed me." I drew in some air, starving for oxygen as I spoke. "And of course, he was right. There is no law in Sky Kingdom that protects me."

Voron listened quietly without interrupting, allowing me to get it all off my chest. And the words poured out of me.

Oh, how they poured.

All the hurt, the fear, and humiliation just spilled over. I didn't even care what he thought of me or what he would do with all that information. I was just glad not to be the only one drowning in all this filth and horror.

"I didn't believe even for a second that my stabbing the king would kill him or even incapacitate him in any way. He's a mighty fae. How could a knife harm him? It wasn't even an iron knife, either. The most I hoped for was that he'd just murder me faster, instead of taking his sweet time torturing me. But he fell and didn't move. So, I ran."

I couldn't tell him about Dove. Omitting her role in my escape didn't distort the story much, but it protected her from the risk of being punished for helping me.

"It wasn't *my* dagger, Voron. I didn't bring it to his bedroom with the intention of hurting him. He kept it there, planning to hurt *me*."

"You said the asshole cut you?" His voice was strained, with a growl tearing through the restraint. His words boiled with anger. Low, but terrifying. Magnus leaped into the air from Voron's shoulder, and the horse flicked his ears nervously.

Instead of being frightened like them, I was relieved. Finally, someone believed me.

Voron didn't tell me to feel honored being selected as the king's favorite. He didn't try to explain how important it was to make the king happy. He didn't expect me to keep the disturbing truth to myself and be grateful for everything the king's favor had brought me.

He simply believed me, and he felt outraged on my behalf. It was the best thing he could do for me in this situation.

"Yes he did. He cut me right here." I pushed aside the cloak on my chest and pulled down the neckline of the tunic to expose the cut on the top of my breast.

The fresh scar was thin, finer than from a scratch by a cat, which was a good thing, considering what the much deeper wound from the dagger did to the king.

Voron lifted his hand to my breast to touch the scar, then promptly moved it away.

"He did it fast, didn't he? Not very deep?"

"Right." I nodded, adjusting my clothes to cover up the scar again. "The king wished for me to *last*, remember? The dagger is new, by the way. He said he just got it that morning. What is that dagger for, Voron? Was it supposed to do to me the same thing it did to the king?"

His arm tightened around my shoulders, and I felt the press of his lips to the crown of my head. But he sounded his usual distant self when he spoke.

"The dagger came from the World of Under. The plane of Nerifir directly beneath the Below. The shadowy dwellers of Under are void of joy. Nothing is sacred to them, not even the spirit of a living soul. The blade was cursed to repel the spirit without killing the body. Little by little, one shallow cut at a time, King Tiane planned to separate your mind from your body and eventually turn you into his mindless plaything. Over time, you would've lost all sense of self. Only your body would have remained, for him to do with as he pleased."

My skin crawled with horror.

That blade had touched my flesh. What if a part of what I was had already departed into the ether somewhere? Was I even still *me*?

"The king cut me with that dagger, Voron." I gripped his hand. "Would I even notice the change if it happened?"

"No. Most likely you would not." He squeezed my hand in response. "But *I* would. I know you well enough to notice if something was missing."

I snapped my gaze to his. "And? Am I still me?"

"Delightfully so," he replied with a shadow of a smile. "With all your parts intact, both naughty and nice."

"Good." I exhaled in relief.

But was it really a good thing? Maybe it would've been better not to comprehend the grim future that awaited me.

"Why did he need to bother with the dagger? He could've just kept taking my memories away. Did you know the king could take people's memories just like you can?"

"I've heard he could."

"Only you keep your ability a secret."

"Not exactly a *secret*," he argued. "I've just never taken anyone's memories other than yours."

"You haven't?" I blinked in surprise. "Why not?"

"There was no need." He shrugged. "Besides, it wouldn't work on fae, anyway. Most fae wear something warded to protect them from magic. But either way, this ability can't be used often. It's not easy to meddle with someone's mind. It takes a permanent toll on the one doing it."

"I didn't know that."

"Taking your memories was just a temporary solution for King Tiane. It didn't grant him full control over you. Clearly, he wanted more."

"He wanted to turn me into a mindless doll that would suffer prolonged abuse in silence." I shuddered, glad I managed to escape that fate, even if I might be facing a death sentence for doing that. "Should I tell the queen the whole truth? Would it help if she knew *why* I did it?"

Voron considered my words for a minute.

"It may. But I advise you to speak with her in private first. Before any public hearing."

"I will." I nodded, feeling just a tiny bit more optimistic.

Queen Pavline had been mostly friendly to me. Maybe she'd be sympathetic, rather than seeking vengeance?

"Maybe if I promise to leave and never come back, she'll spare my life?" I suggested.

The muscles in his jaw flexed. "Is that what you want? To leave Elaros?"

"To leave Nerifir altogether, Voron. To put this entire world behind me. I'd go back to the human realm if that's the only way for me to survive. I just hope the queen will let me."

"Sending you across the River of Mists will be almost the same as executing you. Once you leave, you'd never come back. For all of us here, in Sky Kingdom, you'd be as good as dead."

It sounded so final.

"As good as dead."

But leaving might be my only chance to keep on living.

I heaved a heavy breath. "Just as well."

"If that's what you want, Sparrow, then I will petition the queen to allow you to cross the River of Mists."

"You will? Thank you."

"Rest now." He drew me closer, allowing me to lean my head against his chest. "For I'm not stopping for any more naps, little vixen."

Chapter Thirty-One

VORON

He stormed into his rooms the day after he'd brought Sparrow back to Elaros. His blood was boiling with rage at the news he'd just received.

Sparrow was sent to the dungeon on the queen's orders.

She was supposed to be held in her bedroom at the palace for the duration of the investigation and trial. When and why that decision was overturned, he had no idea. But he was going to find out right now.

"Alcon, get the men ready."

The Head of the Guard rose from his comfy chair by the fire in Voron's receiving room.

"Are we going into battle, my general?" he asked jokingly.

Alcon's merry mood fizzled out, however, the moment he caught Voron's stern look.

"We're going to see the queen," Voron bit out.

Alcon jumped to attention. "Yes, High General."

The queen hadn't summoned him. On the contrary, ever since they came back, she had refused all his requests for an audience.

And now he could guess why. Apparently, Sparrow had been in the dungeon under the palace since yesterday morning. She was sent there just a few hours after setting foot back in Elaros. And no one, not one fucking idiot in this entire place, notified him when that happened.

The answer to that was most likely because the queen didn't want him notified. As far as he knew, there were no preparations for the trial, either. And again, he'd received no explanations as to why.

Queen Pavline chose to exclude him from her plans for Sparrow. She actively avoided him, hiding behind an army of guards placed at the entrance to the king's rooms.

Well, maybe Alcon was right after all, and he had to lead his men into battle to storm the king's chambers.

As he and his men appeared at the doors, two of the guards crossed their spears in his face.

"Queen Pavline asked not to be disturbed while delivering her prayers for the king."

He tilted his head. "She's praying?"

"Yes, she's asking Aithen, the God of Death, to walk King Tiane back to us."

"Sure she is."

Knowing the queen, she'd be likely celebrating the good fortune of the Sky Crown landing in her lap so unexpectedly, not begging for the return of the husband she had no relationship with beyond mutual tolerance.

The guards shifted on their feet uneasily, obviously torn between their sworn loyalty to the crown and their High General, who had earned their respect. He knew that feeling well and sympathized with the guards, but he also needed to see the queen, whether she wished it or not.

"Alcon." He gave the man a signal.

Like a well-tuned clock, his team moved into action. Alcon grabbed the spear from one of the guards, Farion wrenched the spear from the other. Yallar, Raine, and Zinfir slid their swords out, getting into formation to keep the rest of the guards at bay as Voron shoved the doors open.

"You're breaking royal orders, High General," one of the spear-less guards warned.

"Those orders were for you, not for me," Voron tossed over his shoulder, entering the king's rooms.

As he marched into the bedroom, he spotted at least a dozen priests and priestesses keeping vigil by the king's bed. Kneeling or sitting low on their *snakana* tails, their robes pooling like melted gold on the marble floor around them, they muttered prayers to the winged God of Death to spare their mighty king.

Voron averted his eyes from the bed, refusing to look at King Tiane. After what the royal prick did to Sparrow, it was all Voron could do not to charge the bed to strangle him with his own hands.

The High Priest rose on his tail as Voron entered.

"How dare you—"

"The queen?" Voron demanded. "Where is she?"

The High Priest shifted his eyes to the doors in panic, clearly wishing the guards would do something about Voron's sudden intrusion. Unfortunately for the High Priest, the guards reported to Alcon, the Head of the Royal Guard. And Alcon reported directly to Voron. Unless the queen personally ordered them, no one would dare remove him from here.

"Queen Pavline is praying in private," the High Priest said, his gaze flickering to the door to one of the king's private sitting rooms. "She's not to be disturbed. Have some respect."

"My respect has been in scarce supply lately, Holy Father. And now, I'm all out," Voron snapped on his way to the sitting room.

As he stormed in, Queen Pavline jumped from a chair by the table with an open picture book on it. The pictures glowed over the pages, forming images in silver light. Voron recognized the faces of both portraits. One was High Lord Caitore, the other High Lord Bussard. Both were strong, virile men, not bonded and unmarried. Both with a claim to the crown.

If the queen was praying, it wasn't for the restoration of the health of her current husband but for sending her a new one. Not that Voron blamed her. Now that he knew all about King Tiane's perverted tendencies, he wondered just how miserable the royal marriage truly was for the queen.

She quickly shut the book. "What are you doing here?"

"I came to show my *respect*," he quipped.

Her quick, slim fingers tapped on the leather-bound cover of the book.

"Great. You showed it. Now leave."

"In a minute." He took a long look around the room.

She didn't say "I order you," allowing him to view her words as a request or a suggestion that could be ignored at his discretion. So, he ignored it. He sauntered to the nearest white-and-gold couch, lowered himself into it, and stretched his legs, crossing them at the ankles.

The queen leaned her hip against the table and folded her arms under her breasts. Her blue-and-green dress fell in shimmering folds down her tall, slender frame. Her hair was unbraided, draping over her shoulders in thick purple waves. Her appearance was striking even for sky fae.

The low neckline of her dress left the tops of her breasts exposed. As usual, the mating mark was painted on her left side, gold paint glistening against her dark-green skin. The letters P and T, the first letters of hers and the king's names, intertwined in an intricate rosette of vines and flowers.

The royal couple weren't bonded. Yet the queen had the mating mark painted over her heart almost daily to highlight her position as the royal spouse. That mark on her breast, the slim wreath of gilded thorns on her head, and her position at the king's side during most official functions were all that differentiated the queen from any other lady of the court. The king gave her no extra attention. Until Sparrow felled him, Queen Pavline had no official duties, either.

Now, she had it all.

"What do you want, Voron?" she asked.

"I want the one thing I've been begging you for, for two days now—to talk."

"About what?"

"You ordered me to bring Sparrow to you."

"Yes, yes, you did well." She waved her hand in the air. "Do you want a reward? What can you possibly wish for in addition to everything you have already received from us?"

"I just learned Sparrow was thrown in the dungeon." He delivered the words without a flinch, but it took him a gargantuan effort to look unaffected.

"Where else do you want me to put her? She's a criminal. She attacked the king. She belongs in a dungeon cell."

His jaw tightened. He unclenched it, willing his voice to remain calm and even. Showing any emotion would be demonstrating a weakness. The queen would jump on any weakness of his like a vulture on dead meat, and she'd find a way to use it against him.

"There are no preparations for a trial," he said. "Are you even planning to have one for her?"

The queen ran her fingers through the waves of her hair draped over her shoulder.

"Listen, High General, it's been a few very challenging days for me. I didn't plan for any of this to happen. The situation is unusual. The king is not dead. He's still the one who is wearing the Sky Crown. Yet I'm left to make all decisions for the kingdom. I can't even have a proper coronation for myself."

"I sympathize, Your Majesty," he lied. He couldn't care less about which one of the royal heads the Sky Crown sat upon. His promises applied to the rightful ruler of the kingdom. In the king's absence that was the queen. "But there is urgency to this case. Sparrow shouldn't be in the dungeon."

"But that is exactly where she belongs. She stabbed my husband—"

"She *liberated* you. Let's be honest, Your Majesty, and look at things the way they are. Sparrow practically handed the Sky Crown to you. She turned you from Queen Consort to the Ruling Queen. If anything, you should be upset with her for not finishing what she started and not pulling the dagger out of the king's chest to set his spirit free."

"No!" The queen jerked through her entire body. The skin over her high cheekbones darkened in a blush. She lowered her head, hissing through her teeth, "I didn't want any of this to happen. I don't wish for Tiane's death. I didn't plan for his assassination."

"I didn't say you did." He flicked the lace on his cuff, straightening the folds of the ruffle. "But you do benefit from it, greatly. In addition to the Sky Crown, you also get a chance to marry a man who would actually bed you once in a while. You may give Sky Kingdom a legitimate heir after all."

"I said stop it!" She stomped her foot in a lavender silk slipper. "I'm not rejoicing in the situation."

The fact that she denied it so passionately only reinforced that what he said was true. And she knew it.

"I know you can't publicly admit your gratitude to Sparrow for what she's done, but you could show her mercy by letting her choose her punishment."

"That will never happen. The only punishment she can have is death. She dared raise a hand against the king. She went against the crown. She can't have mercy."

"She isn't asking for much," he insisted. "Instead of an execution, she wants to be sent back to her world."

The queen shook her head quickly. "If I let her live, people will think I was in on it with her. That I had something to do with her attacking the king. The Council will use it to cast me aside. There are plenty of High Lords who would help them get rid of me, using any excuse they can find. Everyone with any claim to the throne is dreaming of being the next king right now."

And there it was—the confession. The queen feared Voron

wouldn't be the only one to see the benefits she reaped with King Tiane being out of the picture.

"Crossing the River of Mists is as good as death," he insisted. "Sparrow would never come back. We can make it look like an execution. With a scaffold erected on the main plaza of Elaros, with the verdict read out loud. It'll be a punishment, a banishment not only from the kingdom, but from the entire world of Nerifir."

He saw a wall behind her eyes, impossible to penetrate. The queen had made up her mind. Still, he tried to change it. He couldn't give up on Sparrow.

"It'll be your chance to display leniency. Prove to your royal subjects you rule with mercy, not cruelty like your predecessor did."

She snapped her gaze to his face, her eyes prodding.

"King Tiane wasn't cruel. His reign was just."

"You know what I mean, Your Majesty."

She had to know. The king must have let his violent tendencies slip in front of his wife at some point during their marriage. Voron would go so far as to speculate that might be the reason the queen didn't even try to return to her husband's bedroom.

At the very least, she'd seen King Tiane's "special room." She knew what the king was up to at his leisure.

"If you're talking about the Garden of the Cursed—"

"I'm talking about *all* of it. Tell me where you found King Tiane after he'd been stabbed. Tell me more about the room Sparrow escaped from."

The queen pinched her mouth into a barely visible line. Her eyes narrowed into slits as if he personally threatened her.

"So, the fat little rat has been babbling, hasn't she?" she hissed, lowering her voice. "What did the human tell you?"

He gathered his legs under him and got up from the couch.

"She said enough for me to celebrate your impending widowhood rather than mourn it."

She fisted her hands like she was about to attack him and took a step closer.

"You are not to repeat what you heard from the human girl to anyone outside of this room, do you hear me? I *order* you never to speak about what happened between King Tiane and her in the royal chambers. Never."

That was the route that Queen Pavline had chosen. She decided to play a grieving widow and hide what kind of monster her husband was. If so, Sparrow was doomed.

"The human will die." She stopped his protests by lifting a hand. "I cannot allow a single word of what she knows to leave these walls. King Tiane's reputation will remain unsoiled. His name is forever attached to mine, and both will remain blameless."

"Your Majesty, with all due respect—"

"I want her dead, Voron!" she screeched, stomping her foot. "And I want it done publicly. Let it be the lesson to anyone who dares raise a hand against the Crown of Sky Kingdom. I *order* you to get everything ready for her execution on the main plaza of Elaros City. Now!"

The queen's order was carried out just as she wished.

The scaffold was erected on the main plaza of Elaros City. Draped in red, it was a horrid monstrosity among the glowing whites and soft pastels of the city streets.

Queen Pavline didn't share her husband's fondness for impaling as a method of capital punishment. Instead, Voron had sourced an executioner skilled with an axe from a village nearby.

The executioner was a blacksmith by trade, but he'd delivered enough death sentences during the rule of King Tiane's father to ensure a swift and relatively painless death for Sparrow.

The time of the execution had been set. The announcement

was heralded all over the city and the surrounding area. The scroll
with the verdict had been prepared and signed by the queen to be
read before the crowd.

Voron surveyed the last preparations as a group of workers
cleaned up the construction debris around the execution site.

Alcon landed in front of him, folding his wings.

"All is ready, my general. The executioner will be here in less
than an hour, and the Head of the Council is on his way to read
the verdict."

Voron nodded.

"Good."

He turned to leave the plaza, heading back to the palace.
Alcon caught up with him, matching his wide stride.

"Gather the men, Alcon. What I'm going to do next will at
the very least get me banned from court. At most, it will cost me
my head. I'm not ordering any of you to join me in this. It'll be
entirely your choice if you do."

His direct order was to get everything ready for the execution.
The queen had made it clear what she wished to happen to Sparrow. But she hadn't explicitly ordered him to go ahead with the
execution.

He learned a long time ago to pay close attention to the
wording because words could mean the difference between life
and death.

And in this case, they did.

Chapter Thirty-Two

SPARROW

"Want some more? Here you go, little buddy." I pinched off another crumb of the moldy bread that was supposed to be my lunch and tossed it to the rat in the corner of my cell.

The rat sniffed the air, its whiskers moving rapidly. It then scurried to the crumb and picked it up.

Repulsion rolled through me. I drew my legs to my chest, afraid the rat would come too close. But the rodent had been my constant companion for the past two days, my only companion. Panic no longer jolted me as it did when I first saw it sneak into my cell through a hole between the wall stones. By now, I even found the way it held the bread in its front paws cute, as if they were little hands.

Well, at least someone had the appetite to eat this food. The bread covered in black mold was still better than the bowl of maggot-infested porridge I got for breakfast.

Last night, I was so ravenously hungry, I actually picked at some of the least moldy pieces of my dinner.

Today, my appetite was gone. My stomach felt so queasy, I feared I'd throw up even if the food was good.

It was cold in here, and all I had on was my nightgown. When the guards had dragged me out of bed the morning they brought me here, they didn't even let me get dressed.

"You won't need clothes where you're going," they'd said. "It'll be harder for you to escape this way."

As if I could run away from here. The cell had no windows, only a thick wooden door with a narrow opening in it for the guard to peek through to make sure I was on my best behavior. The door was locked at all times. When they brought me the nasty food, they shoved it through the slit in the door, not bothering to open it.

The rat moved my way, and I squeaked, pressing harder into the wall behind me.

"More bread? Here you go!" I tossed another small piece its way, keeping the rodent at bay and away from my bare toes. Though my feet were so cold and numb, I probably wouldn't even feel it if the rat gnawed on them.

I pulled my nightgown lower over my knees and feet, but the thin material didn't keep my body heat in, and there was no other source of warmth in here. Unless I grew desperate enough to cuddle with the rat.

My teeth chattered, and full-body shudders ran through me every few seconds. My head felt rather fuzzy, too. I was either running a fever or the last dinner had made me sick. Possibly both.

The rat's black beady eyes reminded me of Magnus, as did the suspicious, calculating way the rodent eyed me sideways while eating my food.

The thoughts of Magnus brought the images of his master to the front of my mind.

There hadn't been any messages from Voron. After we'd arrived at Elaros late at night, he'd brought me to my room. The king's guards showed up first thing in the morning, while I was still in bed, and dragged me down here. They gave me no explanation. No one read me my rights or told me if I even had any. And no one came to see me here.

Voron had spoken about an investigation and trial. But I feared I might be left here to rot indefinitely. The queen clearly had no interest in seeing me or hearing me out.

The rat lifted its head again. I tossed it what was left of my bread, but it ignored the food this time. Turning around, it ran back to the hole in the wall and disappeared between the stones.

The noise that scared the rodent away finally registered with me, too.

Stomping feet were approaching.

Then, clashing of metal on metal.

Cries of pain.

Slamming of bodies hitting the floor.

And then...*his* voice, "Find her!"

"Voron." I scrambled up to my feet.

My head swam with dizziness, forcing me to grip the wall for support.

"Lady Sparrow?" The familiar dark face with a pair of bright green eyes appeared in the door opening—Alcon. "She's here, High General."

"Where's the key?" I heard Voron demand from someone in a thunderous voice. "Open that door, and I'll spare your life."

The key turned with a loud screech in the rusty lock. The door flew open.

And there he was, rushing into my dark, filthy cell like a blast of fresh wind from the hills beyond these walls.

"Gods... Sparrow."

He took me in, from my tangled hair down to my bare feet. I smoothed my nightgown that used to be pure white before it'd been smudged by the grime from the floor and the mold from the walls.

I could only imagine what pathetic picture I presented. But I felt lightheaded and too tired to feel self-conscious. I took a shaky step his way.

"Hi."

"Let's get you out of here, little bird." He scooped me up and carried me out of the cell. "Get the fuck out of my way." He shoved aside one of my jailers who had the misfortune of standing too close. "I promised to spare your life, not your limbs."

The terrified dungeon guard flattened himself against a wall, letting us pass.

A horse waited for us outside, with one of Voron's men, Farion, holding the reins.

"We'll fly above you, High General," he said.

Placing me in the saddle, Voron mounted the horse behind me.

"Make sure no one stops us, either from the air or on the ground," he ordered Farion.

Leaning me against his chest, he wrapped his cloak around both of us. I snuggled into his warmth, my whole-body shakes easing somewhat.

"Where are we going, Voron? Where are you taking me?"

He spurred the horse, steering it onto a narrow pathway behind the streets of the city.

"I'm taking you where you wanted to go, little bird. To the River of Mists."

I let his words sink in.

The River of Mists.

He was setting me free, after all.

"What about your promise to the queen?"

He smirked. "All the queen's orders have been fulfilled. She ordered me to bring you to Elaros, and I did it. Now, I want to do something of my own free will. But we need to be quick, before she fires any new orders at me."

"You're taking me without her permission? She'll punish you."

"Oh, she will. But I'll deal with it later. Now, duck and hide."

"What?" I blinked in confusion but did as he said, drawing my head into my shoulders and pressing myself tighter to him.

He drew the cloak over my head. "Shhh. Be a good little bird and don't make a peep."

Noises of a busy street closed in on us from all sides. Rattling of carriages. Shuffling of feet. People yelling, laughing, and arguing.

"The city gates are open, High General." Alcon's quiet voice came from right above us. He must be flying low and very close to us. "Lots of people are arriving to watch the execution. The guards are checking all those coming in, but not those who are leaving."

"Good," Voron grunted, giving me a reassuring pat on the shoulder through his cloak.

One word had struck me. *Execution.*

Whose execution was it supposed to be?

Mine?

I drew in air in rapid, shallow breaths, filling my lungs with Voron's warm, comforting scent. After a while, the noise around us receded, and he drew the cloak back, allowing me to look out again.

We were nearing the forest Trez and I had hiked through, what seemed like a lifetime ago.

It was really happening. Voron was taking me back to where I'd come from. Soon, I could go home. I was going to get what I wanted, after all.

I was getting a chance to live.

The mists hung low over the river as we approached. The gray clouds bloated, rising above the rocky banks. They seemed to merge with the thick dark clouds gathering on the horizon. The pink streak of the River of Mists was barely visible as a slim, shimmering glow deep in the middle of the stormy fog.

Only the first few rows of cobblestone pavement of the bridge emerged from the cloud cover that completely shrouded the rest of the bridge, hiding it from view.

Alcon and two of Voron's men landed but held a respectful distance from us. Two other men remained up in the sky, watching the road.

"Ready?" Voron dismounted from the horse, then helped me down, too.

I clutched his cloak in my fingers, keeping him close while I steadied my shaking legs.

"As ready as I can be." I managed a smile.

He opened a saddlebag and took out a long black shirt, one of his by the look of it.

"From what I read," he pulled the shirt over my head and down my body, "all River of Mists portals in the human world open over a body of water. All known ones are over shallow ponds or creeks, but be ready to swim, just in case."

"Okay."

It was useless to remind him that I didn't know if I could swim. That knowledge was long gone with the rest of my earlier memories. But Voron couldn't do anything about it anyway right now.

Next, he produced a small satchel from the saddlebag and put it across my body over my shoulder.

"There is some food here, sealed in a jar so it doesn't get wet. And these..." He took out a necklace and a pair of matching bracelets. "Human currency is confusing. Throughout your history, you've been using anything from shells, to beads, to some cards, and even pieces of paper, the scrolls say. I'm not even sure how much of that is true. But gold and precious stones seem to be always of value everywhere."

He put the golden necklace that glistened with sapphires and diamonds around my neck, then wound the bracelets around my wrists.

"You got it all ready for me," I said.

"It's not much, but I didn't want the jewels to weigh you down, especially if you do have to swim. Is there anything else you think you'll need?"

I shook my head. My throat tightened. He'd put so much thought into packing for me.

"No. Just... Do you have any water?"

Despite wearing two shirts, I shivered. My mouth was dry. It'd been a while since my last drink of stale water back in the dungeon.

"Here." He untied a water bag from the saddle.

I took a few hungry gulps, then hooked the bag handle back over the horn of the saddle. The water washed the grime of the dungeon out of my throat and cleared the fog from my mind somewhat.

"Thank you, Voron. Thank you so much for everything. If I lived a thousand lives, I wouldn't be able to repay you for what you've done for me today."

He stepped closer, placing his hands on my upper arms.

"I won't ask for much in terms of payment."

"Oh..." I didn't expect he'd want a payment at all. It wasn't like I could give him anything. I had nothing but what he'd just given me. "What do you want?"

He slid a finger up my throat and under my chin, lifting my face to his.

"A kiss, Sparrow. I want to kiss you goodbye before you leave me forever."

My breath halted. I stared at him, finding myself trying to memorize every line, every angle of his face. The stormy sadness in his gray eyes. The stubborn set of his jaw. And his lips, parted for one last kiss.

I tipped my head slightly, granting him permission.

He leaned closer and touched my mouth with his. Our lips connected. His breath mingled with mine. It was gentle, nothing like the frantic, hungry kisses we shared before. He made no attempt to invade my mouth, simply savoring the connection as it was.

The thought that this was our *last* kiss gutted me. We never got a chance to have anything more.

He broke the kiss but didn't move away. His forehead rested against mine.

"Sparrow," he said so softly, his words were almost lost to the wind. "I'm not asking you to stay, but just know you have that option, too. You do have a choice."

I swallowed around a suddenly formed lump in my throat. Thousands of sky fae were currently gathering in Elaros, waiting for my execution. This was hardly a choice. I was literally running for my life.

"Thank you." I gripped the handle of the satchel across my chest. "I should go?" It came out as a question when I had meant it as affirmation.

He removed his hands from me and took a step back. "As you wish."

I couldn't look at him again. If I did, I feared I would break into tears, and it was not how I wished him to remember me. With my head down, I turned around and entered the cloudy mist over the river, heading up the bridge.

The gray clouds quickly hid everything from sight. The riverbank, the forest, and the tall man in the black cloak were all gone.

I staggered up the bridge to the place where the thin filament of pink glistened in the clouds just below the railing. It wouldn't be hard to jump. All I had to do was to climb over the wide stone railing. If I missed the pink, however, I'd fall all the way down to the Below. There was no way to survive such a fall without wings, but if I ever wanted to return to my world, I had to risk it.

I leaned over the railing, staring into the thin line of the shimmering pink. If I did it right, it would take me back home.

Only could I call that world home if I didn't even know how "home" felt?

I was about to risk my life. But for what? To go to a place I didn't miss? To live with people I either never met or didn't remember?

All my memories, every single one of them, were from Sky

Kingdom. And Voron was there from the very first to the very last of them. That was our reality, whether I wished for it or not.

He stripped me of my past. He gifted me to the king. He hunted me down and brought me back for an execution when I ran. I couldn't trust someone like that.

But Voron had also looked after me from the moment we met. Either from the distance, from the shadows, or up close, he had protected me. And now, he'd risked it all to set me free.

His magic-sealed promises never meant much. But I didn't need them. Everything he'd ever told me he'd do, he did without being bound by magic. He was also the one person, in this world or any other, I knew the most. And he knew me the best.

And here I was, ready to jump into the unknown and leave for good what really mattered.

What the hell was I doing?

I turned around even before I'd reached a decision. If nothing else, I simply wanted to take one last look at him, even if that would be looking at his back as he rode away. But when I limped out of the thick fog and onto the road, he was still there, facing me.

His eyes, the color of the clouds behind me, trapped mine.

He gritted one single word through his teeth, "Stay."

"You said you weren't asking me to stay."

"I am. I'm asking you now. Stay." He closed his eyes and added with an effort, fisting his hands at his sides, "Please."

I didn't want to rely on anyone, but I needed help. I had to start somewhere. And for that, I had to know where I stood with Voron, even if that meant making another deal with a fae.

"Give me your trust and your loyalty, Voron, and you can have both of mine in return."

"You want a promise?"

"No." I shook my head. "I don't want to bind you any more than you already are. Just tell me I can trust you, and I'll believe you."

"You'll have my trust and my loyalty, Sparrow. For as long as I'll live," he said without a moment of hesitation.

"It's a deal then." I smiled.

Relief was overwhelming, draining me of strength. The tension of adrenaline was the only thing that had kept me upright. As it drained, I feared I'd fall.

I wanted to ask him how we were going to do it. What would happen if the queen ever found out that he'd freed me? Where would we even go since we clearly couldn't return to Elaros? What would he take as a payment for sheltering me? I doubted it'd be just another kiss.

But I was shaking so much, no words would come out. I was hungry, and tired, and possibly coming down with something. I managed but a single step toward him, then my knees gave in.

I tripped and would've fallen, but he caught me.

"I've got you, little bird. No more flying away." His strong arms tightened around me, holding me to him and holding all my pieces together so I wouldn't fall apart. For once, I felt anchored and safe.

Alcon rushed to our help.

Once again, Voron got into the saddle and placed me in front of him. He swung a side of his cloak and drew it over my shoulders as I leaned against him.

"Let's go, Sparrow." He spurred the horse as Alcon and the others flew up to lead the way. "Let's go home."

Snuggling into his warm, broad chest, I breathed in his familiar scent and let my heavy eyelids drop.

I didn't remember what "home" meant but, I believed, I finally knew what it would *feel* like if I had one.

It would feel like Voron.

Crownless King

CHAPTER 1

It was dark when I opened my eyes. Dark and warm.

I remembered riding with Voron, tacked to his chest under his soft, velvet cloak. I remembered feeling cold, even as my body burned with heat. Someone had given me warm tea to drink. I recalled the touch of a warm, wet cloth against my skin, wiping the filth of the dungeon off my body.

All these memories were fuzzy. Except for the feeling of over-whelming exhaustion. It was so heavy, I couldn't even open my eyes when people had washed and changed me. And after a few more sips of the tea, I remembered nothing at all.

I lay in bed now. In a dark room dimly lit by pale blue crystals entrapped in the semi-transparent black walls. The charcoal gray vines holding the black wall panels reminded me of Elaros, but it didn't look like any room I'd seen in the Sky Palace.

Rising on my elbows, I took a better look at the space. It appeared to be a huge bedroom. The bed alone was almost as big as my entire room back in Elaros. A tall fireplace opposite from the bed would comfortably fit a whole pickup truck. It was unlit. Which was good, as it felt warm without a fire in here.

A couple of dark-blue couches in carved black frames, a chair, and a low table were arranged into a sitting area in front of the fireplace. One of the tall windows was open. A light breeze gently moved the thin white curtains that glistened with *firrian* beetles.

My arms trembled from the effort of supporting my body, and I lay back into the pillows. Rolling to my side, I found a high-backed armchair by my bed.

Voron slouched in it. His long legs bent, knees apart, his head dropped to one shoulder, he appeared asleep. There was something tragic and vulnerable about his position, like he'd been so exhausted, he'd just crashed into the chair, and fell asleep immediately without even bothering to arrange his limbs comfortably first.

I had lots of questions, but I didn't want to wake him.

The familiar staccato of light hooves hitting the floor sounded from the distance. I rose from the cushions again as the door to the room opened, and Brebie trotted in with a small tray in her hands.

"Oh, you're up? Good, good. Drink your water." She set the tray on the bedside table, then handed me a wide crystal glass. "I'll go fetch your dinner right now."

She sounded cheerful and energetic, like always. And just as loud.

"Shhh." I pressed a finger to my lips. "You'll wake up Voron."

"Him?" She waved her hand in the direction of her lord. "Nothing can wake him when he's this tired, only Magnus maybe. But I locked the bird in the library, so that Voron can get some rest. He was up all through last night, pacing here like a man possessed. It's a miracle he hasn't worn a hole in the floor yet."

"Why was he up? Was he worried?"

She nodded. "Out of his mind. He read somewhere that humans are extremely fragile, and was worried sick about you. But look at you." Her voice lifted. "You did just fine, like I told him you would."

"How long did I sleep?" Words scratched my dry throat. I drank the water, emptying the glass.

"You got here late last night. And you weren't really awake when you got here, falling asleep right after we put you to bed. So, you slept for a night and a day. It's your second night here."

"Where *here?* What is this place?"

"Oh, this is Vensari, Voron's family home."

His family home?

I took another look around. It suited him. Granted, I'd only seen this one room, but the rich yet subdued colors of black, dark-gray, and royal blue seemed to be Voron's preferred palette both in clothes and furnishings.

Brebie grabbed my empty glass. "I'll get your dinner now. You need to eat to regain your strength. Poor thing, you couldn't even walk when you got here. Voron had to carry you like a baby."

That must have been the fever that knocked me out so badly. It wasn't surprising I caught something, considering the horrible conditions in the royal dungeon.

I smoothed a hand down the sleeveless satin nightshirt I was wearing.

"Did you change my clothes?"

"Voron and I did. You were like a rag doll. It was like handling dead weight. I needed some help to maneuver you. And there was no way I would let you into the bed as filthy as you were." She shuddered.

My face warmed with gratitude and a whiff of shame for putting them both through all that trouble.

"Thank you."

I debated whether to ask Brebie about the queen and my planned execution, but the matter was probably best discussed with Voron.

Before I could make up my mind about asking, Brebie rushed out of the room. She returned in a few minutes with a steaming bowl of soup and a slice of fragrant sourdough bread. I brought the bread to my nose, inhaling its fresh scent without even a hint of mold.

"It smells so good and looks actually eatable." I tried to smile, but judging by Brebie's expression, failed at it miserably.

She patted my shoulder sympathetically. "King Tiane's dungeon is a horrible place, I've heard. It's mostly empty, though. The king far prefers executions to imprisonment. I'm glad you're out, Sparrow. Safe and sound."

I placed my hand on top of hers. "Me too. I'm really glad to be here instead."

Good food, soft silky sheets, clean air—I'd never take any of it for granted for as long as I lived.

After I'd eaten most of the soup and drank some of the tea she'd given me, Brebie was satisfied to leave me alone. She tucked the sheets around me, gathered the dishes, and left, wishing me a good night.

I turned to my side and faced sleeping Voron again. He really didn't look comfortable, like a broken mannequin damped into the chair. It bugged me.

I crawled to the edge of the bed and straightened his legs, arranging them in front of him. Then I took a small cushion from the pile of pillows behind me. Climbing out of bed, I carefully stepped between his knees and took his head in my hands with the intention to lift it and to stick the cushion between his cheek and his shoulder.

With a soft snort, he jerked and woke up, blinking at me.

"Sorry," I mumbled, still holding his head between my hands. "I didn't mean to wake you."

"Were you trying to wring my neck in my sleep, little vixen?" Despite his biting words, a smile quivered his lips. "How are you feeling?"

"Better."

It was safe to assume he was capable of holding his head up on his own at this point, so I let go of it. I tried to step back, but tripped over his leg and plopped with my butt down on his knee.

"Shit." I made a move to get up, but he stopped me by placing a hand on the small of my back.

"Not that much 'better,' I see." He clicked his tongue disapprovingly. "You're not naturally clumsy like that."

"It's that tea that Brebie made me drink. It makes me sleepy."

He moved a strand of my hair back over my shoulder, then went to stroke down my bare arm but before his skin touched mine, he jerked his hand away.

"You should be in bed."

"You should be, too. It can't be comfortable sleeping in this chair."

"Well, you took my bed." He splayed his hand on my thigh over my nightshirt. Apparently, touching me through the fabric didn't bother him as much as grazing my bare skin.

I decided to test his touching limits by covering his hand with mine. He didn't shake it off.

"Don't tell me this is the only bedroom you have in your house," I said. "I'm happy to go sleep somewhere else."

He grunted, getting up, with me in his arms. "All right, little bird. Too much chirping when you should be resting."

Walking around the bed, he placed me in the sheets, then drew the covers over me.

"Voron, I have questions."

"I know. But they'll have to wait until morning. It'll suffice to say that you're safe here. Safe enough to rest for as long as you need."

"You have to get some rest, too." I patted the mattress next to me. "If you insist on both of us staying in the same room, this bed is huge. I could easily have three men here with me."

"There is no way I'll ever let you roll around my bed with three random men," he muttered under his breath, kicking off his shoes.

I smiled, watching him take off his leather belt and his black vest. He loosened the collar of his white shirt and climbed onto the bed with me, but stayed over the covers.

"Here." He stifled a yawn. "I'm in bed. Will you go to sleep now?"

"Now, I will." I giggled, which earned me an amused glance from him. Come to think of it, I didn't remember ever giggling before, not since I came to Sky Kingdom at least.

He turned with his back to me and stuffed a pillow under his head. "Good night, Sparrow."

But there was one question I needed to know the answer to before I could even think about sleeping.

"Voron?"

"Hmm?

He didn't turn around, so I kept talking to his back.

"What do you want for hiding me here?"

"What do you mean?" Now, he turned. His eyes looked dark blue in the night, reflecting the deep glow of the crystals.

"Nothing is for free," I explained. "In Sky Kingdom, everything has its price. I learned that much."

"Right. Well…" He rubbed the back of his neck. "If you absolutely insist on paying me, I'll take another one of those meringue swans. With a neck to snap," he added with a cold glint in his eyes.

"That may be difficult to do, since I probably won't see the head chef any time soon. How about I'll make you meringue with whipped cream instead? Without a neck to snap?"

I'd ask Brebie to show me how to make meringue. It might take me all day to make it, but I would learn.

"Fine." He turned back around again. "I'll find a way to wring *his* neck instead."

I didn't ask whose neck he meant, but I believed it wasn't the head chef's.

"It's a deal then." I shifted a little closer to him. We were in the same position we had taken a nap in the woods once. Only this time, I had no intentions to run anywhere.

Pressing my forehead to his back, I closed my eyes. "Good night, Voron."

Crownless King is available here:

More in the River of Mists

Kingdom of Under Trilogy

Somber Prince - Coming Soon

Wingless Crow

Crownless King

Fire in Stone

Hearts on Fire

Serpent's Touch

Serpent's Claim

Madame Tan's Freakshow Trilogy

Call of Water

Madness of the Moon

Power of Rage

More by Marina Simcoe

PARANORMAL ROMANCE

Demons (Complete Series)

Demon Mine

The Forgotten

Grand Master

The Last Unforgiven - Cursed

The Last Unforgiven - Freed

Stand Alone Novels

The Real Thing

To Love A Monster

Midnight Coven Author Group

Wicked Warlock (Cursed Coven)

More by Marina Simcoe

SCIENCE-FICTION ROMANCE

My Holiday Tails

Married to Krampus

My Tiny Giant

My Birthday Getaway

New Year, New Planet

Mail Order Mom

My Pumpkin

What Makes an Alien a Dad?

Dark Anomaly Trilogy

Gravity

Power

Explosion

Stand Alone Novels

Experiment

Enduring (Valos Of Sonhadra)

About the Author

Marina Simcoe likes to write love stories with human heroines and non-human heroes who just can't live without them. She firmly believes that our contemporary world could always use a little bit of the extraordinary.

She has lots of fun exploring how her out-of-this-world characters with their own beliefs, values, and aspirations fit into our every-day life.

She lives in Canada with her very own extraordinary hero, their three little offspring, and a cat who is definitely out of this world.

f facebook.com/MarinaSimcoeAuthor

twitter.com/MarinaSimcoe

instagram.com/marinasimcoeauthor

patreon.com/MarinaSimcoe

a amazon.com/author/marinasimcoe

BB bookbub.com/profile/marina-simcoe

g goodreads.com/MarinaSimcoe

tiktok.com/@marina.simcoe

Milton Keynes UK
Ingram Content Group UK Ltd.
UKHW040639301023
431584UK00001B/52

9 781989 967256